BC

✓

A·Y

Penguin Books

A TIME AND A PLACE

Laura Gilmour Bennett is the pen-name of Laura Bennett and
Jean Gilmour Harvey, two Americans based in London who
first met eighteen years ago in West Africa in the wake of the
Biafran Civil War. They began working together seven years
ago, and as part of a collaborative trio known as Justine Harlowe
they produced two world-wide bestsellers: *Memory and Desire*
and *Jealousies*. They divide their time between England, France
and Italy and are currently at work on their next novel.

D0449460

A Time ~and a Place

LAURA GILMOUR BENNETT

PENGUIN BOOKS

PENGUIN BOOKS

Published by the Penguin Group
27 Wrights Lane, London w8 5tz, England
Viking Penguin Inc., 40 West 23rd Street, New York, New York 10010, USA
Penguin Books Australia Ltd, Ringwood, Victoria, Australia
Penguin Books Canada Ltd, 2801 John Street, Markham, Ontario, Canada l3r 1b4
Penguin Books (NZ) Ltd, 182–190 Wairau Road, Auckland 10, New Zealand

Penguin Books Ltd, Registered Offices: Harmondsworth, Middlesex, England

First published by Viking 1988
Published in Penguin Books 1989
1 3 5 7 9 10 8 6 4 2

Copyright © Laura Gilmour Bennett, 1988
All rights reserved

Made and printed in Great Britain by
Richard Clay Ltd, Bungay, Suffolk
Filmset in 10/11 pt Bembo

Except in the United States of America,
this book is sold subject to the condition
that it shall not, by way of trade or otherwise,
be lent, re-sold, hired out, or otherwise circulated
without the publisher's prior consent in any form of
binding or cover other than that in which it is
published and without a similiar condition
including this condition being imposed
on the subsequent purchaser

~ Prologue ~

Prologue

The sixteenth-century villa stood waiting, dreaming in the Tuscan sun, its peeling golden stucco mottled by the shade of cedars and cypresses rising from the weed-choked garden. The closed shutters of the house, once a glossy green, had been scoured silver by decades of rain and wind. Rosy tiles that had tumbled from the roof lay shattered on the terrace below where tufts of grass grew between the cracked paving stones. The rich sun of late autumn bathed the once grand house in splendour, piercing deep grottoes of shade in the surrounding gardens, where giant urns had crumbled and fallen statues lay in pieces, their faces staring at the cloudless sky. In the void left by time and neglect, spiders spun their webs undisturbed on the box hedges which had grown wildly out of shape, and lizards scuttled on the leaf-strewn drive along which horses, carriages and limousines had each in turn been driven over the centuries.

Anxious in case someone would recognize her, Chiara hurried down the overgrown lane towards the villa, her identity concealed by a scarf and dark glasses. A deep-rooted superstition made her conscious that on this day she must cultivate complete anonymity.

When she saw the weathered wall ahead dappled by sunlight, she was startled by the strength of her yearning to see this place. Reaching the locked gates that barred the way to the villa she stopped short and gasped in disbelief at the shocking scene of abandon that lay beyond them. In an instant she guessed what must have happened. The American Marchesa, the elegant ageless woman with the musical laugh and the silvery blonde hair, the glamorous and indomitable Marchesa, must have died, impossible as it seemed. Or, perhaps, old and frail, she had lost her fortune and was now living in obscurity somewhere, having abandoned the villa where she had once lived so graciously.

Chiara stood indecisively for a moment, wondering what to do. Coming out of her daydream she suddenly felt uncomfortable at the deep silence surrounding the isolated villa that seemed to be closing in on her. She was about to turn away when the 'For Sale' sign fastened to the gate caught her eye. The sight of it sent an electrifying chill down her spine. As she hurried away, Chiara couldn't suppress a triumphant smile as a bold new desire sprang to life in the ashes of an old dream.

Later that day, Prospero arrived at those same gates, pausing to study the devastation that time had wrought since the fine summer evening when he had walked proudly down the immaculately pebbled drive with his cousin, the Monsignor.

Until the day before the decaying villa had represented nothing but humiliation and failure to him, but within the last twenty-four hours everything had changed. It was she who had changed him, he acknowledged to himself, the memory of her smile, her touch playing in his mind. Then and there he felt his decision crystallize, gaining a momentum that swept him forcefully along. This house that he had always shunned would ring with laughter once again, with her laughter and that of their children, impossible though that might once have seemed. He marvelled that such absurd romanticism could seize him even after he had tried every pleasure, conquered every obstacle life had to offer.

As he peered into the shadowy depths of the garden, he was filled with exhilaration at the prospect of beginning all over again with the woman he had found after searching for what seemed a lifetime. The emptiness, the disillusionment of the last years, his reversals, his triumphs, were dwarfed by what lay ahead. His eyes flickered upwards to the sign attached to the top of the gate, his talisman. Charged with resolution to make his dreams a reality, Prospero turned his back on the villa and strode down the lane.

Gasping for breath as she ran, Cotton came to a halt at the end of the deserted lane at the rusting gates of the villa. Filled with anger and pain, she made herself look down the tunnel of trees to catch one last haunting glimpse of the peeling yellow plaster, the closed shutters like sightless eyes.

Her intention had always been to come back, yet she never imagined that this long-awaited homecoming would spell the end of the dream that had sustained her life. This house, this old decrepit house, which was beautiful to her even in its sad state of neglect, was hers by right of love. Now, it would never belong to her. She had lost it not just once, but twice over. The radiant past that had always been a pleasure to re-collect, would henceforth be distorted by pain. She wondered where the promise, the tenderness of the day before had gone, as she traced a shaft of sunlight that wove in and out of the shadows. Tears that she had determined not to let fall dimmed the rippling colours of a dragonfly swooping down the path. Releasing her grip on the present, she allowed time to dissolve for an instant, which cast up the colourful splash of a summer dress. In her mind's eye she saw Delilah, her face and silvery hair protected by a wide straw hat as she strolled down the path with a basket of pink and blue delphiniums. Her voice reverberated through the well-tended gardens as she called Cotton's name and in a moment a little girl came running. Their hands linked affectionately before they turned the corner, out of sight.

Pressing herself against the cold bars of the gate, she suppressed an anguished sob as she hardened herself against memory. The combined grief of the day before and of decades ago was so deep that it frightened her. Some day she would have to give in to it, but not now. Taking one last glimpse at the villa which would have to last a lifetime, she wondered how she could let go of a dream that had become a nightmare.

~Book One~

Chapter 1

When Cotton woke up in total darkness, it took her a moment
to remember she had been kidnapped. The sound of her own
breathing echoed in the empty room where she lay on a bare
floor, her hands and feet bound. As her eyes became ac-
customed to the dimness she made out a boarded-up window
that admitted a prism of light telling her it was daytime. At
least they had removed the gag from her mouth when they
dumped her there, tossing her body on the floor like a sack of
coal. As she stirred she realized every part of her body was sore
and bruised. Ignoring the cord that cut painfully into her wrists
and ankles, she struggled to inch her way across the floor and
shift herself against the wall. Breathing heavily from the exer-
tion, she began to think that it was no use. In a moment of self-
pity, tears formed in her eyes, but she held them back, knowing
that weakness, however private, could be fatal.

When she coughed, trying to clear her dry aching throat,
her head began to throb. Had someone hit her? Had they
drugged her with something? She jerked involuntarily at the
rumble of a distant explosion followed by a retort of machine-
gun fire which sent the adrenalin running through her. Her
heart beat furiously at the sound of a distant battle and she
whispered a prayer that her captors hadn't taken her to the
mountains after all. She was still in West Beirut.

From the moment she had been kidnapped, she had lost all
track of time. She had been trussed up and bundled into the

boot of a car for a rough journey that ended with her being imprisoned in this room where she had lain wide-awake in terror the whole night long, her mind spinning anxiously. Trying to stay calm, Cotton began to take stock of the situation.

By now the news of her abduction had probably been flashed around the world. Fame at last, she thought, forcing a smile in the darkness. It was a great story, one which she would have dearly loved to have written herself: twenty-nine-year-old American woman journalist on the *Washington Herald*, veteran of Poland, Nicaragua, Northern Ireland, to mention just a few assignments, kidnapped on her way back to the hotel in Beirut after interviewing American Marines behind the sandbanks near the airport.

The Commodore Hotel, the journalists' headquarters, would be buzzing with rumours that morning. Some of her male colleagues would no doubt think that Cotton Castello had got what she deserved. After all, she had made her reputation by scooping stories from under their noses wherever and whenever she could. She had played being a woman to the hilt if it suited her – a ploy which charmed some people, infuriated others. The *Herald* would wonder who to notify as her next of kin. There was no problem in her case. No Mr and Mrs Castello, parents of the kidnapped journalist, waited anxiously for news of their lost daughter. There weren't even any aunts or uncles, or cousins or grandparents. She was on her own. The only person who might worry about her was William, and she could only hope that he wouldn't find out.

Then she thought of her lover back at the hotel. She had a mental picture of him chain-smoking in his room. By now he probably wished he had stayed in England with his wife and children instead of taking a photographic assignment with a news magazine. Of course he would be frantic. It had taken them a year to line up a long assignment in the same hot spot at the same time. Some romantic interlude, she thought. Ed Broder, her arch-rival on another Washington paper, was probably laughing his head off. She had handed him a juicy story on a platter that would make the front page. Even now she could see the humour in it.

For the thousandth time Cotton cursed her own foolishness. She had been so hell-bent on reaching the hotel in time to get the day's big story on the wire that she had risked taking a taxi alone. Everything had happened so fast that it was disjointed in her memory. The driver had slammed on the brakes when they were ambushed in a deserted side street. But why had the driver taken that side street? Was he an accomplice? She would probably never know. Three dark masked men had sprung from the shadows, probably Shiites. One of them had yanked her from the back seat, making her gasp with astonishment.

All the way to their unknown destination Cotton remembered only one thought piercing her fear: that it had finally happened to her. The magic circle had been broken; the self-created aura of invincibility that had protected her during her career as a journalist had evaporated. In Beirut she had felt safe in the fact that Shiites never captured women. Yet here she was, the exception that proved the rule. Why? There could only be one reason – to exchange her for hostages somewhere, some time. Perhaps they had mistaken her for a man since her hair had been tucked under her cap. Now, her entire being was reduced to flesh and bone which could be used to barter the freedom of terrorists belonging to a splinter group no one had ever heard of. Her captivity could drag on for weeks, months, or more. The knowledge that diplomacy moved slowly tormented her. More than one journalist was still missing after months in captivity, presumed alive, and rotting away in a hole similar to the one she now found herself in. Just the thought made her sweat with anxiety. She had always felt there was one thing almost as bad as death or mutilation in a war zone, and that was being taken prisoner to be used as a pawn in a political chess game.

Her heart pounded when the door flew open and the light came on overhead, blinding her for a moment. She focused on a pair of boots in front of her, then her eyes travelled up a pair of green fatigues, and a revolver tucked into a belt. A swarthy man, whose broad, handsome face was stamped with a thick moustache, was staring at her with expressionless dark eyes as he held out a tray. Just for an instant she sensed his quick scrutiny, the same look that he might have given her in a nightclub or on the street in different circumstances. After all, Cotton told herself, she was a blonde foreigner, and some people thought she was beautiful. She would use every ounce of her sex appeal if it would help, still believing that the strict Muslim Shiites wouldn't molest her. She nearly thanked him in Arabic but stopped herself in time. If her captors knew she spoke even a word of their language they would be on their guard, and there was a chance she might overhear some clue of what they intended to do with her.

'*Mangez,*' the man ordered.

She looked at the tray, flat bread, a chunk of goat's cheese, a cup of water. She was amazed to feel a strong pang of hunger at the sight of food. Looking up at him helplessly with her golden brown eyes she smiled faintly, indicating with a shrug that she couldn't eat with tied hands.

Abruptly he kneeled to untie her wrists.

'*Mais, monsieur, d'abord, je veux faire pipi,*' she whispered demurely.

The expression on his face told her she had caught him off guard.

Nodding curtly, he unbound her ankles and helped her to her feet. Wobbling, Cotton supported herself against the wall, fighting vertigo after being hunched up for so many hours. She stretched her legs, thinking she must be ready to run at any time if she saw the chance.

Following her captor down a corridor, a glimpse out of a window made Cotton realize they were at least four floors up. A glance over her shoulder told her the door to the corridor was guarded by another soldier. She soaked up every detail, thinking it might be her only opportunity, remarking that a ledge skirted the building a short drop from the windows.

When the guard motioned her to the toilet at the end of the corridor, she closed the door behind her. There was no lock, and she hesitated a second before standing on the filthy toilet to inspect the window above. She stayed inside until the soldier shouted for her to come out. About a minute and a half, by her reckoning. She pulled up her trousers and opened the door to find her captor waiting for her, his arms folded as he smoked a cigarette. She remembered to register an envious look as he puffed away, and was rewarded when he handed her what was left of the cigarette.

'*Merci,*' she said gratefully, even though she had stopped smoking ages ago.

When the door closed behind him she saw they had thrown a mattress in the corner. Did that mean they would spend another night there? As she ate, Cotton realized the hardest thing would be to judge time because they had taken her watch. Grateful at least that her hands and feet were now free, she then curled up, determined to get through one minute at a time while she built up her courage for the hour when she would make a run for it. She thought of the ledge that skirted the building. It would be suicide to try an escape at night. She would try the following morning at dawn.

Resting her head on her arm, she decided to try and sleep all day to be ready. As she moved, she felt a reassuring lump in the heavy cotton jacket she wore, one of several she had had made in Hong Kong with an inside pocket that contained her survival kit. Ever since Nicaragua she had carried one as a sort of talisman, until it became a private joke. It consisted of thirty feet of thin nylon cord, a small knife, some matches and a tiny pencil around which was rolled a strip of blank paper and a hundred-dollar bill. She would find use for them all when morning came. She got up and turned off the light, then lay down on the mattress facing the boarded window. She stared at the crack that would tell her when it was light.

The moment she closed her eyes bright garish images of the past month flooded her mind. As if through a photographer's lens she saw flashbacks of children in hospitals, bloodstained survivors of car bombs, buildings going up in smoke. She shifted uncomfortably. The three Ds – the drinking, the drugs, the deadlines – had taken their toll. When it was all over she promised herself she would go to Switzerland where children were rosy-cheeked and smiling, where quaint houses had window-boxes overflowing with flowers. She wanted to breathe fresh air untainted by explosives. She wanted the ordinary, even the banal – just for a while. But that didn't mean she was ready to quit quite yet, she told herself as she sank into sleep.

Some hours later she awoke, her hair soaked in sweat, her heart pounding with the vividness of a recurrent nightmare. The details changed, but the dream was always the same: a jumbled reconstruction of being lost when she was eight years old.

It had happened in Paris, on the Champs-Élysées, packed with people watching the Bastille Day parade. She had pushed her way through a forest of arms and legs to get a better look at the brass band passing by. Her landmark was her mother's bright blue hat bobbing up in the distance. But by the time she had crept back to rejoin Delilah she was no longer where she had been standing before. Cotton had panicked, allowing herself to be shouldered along with the moving crowd until she realized she was hopelessly lost. She had stopped, wanting desperately to cry, but her throat closed with fear. She believed utterly that she would never see her mother again, that she had disappeared from the face of the earth.

From the fragmented memory, Cotton couldn't recall how she had arrived at the gendarmerie, but probably a policeman had spotted her and taken her there. She remembered sitting on a table as she tearfully whispered her story until finally the sound of high heels clicking down the corridor made her heart leap. Delilah burst through the door, immediately recognizable by her blue straw hat.

'My baby darling, what on earth happened to you? My little bunny, you're safe, thank the Lord!' She flung her arms around Cotton and the two of them clung to each other. 'I looked around and my heart stopped when I realized you weren't there any more. I looked everywhere for you, darling. Where were you?'

Cotton was laughing and crying at the same time. The world hadn't come to an end after all as she was enveloped by the frill of Delilah's silk blouse which emitted comforting wafts of Guerlain. It was almost worth getting lost to feel this indescribable joy now that they were reunited.

'Come on, little rabbit. Let's treat ourselves to lunch at

Fouquet's. But first we must thank these perfectly wonderful gentlemen who came to your rescue. Say "thank you" to *messieurs les gendarmes*.'

Cotton smiled at a circle of benevolent policemen, so handsome in their navy uniforms. They were all beaming with approval now the episode had ended happily. Cotton noticed, too, that they cast gallant looks at the blonde, dimpled Delilah, a strikingly chic American in her mid-fifties, which made her feel very proud.

Cotton had all but forgotten about the incident until they left Paris on the Mistral heading south for the Riviera that summer, when she had awakened in her bunk screaming in her sleep. The dream that came back to haunt her from then on was worse than the reality, never ending and always terrifying, of being lost for ever, separated from Delilah. Now, over twenty years later in Beirut, Cotton shivered, thinking that the dream had been strangely prophetic.

She had acquired the habit of banishing the dream by replacing it with a happy memory, an antidote to the pain it caused. Closing her eyes, Cotton followed the past to Florence that summer, where Guido the chauffeur was waiting at the station to take them on the winding drive through the Tuscan hills. She sat on the edge of her seat, straining to see over the dashboard of the Rover with its polished wood and leather interior. When the car slowed down at the magnificent wrought-iron gates hinged to high walls, she knew they had come home to the Villa Robbiano. As the car crawled down the pebbled drive lined with dense cypresses, they passed huge ancient urns and statues tucked away in niches of shrubbery until they reached a carpet of grass sloping to a wisteria-covered pergola overlooking the hills, which were criss-crossed with vineyards and olive groves of dusty green.

'Of course we'll have a party to welcome ourselves back to Robbiano as usual,' said Delilah with an excited lilt in her voice. 'I wonder if William is back from London yet?'

The softening in Delilah's voice told Cotton what everyone already knew, that she adored her lover William Partridge just as he adored her.

The car came round a closely clipped hedge and the old villa sprang into view, its exterior golden in the brilliant sunshine and its dark green shutters flanking the long windows. Cotton savoured the prospect of the summer ahead, when a stream of Delilah's interesting friends would arrive at the villa from all over the world. When the car stopped she leapt out and stood for a moment, consuming the rich familiar smell of the ancient garden, the trilling of birds against the counterpoint of Delilah chattering in Italian with the chauffeur and maid. Cotton was home, in the Villa Robbiano, where she belonged, where she was safe and nothing could ever harm her.

The next morning, when Cotton opened her eyes to see faint light escaping through the crack in the boarded window, she was awake instantly with all her senses fully alert. Leaping to her feet, she felt her muscles tense and her heart pound in anticipation. Opening the door cautiously, she saw one of her captors slouched in a doze at the end of the corridor.

'*Pipi*,' she called, and he nodded.

She walked slowly down the corridor, dragging her feet as if she was in pain. Halting suddenly, she winced and held her stomach, then gave him an embarrassed glance to make sure he was watching. Stumbling into the toilet, she closed the door and made a retching sound as she swiftly removed the cord from her shirt. She expertly tied a mast knot around the pipe of the cistern, something that her cousin Biddle had taught her years ago. As she balanced on the rim of the toilet bowl, she wished her cousin could see the use she had put it to. The thought of him gave her the energy to spring up to the small window ledge. Whipping the cord upwards, she balanced precariously on the windowsill, then slid out, holding on for dear life as her weight dropped. Relief that the knot had held shot through her. She dangled for a second to check there was no window overlooking her escape to the ledge below. Sliding down the cord she had a quick surreal glimpse of the collage of rooftops of Beirut against the smoky pink dawn breaking on the horizon.

As she landed on the ledge, her hands burning from her

hurried descent, she realized that the only escape off the ledge was to cut the cord, tie it to a drainpipe and drop another twenty feet to the roof of an extension below. Her breath seemed to stop with the suspense, but she had the knife out of her pocket even before the thought was half-formed, spurred on by the knowledge that every second counted.

Moments later she crept across a roof from which she could jump down to a balcony out of sight of the window. As she caught her breath on the balcony, she saw she had no choice but to jump into a courtyard below that was behind the building where she had been held captive. Every second brought closer the moment when they would discover she was missing, and she had a sudden terrifying image of enraged soldiers hurtling down the stairs of the building in pursuit.

Taking a deep breath, she jumped. When she hit the stones of the courtyard she swallowed a cry of pain as her ankle twisted. Struggling to her feet, she searched the half-shuttered windows overlooking the courtyard. A dog barked and, at the sight of a woman in a robe peering down, Cotton flattened herself against the wall. Her breathing heavy, her heartbeat bursting in her ears, she heard the woman call out.

Making a run for the exit, she winced at the pain and could only manage to hobble for the first few yards, but as the shock wore off she struggled to appear normal. Sweat poured down her as she walked along the deserted street lined with shell-pocked buildings with overhanging balconies and closed shutters, which projected an eerie emptiness in the cool morning air. She jumped at the noise of a metallic shop front being lifted. Passing two ragged children who held out their hands for money, she could only smile and shake her head. A woman in black carrying a market basket walked by, her head shrouded with a scarf. The sound of a car that wouldn't start ricocheted down the street; she passed a man who had only one leg. Another day was beginning in Beirut. It was business as usual.

It took every ounce of Cotton's will not to run as she made her way down the unfamiliar street that seemed to be closing in on her. She avoided the eyes of people who stared curiously at the obviously foreign, fair-haired woman in a filthy safari suit. In her fear she imagined that each of them was a potential informer. Her mouth dry with terror, she steeled herself against the moment when a soldier would leap on her from an alley, sensing that this time they wouldn't allow her to escape so easily. She tossed the note she had written in case she was captured into the gutter, thinking the odds were pathetically small that it would ever be found.

When at last the narrow street intersected with a busy boulevard, relief flooded through her. The warmth of the morning sun was beginning to touch the dusty streets, even though it was still very early. Dented, rusty cars cruised along and the knots of people she passed shielded her from danger, but she didn't dare to ask directions yet. She walked on as if she knew where she was going, passing shopkeepers pulling up the shutters of their shops, and women already beginning to forage for provisions in the war-torn city. Glancing in a window, she caught sight of a wild-looking woman with a dirty, tear-stained face and matted filthy hair. When she realized that she was looking at herself she suppressed a laugh, knowing it would lead to uncontrollable tears. Just then she spotted a taxi, a grand old Chevrolet, a relic of Beirut in its heyday, and as it cruised by she signalled for the driver to stop. She reached for the hundred-dollar bill in her pocket and flashed it discreetly. Everything about her said she was in trouble, and the time had come to trust someone.

'Hotel Commodore, *la plus vite que possible*,' she muttered, her voice choked with emotion.

The man had a kind face, and she decided she would be safe. As soon as she had got into the taxi and he put the car into gear, she slid on to the floor where she lay in heart-pounding suspense as they headed for her destination – she hoped. As she pulled herself together, Cotton began to wonder if she had made a terrible mistake. Beirut was full of fanatics and crackpots. How did she know the driver wasn't a Shiite sympathizer? How did she know he wouldn't deliver her to the nearest band of soldiers and collect a reward? When at last the car finally came to a halt she was reluctant to get up and see where they were.

'*Voilà, madame, l'Hôtel Commodore,*' said the driver, peering over the front seat.

Cotton blinked at him in disbelief, then dragged herself on to the seat. She let out a gasp of relief when she saw the familiar sand-bagged entrance of the hotel that had been her headquarters for the last month. Getting out of the taxi with as much dignity as she could, she began to shake uncontrollably.

Handing the driver the hundred-dollar bill, she clasped both his hands in hers. Involuntary tears began to stream down her cheeks.

'You have saved my life. *Vous m'avez sauvé la vie. Merci mille fois, monsieur,*' she repeated.

Obviously moved, he pressed the bill back into her hand.

'No, no money,' he said adamantly.

'But you must take it, you must, *s'il vous plaît.* I absolutely insist, *j'insiste!*'

He hesitated, but seeing the pleading look in her eyes he took the hundred dollars from her gratefully. '*C'est très gentil.*'

When he waved goodbye to her, Cotton felt a twist of emotion. The stranger had saved her life in an act of enormous courage, and she would probably never see him again.

Eyes smarting, she walked shakily into the lobby of the hotel, empty except for the clerk behind the desk and a sweeper cleaning ashtrays from the night before. The stale smell of a bar the morning after hit her nose, filling her with elation. It was the most delicious smell in the world, a smell that conjured up the image of living, and banished the fear of dying. The shabby Commodore seemed like a palace all of a sudden. Incredulity at what she had actually done began to overtake her.

The clerk's mouth dropped open when he saw her standing there.

'Good morning, Abdullah,' she said as calmly as she could.

'Mademoiselle Castello — you are safe!' he cried, throwing up his hands in wonderment. 'But what . . .? How . . .?'

'It's a long story, and if you don't mind, I'll tell you about it later.' Her eyes went to Mike's key slot, then to the clock. It was before seven. If she hurried, the time difference would mean that she might make the *Herald*'s morning edition with her story.

In moments like these she had always drawn on a source of inner strength that didn't seem to belong to her. She felt it now, underpinning her resolve and temporarily sweeping away her exhaustion, her craving for a cup of coffee and a shower, and her yearning to see Mike and tell him she was safe.

'Is the telex free?'

'Nobody is here. It's all yours,' said Abdullah in amazement. 'Don't you want to go upstairs first?'

'Soon. In a while,' she replied, adding, 'I could use a cup of coffee, though.'

'With pleasure, Miss Castello,' he murmured in awe, as if she were some sort of heroine.

For the next half-hour Cotton wrote her story. The world narrowed to the keyboard in front of her as she translated the images of the last forty-eight hours into explosive prose. The words seemed to leap on to the pages. When she had finished, Cotton leaned back and brushed her hair from her forehead, the adrenalin still coursing through her. The story of her own kidnapping and escape was undoubtedly the best thing she had ever written.

Walking through the deserted marble lobby, Cotton felt herself descending slowly from an incredible high. Now her job was done, now she was safe, she enjoyed a moment of pure triumph that she had come through it all unscathed, relishing the simple unalloyed joy of being alive. Now it was all over, she was thrilled it had happened. Her stock as a journalist was bound to soar.

Reaching the fifth floor in the elevator, she walked along the corridor to Mike's room and knocked lightly, her heart pounding with a different excitement. When the door flew open and Mike appeared, a towel wrapped around his waist, there was a stunned expression on his face she would never forget.

'Cotton!' His voice reverberated down the corridor. 'Jesus Christ, where the hell have you been?' Without waiting for an answer, he grabbed her and crushed her to him.

'Hush, you'll wake the dead,' she said with deadpan irony as she kicked the door closed behind her.

Chapter 2

Prospero Vallone walked on to the deep terrace of the villa, squinting at the slashes of light that, filtered by tall pines, showered his sun-tanned face and his dark hair. Placing his hands on his hips he regarded the sweep of Portofino harbour melting into the blue Mediterranean.

'I want this piece of balustrade replaced, but it must be exactly as it was,' he said in Italian to the architect who was standing respectfully at his side. Scratching away some of the crumbling plaster he added, 'And match this colour. I want it exactly the same.'

'Yes, Signor Vallone, I understand,' he replied, veiling his annoyance at Vallone's abruptness.

Prospero leaned back to look up at the villa, a rich Venetian red, its windows hung with deep green shutters that had been freshly painted. 'Paint them black,' he said.

'Black? You said you wanted green,' said the startled architect. One sharp look of warning from Prospero, sweetened by the ghost of a smile, caused him to nod.

'And now perhaps you could come upstairs to the master bedroom. There are a few details there, especially in the bathroom, that I would like to discuss with you.'

'I can spare only a few more minutes. That's all,' he said glancing at his wristwatch.

The architect regarded Vallone's expensive watch, suppressing a sneer of contempt at its vulgarity as he reminded himself irritably what it stood for – the kind of money required to restore an old villa in one of Italy's most fashionable harbours.

They passed through the amber colonnaded loggia, and the set of Prospero's mouth conveyed that he was not pleased with the delays. He glanced up at the workmen on scaffolding who were restoring the frescoed ceiling with maddening slowness. Another was carefully brushing the handmade tiles of the floor that had been lovingly laid to look as if they had been there for generations. His own footsteps echoed in the palatial salon whose spaciousness symbolized a certain hollowness of spirit that he struggled to keep at bay. Everyone, even the architect, knew that at the moment Prospero Vallone was separated from his wife who lived in Switzerland with their children. His terseness with the architect hid the shame that the resulting rumour and scandal had caused him in the super-chic little town where everybody knew everybody else's business.

When they had gone upstairs to the bedroom, the architect flung open the shutters to a balcony from which there was an unimpeded view of the harbour dotted with boats.

'Now, we can begin with the bathroom,' said the architect, leading the way.

Frowning irritably, Prospero surveyed the wires hanging from the walls, the fixtures that hadn't yet been installed.

'What is all this? The bathroom was supposed to be done by now.'

'Yes, I know, and I apologize, but . . .'

'But what? What's the excuse this time?'

The architect met the forceful sweep of Vallone's gaze. He preferred to deal with rich aristocratic women who, however whimsical, could be charmed out of their moods and persuaded by smiles and compliments. Unlike them, the Italian–American Vallone was ill-mannered, coarse, and his money had been printed yesterday.

'Something very unfortunate has happened. The onyx we were supposed to install arrived with serious cracks and that delayed everything . . .'

'So? Use something else.'

'But the signora ordered it in a particular shade that is hard to get. Please be reasonable.'

'She's not here to decide,' said Prospero, turning away.

'It would take at least three weeks for another shipment of onyx to arrive.' He was about to suggest that Vallone should hire someone else to do the job.

'I told you. Choose something else. Consult with the decorator. Marble, anything.'

He sighed. 'Very well, I'll take care of it. I'm sure we can find something to suit your taste.'

When they were downstairs in the hallway Prospero said: 'Put in some indirect lighting in the ceiling. It's too dark in here.'

'Lamps have been ordered from Florence, copies of bronze Etruscan horses. They're works of art and will be set on the console table, and there will be mirrors to reflect the light coming through the glass door . . .'

Prospero ignored his protest. 'I want the lights. And make sure there are spotlights outside, too. Tell the landscape designer that I want plenty of lights.' He gestured airily. A note of boredom had replaced his impatience.

'Very well, Signor Vallone,' said the architect curtly.

As if sensing he had gone too far, Prospero abruptly changed his mood. A broad smile lit up his face and he said cheerfully, 'We need light, more light, my friend. I bought this house for pleasure, for enjoyment. Do you know what laughing is? Smiling? Of course you do.' He slapped him on the back. 'And now I have to go. I'm picking up my daughters for lunch in the harbour. And I know everything is in your capable hands, and that you will not disappoint me. I assume everything will be ready by September.'

The architect shook his head. 'I don't know. There's still so much to do.'

'You won't let me down, my friend. You're the best there is, and you're not going to disappoint me. How many Octobers do I have left in my life? Twenty? Thirty? Perhaps far fewer. Therefore, one October is important to me.'

'I'll do my best,' said the architect, trying to resist the famous

Vallone charm. 'Do you have time to inspect the other bedrooms?'

'I'm sure they're magnificent,' Prospero said, dismissing them with a wave of his hand. He didn't want to see them, bedrooms for his children, his brothers and their wives, their children, his cousins, when they came to stay. He was in no mood to think of his extended family housed on another floor of the villa. Least of all could he picture himself in the master bedroom, all alone.

When he left the architect at the door, Prospero was oblivious of the man's eyes boring into his back. Crossing the gravelled forecourt he stopped for a moment to look back at the villa, which was streaked by the shadows falling through the pines that clothed the hillside. A gentle breeze sent a warm whisper through the air as he stared at the exterior of the villa, its shutters like closed eyes. For a second he wished that he had never bought the huge house which had been the fulfilment of a life's ambition. His acquisition of the fine old villa overlooking one of the world's most beautiful harbours was a symbol of how far he had climbed in his life. He banished the dark thought that clouded his dream. No, he was glad he owned the villa, proud. A wish formed in his mind, which he rejected. Wishing was for children. Grown men didn't wish. They went into the world to do, to take, to conquer. He recalled a quote from Pirandello that had stuck in his mind since he had read it not long ago, compelled to commit it to memory when he realized it applied to himself:

> Why have I a house? . . . To grow old somewhere? One can only grow old with one's wife. And for me . . . emptiness, emptiness. Travel. I am a traveller with no luggage.

Singing lustily at the top of his voice, Prospero manoeuvred his Mercedes sports convertible between two big cars in the sun-drenched car park of the Splendido. As Pavarotti vibrated over the car stereo he fiddled with the knob to give it the maximum blast. In a robust tenor, he sustained the last note of *I Pagliacci* until it had died away.

'*Ecco*, heh? Not bad,' he said with a laugh, turning to his two daughters in the back seat. 'Your papa is as good as Pavarotti, don't you think?'

'Papa, hush,' whispered the fifteen-year-old Sophia in English, giving him a sidelong glance. 'Those people in the next car are staring at us.'

'Yes, they are, Papa,' repeated Elysia, now twelve. 'It's so embarrassing,' she added in German.

'Hey, you're in Italy now. No German, remember? Italian or English.'

'*Si*, Papa, yes, Papa,' chirped Elysia obediently, pecking him impulsively on the cheek.

Pleasantly surprised by her affectionate gesture, Prospero put his arm around her as they got out of the car. But the moment had passed and suddenly she had become reserved, more like her mother. Overlooking his daughters' undemonstrative nature which sometimes wounded him inadvertently, he told himself not to be a fool. He proudly regarded their immaculate blonde hair gleaming in the sunlight, their pretty oval faces and the slender arms that would soon be browned by the sun. When a group of chattering Italians passed by on the way to the restaurant, he saw a young boy lagging behind to give Sophia an admiring once-over. It gave him a jolt. In only a few months it seemed that his eldest daughter had become a woman, a fact made undeniable by the swell of breasts beneath her short pink cotton dress, the pretty legs that were beginning to lose their childish slenderness of the summer before.

Sophia and Elysia had retained their reed-like immaturity long past the age when many Italian girls would have burst into womanhood, but now he had to accept that both his daughters were blossoming. He could no longer treat them as children.

'What a lucky man I am to take my two best girlfriends to lunch today,' he teased gently.

'Papa,' began Elysia, ignoring his compliment. Her pale blue eyes were serious. 'I tried to keep it a secret when Alessandro came home for the weekend last week, but he found out we were coming. He was very upset.'

Prospero's face darkened and he said angrily, 'Who told him? Was it you?'

'No,' interrupted Sophia. 'He saw our tickets and passports on mama's desk. There was no way to hide it.'

'I hope your mother explained to him that he couldn't come only because your holidays don't coincide.' The brilliantly sunny day suddenly dimmed as Prospero thought of the six-year-old Alessandro at his special school in Geneva while the three of them were enjoying themselves.

'Yes, but you know what he's like. He doesn't want to understand. He wanted to know when you were coming to see him.'

'What did you say, Sophia?'

'I said I didn't know,' she said with a shrug.

'After lunch I'll call the school and say I'm flying up some time this week.' The moment he said it, Prospero felt the guilt lift slightly from his shoulders though he knew deep down that he was too busy to make the trip. Part of him chafed and worried deeply about his son, while part of him needed to escape from the sobering realities of a life cruelly narrowed by a handicap. Rolling up his shirtsleeves, Prospero glanced around the car park where people were arriving to lunch at the celebrated hilltop hotel. He glanced impatiently at the heavy gold watch on his wrist and adjusted his sunglasses against a sky so blue it hurt his eyes. He searched the car park for some sign of his brother's car.

'Where is everybody? They should be here by now.'

Sophia and Elysia reached into their straw handbags for their sunglasses and all of them waited impatiently. After a few moments a smile broke across his face.

'There they are now. Rico,' he called, waving to the BMW as it cruised towards the entrance of the hotel.

When his brother had parked, two dark exuberant boys under eight leapt from the back seat followed by Gina, Enrico's wife. Prospero went to open the door for his mother who was in the front seat.

'*Ciao, Mamma,*' he said with a welcoming smile, offering her his hand as she slowly got out of the car.

Maria Vallone, still in mourning after thirty years of widow-hood, eased her ample figure from the cushioned seat. Mother and son hugged one another warmly, then Prospero turned to the two boys who pranced behind them. He pulled their wiry little bodies to him with a gruffness that hid his deep affection for his nephews, then embraced his sister-in-law and brother Enrico in turn. Shorter than Prospero, stockier and balding, Enrico greeted his elder brother with a ritual kiss on both cheeks.

'Sophia, Elysia,' Prospero commanded, unable to contain his annoyance that his daughters hung back. 'Come on, come on,' he gestured impatiently, herding them forward to greet the family.

'*Buon giorno, Nonna,*' they chorused, politely kissing their grandmother as she offered them a cheek.

Prospero felt a spasm of annoyance as he caught the critical expression that crossed Sophia's face for an instant, gaping at her grandmother whom she saw no more than twice a year. He knew that his daughter was repelled by her heavily pow-dered and rouged face, her bright red lipstick, and coiled hair dyed the same deep gold it had been when she was young. Neither of the girls knew how Maria Vallone's life had been crushed by misfortune thirty years ago, and Prospero had no intention of ever telling them.

'You've grown a lot since I saw you at Christmas,' his mother was saying to Sophia and Elysia with the reserve she always displayed towards her blue-eyed Nordic granddaughters. She could not feel the same warmth and affection for Ghisela and Prospero's beautiful daughters that she had for Enrico's and Roberto's dark-eyed youngsters.

'Claudio, Bruno,' Prospero called, snapping his fingers at the boisterous little boys who were playing with a football. 'Say hello to your cousins.'

He smiled down at his sister-in-law, the small vivacious Gina whom he had always liked. The gentle swelling of her abdomen under her loose sundress reminded him she was pregnant again.

'Hey, how's the baby coming?' he asked, patting her stom-ach. 'You going to make a girl finally?'

'It better be a girl,' she replied with a mischievous grin. 'I need some help with all these men to take care of,' she added with a laugh, pressing a hand to her stomach. 'But I can tell you I hate being pregnant in the summer in the heat. It's nice to get away from Livorno for a change. And it's good to see you, Prospero. You're looking well, and the girls are as pretty as ever.'

'When the house is finished you could get away by yourself with the children. Enrico can get along without you.'

'Thanks, it sounds like a wonderful idea, but don't think I'm crazy enough to leave him all by himself,' she said with a nod in her husband's direction. 'I don't want him to get any ideas when he's alone.'

Enrico, who had overheard Gina's remark, beamed good-naturedly, and Prospero couldn't suppress a smile at the suggestion that women were lining up to pursue his paunchy, balding brother the moment his wife's back was turned. As he laughed, the sight of the wiry dark Claudio, who was everything he could wish for a son to be, aroused a spasm of involuntary envy. It had come as an unpleasant surprise to Prospero that he could ever envy his self-effacing younger brother who kept the administration of his growing business empire running smoothly. Prospero gave the orders, but he had come to rely on Enrico's sound judgement.

'When will the house be finished?' asked Gina.

'Not soon enough for my liking,' replied Prospero, ignoring the quick look of pity in Gina's dark eyes.

'Well, let's all go in. I'm famished, I can tell you,' he exclaimed.

They entered the cool whitewashed lobby studded with antiques and huge vases of flowers. The proprietor came forward to greet them.

'Welcome Dottore Vallone, Signora Vallone,' he said, expansively, granting Prospero an imaginary title as a sign of his respect. He shook hands with everyone, then led them through the cool lobby to the terrace, shaded by a pergola and suspended above the blue harbour packed with yachts. They seated themselves at the long table draped with white linen, set with *grissini* and mineral water. As Prospero took his place at the head of the table, waiters whipped open the starched napkins. Prospero glanced over his shoulder and nodded to an acquaintance at a nearby table. The clientele of the Splendido were mostly deeply suntanned and attractive Italians who affected a casual elegance that was enhanced by their animated conversation.

'The *antipasto* for everybody,' Prospero said to the waiter. As he reeled off the order, Signora Vallone fanned herself with the menu, causing the diamond and platinum watch on her wrist to sparkle.

'Where is your mother?' she said, leaning across the table towards Sophia.

'She is in Tunisia, *Nonna*.'

'What's she doing there?' she asked, disapprovingly.

'She's paying a visit to some friends there,' Sophia replied coolly.

Maria Vallone exchanged a glance with Prospero who made no reply.

When the waiter served the first course, Prospero tried to ignore the squeamish expressions on his daughters' faces, reminding himself that it always took them some time to unwind when they arrived from Switzerland, and that it wasn't fair to compare them to children who thrived in a happy family. But, noticing Sophia staring with disgust at the coiled tentacles of octopus on her plate, he couldn't contain himself.

'Delicious,' he exclaimed, chewing the octopus with exaggerated enjoyment. Sophia and Elysia exchanged an uncomfortable glance, and he saw his mother scowl.

Prospero's jaw tightened as he felt himself bristling involuntarily. Her silent disapproval deeply irked him, reminding him uncomfortably of hidden truths about his life which he had been struggling for as long as he could remember to keep at bay. He was glad when a waiter interrupted them to serve the pasta.

For an instant the aroma of garlic and crushed basil mingled in the breeze with the scent of the sea and of the flowers carried from the terraces below. In those few seconds, life seemed perfectly arranged. But as soon as the feeling came over Prospero it had gone, leaving acute disillusionment like a bitter after-taste. When he looked up he saw his mother's deep blue eyes, replicas of his own, regarding him critically.

'Why don't you find yourself a real woman – someone like Gina, not some sort of glamour girl,' she muttered, nodding towards the fashionably gaunt women scattered among the clientele of the restaurant. 'You'd never meet a girl like Gina here, or even in Rome, for that matter. Where did Enrico find her? In Livorno, two streets away from your uncle's house.'

Prospero thought for a moment, pouring water into the red wine to dilute its strength. As it turned a deep rose pink, the bitter reply that came to his mind dissolved.

'It's too late for all that, Mamma,' he said quietly, knowing it was true. If he could turn the clock back to the beginning, then it might have been different. Then, he might have married someone like Gina. But as much as he envied Enrico's happy domestic life, or that of his other brother, Roberto, he knew in his heart that it would have bored him after a while. Where would he ever meet a woman who brought him peace of mind, yet who would excite him today, tomorrow, for always? Such a woman didn't exist. But even though he was sure he would never find her, Prospero wondered if he was destined to keep looking. Would he always keep searching, he asked himself, the way he searched the crowded restaurant now? A sun-tanned brunette at a nearby table took off her sunglasses with seductive slowness, and regarded him with narrowed eyes, as if they had met somewhere. Remembering that they had been introduced at a party before he and Ghisela separated, re-membering that the woman was English, Prospero's interest flick-ered for a moment. The woman's glance, cast at him from a distance, was like a stone in a pool that sent a ripple of response through him. But, suddenly, as the pool cleared, Pros-pero saw a predatory smile tug at the corners of her ripe mouth. The implications made him go cold, as if he had seen the steely gleam of a knife, and he glanced away. He turned his attention back to his family in a dutiful spurt of energy. Break-ing off a piece of bread, he dipped it into a pool of garlic-scented oil on his plate and popped it into his mouth without tasting it. Here, at least, among his own clan, he was respected, accepted, if not loved or understood. That, along with wealth, he told himself, should be enough for any man.

Later that afternoon when Gina and Maria Vallone had gone to rest in the apartment he had rented while the villa was being completed, Prospero was at the wheel of a speedboat moored near his eighty-foot yacht, the *Elphiandro*, named for all three of his children. He had changed into white swimming-trunks and the thin gold chain around his neck glinted in the dark hair on his chest. The engine idled in the choppy water churned up by the passing boats as Enrico untangled the line for Claudio to water-ski while the others waited their turn. He leaned back and patted Elysia on the cheek, thinking she was as pretty as a doll with her hair drawn back and her cheeks already rosy from the sun.

'Here, put some of this on,' said Sophia, handing her sister a tube of sun cream.

Prospero had regarded her with amazement when she had emerged from the changing-room on the yacht that afternoon. In her tight black bathing-suit, his eldest daughter looked startlingly like her mother when he had first met her.

'Mother says the sun dries your skin up like a prune and that we should always use lots of sunscreen,' Sophia pronounced.

'Bah, nonsense,' retorted Prospero. 'Sun makes you grow, sun makes you happy. Anyway, your father likes you gold-plated.'

His two daughters broke into uninhibited giggles. Prospero knew that if only his daughters were with him more often they would learn to respond to him in the open-hearted Latin way, proving that they loved their papa.

When he turned around and saw Enrico still struggling with the rope he said impatiently in English, 'Hey, are you ready? Let's go.' His attention was diverted by the eager young Claudio, who was waiting excitedly for the boat to start as he bobbed in the water, his skis poised in readiness.

At the sight of Claudio's sturdy little body waiting to ride the power of the boat, a feeling of having been cheated by fate swept cruelly over Prospero. Alessandro, two years younger than Claudio, should have been there in his place. Pushing down the throttle after Enrico had given the signal, Prospero was compelled to turn and watch Claudio rising from the wake. Claudio wobbled for a moment then raised his fist triumphantly as he gained his balance, eliciting a rousing cheer from his father. Prospero couldn't help but notice the look of pride that magically transformed his brother's face, making him almost handsome.

Chapter 3

HOLLYWOOD

The actress Chiara Galla had read somewhere that white was the colour of mourning in India, a piece of information which had immediately appealed to her. Now, as she stood slightly apart from the horseshoe of mourners dressed in black at her husband's funeral, she felt triumphant, like a swan among ravens. She consoled herself with the thought that her late husband would have preferred to see her thus, in a beautifully tailored white linen suit sheathing her perfect body like gauze over the Venus de Milo, rather than smothered in widow's weeds.

She pointedly ignored the hostile glances of Abner Wolfe's children. If they didn't approve of her, so be it. They never had. Myron, the eldest, cast a dull, contemptuous eye over her body, the hated symbol of his father's alienated affections as well as his vast fortune. In Myron's eyes she was little better than a whore. His loathing of her was shared by his two middle-aged sisters whom Chiara had always particularly disliked. Designer clothes and cosmetic surgeons had not been able to transform their fat ankles or beady eyes. During the stilted family occasions Chiara had endured in the past twelve years, she had masked her contempt for Abner's dreary children with a thin veneer of charm that had passed for affection; but now she couldn't be bothered to keep up the pretence.

Placing one beautifully shod foot in front of the other, Chiara blotted out the monotonous droning of the rabbi as she stared directly ahead at the marble vault where Abner's ashes had been laid to rest. In spite of the flowers, the decaying smell of his decline still seemed to linger in her nostrils. Repulsion passed through her as she recalled the indignity of Abner's passing. His children might despise her, but she wondered if any of them would have been prepared to endure what she had experienced during the last months, spoon-feeding their father throughout the day, supervising injections, imprisoned in a stuffy room, even providing the sexual stimulation that he had occasionally demanded.

If Abner's children contested his will, then they were even more stupid than she thought. All of them had plenty of money. They had been born rich. Abner's money belonged to her because she had been his beloved wife, in sickness and in health, and now she was going to go out and spend it. She would buy whatever her heart desired, unchecked, unheeded. A little smile played about the corners of her mouth: if Abner's children only knew that she had already made her first purchase with the Wolfe millions! Even now, she carried a dog-eared copy of the book in her handbag for luck. It filled her with excitement to know that she owned the film rights to *Village in the Sun*.

When the funeral was over there was an awkward pause during which Chiara drew attention to herself by pressing a lace-edged handkerchief to the corners of her eyes to wipe away the tears which she could summon with no trouble at all. She took one last look at the vault, intending never to set eyes on it again. But just when she thought she had wrenched free from the past, an unexpected sadness took her by surprise. In a way, everything she was she owed to Abner Wolfe. Not liking the feeling of genuine regret at all, she pushed it aside, telling herself not to be so sentimental.

As the widow, she was the first to leave. Without saying a word to any of the small group of friends or family she stalked towards the black limousine that awaited her. As she passed by Abner's children she entertained the pleasurable illusion that they were like galley slaves straining at their chains with impotent hatred for the taskmaster who wielded the whip.

As Chiara Galla opened the bedroom doors of her suite at the Hassler, the tap of her kid shoes announced her presence in the drawing-room, which was lined with long windows that filtered the Roman sunlight. With the timing of a born actress, she paused just long enough to focus attention on herself, then elegantly entered the room.

'Miss Galla, this is Nancy Rogers from *People*,' said her secretary, springing to attention.

'What a pleasure to meet you, Miss Rogers,' she said in faintly accented English as she extended her hand. With a shrewd eye she summed up the journalist whose platinum blonde hair was tied back by a black ribbon, remarking that her chic black linen dress flattered her bony figure. Though a vivacious smile lit up her nearly unlined face, her freckled, thickly veined hands told Chiara she was sixty if she was a day.

'And I'm so thrilled to meet you, Miss Galla,' replied Nancy, adding her stock opening phrase to actresses: 'I've always been a fan of yours.' Mentally she jotted down notes she would later pour into her portrait for *People*. 'Dipped in gold,' was the opening phrase that came to her, inspired by Chiara's golden bronze hair, her velvety tanned arms against the simple gold and green ensemble she wore, accentuated by heavy gold jewellery.

'You've met my director, Sandy Vincent?' said Chiara as he crossed the room to greet her. 'Sandy, darling,' she exclaimed, as he kissed her on both cheeks.

'Oh Lord yes, we've known each other for years, haven't we, Sandy?' bubbled the journalist.

'I've carried a torch for Nancy as long as I can remember,' said Sandy in a Brooklynese accent untainted by living thirty years in Rome.

Nancy gave a girlish giggle. 'And he still remembers to say the sweetest things.'

Chiara settled on a brocade couch opposite Nancy, with a sunburst of yellow roses between them. Sandy gave her a reassuring smile that said he knew how nervous she was about her first interview in a decade. Years of good living in Italy had mellowed the wiry, energetic director Chiara remembered from her days as a starlet into a pot-bellied, balding man with a deeply lined humorous face. After the lean years of being black-listed in Hollywood in the fifties, Sandy had now earned an international reputation which gave confidence to the investors backing Chiara's mini-series.

Fishing in her bag for her glasses, Nancy's ivory bracelets rattled. 'What an amazing feeling it must be for you to be back here in Rome, Miss Galla,' she said breathlessly, gesturing towards the windows which commanded a sweeping view of the city.

Chiara cautioned herself not to be fooled by Nancy's enthusiasm, knowing she could annihilate her with a few well-chosen words.

'In fact, my family isn't from Rome, so it has never really been home to me,' she began hesitantly.

'But you did live here during the years you worked at Cinecittà, didn't you? In the late fifties?' she added pointedly, trying to fathom Chiara's exact age.

'You'll find everything in the press release my secretary sent you,' Chiara gestured airily, her mouth melting into a smile.

'All the same, it would be interesting to hear in your own words how you began in the movies,' persisted Nancy.

'I'm ashamed to say it's very dull, really. I had a small part in a movie directed by Sandy. He chose me from hundreds of girls. Then I had to learn to act. I struggled like any other young actress, learning my profession. But my life, my career, really began when I went to America.'

Her resolve to say no more communicated itself to Nancy, and belied her air of soft-spoken modesty.

'Tell me about your other two marriages before you met Abner Wolfe. You've had three husbands, all Americans, haven't you?'

She thought for a moment. 'Well, my first husband was a stuntman. That's how I got to Hollywood in the first place, when we went together. Then we were divorced and I married Todd Freeman the actor, as it says in the press release. Then Todd and I were divorced. That's all.' She shrugged sweetly.

'I'm still very good friends with both of them, and always will be,' she added, even though she hadn't set eyes on either of them for years.

Chiara gave a warm-hearted laugh as Nancy scribbled. 'It's always been my philosophy to live in the present, not the past. Since my husband died I am looking forward only to the future, and that's what I hope to discuss in the short time you're here.' She glanced at Sandy, who signalled his approval.

Chiara launched into the speech she had prepared about her plans for filming *Village in the Sun*, how she had fallen in love with the story and with the character of Isabella, a poor Italian girl who becomes the head of an international banking empire.

'It's a very ambitious project, Miss Galla. I mean, you've been out of the limelight for a very long time. One can only wonder why you don't choose to sit back and enjoy the wealth that your late husband reputedly left you,' said Nancy in a silky voice.

Chiara gave her a generous smile, tinged with condescension.

'This project is really in memory of my husband.' To make her point, she turned towards the framed photograph of a smiling white-haired man thirty years her senior, on a nearby table. Her eyes then moved to Sandy who gave no indication that this was the first time she had mentioned Abner since her arrival in Rome the previous week.

'Yes,' Chiara continued, warming to the theme. 'During my husband's illness I lived like a recluse, devoting myself to him. But he always encouraged me to return to Italy one day, to make my childhood dream come true.'

'And what's that?' Nancy inquired, gazing over the tops of her glasses.

'To make an important film in my country. And now at forty, I've found the part I've been waiting for all my life.'

At the mention of forty, Nancy Rogers suppressed a wry smile. Was she really expected to be so gullible? 'I've read the book, of course. But then, hasn't everybody? Are there any parallels between the heroine, Isabella's life and yours?'

A faraway look came to Chiara's eyes as she began to reminisce.

'Unlike Isabella, I had a wonderful childhood. My mother was a brilliant pianist who gave up her career when she married my father who was a professor of languages. She died when I was very young and my father and I lived like vagabonds for years, travelling to foreign places. Those were wonderful, wonderful years. My father died young, much too young,' she said sadly. 'Naturally I wanted to follow in his footsteps, to be a teacher. But fate intervened. I think I would have made a very good teacher,' she added brightly.

Nancy cleared her throat. 'As everybody knows, you made your mark in the television series, *Ciao, Senator*. Lord, how I used to enjoy it,' she said with genuine enthusiasm. 'Of course we didn't get it here until years later, when they were doing re-runs in the States. I'm just wondering why you never returned to your native country before?'

Chiara was frowning inwardly at the tactless reference to re-runs, a word that made her sound like a has-been. With a philosophical shrug she said: 'I always meant to come back. But my husband and I postponed it until it was too late. Now I have promised myself not to put off living. Living is for today, not tomorrow.'

Nancy pursed her lips, irritated as she took down the clichés that she would have to change later to jazz up her article. She was forming an idea about the riveting piece she would do on Chiara concurrently with the one for *People*, a sensationalized exposé that she would sell for a fat fee to an Italian gossip weekly under a pseudonym. Chiara stubbornly fielded the probing questions about her present love life, her fortune, reputed to be more than thirty million dollars, inherited from Abner Wolfe. As Chiara talked about herself, the journalist studied her, concluding that she had had a face-lift, a nose job, silicone implants.

'Let's talk about love,' Nancy asked in an intimate voice. 'When all the glamour is stripped away, how do you view a relationship between a man and a woman? Are you a romantic or a realist, who thinks that love needs a practical basis?'

'I'm a romantic, definitely!' Chiara enthused. 'My husband and I were very romantic together. A man and a woman are bound by destiny like the strands of a rope. Separate them, and you'll find one has taken the shape of the other. That's how it was with my husband and me,' she said, avoiding Sandy's eyes.

Nancy sucked in her breath impatiently. 'What does the future hold for you? What does love hold for you?' she said with dramatic emphasis that demanded an answer.

'Ask me that when the future arrives, tomorrow, next week. A widow needs much tenderness and more understanding than an ordinary woman.'

A poignant note crept into her voice which the journalist didn't seem to catch. Chiara was jarred by a peal of brittle laughter that suggested Nancy found her sentiments more naïve than touching.

'I sincerely hope you find what you're looking for here. The Italian male is a subject I would love to discuss at length. Take my advice and tread warily now you're in your native country, otherwise you may be in for a rude shock.' Her blue eyes went dead.

Chiara gave a sparkling laugh. 'I don't know any Italian men. None at all.'

'Well, now you're here, no doubt they'll be beating your door down. Keep it closed until you know who's on the other side, believe me.' Sensing she had said enough, Nancy returned to her notebook.

When the time allotted for the interview came to an end, Chiara rose and nodded to her secretary.

'What a pleasure it was to be interviewed by a woman who is so charming, so sensitive. You and I are so much alike. We've traded one country for another, haven't we?' she reflected wisely.

The moment the door closed behind Nancy, Chiara's smile hardened to a frown. 'What a terrible woman! I hate to think what kind of bitchy article she will write about me.'

'Don't be too hard on Nancy. She's not a bad old broad, really. She's an institution in this town.'

'Like you, you mean?' replied Chiara with a laugh. 'At least you're not bitter.' She called to her secretary, 'Diane, order some sandwiches from room service. Chicken with no mayonnaise.

Go on, do it now,' she said irritably when the secretary didn't get up immediately. 'I'm exhausted,' said Chiara, sinking into a chair and kicking off her shoes. 'And the day is just beginning. We have meetings, more meetings; then I'm looking at some houses to rent later in the day.'

'Tired of the Hassler already?' asked Sandy, pouring himself a bourbon from the bar.

'Yes, tired, sick and tired. I need space, room to breathe. There's no privacy here.'

Sandy raised an eyebrow, but said nothing. In the short time Chiara had been in Rome he couldn't help but notice that she would do anything to avoid being alone. She demanded the constant attention of the entourage she had gathered around herself, including a personal maid and masseuse, her secretary and a chauffeur. Whenever she was lonely, at any time of day or night, she would phone him on some pretext or other.

There had been a very long gap in their friendship when Chiara left Rome for the States in the sixties; but when Sandy started going to Hollywood again and Chiara was living in luxurious seclusion with Abner Wolfe in Bel Air, she had latched on to him as a last tenuous link with her native country, a role he had taken on good-naturedly. Now, years later, she had rewarded him by nominating him as director of her mini-series.

'How do you know Nancy Rogers?' Chiara asked as he sat down beside her. 'What reason has she to be so bitter?'

'I guess she's got a few reasons. I remember one night she cried on my shoulder after she made the mistake of falling in love with a young gigolo. He was a real ladykiller, that one. Nearly broke her heart when he married a rich European girl. Nancy took too many sleeping tablets and tried to end it all. Life is funny, isn't it? Would you believe, he's a good friend of mine now. In fact you'll probably meet him the night of the party at the Osteria del Orso. His name is Prospero Vallone.'

Chiara leaned forward and plucked a wilted leaf from the spray of roses. 'He doesn't sound like the kind of person we want to invite – an ex-gigolo.' Her voice was coolly disapproving. 'Cross him off the list. An opportunist. If there's anything I don't like in a man, it's that.'

'Hey, I can't do that. He's an old friend of mine, and besides he's an important guy now. He's just bought a chunk of the network that might run the series here. Besides, the invitations have been sent.

'Christ, I wish I hadn't mentioned him,' Sandy muttered under his breath.

'I don't want you to invite him,' she said adamantly. 'We agreed we would keep the party select. You're giving the party for me, to introduce me, to get publicity for the film. Somebody with a shady past is not welcome as far as I am concerned . . .'

Sandy's eyes narrowed. 'Chiara, everybody has a past. Me, Vallone, you . . .'

As their eyes met, she was reminded of all the little lies, the deceptions she had perpetrated in the interview. She wondered if Sandy had noticed her nervousness when Nancy Rogers had strayed perilously close to the subject of her early career. There'd been a couple of years when, out of desperation, she had made a string of low-budget porn movies. Sandy was one of the few people who was aware that Abner had paid a large sum to have the negatives destroyed before her American television show, just after they were married.

'If you insist about Prospero Vallone, then you leave me no choice,' he said with a shrug. 'But I think you're making a big mistake.'

She frowned for a moment, and he could see her wavering one way, then another. At last she murmured, 'I don't care. Do what you want.'

His face broke into a broad smile. 'You won't be sorry, believe me. You'll like the guy. He's separated now from his wife, so he's a bit lonely. Say, I haven't told you yet how well I thought you handled the interview,' he added to sweeten her mood. 'Congratulations. You handled it like a pro.'

'Don't try to flatter me. I know I was bad,' she said with a shrug that said she appreciated his compliment all the same. For an instant her eyes revealed all her fears.

'No, you were good, just right, and I want to tell you so. Isn't that what friends are for?'

'I know they are for something, but I can't remember what.'

'You're heartless, Chiara, but I love you. By the way, that colour you're wearing – I like that colour. You should wear it in the reunion scene with Isabella and Klaus.'

He visualized Chiara through the lens of a camera. Her sculpted hair dishevelled by the wind, her make-up played down, not immaculately applied as it was now. He mentally stripped away her jewellery, modified her beautifully cut gold-green dress, transforming it into a simple garment that displayed her curvaceous body to perfection and made her flawless skin glow.

The camera would capture all that and more, but it would fall in love with her wide sensuous mouth and long dancing eyes set in a little girl's face, a face that had changed greatly with the years, but that had not aged. One minute it registered a shocking petulance, the next a mesmeric femininity, a strange duality that had captivated Sandy Vincent from the moment he first set eyes on Chiara. It seemed to him that two beings still warred within her, one the vulnerable adolescent, the other a shrewd, grasping woman who let nothing stand in her way.

'You know, Chiara, sometimes I can sense in you the same kid I picked out from a crowd of hopefuls in the Piazza Navona,' he remarked as she stared vacantly into the distance, her chin resting on her hand.

She looked up sharply. 'Can you? In that case, if you think I look as young as that, why don't you want me to play Isabella as a young girl? Can you tell me why?' she insisted, reverting to a subject about which they had argued incessantly.

'That's dirty pool. That's not what I meant, and you know it.'

'But you can see the logic, can't you?' she countered.

'Chiara – listen. Beautiful as you are, nobody will believe you're eighteen. You know I love you, but be realistic. They want someone young and hot. Now, we've been through all this. The Germans, the Italians will back out if you insist on playing both roles.'

'What about Stefanie Powers? She played a girl of eighteen and a woman in her forties in *Princess Daisy*.'

'Honey, Stefanie Powers is a bankable name. She's a star. Everybody knows her name. Sad to say, good as *Ciao, Senator* was, it was too long ago. You'll come back again after this series, believe me, but not playing both roles. You're a voluptuous, beautiful woman, so use it for all it's worth. Anyway, Isabella the grown woman is the meaty part, and you've got it.'

Still unconvinced, she bit her lip. 'But that means I won't even be seen in the first episode.' A troubled expression darkened her eyes.

'Is that what's worrying you? Why didn't you say so? This new script is going to have the young Isabella in flashback interwoven with the grown-up Isabella, so you won't be absent from the screen for more than a few minutes at a time.'

'I'm not so sure. You're exaggerating just to please me, aren't you?' she said, slightly mollified.

'No, of course not. Anyway, we can't change everything now. I've already spent six months of my life so far getting this package together.'

'You cast the role of the young Isabella behind my back,' she reminded him.

'I did it for one good reason. For the hundredth time, it was the only way we could come up with the money from German and Italian television. Unless you want to put up all the money yourself. At one point I reckoned it would cost five million per hour per episode, maybe more with cast over-runs. I wonder if you want to do that? It's not too late, you know. That's another six million on top of what you paid for the book, and your fifty-one per cent stake. Is that what you want?' he said, knowing he touched a delicate nerve.

The look she gave him suggested that where money was concerned Chiara was as suspicious of the future and its depredations as any old peasant woman clutching her purse. For just an instant, Sandy had a glimpse of what she might be like in old age. But instead of hiding her money in the lining of her coat or underneath the floorboards of a cottage, Chiara had securely invested the bulk of the Wolfe millions. She had already proved her shrewdness when they went over the financial details of the mini-series budget, showing the same relentless attention to detail with which he knew she handled her personal finances. The clashes that had ensued had already begun to try Sandy's patience. Softening the anger he felt, he said,

'Chiara, there's a lot I don't know about you. Something in you will always remain a mystery to me, but sometimes I think underneath it all you're still the same frightened young girl who had her purse stolen by a thief on a Vespa and who is determined not to let it happen again.'

She looked questioningly at Sandy, her mind instantly reverting back to the incident. With no effort at all, Chiara could evoke the terror of that day in Rome when a thief had snatched her handbag containing her life savings. She could still hear the menacing whine of the motor scooter as it died away down the narrow, dark alley, and the rising beat of her heart as she realized she was penniless. Ultimately, the loss had proved to be a golden link in a chain of circumstances that determined the course of her life. If she hadn't needed a job, she wouldn't have met Sandy, which would have meant she wouldn't be here at this moment. Her mind stretched back to the past, to the very beginning.

She had just folded her white apron and hung it on the door of the linen room in the depths of the Hotel Inghilterra not far from the Spanish Steps. After hurriedly slipping out of her checked uniform and into the deliciously cool blue summer dress she had bought with her first week's pay as a chambermaid, Chiara rushed up the stairs and out of the service entrance, where her dark, plump friend Giuseppina was already waiting for her.

The two girls walked down the street, chattering excitedly about the event that had occupied their minds for days – the movie being shot in the Piazza Navona which needed several dozen extras.

Waves of summer heat fragrant with coffee mingled with the cool currents that wafted from the ancient stone courtyards and doorways as they hurried along. Tossing her hair, Chiara adopted an air of careless disregard to fend off the caressing eyes of men who clicked their tongues and whistled as she passed. After three months in Rome she had grown used to the constant attention. In the correct atmosphere of the hotel she played the role of a demure chambermaid, making beds and pressing clothes for rich Americans and Europeans; but once she escaped into the streets she played the provocative young seductress who left a trail of male admiration in her wake.

'*Ciao, bellissima,*' called a brawny young labourer, resting on his shovel as he ogled her. Another smacked his lips as he sped by on a scooter. She allowed only a shadow of a smile to express her acknowledgement.

'When we're out together they all go wild, but when I'm on my own nothing happens at all,' complained the plump dark Giuseppina as she looked at her ravishing friend.

'You're not doing the right things,' counselled Chiara, looping her arm through Giuseppina's. Her plain, good-natured companion had proved to be a treasure-house of information, from where to get a room for next to nothing, to the location of the cheapest and best shops and trattorias in the vicinity. 'You want to lose a little weight and wear a little make-up. That's all.'

'It wouldn't make any difference,' she replied with a sigh, envying Chiara's liquid eyes, her slender arms, her figure barely contained by the tight summer dress.

As Giuseppina chattered, Chiara's thoughts leapt to their adventure, and to the giddy prospect of escape from anonymity if she became an extra in a movie. For a moment the expensive boutiques along the Via Condotti interrupted her fantasy. The two girls stopped in the cool shade cast by striped awnings to feast their eyes on fine leather goods, delicate lingerie and evening gowns locked behind the plate-glass windows where every luxury Rome had to offer was on display. Chiara imagined herself the proud possessor of everything that she saw, and on that sunny afternoon her dreams seemed within reach. As she pressed her nose to the window of a renowned jeweller, a necklace worth millions of lire danced close to her throat.

Several times that summer Chiara had been approached by suave, well-dressed young men who had made lucrative propositions disguised by effusive flattery. Some were pimps trying to recruit whores. They cajoled her with the most tempting promises of ease and luxury, even of love. If she were to believe them, she would be rich enough to buy necklaces like the one she was looking at now. Beneath the wheedling promises of these smooth men, however, Chiara sensed a threatening undercurrent which held her back. At times like this, strolling with Giuseppina past the luxury shops from which she would never be able to afford to buy a single item, she always reflected again, wondering if she was a fool not to take the easy way out rather than to remain toiling at the hotel for such low wages.

They crossed the busy street towards the piazza where the filming was in progress, bringing the traffic to a standstill and causing chaos among the curious passers-by. Chiara's heart fell when she saw the competition. There were literally hundreds of girls swarming at the meeting-point, where a man with a megaphone was trying to organize them into some sort of order.

It seemed that every girl in Rome had the same consuming desire, and as Chiara observed the others she lost hope. Her simple dress seemed absurdly understated compared with the fashionable frocks worn by some of them. Her hair, too, was all wrong, she realized, envying the elaborate sprayed styles concocted by expensive hairdressers. Women's chatter, the smell of their perfume and sweat filled the air as she and Giuseppina joined the queue. Girls with heavily made-up eyes flashed dark contemptuous looks at her, and she returned their hauteur with an icy stare.

The line moved along, and she and Giuseppina squeezed each other's hands for luck. Ahead, she could see a man seated in a chair who gave each girl no more than a few seconds' glance, sorting them into groups like piles of laundry. When it was her turn, she dabbed her face with her handkerchief to blot off the perspiration, then walked confidently in his direction, her head held proudly. Her heart pounded excitedly when he nodded for her to join a group of other anxious hopefuls. They waited interminably in the blazing sun, until her dress was clinging to her back. Finally, there came a shout from the man:

'Hola, hey, you there. The one in the blue dress.'

Everyone seemed to be looking at her. 'You mean me?' Chiara replied, looking at the others.

'Yes, you, dumb-bell,' hissed a jealous rival.

The man strode up to her. 'You want to be in the picture?'

She nodded, too startled to reply. 'This way, then. That woman over there will tell you what to do.'

An efficient-looking woman in a plain dress and glasses led her to a man seated at the centre of the confused scene.

'Signor Vincent, is this the one you want?'

He rose with a smile and put his hand lightly on her arm, almost in a fatherly way.

'What is your name?' he said in Italian, with an American accent so thick she could barely understand him.

'Chiara. Chiara Galla.' She spoke in a whisper.

'Now, Chiara, when I tell you, you are to walk towards the end of the street,' he explained, leading her to an alley where a camera had been stationed. 'I want you to walk along just normally, without looking back. Do you understand?'

She nodded, agog for his every syllable.

'We're doing it in one take, so you must do it right the first time.' Now he spoke impatiently in English, and the female assistant translated.

Chiara waited an interminable time as the sun passed overhead. She had begun to think they had forgotten about her when the assistant director, a small hairy man with a dictatorial manner, grabbed her by the arm and led her in front of the camera, where a woman thrust a basket of flowers into her hand.

'All right, now,' shouted the man.

She walked forward, but it seemed to take for ever to reach the corner where she was supposed to disappear. Then a terrible thing happened. As she turned the corner, the basket slipped on her arm, causing some of the flowers to tumble to the ground. Unthinkingly, she bent down and turned her face towards the camera. When she looked up in alarm, she found herself staring into the handsome face of the star of the movie, Marcello Mastroianni.

'Cut!' boomed the enraged assistant. '*È pazza, la cretina!* We'll have to shoot it again.'

Sandy Vincent calmly wagged his finger.

'No, it will be all right.' He gave Chiara a smile before turning away.

Chiara felt as if a great weight had been lifted off her chest now that it was over. A girl with a notebook took her name and made her sign a register. She was surprised to be paid anything after the blunder she had made.

'You can come and collect your money on Friday.'

'I can't come on Friday. I will be working at the Hotel Inghilterra.'

'Never mind. I'll send a messenger over with it. It'll be twenty thousand lire.'

She gasped. It was more than a month's pay at the hotel, including tips, and it seemed like a gift to compensate for her stolen money which she still grieved for.

That Friday the manager of the hotel handed Chiara an envelope with her name on it. She tore it open and found four crisp five-thousand-lire notes. Putting them back into the envelope, she saw there was a message inside.

'What is it?' asked Giuseppina impatiently as she read the paper with open-mouthed astonishment.

'It's a note from Signor Vincent. He wants me to go to Cinecittà for a screen test next week,' she murmured.

Later that afternoon Sandy and Chiara were in conference with the location director in the hotel suite. When the phone rang, the secretary got up to answer it.

'Mr Vincent, it's for you.'

Sandy came back to the table rubbing his hands. 'Guess who that was? It looks like we've got it all ironed out with Felix Hartman's agent – he's signing. I can just see those Emmys lining up on the mantelpiece right now. I can see it, I can taste it,' he enthused. 'Isn't it fantastic, Chiara?'

She gave a rich laugh. 'I never had any doubt he would sign.'

'If we can just clinch the deal for Romano Girardini to play Naldo, then we've got it made. Getting back to Nino,' he said energetically, 'what do you have to tell us about the locations?'

The handsome young Italian, who had been eyeing Chiara from the moment he shook her hand, said: 'There are a number of ideal places on this list. Here – you can see for yourself. I've narrowed it down to five,' he said, handing them a list of villages he had already scouted, accompanied by detailed descriptions and photographs.

'It must be in Tuscany,' pronounced Chiara. 'After all, that's where the book takes place. It would be more authentic. I want to inspect all the places myself,' she added, thumbing through the details. 'What's wrong with this one? You've crossed it off.'

'We'd have to build a fountain for the shooting scene and it would be expensive.'

'It's a pity,' said Sandy, gazing over Chiara's shoulder at the photograph. 'The piazza looks perfect.'

'It's not so bad. There's another better one with a bigger piazza – San Treviano. But the church isn't so good.'

'Maybe we could do just the one church scene here – let's think about it.'

After they had discussed several other locations in detail, Sandy glanced at his watch. 'Hey, everybody, time's up.'

'Yes, I have things to do. I'm supposed to be looking at a villa to rent this afternoon. Call the agent and tell him I want to come at four,' said Chiara to her secretary.

'Not so fast – I've got a big surprise for you, Chiara. One that's well worth waiting for.' Sandy zoomed to the television set and began to twiddle the knobs. 'Sit down, everybody, sit down,' he ordered with a mischievous smile as a soap commercial came into focus.

Chiara was giving a string of orders to Diane when the notes of a familiar song filled the room. She stopped in mid-sentence, her eyes widening in surprise as she stared at the television. Clapping her hands to her mouth, she exclaimed:

'What? What's this? Is it . . .?'

'That's right,' said Sandy triumphantly. 'It's none other – ta-da,' he cried with a flourish.

'*Ciao, Senator*' in bold red and green letters flashed on to the screen against a shimmering backdrop of the Trevi fountain.

Darting closer to the television, Chiara threw her arms around Sandy and burst into delighted laughter.

'But how did this happen? Tell me, you're wonderful,' she said with a sigh, giving him a kiss.

'A little of this, a little of that,' he said, rubbing his hands together. 'But no, to be honest, I can't take any credit. They were going to re-run it anyway some time soon. I just bumped into somebody who helped it happen a little sooner, that's all.'

Chiara hadn't heard a word he said. Putting her finger to her lips, she grabbed a chair and stationed herself in front of the set, completely absorbed as the credits rolled by. There was Chiara Galla of fifteen years ago, with dark smooth hair lacquered stiff, her stunning figure all curves and legs in a dress that ended well above the knees. The montage of shots that unfolded showed her with Senator George Kirkland, played by a well-known actor with a handsomely chiselled face. A quick, condensed version of his romance with Gina, the Italian interpreter, flashed by, set against the Colosseum, the Forum, ending with the two of them hand-in-hand in St Peter's Square, feeding the pigeons. As the senator carried his Italian bride over the threshold of their Georgetown home, the scene dissolved into the opening of an episode.

'My favourite! This one is my favourite!' Chiara exclaimed to no one in particular. The plush suite of the Hassler Hotel ceased to exist as she lost herself in the zany antics of Gina Kirkland giving her first Washington dinner party. She sighed, she laughed, completely reliving the moment when Gina marched proudly into the dining-room bearing a platter of her favourite spaghetti.

'Watch this – watch the senator's face. He's so angry that I made spaghetti instead of a roast. It was the only thing I knew how to cook. My husband is trying to impress all these important people with his new Italian wife. She cooks spaghetti and they're all wearing tuxedos. Isn't it funny?' she cried, glancing at Sandy. She dissolved in laughter as the Americans tried to attack the spaghetti with knives and forks. 'This is the good part – watch this. It's where I teach them all to eat spaghetti Italian-style.' There was a lingering close-up of Chiara's puckered mouth as she twirled spaghetti dripping with sauce on to her fork and launched it into her mouth. The hotel suite was filled with the brassy ring of canned laughter.

'Watch me, watch my eyes as I look around the table at all those clean white shirts, those silk dinner dresses!' Like a storm breaking, Gina's face fell at the catastrophe she saw was about to happen. With an exclamation in Italian, she leapt from the dining-table and the camera followed her as she ran upstairs to the nursery where she frantically grabbed a handful of freshly laundered nappies, then ran back downstairs.

'Gina ties them around everybody's neck. The best shot is with the big fat senator. Look at his funny expression when I lean forward in my low-cut dress. For television in 1971 this was very sexy,' she informed them with a peal of laughter as she clapped her hands in delight. Canned laughter echoed in the room for the next twenty minutes as the episode unrolled, culminating in the guests leaving the dinner party, all smiles. It ended, as did all episodes of the series, when the door closed and Senator Kirkland embraced his irrepressible wife.

When it was all over Chiara came back to reality. Sandy, the locations manager, her secretary, were all regarding her silently with fixed smiles. It was Sandy who broke the silence.

'What a great show – terrific! It was one of the best. It should have run for ever. There should have been that sequel they talked about in the beginning, *Ciao, President*.'

Chiara stood up with a shrug and silently left the room. Sandy's eyes followed her towards the bedroom and focused on the photograph of Abner Wolfe. His impish, appealing face didn't disguise the metallic strength of his personality that was legendary in broadcasting. With the consuming zeal of a self-made Titan, he had created a television empire from a single small radio station. Sandy realized that Wolfe Productions had probably failed to pick up their option on *Ciao* and that Abner Wolfe had quietly nipped his wife's career in the bud with the same self-serving instinct he had used to destroy the negatives of her undesirable films. As she closed the bedroom door behind her, Sandy was reminded once again of the child–woman whose treasures had been snatched by a thief.

For a moment Sandy stood in a pool of filtered light absently listening to the muted sounds of traffic coming from the street below as he thought about Chiara. In the three decades of their friendship he had witnessed the birth of several Chiara Gallas. He had known her so long that one had merged into another in his mind, but on reflection he wasn't sure that he didn't prefer the young girl he had first met when filming in the Piazza Navona. He had never imagined at the time that he was starting her down the road to stardom on another continent. After all these years he wouldn't disillusion her by telling her that it was nothing more than pure chance that had led to her first bit part in his movie. He indulgently allowed her to perpetuate the myth that he had been struck by a thunderbolt the moment he laid eyes on her. In reality he had been too harassed, too hot, too preoccupied to give more than a few seconds to the final selection of a young girl for a minor scene. He might have liked the colour of her hair, her dress, anything. It wasn't until afterwards when he was watching the rushes that he recognized that she might have something special. Whether she had dropped the basket of flowers she was carrying on purpose or not, nobody knew, but it meant that her young face had been frozen for an instant on film, just long enough for him to get a look at her.

She had proved a remarkable pupil though she quickly lost the innocence he later remembered with nostalgia, and metamorphosed into a sinuous bombshell at Cinecittà in the early sixties. The promise he had seen in her in the early days had never quite materialized, and then, when she got her ticket to Hollywood as the wife of an American stuntman, he lost track of her. They had been unexpectedly reunited ten years later when she called his name across the lobby at the Academy Awards. At first, he couldn't place the super-glamorous beauty on the arm of the legendary Abner Wolfe, an ageing magnate with a boyish smile and white hair, many years her senior. She was resplendent in black velvet and silver lamé with easily a half a million dollars' worth of diamonds around her neck and wrists. No longer a sultry young starlet, she was now aloof, regal and elegantly turned out, her interpretation of the class that went with her new status.

'Sandy, don't you remember me? It's Chiara — Chiara Galla. Don't try and fool me. I'd know you anywhere.'

He stared at her uncomprehendingly for a moment, struck speechless by what he saw. The Chiara Galla he had known didn't speak such fluent English in a low melodious voice and only a trace of an accent. Everything about her had changed — from her teeth which he guessed had been skilfully capped, to her slightly imperfect nose that had been beautifully rechiselled by the best surgeon Hollywood could offer.

When she saw the look of shock in his eyes, Sandy guessed that Chiara probably regretted her impulse. Taking the hint he quickly regained his self-possession and kissed her on the cheek whispering, 'Ciao, bella,' as if they had only just parted. Thinking about it later, he realized that it wasn't just her physical transformation which had made her almost unrecognizable: the hungry ambition which had burned in her eyes when he first knew her had vanished to be replaced by the apparently impregnable self-confidence that Chiara had gained during her years in Hollywood. But, as Sandy got to know her all over again, he became aware that Chiara's dignified and commanding presence concealed a pathetic lack of direction.

Coming back to the present he wondered what the next transition in Chiara's life would bring now she was a rich and independent woman. He couldn't help wondering whether she knew herself.

Chapter 4

ETHIOPIA

Under the burning Ethiopian sun, Cotton stood to one side as the photographer who had accompanied her on an assignment snapped his Nikon in the direction of a pack of pot-bellied, ragged children scavenging over a rubbish dump. In a T-shirt and loose trousers, she folded her arms and glanced up at the vultures wheeling overhead and casting jagged shadows on the dry earth while she searched for the words to begin her next story for the *Herald*. When the opening words formed in her mind, she pulled her tape recorder from her canvas shoulder bag and spoke into the microphone, training her gaze on the distant blue hills that ringed the valley.

> This is where it all began, and in Makele, as elsewhere in the country, the underlying causes of famine remain untouched. The city of white tents that has all but usurped the valley rises against the blue hills like an ice floe, and like an ice floe seems impervious to the frail human efforts to melt it. Makele symbolizes the power of an extraordinary global response – of people who have shown they care. But filling empty cups is not enough. Roads must be built, crops must be coaxed from the parched earth, wells must be dug unless we are to see an entire civilization discarded on the scrap heap.

Chris aimed the camera at her. 'Hey, hold it – you look great in that light. I want to get a couple of you just like that.'

She continued to talk into the microphone while looking into the lens. As he kept snapping, her composure broke. 'What is this, anyway? I must look like hell.'

'This is for the book jacket when you write your memoirs. Trust me.'

'I've heard that one before.'

He caught her face in transition as the expression in her intelligent eyes changed to amusement. It was a face too powerful to be conventionally beautiful, with challenging angles that suggested strong character. Her darkly sketched eyebrows above long amber eyes were in startling contrast to her wheat-coloured hair. Chris kept trying to allay Cotton's scepticism, waiting for just the moment he wanted.

As he put the lens cap on his camera, Cotton said peevishly, 'Sure you've got enough?'

He gave her a look that said she was trying his patience, then mopped the sweat from his receding hairline. She reached into her bag for her sunglasses to ward off the glare that had already given her a headache.

'Yeah – that's it.'

'In that case, we could wrap it up for today,' she said as they walked towards the Land-Rover they had driven to the rubbish dump.

'Yeah, good idea. Why don't we have a few beers? It's nearly noon, you know.'

She shook her head. 'I want to catch a few more of the volunteers back at the camp. This is a good time to do it. I'll meet you back at the house later, and in the meantime maybe you could drop me off at the Red Cross headquarters. I'll find my way from there.'

Chris stroked his beard thoughtfully. 'I think I'll come out here at dawn and get some shots of those tents at sunrise in colour, just for the record.' He gazed at the sea of white pyramids where the refugees were camped in their thousands. 'I'll have to time it just right. Father McGuire can probably tell me what time the sun comes up.'

'You can borrow my alarm.'

'I have a better idea. Why don't you come to my tent before

sunrise for breakfast in bed – or something even cosier if you'd rather. I hate waking up alone.'

'I'm terribly accident-prone. You might get a cup of scalding coffee poured down your silk pyjamas,' she retorted with amusement. She and Chris had had a fling years ago when they were on a story in Spain, and they were still good friends.

Opening the door of the Land-Rover he said: 'If you change your mind I wouldn't hold it against you.'

'You wouldn't hold what against me?'

He chuckled and put his arm around her affectionately.

'Are you still involved with that no-good Englishman?'

'Do you mean Mike? Lord, no. That was over ages ago,' she replied, thinking it seemed like ages even though it was only three months.

'I'm glad to hear it,' said Chris. 'Last time I saw you you were talking about cottages in the country. That's not your scene at all, no way,' he remarked sagely.

'No, Chris, you're wrong about me. Lately I've had this fatal urge to stay in one place for more than a month.'

'That *is* serious. Better get to a doctor and ask for something to cure it,' he said over his shoulder, taking off his cameras one by one. 'Are you winding down or something? This isn't the Cotton Castello I remember.'

'Not winding down. Changing.' Cotton didn't comment further, but since Beirut six months before, her life seemed to have shifted on its axis. It was something she hadn't discussed with anyone. Change was a subject she didn't particularly want to think about, and she was glad when the sound of a motorbike interrupted their serious train of conversation.

She and Chris turned to see a trail of dust coming up the hill towards them. As the motorbike approached, Cotton saw the rider was a brawny young man with square shoulders and a mop of black curly hair. He roared to a halt in front of the Land-Rover.

'Hello,' he called, leaping off the bike. 'I'm Seamus Mahony of Aid Network.' He extended his hand to each of them.

'Cotton Castello,' she said with a nod. She was struck at once by Seamus Mahony's beguiling Irish face and bright blue

eyes, and she knew instinctively that he would feature somehow in one of her stories.

'You two are from the *Herald*, aren't you? I heard you were
up here and thought I'd say hello. Are you finished in Makele?'

'We'll be wrapping it up in the next day or two,' said
Cotton.

'If I can be of any service just let me know. Have you seen
the maternity unit on the other side of the camp? When I heard
from Father McGuire that you were here, I said I thought it
would be a shame to leave Makele without seeing it. It's run by
Irish sisters. Would you like to have a look?'

'Ask her. She's the boss lady,' said Chris.

'Yes, why not? Can you take me there now? If we use it,
Chris could come over tomorrow and get some pictures.'

'In that case, why don't you hop aboard?'

When he had started the bike, she hitched her bag over her
shoulder and hopped on. Clinging to Seamus's torso, she held
tight as he accelerated down the road.

'Been here before?' he called over his shoulder.

'No, not to Makele. I went to Lalibela last year, just briefly.
We were in Wollo last week. What about you? Have you been
here long?' With one hand she brushed a strand of hair from
her eyes.

'Since the Flood, it seems to me,' he replied, making her
smile.

After a bumpy, dusty drive they arrived on the other side of
the valley and Cotton jumped off. As they walked along
Seamus filled her in on the project they were going to see,
housed in a mud-walled building roofed with tin.

'Some people think that famine is nature's way of checking
population growth, but they couldn't be more wrong. Death
makes people breed even faster, as if to preserve the species – a
kind of perverted logic.'

Cotton fished out her tape recorder and said a few words to
mark their entry into the maternity ward. For the next hour
they toured the hospital, accompanied by a nun in a short
white habit. Cotton sensed the despair in the stiflingly hot ward,
where uncomplaining mothers administered to whimpering

babies on mats on the floor. They didn't bother to shoo away the flies from their noses and mouths. She watched a gaunt woman smiling tenderly at a pathetically undersized infant in her arms who seemed to have no desire to suckle her shrivelled breast.

Suddenly, without warning, Cotton was struck by a powerful wave of maternal tenderness. She was acutely aware of patient dark eyes following her as she moved among the mothers shrouded in their *shammas* while the sister delivered a quiet commentary. Cotton paused by a mother trying to comfort a baby whose cry seemed strangely hollow.

'May I hold him?' she asked impulsively. Looking at the nun she added, 'Do you think she'd mind?'

'No, not a bit.' She spoke in Tigrean to the mother.

Cotton gently took the baby boy, naked except for a small necklace of beads. She knew the unexpectedly poignant moment would always remain stamped in her mind. To her surprise, the child stopped crying as she hugged him to her. A lump came to her throat and tears to her eyes when she comprehended the resignation in his dark eyes set in an old man's face.

The mother touched her trouser leg and uttered something in a beseeching tone.

'What did she say?'

'She wonders if you would like to have the baby,' said the sister.

For a moment Cotton didn't reply, but stared helplessly into the mother's eyes. With difficulty she said, 'Please explain that I'm very sorry, but that I can't take him with me. Would you say it's impossible because I'm working.' Feeling like a fool, she exchanged a glance with Seamus. Why couldn't she take him home with her, him and a dozen others?

When the sister spoke to the woman, a look of dull acceptance passed across her face; there was no disappointment. Cotton unfastened a gold chain she wore around her neck with a blue enamelled St Christopher's medal, which Mike had bought her in Beirut after her kidnapping, and pressed it into the mother's brown tapered fingers. As they moved on, Cotton saw her regarding it blankly, turning the medal over and over.

When they left the hospital, she and Seamus stood in the shade on the verandah.

'What do you think? Would you like to come back tomorrow morning and get some pics?'

'Yes, I would, thanks,' she replied. 'I'll tell Chris.' Her mind was crowded with images of squalid, pathetic humanity huddled together in the refugee camps she had visited.

'You know, Seamus, I've seen a lot of disturbing things in my career, but this is without doubt the worst. I don't know how you stand it.'

'You get used to it,' he said cheerfully.

'What do you usually do for a living?'

'Before I came out here I was a cinematographer in London. The ad agency I was with went broke. How about coming to the market and having a few glasses of local beer? I know a place that sells the best *talla* in Ethiopia. It's a well-guarded secret.'

'Great. I haven't had a chance to see the market yet.'

They walked through an alley of closely packed stalls made of sticks and roofed in tin or matting. The pungent odour of decay assaulted Cotton's nose. Cotton shooed away a swarm of flies from her face.

They paused at a stall where a wizened old man was sitting on his haunches wrapped in a dun-coloured cloak. The cry *'feranj'* volleyed through the lane from a pack of barefoot children who had spotted Cotton and Seamus.

While Seamus chatted with the old man in Tigrean, Cotton regarded the jewellery spread out on a blanket in the dust. She bent to touch the precious Coptic amulets wrought in silver, rich dollops of amber strung together, corals and turquoise.

'These must come from the refugee camp.'

'Yes,' said Seamus. 'They sell them for a song to any trader who will give them cash for food. I'd like you to choose one to replace that necklace you left behind in the ward.'

'You're not serious?' she said with a laugh.

'I am indeed. We must support the local economy, don't you agree?' he said, with a mischievous glint in his blue eyes.

'Well, if you put it that way.' Something about his

expression made up her mind, even though she suspected he could ill afford it.

'Are you sure this won't cost you a month's salary?' she said, picking out a small amulet of Coptic silver.

'It's all for a good cause,' he answered, taking the money from his wallet.

'Thank you very much. It's something I will always cherish. But you didn't need to, you know.'

'I wanted to,' he said simply.

They came to a row of whitewashed mud buildings where a tall tree cast a fine shade over rough wooden benches and tables where men sat drinking beer. When they sat down Cotton realized her knees were shaking from the accumulated emotion and fatigue of the last two weeks.

'A cardinal rule of my life has been not to get involved emotionally with my subject,' she said. 'In this case, I'm afraid I am involved. I suddenly feel that I've come a long way from home, wherever that is.'

'Where is it, anyway?'

'London, but that's just my base. No, home is somewhere else,' she replied, not allowing herself to examine the image the word implied. 'I suddenly feel like talking. Do you mind?'

'I'm here to listen,' said Seamus.

She found herself opening up to him, talking about herself as she never would to someone in the closed world of news teams. Memories of the last years surfaced as she recalled Poland under martial law, violence in Ireland, terrorist attacks in Paris, assignations in Spain, Nicaragua, the Philippines. Several glasses of strong local beer loosened her tongue as she unburdened herself in a tranquil patch of shade surrounded by a welter of despair.

'Feel better now?' asked Seamus, as he watched her gulp her beer.

'Yes, much. You've soothed my troubled spirit,' she said, hoping it didn't sound trite. 'I think it's time for R and R. Things must be getting on top of me,' she added by way of explanation. 'Lately I've been lying awake nights wondering what I'm doing. Before I came here I covered Mrs Aquino in the Philippines; before that I was shuttling all over Europe; before that, Beirut.'

'Don't you ever slow down?'

'Rarely. I took a couple of weeks' break at Christmas. Went to Switzerland by myself,' she admitted, feeling ashamed of herself when she recalled that Seamus hadn't had a break for eighteen months. An excuse sprang to her lips. 'It was a reward for being held hostage in Beirut in September.'

'I see.' Sensing she didn't want to elaborate, Seamus didn't pry.

'Where are you staying?'

'The hotel was full so the Red Cross managed to find us a house with some spare rooms.'

'What are you doing tonight? Busy?'

It seemed to her his reserved expression concealed a gnawing loneliness she understood and that made them soulmates even for only a few hours.

'I'm not doing anything, unless you call sharing rations with the German Red Cross busy. But I could easily give that a miss.'

'I do an outstanding gourmet dinner on my primus stove. It's a sight to behold with flames leaping to the ceiling – a bit like *crêpes suzettes* at the Ritz. If you come I'll throw in a bit of Spam.'

'That does it. I'm coming,' she said with a laugh.

That evening Cotton left the house at the edge of town where she was staying with Chris and the ABC news team. The heat of the day had vanished, and a biting wind now swept across the straggling town of Makele. She zipped up the padded jacket over her safari suit and picked her way carefully down the road lit only by reflected light from the houses tucked away in eucalyptus groves that had once been inhabited by Italian colonists. She remembered meeting some of those exiles when she was growing up in Italy. At the time she had felt sorry for them, knowing there was nothing worse than being banished from where you belonged.

She passed people huddled around fires, their slender limbs

protruding from the blankets wrapped around them. She observed a dark, graceful woman preparing the evening meal before a fire. Her elegant movements made tall shadows against a wall as she served her husband who was giving titbits to two children waiting patiently at his side.

Turning a corner, Cotton was reminded of the greater reality of Makele when she caught sight of the camp in the valley, its thousand white tents like rugged mountain peaks against the gold-crested line of hills rising in strange shapes against the sky set with bright stars. She stopped a moment in a hissing grove of eucalyptus to contemplate the awesome beauty of the highlands. The stars in the purple dome of the sky had a piercing clarity and seemed to pulsate with a cold twinkling lustre as if they were being spun by the wind.

Cotton was gripped by an aching, desperate loneliness which lodged like a pain in the centre of her being. Over the years she had built up an immunity to it, but now and then it penetrated the tough façade she had woven around herself to combat the horrors accumulated in her mind.

She knew she had come up against a blank wall, after five years on the job, with a dark tunnel looming behind her. The reel spun backwards, recounting her life from the moment she was in the hospital that afternoon. She remembered camps, death, sickness, corrupt officials. She recalled being threatened by armed soldiers in a dozen countries. She had hidden from the police in a cupboard in Warsaw for three days, been sniped at in Belfast, walked in funeral cortèges for victims of assassinations, been blown up in Nicaragua. She had gone from country to country picking the bare bones of disaster, then leaving for the next.

Between the horrors, there had been pleasure – weeks lying on beaches in Greece or Spain, living it up in London or Paris or Rome, or hitting the town with her friends in New York. With her fat salary she had bought antiques and clothes with abandon when she wasn't chasing a story. She had denied herself nothing. If she wanted a brief encounter, there was never a shortage of men, and before Mike one had followed the other with dizzying frequency. She had enough money in the bank to live on for a year, or even two. She was at the top of her profession, and world-famous following her kidnapping in Beirut. The combination of confidence, good looks, intelligence and ambition had earned her celebrity status. Yes, she had surpassed what she had dreamed for herself all those years ago when she decided to *be* somebody. And yet, thinking of Seamus, she could think of nothing to say for herself at all.

A dog snarling in the darkness brought her back to the present and she returned to the road glad that she would be seeing Seamus. Suddenly, she craved, more than anything in the world, to be close to a sympathetic human being, far from the black humour and the jargon that journalists used to keep their emotions at bay.

When she finally found Seamus's house, she had the fleeting sensation of being home and safe, however illusory. It was a feeling she sometimes had when a man opened his hotel room door for her late at night, but it had always faded by morning.

Knocking at the door, she pulled herself together, determined to look like a confident journalist prowling around for interesting contacts. When Seamus greeted her with a bright smile Cotton gave no clue to the emptiness that had touched her on the way there.

'It's not much, but it's home,' he said, ushering her into the sitting-room.

She laughed at this obvious truth. The only furniture was two camp chairs and a table made of packing cases. A kerosene lantern cast wavering light on to bare floorboards, its flame moved by the draught seeping through the badly fitting windows.

'Cocktail?'

'Mmm. A frozen Daiquiri, please,' she replied as he handed her a mug of cloudy local beer. Taking a sip she said, 'Not bad. I'm getting used to it.'

'Come on in the kitchen while I get supper ready. It's the cook's night off.'

She stood in the doorway as he prepared supper over a primus stove on packing cases.

'Tonight is a two-lamp night,' he said, nodding to the lantern hanging on the nail above. 'I usually have only one burning. Kerosene is like gold, and so are the tins it comes in.'

She watched his shoulders move beneath his shirt as he bent his curly head over a tin bowl and cracked the eggs. Sensing he was being observed, he said,

'It's been so long since I had anyone to dinner I've forgotten how to cook.'

'Don't you cook for yourself?'

'Yes, but not like this.'

'I'm honoured to be your guest.'

As she watched him chop up a purple onion, Cotton's mind was working. She had come to a decision that she couldn't leave Ethiopia as she had every other place after she had finished her series of stories. She couldn't adopt a baby but, she mused, there were other things she might do to give her peace of mind, satisfaction that she was making a contribution. She mulled over the possibilities.

While they ate dinner on the packing case covered with a dishcloth Seamus began talking about Makele.

'The trouble is, people come in here, shoot miles of film, and it all ends up shelved, except for a few harrowing frames. There needs to be more documentaries made for television. I know exactly the kind of film I would make. I have a clear vision of what I'd do if I had the chance. It would be spectacular, but very simple, based on a few real-life people who would become characters in the drama as it unfolded.'

'Seamus,' Cotton interrupted, feeling as if she had been struck by lightning. 'Why don't you make your film?'

He rubbed his fingers together and smiled wistfully. 'Money.'

'How much would it take?'

He named a hefty figure.

'That much?' she asked.

'I might be able to do it for less. Working out here is not cheap.'

'We'll talk about that in a minute. Seamus,' she said, folding her arms across her chest, 'I'm going to raise the money for you.'

'Don't tell me you're some sort of philanthropist disguised as a journalist. Jesus,' he whistled, and leaned back to laugh. 'The *talla* has gone to your head.'

'No, you don't understand. Here – look,' she said, taking the amulet he had bought her that afternoon. 'What if I swear on this cross that I'll do what I say?'

'Swear away.'

'I swear.' She reached out to shake his hand. 'Trust me, and you're as good as in business.'

He smiled shyly. 'When you came here, tonight, I admit I had hopes, but not for you to fund a movie.'

Laughing at his endearing frankness, she was tempted. It would not be mere love-making, but a reaffirmation of life.

'Would you accept some film finance as a consolation prize?' she said after a moment.

The wind howled through the cracks in the windows.

He nodded with amusement. 'Sure. By the way, where are you going to get the money, as a matter of interest?'

'I haven't the faintest idea,' she replied, noting the scepticism on his face. 'But I'll get it, whether I have to beg, borrow or steal.'

Chapter 5

ROME

No one recognized Chiara Galla in faded jeans and a white leather jacket as she left the Hassler Hotel to fulfil a promise she had made to herself a long time ago. She had tucked her hair into a pink and white silk scarf, and gold-framed sunglasses concealed her eyes. She crossed the Piazza della Trinità dei Monti beneath the blue April sky.

Chiara paused at the balustrade overlooking the Spanish Steps, her heart beating with an unpredictable rhythm of dread and anticipation at her new-found sense of freedom. She breathed deeply of the air of Rome, with its faint suggestion of woodsmoke, coffee and herbs. Scanning the domes of a hundred churches thrusting through the patchwork of terracotta rooftops, a private smile crossed her face as she adjusted to the novel sensation of being anonymous in a crowd. There was no limousine with bullet-proof glass to protect her, no bodyguard or chauffeur as had always accompanied Mr and Mrs Abner Wolfe wherever they went. Glancing down at her feet, Chiara was still surprised that she had dared to discard her usual high-heels for a pair of running-shoes that her secretary had bought on the Corso. Today she was determined to discard glamour, intending to walk all over Rome until she was exhausted. She was going to explore all the streets and quarters, all the piazzas and wide avenues that she hadn't seen for twenty-five years. From the moment she had set foot in the city, she knew she would some time, somehow, be compelled to make a pilgrimage into the past.

Students were already beginning to collect in the sunshine on the famous Steps, and she felt strangely apprehensive as she began to pick her way down to the bottom, zig-zagging among them. After living so many years sealed away from the world with Abner Wolfe in Hollywood, the sights, sounds and smells of humanity filled her with the slight tingling of danger. It was as if one of the long-haired students with beer on his breath would reach out to drag her down to his level.

Inwardly shrugging off her absurd paranoia, she quickened her steps, trotting past young men and girls in jeans and T-shirts, with radios blazing pop music, playing guitars, drinking wine straight from the bottle, and munching hamburgers and chips from the McDonald's off the Piazza di Spagna. It was the wrong time of year for the colourful flower market and she wished the banks of yellow chrysanthemums, the rich red carnations and roses that she remembered so vividly beneath the Roman sky would magically reappear.

At the bottom of the Steps she paused at the marble fountain of Neptune, a trembling blue in the sunlight. She hesitated, wondering which way to turn. Ahead lay the fabled shops of the Via Condotti and the Via Babuino, where she had once spent hours and hours coveting all the things she could now buy effortlessly by flourishing her chequebook. She almost wished that heightened yearning to own beautiful and expensive things would come back; that impulse had once been stronger than lust within her, more durable than love. The craving to own, to possess what was rare, beautiful, expensive had driven her for years, yet now curiously it seemed dormant. She still went through ritual spending sprees but lately it had been a reflex more than a need, and it had been all but satiated. She had read somewhere about people who lost their sense of taste after a car accident. So with her the accident of wealth had dulled her appetite for jewellery, clothes, antique ornaments.

Choosing the Via Condotti, Chiara strolled past the familiar cafés, boutiques, many of which had lost some of their remembered lustre after years of shopping on Rodeo Drive in Beverly Hills. But just as she was nursing her disappointment, as if released by time's chrysalis, there appeared a girl who reminded her strongly of herself when young, staring hungrily into a brightly lit boutique window. The poignant memory of the girl she once was faded as a handsome young boy slipped his arm around the girl's waist and buried his lips in her hair, whispering something that made her arch towards him with a laugh. The two of them wandered away, rich in love and promise, leaving Chiara with a stinging discontent that threatened to disturb her already fragile equanimity. A glance at her jewelled watch told her that only minutes had passed since she had left the hotel, instead of hours as it had seemed. Time, she realized, was beginning to hang heavily on her hands. Until a production meeting at the hotel next morning she had nothing to do, no one to phone or meet. The shadows of the Via Condotti were chilly in April, and she pulled her leather jacket tightly around her.

Walking on, she came to Bulgari, her mind reverting to the young lovers she had seen earlier. As she scanned the dazzling display of jewellery in the shop window she thought of Sandy and the party he had thrown earlier in the week at Rome's most glamorous nightclub, the Osteria del Orso. Towards the end of the evening, when he had drunk too much, he had made a remark that still came back to haunt her.

'Was it worth it, Chiara, all those years with Abner?' he had muttered, his eyes fastening on her magnificent diamond necklace, the pride of her collection.

It was a startling question coming from Sandy, a question that he had no right to ask and one to which Chiara knew he had guessed the answer. He was perhaps the only person still in her life who understood just how far she had come, and what drove her. Only someone who had once been as desperate as she had, someone like Sandy, could appreciate that wealth represented the only wall between her and that tidal wave of want, and that the older she got, the higher the wall had to be to withstand the depredations of age and time. And yet, she recalled with annoyance, he had seemed remarkably unsympathetic.

She turned hesitantly, not quite knowing which direction to

take as she surveyed the long narrow street filled with people. She had lost her taste for exploration. What had begun as an adventure had become a tedious meandering. She paused by one shop, then another, as she fought the urge to return to the hotel. She was just about to enter the Café Greco when she spotted a familiar face that alerted all her senses. A man she had met before passed by and on impulse she followed him as he strolled along the street. Whenever he slowed his footsteps to gaze in a shop window, she would stop, pretending to browse herself. A surreptitious study of the man's elegant but casual clothing told her he wasn't on business, but wandering as aimlessly as she was. His walk, the angle of his head on his broad shoulders, the strong lines of his mouth and chin suggested the virile determination in Prospero Vallone that had made him stand out in the crowd on the night of the party at the Osteria del Orso. He had drawn her then, as he attracted her now, against her will and better judgement.

She followed him discreetly, concluding from his interest in jewellery that he might be choosing a gift for a woman, and that he appreciated the very best. As Chiara became more and more engrossed in her pursuit, she began to enjoy the game. The more she looked at Prospero, the stronger became her impulse to contrive a meeting as if by chance. It was suddenly clear to her that he was the vital element of risk that was missing in her life.

When he entered Bulgari, she followed him in, her heart beating with the excitement of the chase. The two of them stood next to each other for a moment, gazing down at the illuminated glass counter, and she pretended to be absorbed by the sparkling gems strewn on velvet.

When the assistant greeted them with a smile, Chiara indicated that he should take care of the gentleman first.

'*Buon giorno, Signor Vallone*,' he said warmly, making clear to Chiara that Prospero was a good customer.

Prospero withdrew a watch from his pocket. 'Could you put a new battery in this while I wait?'

'Yes, of course. It will only take a moment, signor.' Then, turning to Chiara, he added, 'Someone will come in a moment to attend to you. Is there anything you wish to see?'

'I would like to look at some diamond earrings,' she said almost in a whisper. As she spoke she could feel the heat of Prospero's glance. While the two of them waited in silence, she wondered how to attract his attention.

The assistant returned to unlock the case, then took out a tray of earrings which she pretended to examine. She moved the tray closer to the edge of the counter to inspect them just as Prospero folded his arms, causing it to tumble to the floor where several earrings rolled on to the carpet.

'Oh – I'm so sorry,' she exclaimed.

The assistant leapt from behind the counter. 'No, please, don't touch them. I'll pick them up,' he cried, softening his alarm with a smile.

With an ironic shrug, Chiara met Prospero's deep blue eyes as she removed her sunglasses.

He returned her smile with a grin. 'The poor guy thinks we're about to rob the place,' he said in English.

Her laughter told him she had understood.

'No, no, please, *scusi*, Signor Vallone – signora,' said the flustered assistant. 'It was not my intention to imply . . .'

Prospero inclined his head invitingly towards her as she studied his face, pretending that she couldn't quite place where they had met.

'Have we met before?' she asked hesitantly.

'Yes, we have. You probably don't remember me, but I remember you. We met at Sandy Vincent's party last week, the one he gave in your honour.'

'I'm very sorry, but there were so many people there that I was confused,' she said in English, unsure whether to speak Italian with him. Prospero's friendliness gave no indication that she had been extremely cool when Sandy made the introductions, something she now preferred to forget. She gave him a warm, inviting smile as if they were old friends.

'You're obviously incognito today,' he remarked, glancing at her running-shoes.

'It's true,' she said with a laugh, wishing she had worn high-heels and a pretty dress. She no longer wanted to be anonymous; she wanted to be Chiara Galla again. 'Sometimes it's nice to be simple,' she added by way of explanation.

The assistant came back to the counter with Prospero's watch. 'Never mind about the earrings,' she was quick to say. 'I'll come another time.'

They walked out of the shop together, but when they were on the pavement doubts overtook her and her heart started pounding.

'Sandy said you haven't been to Rome for years. It must seem odd to be back,' he said as they walked up the street.

'Yes, it is. Do you mind?' she asked abruptly. 'I'd rather speak in English. My Italian is so rusty.'

'I know what you mean. I've gone through the same thing myself. I came back here to live about six years ago after years in New York.'

He stopped, his hands on his hips as he gave her a quick scrutiny, his eyes kindling with interest. Beneath the façade of a powerfully handsome man in his prime lurked the flirtatious suggestion of a teenage boy picking up a girl on the street, which conveyed itself to Chiara.

'Listen, I don't know about you, but I don't have any important plans for the day. Why don't we do something together?'

Chiara looked thoughtful, finding it hard to admit that she had no plans whatsoever.

'I'd have to go back to the hotel and check with my secretary first,' she said evasively.

'No – don't do that,' he said, his hand closing on her wrist. 'Either you're free or you're not free. And if you're not, make yourself free.' His voice had a commanding undercurrent that killed all her feeble objections.

'Yes – why not? All right, I'll come,' she exclaimed, embracing chance like a kite catches the wind.

An hour's drive north of Rome, Prospero turned the B M W off the motorway just as they entered the heart of a shallow green valley. Slowing down, he took a sharp bend into a long straight road lined with poplar trees, their newly opened leaves moving in the breeze.

'It's been so nice to let down my hair, to talk to you about my problems,' said Chiara, releasing her pent-up emotion with a sigh.

'I have to admit I was surprised by what you've told me,' Prospero replied, his voice full of sympathy. 'You mean you didn't have an idea how much your husband was worth?'

They had been talking about investments, taxes and Chiara's fortune during the entire drive, which had distracted him from her disturbing presence. Glancing at her exquisite profile, Prospero wondered if Chiara could really be as naïve as she appeared.

'I know, I know it must sound very strange, but it's true,' she said in a small voice.

'What you did, coming back here to start all over again and do this mini-series – well, I find that very courageous. As soon as I get back to Rome I'll put you in touch with my investment adviser in Geneva, if you want.'

'That would be very kind.'

'You want to make sure you have very sound advice about taxes because, though you're an American citizen, you'll be residing here for a full tax year. With the proper advice you could plough back a percentage of your profits into a new production company. That is, assuming you intend to do other projects.'

'Oh yes, I do, of course,' she replied vaguely. 'I want to work – I have to. Otherwise I will get so bored.'

'If you like, I'll go over the budget details with Sandy. I have a couple of ideas that might save you production costs.'

'Oh would you? That would be so kind. But I don't want to trouble you, Prospero.'

'No trouble at all,' he replied with a smile that showed he meant what he said. He kept to himself his opinion that he considered Chiara's project one of the shakiest ways in the world to invest six million dollars. As if reading his mind, she said with a throaty laugh,

'You must think I'm crazy.'

'Crazy? No,' he said cautiously. 'All in all, it seems to me that you've been lucky up to now. You've kept the controlling interest in the production. You've hired Sandy, who is one of the best in the business. Still, six million is six million,' he mused.

'There was a time when I thought I wanted to produce the series myself, but Sandy persuaded me we needed other backers to make the package attractive to Italian and German networks. This way, we're sure it will be shown everywhere.'

She broke off, reluctant to plunge too deeply into the mechanics of television. Over the years Chiara had acquired a detailed knowledge of the workings of Wolfe Productions which it seemed unnecessary to divulge. Looking at Prospero's strong hands on the steering-wheel, she suddenly craved his protection, protection which he wouldn't offer so readily if she presented herself as the consummate businesswoman she had become. It was a lesson she had had to learn over and over again in life, reminding herself each time that a man needed the illusion that he was her master, her superior.

As she glanced at Prospero's strong jawline and determined profile, Chiara was overtaken by an unmistakable yearning that began in the pit of her stomach and radiated downwards, heralding desire that she hadn't felt for as long as she could remember. The only time in recent memory that she had experienced anything even resembling the sensation she felt now had been years ago when she had had a discreet rendezvous in a motel in Beverly Hills with a virile young handyman who worked on her husband's estate. But then her anxiety that she had been followed by a private detective employed by Abner was so strong that she had hurried away after a few passionate kisses and a tussle on a king-sized bed that had left her with a gnawing frustration for days afterwards. She leaned back luxuriously in the cushioned seat of the car, enjoying the realization that this time there was nothing to worry about. She was alone – she was free. There was no one to punish her, to torment her, to spy on her.

'Look at that lovely stream just there through the trees – and that pretty village on the hill. There's no place like Italy, is there?' she remarked wistfully.

'It's not much further now,' said Prospero, his mind still on money. 'The laws in California favour the wife – community property. You must have known that you would inherit your husband's money, his share in the studios.'

'I just assumed he would leave most of his fortune to his three children, so I never inquired. I didn't want to compete. I didn't want them to feel bitter when he died. Peace and harmony in the family at any price, I said to myself because, after all, I have no family of my own. I inherited one through my husband. Myron's children, that's Abner's son, are like my own,' she said, half-believing it. 'Oh yes, Abner was very old-fashioned,' she added warming to the idea. 'He was just like my father, who treated my mother the same way. He protected her from the worry of investments, of interest rates, of stock portfolios – even of knowing how much money they had in the bank. So I assumed that's the way it was between a man and a woman. The woman took care of the house, the man took care of the money . . .'

'But what happened to all the money you earned from your television show? I don't mean to be nosy, but you must have had money of your own.'

'Not as much as you think,' said Chiara, with a trace of bitterness she couldn't conceal. 'I was almost unknown when Wolfe Studios signed me, and my agent didn't work out a very good deal for me. But still – why complain? I bought a powder blue Jaguar, a fur coat, some jewellery. Foolish, wasn't it?' she said, thinking of the small, exclusive hotel in Westwood in which she had also invested her earnings.

'And then,' she continued, 'when my option was renewed by the studio for another year, by that time I was married to Abner so I didn't worry too much about a salary. After all, indirectly, he was the one who was paying me.'

'I see,' he nodded, realizing that Chiara was a typical child–woman who had married a surrogate father. 'But you do have advisers now, a good firm of accountants to help you manage your money.'

'I'd still be most grateful for any advice. I often wish I had been brought up differently, that I was one of these modern girls who speak the language of money as easily as the language of love. I learn very quickly, however . . .'

'I'm sure you do,' said Prospero with a laugh. Seizing the opportunity, he reached out to touch her hand for a moment. 'I admire a woman with guts, I really do. I'm not a typical macho Italian.'

'Not even just a tiny bit?' she teased, wanting Prospero to be at that moment all the things in the man who could tame her, masterful, courageous, afraid of nothing and no one. When the time came she would mention that before leaving Los Angeles she had had a four-hour meeting with Abner's accountants whom she had fired on the spot, transferring the bulk of her investments to a larger, more aggressive firm. Some day, when they knew one another better, he would discover that she had the *Wall Street Journal* delivered every morning with her breakfast tray. She would reveal her true nature slowly, so it wouldn't come as a complete surprise.

'I'm so glad to hear you don't think I'm crazy,' she said with a sigh, still aware of the way his hand had touched hers a moment ago. 'They all say I could end up losing everything. It's such a gamble.'

'Of course, but you don't want everything to be safe. Risk gives life its edge, its meaning. I've done the same thing myself, withdrawing comfortably invested capital and shoving it into something risky just for the hell of it.'

'I like that kind of spirit. And does it pay?'

'Sometimes. And sometimes it backfires. That's part of the game.'

'You and I are really alike, aren't we?' she replied thoughtfully. 'You understand what I mean, but so many people don't. They say, Chiara, relax, enjoy yourself and the money Abner left you. Why do anything at all? I'll tell you – because I have ambitions, plans, dreams. They don't die when you have money. Didn't somebody once say that work and love are the dynamos of life? It seems very wise to me,' she said, narrowing her long golden-brown eyes. Her voice had dropped to a whisper. 'What about you, Prospero? Do you have all of life's riddle solved?'

'Not entirely,' he replied, knowing it was his cue to tell her about his separation. But he remained silent. If he talked about

Ghisela, he would have to talk about his children, his son Alessandro. And he could not do that without a much deeper level of intimacy than he had yet reached with Chiara that blustery spring day. 'How did you meet your husband?' he asked, returning the subject to her.

She sighed deeply, as if she found the recollection painful. 'I was divorced, living alone in Malibu, working mostly in the movies but occasionally in television. I preferred the quiet, simple life there to the glamour of Hollywood. You see, I'm really just an ordinary woman who likes to cook and look after a man, and I think that's what my husband recognized in me. He was a lonely man, who had had no home life after his wife died. When we got married, we spent most evenings watching videos. But that was later. When I met him, the studio was looking for somebody to play Gina in *Ciao, Senator*. Finally, they thought of me. Whenever Cardinale, Lollobrigida or Loren weren't available, I was the one they called. They tested me as Gina, and then I was signed not long after.'

'I'm aware the show was a success, though I have to tell you I never saw it,' Prospero admitted.

Chiara thought of the re-runs on television, and looking at her watch she realized she would be missing an episode. Until that day she had consecrated every afternoon to watching herself in *Ciao, Senator*.

'So what happened?' he prompted her, slowing down the car as they drove the last kilometres down a narrow road pitted with potholes.

'I realized quickly that you can't be a star and a wife.'

'Come on – was that really it?' he said in disbelief.

'And I admit I'm a bit lazy sometimes,' she said with a laugh. 'But no, it's true. Hollywood marriages fail because both people have careers. Abner was an older man, an attractive man, and I knew lots of other women would like to take my place if I neglected him.'

And rich, Prospero thought, with a smile. As he listened to Chiara's chatter, he sceptically filed away everything she told him. His mind kept wandering from what she was saying to the way she said it. Her full lips forming the words fascinated him, and the little circles she drew with her pretty hands as she talked gave her conversation an irresistible femininity. He found himself aroused by her soft cajoling voice. It didn't matter that she was vain, capricious, inconsistent, all of which he had summed up at one glance. Chiara Galla was one of the most desirable women he had met in a long time. And though she was no longer young, her voluptuous maturity drew him. He could sense that she was both eager for and afraid of love, a paradox that challenged him.

Shifting gear, his eyes fell on her thighs and the swell of her hips encased by tight jeans. He was half-aware of the tiny waist partly hidden by her leather jacket, and the full, firm breasts beneath wide shoulders that he guessed were magnificent. There was so much behind Chiara's story that she wasn't telling him, and he wondered why she felt compelled to paint a picture of nuptial bliss with Abner Wolfe. Even a child could see that Chiara was spinning some kind of fantasy, but as he made monosyllabic replies to her frothy little monologue, Prospero found himself laughing in a relaxed way. When he had least expected it, he found welcome escape in her diverting company. She had the quality of a pretty musical box that played a simple but enchanting tune, and he was only half-tempted to lift the lid and discover the inner workings that moved beneath the surface.

'We're here – this is the turn-off,' he said, shifting into low gear as they climbed a rocky drive. Arriving at a grassy knoll crowned by olive trees, they found a low rambling restaurant roofed in tiles that had faded to a deep rose with age. Pergolas covered with vines sloped down the terrace beyond.

'Isn't this charming,' Chiara exclaimed as she got out of the car. 'Breathe the air – it's so fresh and clean after Rome. Thank you, Prospero, for bringing me here,' she said, looping her arm through his. Realizing she had struck the right note with Prospero, without even trying, she was glad she had worn jeans.

'A lot of people come here in the summer, but it's practically empty now,' he said with a shrug, pleased by her enthusiasm.

The owner greeted Prospero effusively and led them to a

booth containing a table draped with a checked cloth. They drew up the raffia-seated chairs as the waiter brought the menu.

'There aren't many people here today. This is the best time to come,' said Prospero, folding his hands. 'You should try the *gnocchi alla Romana*. It's famous.'

'That's exactly what I want. Exactly,' she exclaimed, clapping her hands.

'For me too,' he said, ordering in Italian.

He ordered *piccata* of veal for both of them, and when the waiter had filled their glasses with full-bodied country wine Chiara said:

'You speak like a Roman.'

'Now, maybe. But I get impatient. I express myself much better in English.'

'There's so much I don't know about you. You haven't told me your life story yet.'

'There's no hurry, is there?' he said, allowing his eyes to linger on hers.

'No, none at all. I'm very glad that you enjoy the simple things of life. Living in Hollywood for so many years, this is what I've missed, places like this.'

'Good – I'm glad you like it.' He had instinctively avoided the elegant restaurants of Rome, bringing Chiara to the most basic place he could think of. The bustling warmth of the family-run country trattoria symbolized the man he had had the courage to become only after he had earned the money to buy anything his heart desired.

Chiara was adjusting her leather jacket over her shoulders as a boy with wide, curious eyes brought a bottle of mineral water to the table.

'*Ciao,*' she said with a friendly smile as he gaped at her.

'*E bella, si?*' Prospero asked the boy, who nodded and blushed. With a shy smile, he turned and ran away. 'He's never seen anyone like you in his life. And neither have I,' he said, reaching for her hand. 'You've got a faraway look in your eyes. What are you thinking about, tell me,' he coaxed.

The luminous softness in her eyes faded as she focused on him. She shrugged.

'It sounds ridiculous, but you remind me of somebody, a boy I once knew. He was my first love, an art student in Vienna when I lived there with my father.'

He laughed at the suggestion. 'You didn't know me when I was young, so believe me, nobody could have taken me for an art student, no way.' The thought that had been only half-formed in his mind came to the surface. 'It's funny you should say that, because the night I saw you at your party I had the feeling we'd met before. But I admit I don't know where or when.'

She laughed doubtfully. 'That's a wonderful line, but not very convincing.'

'Yeah, pity you beat me to the punch. If I was on the ball, I would have used it first, on the night of the party. Just think of the time we've wasted.'

She sighed as he took her hand. 'I guess we'll never know where it was – on a plane, in an elevator. But then, you must have known many, many women.'

'A few,' he admitted, with the suggestion of a smile.

'Tell me, do you live alone?' she asked after a moment.

'Now, yes. My wife and I separated about six months ago. She lives in Switzerland with my two daughters, and my son.'

Chiara smiled slightly, pleased she had forced him to say what she already knew. The tone of his voice reassured her that he no longer cared about his wife, who Sandy had told her was very rich and beautiful.

'What are you doing tomorrow night?' he said, his eyes on hers as he toyed with her hand.

'I don't think I'm free at all until next week.' The pace of the duet she dreaded yet longed for was proceeding much too fast. If Prospero had been a young actor or a technician at Sandy's party she would have capitulated instantly. But a lifetime of experience told her that Prospero Vallone was a powerful personality who expected, who needed to pursue a woman if he were to value her. Softening her refusal with a flirtatious glance, she said impulsively,

'I'm having a dinner next week to celebrate moving into the villa I've rented. Could you come then? On Tuesday? My secretary will ring you with the address and time.'

When the *gnocchi* came Chiara attacked her food with gusto.

'It pleases me to see the way you eat, as if you were really enjoying it,' Prospero said, swallowing a mouthful.

'What do you mean? Have I done something wrong?' Her forehead creased in consternation like a little girl's.

'No! Just the opposite. I like a woman with a good appetite.' He was reminded of his wife's finicky appetite, and fastidious ways, so different from Chiara. 'Let's face it. Deep down, you and I are a couple of peasants. It took me years to value the strength that comes from knowing who you are, but now I'm not ashamed of who I am and where I come from.'

A flash of displeasure crossed her face, which she couldn't dispel, giving him a sudden telling insight into her character. He had wounded her pride in spite of all her protestations that she loved the simple life.

'I'm afraid you're quite wrong about that,' she said. The flirtation had vanished from her eyes, putting a sudden distance between them.

'Am I?' he replied, clutching her hand roughly across the table to tease her.

'I don't know what makes you say it but, if it pleases you to think it, then . . .'

He leaned back in his chair and gave a low laugh of private amusement, thinking to himself that, if Chiara Galla wanted to play the great lady, so be it. He was sure that she would drop the act once he got her into bed, sure that though she might not know it, she was capable of making love with the same lack of inhibition with which she stuffed the *gnocchi* between her lips.

The following week Prospero drove up to some high gates on the Via Appia Antica, and identified himself on the intercom. As he swung his car into the forecourt of the grand old Roman villa he was surprised not to see a line of cars parked there already. A light spring rain was falling, and as he got out of the car he threw a raincoat over the shoulders of his dinner jacket and raced up the tiled steps glistening in the light cast by two huge lanterns on either side of the impressive entrance. Ringing the brass bell, he caught an intoxicating whiff of the scented air, suggesting violets and freshly tilled earth, which arose from the depths of the dark garden. He breathed deeply, letting his lungs expand, as he savoured his keen anticipation of the evening ahead. Tapping his foot impatiently, he glanced at the marble plaque near the door, engraved with the legend, 'Villa Flavia', confirming that he had come to the right place. He was wondering if he had misunderstood Chiara about the time when the door swung open and he saw a butler in a striped waistcoat.

'*Buona sera*, Miss Galla is expecting me. Vallone is my name.'

The butler nodded. 'Signora Galla will be down in just a moment, signore. May I take your coat?' His footsteps echoed down the marble hallway as he went to put Prospero's coat away. In a moment he reappeared and started up the stairs.

Prospero straightened his tie in front of an elaborate Venetian looking-glass. Turning, he studied the palatial entrance hall with its curved polished staircase in pink marble. He smiled to himself, thinking it was the perfect staircase down which to make an impressive entrance. Noticing that the drawing-room doors were closed, he wondered what Chiara had planned for the evening.

Viewing her multiple image before a triptych of scrolled mirrors, Chiara studied her face at every angle as she sat at her dressing-table. With a thick sable brush she put the finishing touch to her make-up, dusting her chin and forehead and the tip of her nose with a fine gilded powder that gave her face a luminous clarity.

As she moved, the big pink diamond solitaire she wore on her left hand, a gift from Abner, blazed in the light, competing with the jewels at her throat. Reaching for a dark bronze pencil, she outlined her full lips once more, then sat back on the stool to regard herself. Midnight-blue velvet was most becoming, she decided, smoothing the off-the-shoulder gown that she had bought for the opera. She was still regarding the triple cameo of herself with rapt attention when she heard the butler tapping at the door.

'*Si?*' she called.

'Signor Vallone is downstairs, signora.'

'*Un attimo*,' she called back, her heart leaping. Her eyes darted to the porcelain clock on the dressing-table. Prospero was, as she had expected, exactly on time. He was still more of an American than an Italian, she thought to herself. An Italian would doubtless have been fashionably late. Rising from her seat, Chiara stood in the centre of the room for a second to reassure herself that everything was in order and to soothe her nerves.

The carved rosewood bed with its peach brocade pelmets and hanging silk tassels was made for love. The maid had turned down the linen sheets and plumped up the lace-trimmed pillows. The room was softly illuminated by gilt cherub lamps with fringed shades. It was the bedroom of a courtesan, with walnut commodes and lace curtains peeking from the burgundy damask draperies closed against the night. Chiara stood on the floral tapestry carpet, regarding every detail as she heard the clock tick the seconds away. One look at this bedroom had assured her that it was the perfect setting for what would – if all turned out as she planned – be her first affair in seven years.

Just knowing that Prospero was waiting impatiently for her downstairs was part of the elaborate ritual that had begun several hours ago when she had bathed in scented oil, then stepped into black lace lingerie – a ritual which could culminate, depending on her mood, with the two of them slipping between her perfumed sheets.

Laughing nervously at her own lack of composure, Chiara went to the bed and quickly smoothed the pillow, lifting the case to make sure the maid had hidden a little bag of potpourri underneath as she had been told. Realizing she could delay no longer, Chiara glided towards the door, telling herself that the fantasy of love-making could well be more exciting than the reality.

Prospero was just beginning to feel irritated at being made to wait when the sound of footsteps on the marble and the rustle of a gown made him look towards the landing.

'Good evening, Prospero,' Chiara's voice lilted through the marble hall. She came sweeping elegantly down the staircase in a cascade of blue velvet which made an instant impact on Prospero. Looking at Chiara, he felt the same desire to possess her that had first stirred in him on the day they lunched in the country. The lines of her figure as she moved gracefully towards him, the transparent gleam of anticipation on her matchless face made him forget his impatience with her coy little games.

She came towards him with her hands extended. Drawing her close, he lightly kissed the corners of her mouth as her musky perfume filled his nostrils. For a second his attention was distracted from her eyes to the fabulous diamond and sapphire necklace at her throat.

'I'm so glad you could come,' she said, dropping her eyes.

'Nothing would have kept me away, Chiara.'

She drifted away and he followed her through the marble-framed doors into a huge drawing-room decorated in baroque splendour with vast tapestries and gilt furniture upholstered in velvet brocade. An ornate marble mantelpiece framed a crackling fire.

'Well, do you like my new house?' she asked, looking round proudly.

'Yes, it's really something,' he acknowledged, pretending more enthusiasm than he felt. He found the richness of the décor somewhat suffocating, but it seemed an appropriate setting for Chiara Galla, the star, the woman.

'I'm so glad you like it. I couldn't believe how lucky I was to find a house to my exact taste. Of course there are things I would change. I would redecorate from top to bottom if I owned it, but it suits me for the moment. Abner's taste was very modern, so this is a release for the inner me, the woman who loves beautiful things . . .' she broke off breathlessly.

'Yes, the houses on the Appia Antica are wonderful. Are you thinking of buying it?' he said, noticing Chiara's undercurrent of nervousness as she faced him across the drawing-room.

'Maybe, maybe not. I have to see what the tax implications would be if I had a house here. I don't know, really. I've always liked the coast — Sabaudia, perhaps, or some place like that. Where did the butler go?' she said with a questioning smile, disguising the fact that she had told him not to appear until he was called. 'Can I get you a drink? Whisky? Vodka? Gin? Or maybe you'd like some champagne?'

With one eyebrow raised, Prospero glanced towards the fireplace in front of which a small round table was elegantly laid for two.

Following his eyes, Chiara said,

'I hope you're not disappointed. It turned out there wasn't time to arrange a party, and anyway, I thought it would be nicer with just the two of us. Since that day we had lunch we've hardly had a chance to speak, so I thought . . .'

'Why not? It sounds cosy to me. I'll have a whisky and water with no ice,' he said, approaching the bar where she stood. 'It's a cold night outside.'

'Is it?' she said.

As she poured him a drink, he regarded her back and creamy bare shoulders against the dark velvet that dipped invitingly. Seeing her hurried movements, he was suddenly amused by her nervousness.

When they had settled on a brocade settee her proud expression returned, telling him more than she intended. The quick turn of her head, the too ready smile, her tinkling laughter at his little jokes were all clues to her state of mind. She picked up a silk cushion and placed it between them, a ridiculous gesture that added to his amusement. He made up his mind that he wouldn't leave the house until he had made love to her.

'I only moved in at the weekend. You have no idea how difficult it was to find a house like this, so I immediately said I'd take it for six months with an option to extend the lease, which should cover the time I'll be in Rome until we start filming.'

He sat back sipping his whisky and let her chatter about the latest developments in the production of *Village in the Sun*. Finally, he interrupted,

'Chiara —' he said soothingly, reaching for her hand. The

sound of him speaking her name brought her nervous prattle to a halt. 'You are a magnificent woman. Many, many men must have told you that. I shall tell you so, again and again. You're beautiful, Chiara, and I find you very exciting.' Drawing her hand to his lips, he caressed her fingers which she tried to pull away. He held on, opening her palm like a flower and pressing his lips down gently as he stabbed his tongue suggestively between her fingers. She stirred and gasped involuntarily.

He raised his eyes. 'How long has it been for you?'

His words stripped her of all pretence, his penetrating blue eyes demanded a serious answer, not a flirtatious reply.

'Does it matter how many months or years? Much too long,' she admitted in a rush, forgetting the stories she had rehearsed about her string of admirers in Hollywood.

Prospero was surprised to notice that tears had sprung to her eyes, suggesting the vulnerable and unsure woman beneath the glamorous façade.

'You don't have to pretend with me, Chiara.'

She considered his directness for a moment. 'Yes – I must have sensed that the day we had lunch. Maybe that's why I asked you here alone tonight. I feel I can talk to you.'

As their eyes locked he wondered if they would ever be closer than they were at that moment.

'Is that the only reason you asked me here?'

'No, not the only one.' Her voice was guarded as she realized her careful plans for the evening were being overturned. Prospero seemed to be leading her from the seclusion in which she had lived securely for so many years. It was a strange unsettling sensation, one that she didn't want to resist.

As the two of them regarded each other across a chasm of silence, Prospero sensed that honesty didn't come easily to Chiara. He could almost see her mind working as she weighed her words, filtering out anything that was unpleasant or revealing without realizing just how transparent she really was. There was only one way to start finding out the truth, he thought as she rose abruptly and went to refill their glasses. Rising to follow her, he brushed close as she picked up the decanter.

'I want you, Chiara. I don't want to wait. I want you now,

this moment.' Stooping to kiss her shoulders, he moved to the nape of her neck with smooth, gliding kisses. At the touch of his lips on her bare skin, the last shred of self-control left her. She turned to face him, her eyes feverish with expectation. Cradling her chin in his hand, he filled her mouth with sensuous kisses, plunging his tongue deeper and deeper, sucking her breath into his. As he felt himself harden, he wedged her against the table to convey his rising urgency. At this signal of his desire she struggled for a moment, then gave in with a melting sigh as they kissed.

'Come on – let's go upstairs,' he said gruffly, loosening his tie. She nodded, without pausing to think.

He followed her up the stairs, his eyes travelling up and down the length of her swaying figure, experiencing a rush of excitement as he vividly imagined her nude body from the dips and swells suggested beneath the velvet gown. When he followed her into the bedroom and closed the door behind him he reached for her, but she stepped back.

'Love is a ritual. We must not hurry it,' she breathed, suppressing the flutter of panic that turned to tense expectation as he encircled her waist with his hands. He traced her pubic bone suggestively with his thumbs, circling slower and slower until she gasped.

He lowered his chin and regarded her intently. 'I'm impatient, aren't you?' Taking her hand, he guided it towards his erection.

She gave a moan that ended in a little laugh. 'No,' she chided. 'First we must have a bath. I'll undress you – slowly. Then you can undress me.' She turned away with a fluttering motion like a butterfly panicked by the net.

He pinned her down with his deep blue eyes. Besides his ardour it was his impatience that excited her unbearably, he knew. As he unzipped her dress, Prospero guessed that Chiara was pleading not for love's ritual as she had said but for time, more time, until perhaps she changed her mind. With that thought uppermost, he kissed the length of her back, murmuring soft phrases in Italian, conjuring up erotic images to excite her further. When her dress had slipped down, he nudged against her firmly, encircling her breasts with his hands. She arched as he kissed her neck, then slipped away.

'I'm going to prepare the bath,' she called over her shoulder, crossing to the ornate marbled bathroom where she poured a bottle of scented oil into the jet of foaming water filling the deep sunken tub. Closing the door behind her she peeled off her black lace underwear, watching her body in the mirror. When she was naked she paused to observe her own image repeated in the mirrored walls, then, slipping on a cream lace *peignoir*, she came out of the bathroom to call Prospero. She was startled to see him lying naked on the bed with his erection very obvious indeed from across the room. As she came closer, he slipped from the bed and began to walk towards her, a conquering smile on his face. Chiara almost stopped breathing as he parted her *peignoir* with deliberate slowness, allowing his eyes to travel down the crevasse of tawny flesh bordered by the lace. The breath catching in his throat conveyed how her body thrilled him.

'Won't you come to the bath?' she coaxed in a throaty voice. Something in her yearned to eke out the last drop of romance before surrendering to the passion leaping inside her.

'No, I want you now, just the way you are.' Pressing his lips to her hair, he brushed against her. 'Forget you're here in this villa. This bed is a field of grass, the canopy the trees overhead with sunlight filtering through . . .'

Closing her eyes, she was enveloped by the vision he suggested. His touch sent an aching response up her thighs that made her feel she was falling, falling. He lifted her on to the bed where they tossed for several moments in a passionate battle which was won when he pinned her breathlessly beneath him. Her glazed eyes showed that she was ready, that she couldn't wait for him. She arched towards him as he entered her, forging his way into the darkness where her desire still lived. Tears of joy flowed down her face as she gave herself up completely to his strength, drowning in the taste of his kiss, the smell of his sweat, the sound of his rapid breathing. Her limbs pounding against his, she sank yet swam, soared yet fell as they were speared together by a shudder that dissolved all her senses.

When their passion had subsided, Chiara lay stunned in Prospero's arms, reluctant to move. She realized by the sound of his breathing that he had fallen into a light doze and moved to turn off the light and pull up the covers; but he drew her back fiercely, a possessive gesture that seemed to her more ardent even than all the love-making that had preceded it. Looking at his dark hair tousled on the pillow, she felt drugged with happiness. Returning gratefully to his side, she stretched full-length against him, welding their bodies together at pulse points that joined them in one unified heartbeat.

As she stroked him lightly, her face blank with disbelief at what had happened, he kissed her and whispered:

'Aren't you hungry now? Maybe we should go down and have dinner.'

'No,' she cried with a gust of laughter that triggered tears of emotion. 'I mean yes – yes.' Reaffirming her need that had slain every mundane fear, she took his hand and slipped it between her legs. 'It's you I'm hungry for, Prospero, you . . .'

With a burst of energy, he was instantly aroused, chanting her name softly: 'Chiara, Chiara . . .'

Chapter 6

Shaking her wet hair, Cotton propped her bare feet on the wrought-iron balcony, closed her eyes and turned her face towards the sun. It seemed she had slept for most of the thirty-six hours since she had arrived at Fiumicino, where she had been met by Archie and Chiquita Bowles, friends with whom she shared a long, happy history. Reaching for her coffee cup, she glanced down at her broken nails and torn cuticles, reminding herself to do something about them before the party that night.

'You've really let yourself go to seed, Cotton old girl,' she whispered to herself. As the memory of her three weeks in Ethiopia seared her consciousness, she knew her preoccupation with nails was ridiculously trivial, hardly worth consideration. Yet here she was in another world, light years away – in Rome. Gradually the disturbing images that had kept her awake at nights had begun to subside. But this time, before going straight to another assignment or back to London, she was glad she had begged time off to come to her spiritual home and commune again with the things she loved.

The very air wafting its way up from the gardens of Parioli below coaxed her senses achingly to life with its exotic scents from the herbs and flowers tumbling from pots on the balconies. A feeling of luxurious indolence descended on her as she heard the pure scale of birdsong – was it a nightingale? – in counterpoint to children's shouts and laughter somewhere in the distance. Which reminded her of Seamus. She had to do something about her extravagant promise to raise money, before she could consider herself legitimately on holiday.

Leaning back, Cotton stretched her arms over her head, feeling the languor of a cat who has found a quiet place after chasing through the night. It was one of the addictive contrasts of her frenzied existence, to unwind slowly, feeling no guilt, no hurry to be anywhere at any particular time. Opening her eyes, she was met with the arresting palette of ochres and ambers of the houses and apartments juxtaposed against the bluest sky she had ever seen. She wished for a moment that she could paint, a yearning that brought with it a reminder to contact her godfather, William Partridge, in Florence. The tug of Italy was becoming stronger year by year, a need to come back, a yearning that only the sights, sounds and smells of her native country could satisfy even though she hadn't lived there for decades. Even the colourful faience cup evoked a sense of satisfaction. There was a pleasing rightness about the broken roll and the curls of unsalted butter on a plate, the bitter fragrant coffee that she now sipped, which summoned an entire world that lay timeless in her memory.

'Go ahead, daydream to your heart's content,' came a voice.

Cotton smiled at Chiquita, who had come on to the balcony, balancing her six-month-old son on her hip. He put out his arms to Cotton.

'Come on, Hadrian,' she said, hoisting the chunky baby on to her lap for a moment.

'You were lost. I remember the good old days when I used to do that before Hurricane Hadrian appeared on the scene,' Chiquita said good-humouredly. 'Just hold him for a minute while I mash this banana up.' Chiquita, a vivacious dark Hispanic who had been Cotton's room-mate at university, rapidly peeled and pulverized the banana.

'You still move as though you had only a day to change the world,' Cotton observed, kissing Hadrian's downy temples.

'You learn how to move, I can tell you, when you've got a little bag of energy like him around. Come on, sweetheart, come and have breakfast.'

'How do you find out what a six-month-old baby likes, anyway?' asked Cotton, handing her the baby.

'We mothers have a special understanding. We just *know* what they like.'

'Don't give me that earth mother garbage,' said Cotton with a laugh.

'I'll tell you how – they spit out what they don't like, all over you. I've got a whole wardrobe with assorted stains to prove it.'

'Babies are a total mystery to me,' Cotton remarked. 'But I find them absolutely fascinating.'

'Uh-oh, watch out,' said Chiquita, arching an eyebrow. 'That's one of the danger signals. That's exactly what happened to me.'

'I was dumbfounded when I heard you were having a baby. I mean, you and Archie were going strong in the State Department with matching careers the way some couples have matching sheets and towels.'

Chiquita laughed. 'That's before we went to Hadrian's Villa.'

'What a spectacular way to begin life – conceived in Hadrian's Villa. I don't know how you ever got away from the guides. Think what fun it'll be telling him all about it when he's grown-up.'

'It wasn't exactly at the villa. There's an abandoned olive grove behind the wall, where you can park. And after a picnic with a bottle of wine, well, you summon up the Roman goddess of fertility and whammo, you get one of these.'

'He's a dream, he really is. I've never seen you so happy.'

'I only hope we'll stay put in Rome for a while. But knowing the State Department, we'll probably be transferred to Lapland as soon as my Italian is nearly fluent.'

'When I think how you used to love dancing until dawn! You, the outspoken extrovert, campus radical, married to a shy intellectual who's a real Wasp. Do you ever fight, you two?'

'About once a month we have a real shiner, and then when I get it off my chest things go back to normal. Archie understands me. Don't ask me why, or how, but he does – always has from the moment we met.'

Glancing at the baby in the playpen, the attractive living-room of the apartment stuffed with books and mementoes from foreign postings – rugs from Peru, Indian carvings, African bronze heads, Archie's fine collection of drawings and watercolours – Cotton wondered what it would be like to be so comfortable, so sure of somebody as Chiquita was of Archie. She thought of her own soulless apartment in London.

'Speaking of the night you met Archie, do you hear anything of Herron Easton these days?' said Cotton, pouring herself another cup of coffee.

'Herron? What made you think of him?' asked Chiquita, a startled expression on her face. She looked thoughtful for a moment. 'No, haven't heard a thing.'

'I just wondered. Not that I ever think of him. I just like to catch up on the news.'

'Sure that's all?'

'Oh Lord, yes. He's married with two kids now. You know that.'

'Men can get unmarried.'

'Not with me, they don't.'

'That reminds me. You haven't gone into details about Mike. What happened? Everything looked so great after you were kidnapped. You said in your letter he was a changed man.'

'Oh, he was for a while. Then he changed back again. He went all to pieces when I was missing.'

'I'll have to remember that when Archie cools off. I'll put a ransom note on his pillow: "Smarten up your act, kid, or we won't bring her back." I felt sure you two were going to move in together.'

'We came close, I guess. You can imagine all the heavy emotions churned up by a situation like that – then, once he got back to London, the wife and kids must have looked awfully good . . .'

'Come on, Cotton. You're a knockout and you're very successful. He was just the wrong guy, that's all.'

'I wish I'd remembered that when I was waiting for him to come to Switzerland after Christmas. His kids came down with the measles, and by then I'd had enough. Christmas – that's the worst time.'

'You can always come and stay with us.'

'Thanks, Chickie. In a way there's nothing I'd love more, and yet in another way, well, I think you understand.'

'Yeah, I know. All this family togetherness gets a bit heavy, doesn't it. But honestly and truly, Archie and I must seem like colossal bores. We're so damn domesticated. How can you bear being with us, anyway?'

'You and Archie may be domesticated, but you're different. That's why I love you. There are different courses for different horses, that's my philosophy.'

'Oh, I get it. We're a couple of draught horses hitched to a plough. Well, there's no doubt about it, you're the thoroughbred out there in front getting garlands and ribbons instead of baby food all over you, sure enough.'

'It looks fun, feeding baby. But it's not for me, let's face it.' Just then Hadrian turned his head and stared at her with large serious eyes. 'He understood, did you see that? Smart kid, that one,' Cotton said, laughing.

'He didn't like that remark one bit, did you, Hadrian?' said Chiquita, kissing his banana-smeared cheek.

'One of these days, Cotton, you're going to walk into a room and the cannons are going to go off, and the cymbals, the drums, the whole works, and you won't be able to do a damn thing about it. What I wouldn't give to be a fly on the wall when that happens. Some unlikely Adonis is going to make mincemeat out of big tough Cotton Castello, and I hope I'm there to see it.'

'Don't hold your breath, that's all I can say,' Cotton grinned ruefully.

'What are you going to wear to the party tonight? Have you decided? Why don't you go out and buy something new?'

'Say, what is this? You haven't got me lined up or something, have you? The way you've been talking up that party, you're making me suspicious. I'll have to go out shopping.' The minute she said it, Cotton made up her mind to hit her favourite boutiques and blow a small fortune. She'd buy an evening dress, maybe a leather suit and handbag, some jewellery.

Chiquita smiled mischievously and looked as if she was about to say something, then thought better of it. 'By the way, I hope you're staying a good long time with us. You need a rest.'

'A week at least, if you want me. I'm on extended leave from the paper until further notice.'

'Well, don't you think it's time you finally went back to Robbiano?' Arms folded, Chiquita gazed thoughtfully at her friend.

'First, you proclaim the joys of true love, and now I'm supposed to go back to my roots. I've never known you to be so damn bossy,' said Cotton, giving her a hug. 'The thing is, I don't know if the time is right yet.'

'There's no time like now – sleep on it. By the way, that reminds me, I thought you might like to have a look at this,' she said, tossing a magazine on the table. 'Excuse me a minute. Time for a nappy change.'

Cotton gazed unseeingly at the magazine, her train of thought disrupted by the mention of Robbiano. Chiquita, who knew her so well, had touched a raw nerve. She promised herself she must go back soon. Next week perhaps. Or next time. But one thing she knew, she didn't want to go back alone. Draining a last mouthful of cold coffee, she thought how ironic it was that Cotton Castello, award-winning journalist, world traveller, veteran of innumerable global conflicts, couldn't face going back to the town where she had grown up.

She picked up the recent issue of *L'Uomo* Chiquita had left on the table and focused on the interview she had circled, accompanied by a photograph of a man who looked familiar. Emanating waves of money and power, he was standing behind a massive boulle desk, his hands in the pockets of his grey suit, his sardonic smile aimed straight at the camera. She didn't have to read the article to know it was Prospero Vallone.

'What do you think?' Chiquita asked, returning to the balcony.

'Interesting,' she murmured, skimming the paragraph that outlined his philosophy of life, love and women. She smiled in amusement at what she read.

'I knew you'd get a kick out of it, so I saved it for you.'

'I haven't given him a thought since the day he dropped his

lawsuit against me. Listen to this hype – it's incredible: "The only real women left in the world are European women. They're tough, sensuous and vulnerable, all at the same time." And listen to this: "He believes in leading a balanced, harmonious existence",' she twanged, imitating his Brooklyn accent. '"His tastes are simple" – oh, sure, very simple, house in Portofino, duplex in New York. Who's he kidding?' Cotton laughed.

'You didn't know him at all, so how do you know what he's really like? Anyway, all that stuff in the article is probably rubbish. You're a journalist and you ought to know they never print the truth.' Gazing over Cotton's shoulder she added: 'I think he's pretty cute myself. You never mentioned that when you had a run in with him years ago.'

'Cute?' said Cotton incredulously.

'Well, what would you call him, then?'

'He's not bad, I guess,' she said, censoring the word 'attractive' that had been on the tip of her tongue. 'I wonder if he's still married to that Swiss heiress,' she mused.

'Here's a bit of gossip for you. I read the other day that they're separated and that he's having a big romance with some Italian bombshell who used to have a TV show in the States in the seventies. Chiara Galla – remember her?'

'I can't say I do,' Cotton replied. She was still staring at the photograph of Prospero. As her mind ticked over, she felt an irresistible spark of mischief ignite. 'It says here he lives part of the year in Rome. Isn't that interesting . . .'

'Cotton – if I don't tell you something soon I'm going to burst.'

Cotton looked up in surprise at the undercurrent of excitement in Chiquita's voice.

'Archie wanted it to be a surprise, but I can't help it – you have to be told. Guess who is in Rome and is going to be at the reception at the Embassy tonight?'

'Give me a hint – friend or foe?' said Cotton suspiciously.

'Herron Easton,' she burst out.

'What? Herron? You're kidding. Why didn't you say so?' shrieked Cotton. 'I don't believe it,' she murmured, sinking into a chair. 'After all these years . . .'

'Chiara, I don't want to stay at the reception very long,' Prospero was saying as he accelerated his BMW. As they drove through the Borghese Gardens, the tall pines were etched in black against the lemon-coloured sky.

'What do you mean you don't want to stay long? I want to meet people, have a good time,' she announced. She folded her manicured hands on her white lace suit. Clusters of diamonds glinted at her ears and wrists.

'I promised Ghisela that I'd phone this evening to ask how her father is, so I don't want to be too late.'

Chiara took a tissue from her gold kid clutch bag and snapped it shut irritably. The car was filled with the musky perfume that was her trademark. 'Anyone would think you were still married to her.'

Prospero ignored the challenge in her voice. 'The doctors say he won't last long. I'll be flying up there this weekend if his condition gets worse.' Prospero also wanted to see Alessandro, which Chiara knew and it annoyed him that she pretended not to understand.

Chiara thought for a moment, then said: 'You know, Prospero, I can't understand why, after being separated from Ghisela for so long, you have to rush to her side because her father is ill. After all, it's her family, not yours. How do you think it makes me feel? It makes me feel like hell. Anyway, I might be travelling to see villages for locations next weekend. I assumed that this weekend we would be together, that you would go to the trouble of arranging your affairs as I have mine . . .'

'Unfortunately, *cara*,' he interrupted, 'I can't ask Otto Schmidt to postpone his date with the Grim Reaper in order to please you,' he replied. Whenever Chiara's temper began to rise, he treated her with the patience he would use with a small child.

'You seem to forget that I arranged a dinner on Saturday. Sandy and his wife are going to be there. They'll ask: "Where is Prospero this weekend?" I reply: "Oh, he is with his wife. She's sad because her father is ill and he went to comfort her." It makes me look like a complete fool.' Her voice rising a note, she added: 'You can put it off until the beginning of next week. Then I'll be away; then you can go.'

He turned towards her in disbelief. Her nostrils flaring with anger, her eyes blazing, she looked compellingly beautiful.

'Thank you very much for your kind permission. Thanks for being so considerate,' he said sarcastically.

She didn't seem to catch the dangerous undercurrent in his voice. Toying with his wrist, she crooned softly, 'You are too used to being alone, to doing what you want. Now you and I are together we both have to learn to compromise. Isn't that what you want, to be with me only, my darling? That's what you whispered to me last night lying in my arms.'

Sudden meekness after a display of temper came easily to Chiara. It was a gift she had developed during the years she had been married to Abner. It was a little game she had employed to amuse herself and to make him feel indomitable; but Prospero seemed indifferent to her playfulness. She turned away sulkily when he drew back his hand.

'Chiara,' he said abruptly. 'I want to make one thing clear. I will go to Geneva if and when it suits me. Do you understand?'

Chiara's eyes widened in surprise and she sucked in her breath with genuine anger. Her instincts had failed her – she had gone too far.

A break in the high wall surrounding the Villa Taverna, the American Ambassador's residence, showed that they had arrived. Joining the queue of cars, Prospero rolled down the window and handed the invitation to the Marine guard when his turn came. They drove in silence down the avenue of illuminated ilex trees. As they approached the portico of the old villa, Chiara said in a contrite child's voice:

'Let's not argue, yes? I don't like arguing. I find it exhausting.' She was looking at him with mock repentance as the valet came to open the door.

'Yes, all right, *cara*,' he replied briskly. 'Please get out. The man is waiting.' He watched her alight and hover at the edge of the portico, every inch the movie star in white lace and diamonds, with a radiance that attracted looks from the arriving guests. But for Prospero her loveliness was tarnished by the scene in the car, one like many others during the last few weeks of their affair. Disentangling himself this time wouldn't be so simple. The thought of Chiara's fierce possessiveness exasperated him, but it also pleased him in a way he had never paused to examine.

He had a fleeting glimpse of her as he passed under the portico. She waved and smiled, which made him shake his head and laugh. In spite of himself he felt a rush of pride that he, Prospero Vallone, was attending an American Embassy reception with Chiara Galla on his arm.

At that moment, Archie Bowles was leading Chiquita and Cotton through the marbled foyer of the building towards the crowd waiting to enter an adjoining room where the Ambassador was receiving his guests.

'Is this really the same world-weary correspondent we picked up at Fiumicino two days ago?' he said to Cotton with an admiring glance.

'I'm one of Rome's more successful make-overs,' she replied, her confidence soaring. That afternoon on the Via Condotti she had discovered a shell pink sheath with a slit up one side, the perfect dress for her narrow-hipped, leggy figure. It was cut to display her suntanned back and arms and rippled sinuously as she moved. Her normal hurried stride was restrained by high-heels of latticed gold leather, and huge disk earrings of gold and pale coral gleamed from her thick streaked blonde hair. When the occasion demanded, Cotton could dazzle, and tonight she knew she had good reason.

Chiquita, in electric blue silk trimmed with sequins, said in a sarcastic whisper as they entered the crush of the anteroom:

'You're a cruel bitch, do you know that?'

Cotton gave a peal of laughter. 'You got it.' She found herself scanning the crowd for Herron Easton while trying to look blasé. 'Anyway, what does it matter? He's married.'

'Ever heard of divorce?'

Cotton laughed nervously. 'I've got butterflies, dammit.'

After shaking hands with the Ambassador, they took a drink and passed on to the crowded terrace that overlooked the breathtaking illuminated gardens of the villa. She was glad when Chiquita and Archie were immediately claimed by an acquaintance, giving her time to collect herself as she combed the crowd for Herron. There was no sign of him yet. Her heart pounded with expectancy, and her imagination was teased by the intervening years. What had happened to him? How had he changed? How had she?

Cotton found herself staring into the bold blue eyes of a man whose face jarred a memory – not Herron, but someone else. Those same eyes had bored through her once before. As his identity dawned on her, Cotton returned Prospero Vallone's stare with a smile, realizing by the undivided attention he was directing at her that he had no idea who she was. They seemed to breach the space that separated them at the same time, but it was Cotton who spoke first. Extending her hand, she said with a friendly smile,

'How do you do? I'm Cotton Castello.'

At the sound of her name a shutter seemed to fall between them. The frank admiration in his eyes dissolved to hostility and she could feel his hackles rising. She knew she couldn't expect anything more after what had happened between them, but none the less her ego was bruised.

'How do you do,' he said with polite frigidity, turning his eyes on the crowd.

He had aged handsomely and well, she decided, calculating that by now he was in his mid-forties. His aggressive, rather rough-hewn face was illuminated by his extraordinary deep blue eyes, their brilliant colour heightened by his nut-brown tan. He possessed a fine, sensitive mouth, framed with deep laughter lines at the corners. His hair was flecked with grey at the temples and he was dressed with the discreet elegance that Italian men cultivate with such ease. His voice surprised her – she had assumed he would still speak with a thick Brooklyn accent.

'Do you live in Rome?' she asked blandly, recalling the facts she had read about him in the magazine that morning. The picture hadn't done him justice, failing to capture the animal magnetism which she had almost forgotten. Meeting him like this saved her the trouble of seeking him out. Whether he had been enemy or friend she knew he would be perfect for what she had in mind.

'I divide my time between Rome and other places. What about you, Miss Castello? What brings you to Rome?'

His formality irritated her. She would have preferred it if he had been openly rude.

'I'm just visiting some friends between assignments,' she said flippantly.

'Very pleasant for you.'

'Yes, there's no place like Rome,' she said, not intending to be funny, but when he gave a little chortle of laughter she was pleased. Suddenly thrown by his cultivated aura, she felt as awkward as a schoolgirl. Even now, as he observed her, she was sure he had no idea just how far they stretched back to the past. She resisted the memory of stroking his forehead in another time, another place.

'Are you still in journalism?' he asked, his voice warming slightly.

'Yes. Yes, I am.'

'It must be a fascinating profession.'

'It has its ups and downs.' Her gift for repartee seemed to have died and all she could think of were lame clichés.

'Have you ever been to the Embassy before?'

'No, never,' she said brightly, latching on to the topic. 'My mother told me wonderful stories of the days when Clare Boothe Luce was Ambassador here, though, so I'm especially pleased to see it for myself.'

He smiled, and raised his glass to his lips as he took her in. As she returned his scrutiny, she couldn't help but recall the gauche young man she had met years ago in a cheap, ill-fitting suit with flashy cuff-links. The transformation in Prospero Vallone fascinated her and she longed to know the story that lay behind his incredible climb. He was talking about the Embassy, continuing the myth that they were perfect strangers.

'I don't know if you noticed the twelve trees planted along the approach to the villa? Well, they symbolize the twelve apostles.'

'Really? How interesting. I'll remember to look on the way out.'

Fixing her with his eyes, he added pointedly: 'When you do,

be sure to notice that one tree is slightly out of alignment. That represents Judas.'

Cotton's mouth parted in shock and she blushed, wondering if he was referring to her. But then she felt two hands firmly grip her bare shoulders.

'Cotton.'

Whirling round, she found herself looking at Herron Easton.

Oblivious of the crowd around them, they threw their arms around each other in a warm reunion, punctuated by peals of laughter.

'I can't believe it,' Cotton gasped, breaking away to look at him. He had laugh lines in all the right places and his sandy hair was greying gently, somehow making him even better looking than the picture she had carried of him in her mind all these years.

'Let me look at you. My God, how did I ever let you get away?' he exclaimed.

Suddenly remembering Prospero, Cotton turned, flushed with emotion from her reunion with Herron. She was about to speak when she realized he wasn't there.

'He's gone,' she said, bewildered.

'Who's gone? You mean the guy you were talking to? Do you know, for a moment I thought it could be Prospero Vallone. I never forget a face . . .'

'It was him,' she interrupted.

'What a shame he didn't stick around to shake hands.'

'I'd love to have seen that,' she replied, still smarting with disappointment that he had left so abruptly.

'He probably still holds a grudge. What's he doing here tonight anyway? He's the last person I would expect to meet at an Embassy reception.' Herron couldn't disguise the disapproval in his voice.

'Apparently he's quite a big shot now. These days he's strictly legitimate,' she added, somehow feeling the need to defend him.

'Well, well, this really is old home week,' said Herron expansively. 'Come on – let's you and I wander away for a moment. We've got a lot to catch up on.' Putting his arm around her shoulder, he led her away from the terrace down a narrow path bordered with clipped hedges, towards the narrowing vista that ended in a gushing fountain.

'It's really good to see you, Herron. You look absolutely wonderful. Being in the Senate obviously agrees with you. But then, it was what you always wanted, wasn't it?'

'And you — you look simply sensational.' There was an affectionate catch in his voice.

Silence fell between them as they strolled along the moonlit path past the fountain, accompanied by its flowing water and the trilling of crickets.

'This place is huge,' Herron remarked.

'Seven acres — built over some catacombs, apparently. Do you hear the lions roaring? The zoo's not far from here.'

'Maybe I should have gone into diplomacy instead of politics. Look where I could be living.' He laughed, then his voice went serious. 'You know, Cotton, I've thought of you so often in the past few months . . .'

'Have you?'

'Yes, I have. I read all about that near miss you had in Beirut. I came down to breakfast one morning and opened the paper, and there was the account you wrote of your own kidnapping. I was scared for you, proud of you, cheering, all at the same time, but mainly I was so damned relieved that you were safe. I had tears in my eyes when I put the paper down. It was a brilliant story — congratulations. Naturally the happy conclusion had a very personal meaning for me.'

She shrugged, not quite knowing what to say. 'Did you ever get a telegram from me when you were elected?'

He nodded. 'I did, and thanks a lot. I wrote you a note, but you were probably globetrotting somewhere and didn't get it.'

Cotton had a sudden picture of Herron's attractive wife. Chiquita had sent her a clipping of their wedding photograph from *The New York Times*.

'Is your wife with you on this trip?'

'No, she isn't,' he replied, hesitation in his voice. 'I guess there's no reason why you should know about it, but Betsy and I separated several months ago.'

'I'm terribly sorry to hear it.' Cotton was taken aback at the unexpected news that his life hadn't gone according to plan.

'It's just one of those things, not worth talking about really. In fact it had been coming for some time. She's living out at Chevy Chase with our two boys and I've moved back to the little house in Georgetown. We did everything we could to work it out, but in the end we conceded defeat.'

'It's terrible for you on a personal level, but nowadays divorce or separation doesn't have to affect your career,' she consoled.

'That's true, and I'm glad for that at least. Betsy is a great girl, but looking back I realize I must have married her on the rebound.'

Cotton thought it was better to let the comment pass, but coming from Herron it was a surprising admission.

'You know, Herron, you've changed since I knew you, and the change is for the better. You seem much more . . . what should I say, well, introspective, I guess. It touches me, it really does.'

He laughed pleasantly. 'And you, Cotton, you're the same marvellous girl you always were. But seeing you tonight, so far away from home, I can sense things about you I think I neglected to appreciate. In days gone by I suppose I was too busy running too far too fast,' he admitted with a regretful smile.

'Still have your eyes on the White House?'

'If it happens some day, I'm ready for it, but I've done a lot of running and now I'm ready to stroll a bit.'

'That should appeal to the voters,' she said, squeezing his arm affectionately.

'I'm not so obsessed by that any more. I see life in proportion now, I hope.'

Turning back, they walked through pools of moonlight beneath the trees. Glancing at Herron's profile, Cotton conceded to herself that she preferred the man he had now become, his drive scaled down, his values humanized. Consuming ambition, hers and his, was what had come between them. As they approached the crowded terrace the sound of the orchestra reached them above ripples of conversation in Italian and English.

'Archie tells me you're posted to London now,' Herron said, pausing by an urn spilling with flowers. 'Do you ever get home?'

'Now and then, but not very often really.'

'I gather you're no longer in touch with the Townsends.'

'I'm afraid that chapter in my life is over and done with.'

He nodded thoughtfully. 'What I really mean to say is, I guess, that I hope you do come home soon.'

'Do you?' Cotton felt a twist of tenderness for Herron. The cord of old-established friendship had tightened unexpectedly between them.

'How long are you going to be in Rome?' she asked.

'A few days more. Probably until early next week. Then it's on to Brussels, and then home. Why don't we try and get together?'

'Yes, good idea,' she said, liking the thought more than she wanted to admit.

'And let's plan for you to come to Washington.'

'I'd love that. I really would.' She had a quick vision of his little house on P Street in Georgetown where they had spent so much time together.

'And in the meantime I'll have to fabricate some burning international issue to take me to London. I'm sure it could be arranged.'

As they returned to the terrace, Cotton saw Chiquita cut her way through the crowd towards them, a triumphant gleam in her eye.

'I've been looking all over the place for you two. I'm told this garden has no end of wonderful hiding places.'

Herron and Cotton exchanged a smile just as Archie appeared.

'Why, Herron,' he said in a flustered voice. 'Where the hell have you been? Ambassador Clarke has been asking about you. You had vanished and I was running out of excuses. He wanted you to meet the new man the Premier has picked to go to Washington.'

'Looks like I'm in trouble,' said Herron.

'I'd better take you to him right away. But before I do, Chiquita and I were thinking it's time the four of us had another double date, like old times. What do you say we go over to Trastevere after the reception ends?'

'Damn, I've been roped in for a working dinner with the Minister for Industry.' Glancing at Cotton, he added, 'But I'll duck out of it somehow.'

When the two of them had gone Chiquita asked Cotton, 'Well? What happened?'

'We're getting married, next week,' said Cotton, with a comic gleam in her eye.

'Cotton, this is no joke – this is serious,' she chided.

Cotton gratefully took a drink from a passing waiter and looked around with a sense of pleasurable unreality as the time, the place merged together in her mind. The musical pitch of Italian meshed perfectly with crisp, rather flat American voices, creating a melodious buzz in her ears. The cool air on her bare shoulders brought with it the evocative smell of the dark cloistered gardens of her childhood. Blurring her eyes for a moment, making the lights and colours run into a pool of darkness, she found it almost possible to believe that she was twelve again, that this time, this place had expanded, reached beyond the walls.

When she opened her eyes again, Cotton saw Prospero Vallone, standing alone at the edge of the terrace. She felt a compulsion to speak to him again. She told herself some excuse was bound to spring to her lips now she'd had a couple of drinks. She glided up to him, wondering what lay behind his unsmiling expression. As their eyes met she began to sense what it was that drew her to him. He and she were outsiders, individuals, who observed life eddying around them. This common strand bound their characters, their lives, together if only for a moment, and she had to pursue it. Taking a deep breath, she said:

'Mr Vallone.'

'Miss Castello,' he replied with a polite nod.

'I would very much like to see you again. There's something that I'd like to discuss.'

He registered no surprise whatsoever at her request. Reaching in the breast pocket of his suit, he withdrew a card.

'Perhaps you'd like to come to my office, say tomorrow morning about eleven? Where are you staying?'

'In Parioli, with friends.'

His tone was warm, as if he had decided to forgive everything. 'I'm just a short walk off the Via Veneto, not far from the Excelsior Hotel.'

As he gave her his card their fingers touched for a second. Slipping it into her handbag, she was tempted to ask if he wasn't curious why she wanted to see him; but a strange little *frisson* of expectation told Cotton they were thinking along the same lines. They had so much to discuss. She reasoned that an eleven o'clock appointment could easily run into lunch, especially if you had half a lifetime to fill in.

'Just one thing.'

'Yes?' she replied hopefully.

'You don't call yourself Mrs Easton. Any special reason?'

She laughed, realizing that all these years he thought she had been married to Herron.

'A very good reason. We're not married.'

Some time later she was talking to Herron again, after he had done the official round of meeting Italian officials.

'I saw you and Vallone in a tête-à-tête. I was tempted to come over and break it up.'

'Well? Why didn't you?'

'Frankly, I wasn't sure I'd get a warm reception from either of you,' he said with one quizzical eyebrow raised.

'Surely you don't think . . .? No, that's ridiculous.'

'I hope so. Because I have other things in mind for you.' He chucked her playfully under the chin.

'You do?' she inquired, beginning to enjoy what seemed for a moment like jealousy.

'I do. A candlelit dinner for four and a dark little club somewhere with an orchestra, where a boy and a girl can dance cheek to cheek.'

Just then the Ambassador forged his way through the crowd with Chiara Galla on his arm. People stepped back spontaneously as the two of them approached Herron.

'Now that's what you call star quality,' whispered Chiquita, who had drifted to Cotton's side.

Along with everyone else, Cotton found her attention riveted on Chiara. The moment she set eyes on her she perceived that this was true Hollywood glamour. The dazzling image was so far removed from reality that she might have come from another planet; but beneath the sculpted bronze hair, the make-up carefully applied, the lace suit that must have cost the earth, the small fortune in diamonds casually clustered at her ears and wrists, Cotton could see there lived a durable natural beauty who had basked in admiration all her life. She had a rich, sensual smile that suggested an inner amusement, and her dark eyes were stamped with glistening stars as if she were regarding spotlights. Cotton caught her glance just for a second as her eyes swept the group, and she felt a twinge of confusion as she recalled that Prospero Vallone was supposed to be madly in love with her.

'I wonder what it's like to look like that,' whispered Cotton to Chiquita as the Ambassador began the introductions.

'What's it like to be worth so much money, you mean. I read she inherited a cool thirty million when her husband died.'

'It's obscene,' Cotton muttered. 'Nobody needs that much money.'

'How do you know till you've tried?'

'I was wondering,' the Ambassador was saying genially, 'if we could borrow Senator Easton for a moment for a few photographs.'

Cotton noticed that Chiara Galla extended her hand only to Herron, dismissing everyone else with a glance. Passing her eyes over him approvingly she murmured:

'I hope you won't consider me too vulgar to suggest it, but I wanted to pose tonight with a real live senator, as the Ambassador has given permission for a press photographer to come in for a few moments. Do you mind very much?' she said with a kittenish smile at Herron.

'Mind? Not at all – I'd be glad to be of service,' Herron

replied. 'Miss Galla, it's a pleasure to tell you in person that I'm a great fan of yours . . .'

'Get that? *Is* — not *was*,' whispered Chiquita in an aside to Cotton. 'It must have been a decade since she was on TV.'

'You know,' Herron was reminiscing, 'I don't think I ever missed an episode of *Ciao, Senator*.'

Cotton watched Herron's ingratiating manner in amazement, telling herself he was just as susceptible to celebrity sex appeal as the next man. *Ciao, Senator* was so long ago that she could barely remember it, and she was sure Herron didn't either. She looked on in fascination as Chiara came alive in front of the photographer, looping her arm through Herron's, smiling up at him.

A few moments later, after Cotton had talked with the Ambassador, she noticed that the two of them were still locked in conversation. Chiara's musical laugh echoed through the night in counterpoint to Herron's deep chuckle. It struck her that they made an unlikely but striking couple, and that tomorrow when the paper was plastered with their photographs they would both bask in the publicity. Cotton, who didn't want to look as if she was prying, turned and ran straight into Prospero. His low gust of laughter sent a little shiver down her spine.

'We meet again, Miss Castello.'

'Please call me Cotton.' Before she had a chance to say more, Chiara interrupted them.

'Prospero,' she said breathlessly, 'I don't think you've met Senator Easton yet. Please allow me to introduce the two of you.'

Cotton looked from one to the other of the men, holding her breath while she waited to see what would happen. When Chiara pointedly ignored her, Cotton stifled her annoyance.

'Senator Easton, I'd like to introduce Prospero Vallone, a very dear friend of mine . . .'

'Prospero and I have met already, haven't we? It's been a long time, Prospero,' said Herron, magnanimously extending his hand.

'Not long enough,' Prospero retorted sharply.

Cotton lurched back as his fist shot out and smashed into

Herron's jaw, sending him reeling painfully into a pot of flowers.

Chiara let out a scream as he stumbled backwards, his mouth slack with shock. Conversation on the terrace was suspended; then there were ripples of shocked disbelief.

'Prospero!' Chiara screamed shrilly, then launched into a tirade of abuse in Italian that brought the party to a standstill.

Coolly straightening his jacket, Prospero was regarding Herron with flushed defiance. He paused only long enough to shoot a warning glance at Chiara, then turned abruptly and strode away.

Cotton stood gaping at the astonishing scene. As she watched Prospero disappear into the house, she felt her knees go weak at the thought that she would be seeing him tomorrow. She couldn't help but feel sorry for Chiara who was leaning on Herron's arm, tears streaming down her face. But beneath her tragic expression Cotton could sense her satisfaction, and she realized that Chiara had jumped to the erroneous conclusion that Prospero had punched Herron out of jealousy.

Chiquita grabbed Cotton's arm. 'What happened? I didn't see because I was too far back.'

When Cotton told her she groaned. 'Oh, God, he'll never be invited back to the Embassy again.'

'Something tells me he thinks it was worth it,' she replied, adding ruefully, 'do you know, Chickie, I'm the one he should have punched.'

Bars of early morning sun slanted over the Via Veneto as Cotton darted through the traffic. Stealing a look over her shoulder at the view of the serpentine avenue lined with trees, she was startled by the deep honk of a Maserati. Whirling around, she peered over her sunglasses and smiled at the rakishly handsome driver who leaned his head out of the window.

'Ciao, bellissima!' he called.

She proceeded across as he called after her, extolling her beauty to the skies and begging for her phone number. She laughed at the suggestion, knowing his enthusiasm would wane if he could see the puffy eyes behind her sunglasses. The cold compresses she had applied earlier had had no effect and the three cups of strong coffee she had gulped to cure her wicked hangover had merely made her feel jumpy. She had dragged herself from bed reluctantly, with a pounding head and a dry mouth, wishing there was some way she could postpone her appointment with Prospero Vallone. But she could not regret the night before which had ended in Trastevere with Archie and Chiquita, she and Herron singing in the streets after innumerable bottles of Chianti. Herron, who never got tight, did a rendition of *I Pagliacci* that would have astonished his colleagues in the Senate.

Cotton hastened her pace and walked briskly past the bright scalloped awnings of the pavement cafés already full of people dawdling over espressos and newspapers. Deciding she was in too high a gear for the unhurried tempo of Roman life, she abruptly slowed to a leisurely stroll. Catching sight of herself in a shop window, she was satisfied that her sage green suit and black accessories projected the correct businesslike image. She had tied back her hair with a ribbon at the nape of her neck and wore only a touch of make-up, sensing it was futile to try and conceal the ravages of the night before. She rubbed her chafed chin, knowing it was a dead give-away. She and Herron had necked passionately in the back seat of the car on the way back to his hotel, like two teenagers, calling up sensations that had taken her by surprise. He had left her with a promise to free himself as much as his last busy days in Rome would allow.

When she turned off the Via Veneto she felt tension coil inside her at the prospect of meeting Prospero, yet wondered why she should care at all. He would say either yes or no to the proposal for Seamus's film which she carried with her in a folder.

Seamus had surprised her before she left Ethiopia, with the entire package neatly laid out, including the shooting schedule, the locations and a detailed account of the costing. As she approached the Via Aurora, she began to work up the white heat of enthusiasm needed to sell Prospero the idea. The address on his business card turned out to be an old Roman house with a brass plate set in the stone deeply etched with 'Vallone Enterprises SA'. Cotton rehearsed her opening remarks as she walked under an archway to an interior courtyard where a gargoyle spouted water into a stone basin. Entering through modern glass doors fitted into the old lintel, Cotton was enveloped by the subtle luxury of the fine old building, carefully restored and decorated.

A chic young secretary sat behind a word processor, in the foyer of the elegant office.

'*Buon giorno*. I'm Cotton Castello. I have an appointment with Signor Vallone at eleven.'

'Please take a seat,' said the secretary, pressing the intercom.

Cotton sat down on a cream leather sofa. Pretending to thumb through an issue of *Apollo*, she looked at an interesting abstract above a marble urn filled with plants, the slabs of glass set on stone columns and a lamp made from a fine bronze statuette of a discus thrower, all signalling that no expense had been spared at Vallone Enterprises. Prospero Vallone had money and plenty of it, and she calculated that with a bit of persuasion he might part with enough to finance Seamus.

'Signor Vallone will see you now,' announced the secretary.

Cotton got to her feet as a pair of carved doors opened and Prospero appeared. He was immaculately turned out in a dark blue suit and she was uncomfortably aware that there was no sign of a hangover on his suntanned face. As she brushed past him she noticed every detail of his appearance, from his sharp blue eyes to the smoothly brushed black hair that just touched his collar. He smelled beguilingly of an expensive shaving lotion.

'Good morning, Miss Castello,' he said, closing the doors behind him.

'Good morning, Mr Vallone,' she replied, wondering impatiently why he couldn't call her Cotton.

She seated herself in a leather and chrome chair across from the boulle desk that she remembered from the photograph, empty except for a telephone, a silver letter opener and a large blotter. She eyed the bronze sculpture of a leaping wolf near a bookcase full of leather-bound volumes, a telling symbol of

Prospero's own leap to power and riches. Now that she had penetrated to the heart of his domain, the scale of his achievements began to dawn on her.

'Would you care for a cup of coffee, or maybe something else?'

'No, thank you,' she replied, wishing she had the courage to ask for a double Bloody Mary. But she didn't want to give herself away. She couldn't avoid his direct blue eyes as he sat down, hands folded, and waited for her to speak.

Crossing her legs and leaning forward, her carefully prepared introduction vanished. Instead she heard herself saying,

'Before I go into why I'm here, there's something I really have to mention.'

'By all means, go ahead,' he said with a gesture, indicating he was in no hurry.

'I realize that you and I have met before. That is, we met that time in New York. But I don't think you're aware that we go even further back. Quite a bit further.'

'You and I met before that time? Really?'

'Oh yes, ages ago, when I was twelve years old. Of course I wouldn't expect you to remember me . . .' She broke off, wishing she hadn't brought it up. He seemed to be regarding her with a closed expression, not the friendly curiosity she had expected.

'Please go on. Tell me where we met, as I have no recollection.'

'Presumably I've changed since then,' she said, raising an eyebrow, which elicited a smile. 'Do you remember the Marchesa di Castello di Montefiore?'

'Why, of course I remember her,' he replied, inclining forward.

At last she was getting somewhere. For a moment she enjoyed the suspense as he regarded her with a puzzled expression.

'Well, in the summer of 1968 you came to the Villa Robbiana one night with your cousin who I remember was a Monsignor then – Cardinal Giannini.' When Prospero nodded but still didn't speak, she stumbled on. 'It's very vivid in my mind still. It made a great impression on me at the time – I mean, you did.' As she said it, she felt as gauche as Prospero must have felt the night they met. 'I remember you talking to a journalist, Nancy Rogers, a friend of Delilah's.'

'Oh yes, Nancy,' he said with a non-committal smile.

'You see, I'm the Marchesa's daughter.'

He shook his head as if he was trying to place her. 'You'll have to forgive me, but I can't remember. It was a long time ago. And is that why you came to see me this morning, to renew our old acquaintance?'

She flushed at his coldness, while the undisguised boredom in his voice ignited her determination. Ignoring his rudeness, she took a grip on herself.

'No, that's nothing to do with it, really. I just thought I'd mention it in passing to break the ice. After all, it seems such a coincidence that we've met not once, but three times quite by chance. Anyway, as I mentioned last evening, I'm visiting friends here, but at the same time I'm trying to raise money for a film for television about Ethiopia in order to keep the situation there very much in the public eye. The idea for the project has been put forward by a brilliant young cinematographer who has become a relief worker in Makele, and his passionate conviction is something to behold, Mr Vallone.' She almost said 'Prospero'.

She was suddenly articulate now she realized he preferred to keep the meeting strictly on a business footing. The expression on his face hardened, which she interpreted as interest, and she launched into the speech she had prepared, mentioning her own journeys to Ethiopia, and the desperate need to keep the cause alive in the world media.

'When you look over the material in this folder,' she concluded, 'you'll see for yourself that the film has every chance of recouping the original investment and making a healthy profit when it's sold worldwide for television, so you'd be killing two birds with one stone, so to speak. It's both philanthropic and commercial.'

Prospero was now regarding her with what she realized was inexplicable hostility. She added: 'I suppose you're wondering why I came to you. The thing is, I'm aware that you're a person of means.' He remained silent. 'I've heard you're involved in quite a number of charitable causes,' she lied, wondering wildly whether it was true or not. 'So it occurred to me that you're the right person to approach. It's all there in the folder if you care to look it over. Perhaps we could get together again after you . . .'

He rose abruptly, cutting her off.

'You have one hell of a nerve walking in here and asking me to finance one of your pet projects. Just who the fuck do you think you are, anyway?' He slammed his fist down on the desk, making it shake. 'I was under the erroneous impression that you came here to apologize for all the havoc you caused to me and my family all those years ago — you and that eager beaver Easton. I had the satisfaction of proving last night what I thought of him, and now it's your turn. Little Miss Rich Bitch, you're dealing with the lives of human beings here, not paper cut-outs — the lives of my children, of my wife, degrading us by those cheap jibes you made in the press. I can tell by that smug look on your face that you think I've forgotten all about it. Do you ever think about the effects on other people when you write your stories? What it does to them? Last night should have convinced you that I mean business . . .'

She leapt up. 'Just a minute! What I did was my job and I have no reason to apologize for it,' she cried. 'If you're careless enough to go out and get shot up by the Mafia because of some dirty dealings, then I'll tell the world about it. That's what I do for a living, and I'm proud of it.'

'Oh yeah? You're proud of what you do? Well, I'm proud of what I am, where I came from, and what I've made of myself. See all this?' he gestured. 'I built all this and what it stands for from nothing, nothing. Everything you're looking at came from nothing. As for you, you were born with a silver spoon in your mouth, but it takes more than that to impress Prospero Vallone. I don't give a shit about all that stuff.'

'Impress you?' she gasped. 'Why would I want to impress you? What a laugh! You stand there making all these assumptions, but you know nothing about me, absolutely nothing.

The difference between you and me is that I don't have a massive chip on my shoulder, that's what.'

As the anger ricocheted between them Cotton glowered at Prospero. Snatching the folder she had placed on his desk, she stuffed it into her bag.

'Why I bothered to even think that I could speak to someone like you, I can't imagine. I must have been completely crazy to come here, insane, out of my mind . . .'

'Yeah, you could say that,' he growled, 'and a few other things.'

With queenly dignity she turned abruptly and swept towards the carved doors in a few long strides, her hair swirling. Wrenching violently at the door handles, she nearly fell when they wouldn't move. Recovering her composure, she said crisply,

'Would you mind opening the doors?'

'Not at all. Goodbye, Miss Castello,' he barked, pushing a button.

When Cotton had slammed the doors behind her, Prospero brought his fist down on the desk and cursed under his breath. With a snort of anger he thrust his hands on his hips and turned to the window overlooking the courtyard. In a moment he saw the flash of Cotton's blonde hair below. He watched her intently as she crossed the cobbled yard, propelled by outraged dignity. He didn't stop staring out of the window until her shadow had disappeared from sight.

Sinking back into his chair, he cupped his chin in his hand, his mind pulsating with the many faces of Cotton Castello, alive with passionate conviction one minute, smarting with anger the next. He remembered her in the garden of the Villa Taverna the night before, an attractive, confident smile belying the hesitation in her eyes. He hadn't realized until that morning that her eyes were a soft golden brown which changed colour as the pupils widened. He summoned up the image of her grand exit, her head held high on straight, square shoulders, turning it over and over in his mind like a jewel. When she had tugged furiously on the doorknobs he had been looking at her legs. Amusement crossed his face when he remembered her outraged expression. The locked doors had deprived her of a dramatic exit, like an actress who broke up the house when the set door jammed. He leaned back for an instant and roared with laughter as the humour of it sank in. When his smile had faded, he rang his secretary.

'Paola, cancel that table you booked for lunch, will you? Try and get Cimolai Steel on the phone, then you can bring in those telexes on the bridge contract.'

'*Sì*, Signor Vallone. Miss Galla called again while you were occupied. I told her again that you were out, but she didn't seem to believe me. She said she called to remind you about dinner on Saturday.'

'Paola, don't call her now, but when I've gone to lunch. Tell her that I'll be in Geneva and can't make it. I don't want to talk to Miss Galla, is that clear?'

When he had rung off, he tapped his fingers impatiently on the desk as he thought of Chiara. After he had punched Herron Easton he had left abruptly and waited for Chiara in the entrance hall of the Embassy. People leaving the party glanced at him uncomfortably as they passed by, but he ignored them, triumph at what he had done still pumping through his veins. Whoever said vengeance was empty had obviously not waited years to plant his fist on Herron Easton's chin, he thought with satisfaction.

On the way home the silence between himself and Chiara was soon broken by a violent argument during which she had called him a boor and a peasant. She had also accused him of being unfaithful with a string of women. The end of their affair had come, as had so many others, without warning. He had taken one last look at her beautiful face illuminated by the lanterns of her villa, then had opened the car door with a sense of finality that had obviously not communicated itself to Chiara. The thought of what she would do when she discovered their affair was over made him feel uneasy. It occurred to him that he owed her a letter, or at least a phone call; but he had nothing to say. For him, the only dignified end of a relationship was complete silence.

As he waited impatiently for his secretary he felt flat,

disappointed. Since the evening before, when he had met Cotton Castello at the Embassy party, the thought of her had been teasing him. She was intelligent, she had an unusual sort of beauty enlivened by her quixotic nature. She had directness, a challenging manner, a firm, good body, and he desired her. Overnight he had developed a craving to know her better. Before she had even spoken to him in the Embassy garden, he had been watching her, thinking of how he might introduce himself without appearing too smooth. He could tell the minute they spoke that she too felt the chemistry, but he knew it might take him a long time to get her to admit it. When she had asked to see him, he had assumed she had come to apologize for what she had done years ago. His damnable, savage pride which had only grown with the years kept him from treating the whole thing as a joke. She had been surprisingly nervous when she came into his office, and he knew he should have cajoled her along as she made her confession, even steered her into an apology himself, using the charm and tact he knew he possessed in abundance. Instead of the olive branch, he had offered her contemptuous silence and she had reacted in the only possible way she could, storming out of his office, out of his life, perhaps.

He had had it all planned – how he would shrug off her apology gracefully, how they would drive to a quiet, remote restaurant where they would talk the afternoon away under a pergola over a long lunch and a bottle of wine. When they drove home in the late afternoon, he had planned to invite her to the apartment on the floor above his office, with its sweeping view of the hills of Rome. As the lights were beginning to stud the seven hills, he would slowly draw the curtains and take time undressing her. With slow burning passion he would make love to the complex, responsive woman his instinct told him lay beneath Cotton's cool exterior. He imagined her responding to his touch, his kisses in the filtered light of evening. He knew her better than she realized, oh yes, he knew her. Every detail of that evening in the Villa Robbiana, the night that had changed his life, was preserved in his memory, including a vivid recollection of the Marchesa's daughter, Cotton.

Contrary to what he would have her believe, he had never forgotten the precocious child who in one glance had detected the gauche greenhorn that he had known himself to be. Over a decade and a half ago he had smarted with crushed pride as she sized up his cheap, gaudy clothes, the pointed shoes which, the following day, he had thrown away before leaving Florence for Rome in Nancy Rogers's open-topped Alfa Romeo. Cotton Castello the woman, the child, had churned up memories of a time and a place he hadn't thought of in years.

~Book Two~

Chapter 7

Prowling restlessly like a young lion, Prospero wandered away
from the wedding in the brightly lit village piazza. Stationing
himself on the dark corner of a cobbled side street, he took a
packet of cigarettes from the pocket of his white silk suit. He
was safely out of sight of his mother who insisted he was too
young to smoke at fifteen. Folding his arms across his chest, he
flexed his muscles nervously as he waited, half listening to the
band in the piazza.

Tonight the village of Robbiano was like a carnival, but it
wasn't like this every night. He swore to himself that he would
never be content to live and die in a dump like this. Until that
moment he had never fully appreciated the courage it had
taken his father to get out of Italy and start a new life in
America. As he waited for Anna, glancing down the narrow
dark street, he found himself imagining that they were back
home, in New York. Dressed fit to kill in his white sharkskin
suit, he would take her somewhere swank, to a nightclub
maybe, or dancing at Roseland. On the way home they would
find a dark corner where they could neck. He knew plenty of
dark corners. He imagined himself slipping his hand up Anna's
skirt and felt himself go hard at the thought.

Tension gripped him as he heard her hurrying towards him,
the outline of her face caught in a square of light. He had a
tantalizing image of her soft brown hair tumbling around her
shoulders, her red dress cut provocatively low. She excited him

more than any girl he had ever met, though he didn't know why. Back home in New York there were plenty of girls more beautiful than Anna, but none of them exuded her sexual magnetism.

'Anna,' he whispered hoarsely, catching her wrist.

She gasped, then broke into a laugh when she saw who it was. '*Gesú Maria*, you startled me.' As she stepped from the shadows, a look of recognition passed between them.

'What kept you so late? I've been waiting for you.'

'I couldn't leave the house until my grandfather went to bed. You know what it's like.' She slipped off the black sweater she had thrown over her bare shoulders and the gleam of her throat and arms caught the light.

'You look sensational tonight, sensational,' he whispered, circling his hands around her waist. He moved his thumbs downwards towards her belly, and even several layers of material couldn't stifle the message he conveyed. Anna drew in her breath sharply, then, seeing the look on his face, allowed her full mouth to break into a smile. Immediately, from habit, she covered her mouth, hiding her small uneven teeth.

The sight of her gave Prospero a soaring feeling in his chest. He had felt that way from the moment he first saw her two weeks earlier, when he had arrived with his mother and two brothers for the wedding of his cousin. Her brothers had told him that Anna Gagliani had been transformed from an ugly, skinny kid to a knockout almost overnight, and he still found it astounding that she was only fourteen.

'Do we really have to go to the piazza?' he asked, pushing her against the wall.

'Hey, you're crushing my new dress.' Arching her back, she slid away from him.

'We'd have more fun alone, just the two of us,' he said urgently. The way she lowered her dark-fringed eyes had driven him mad with desire. His eyes traced the line of her neck to the shadowy cleft between her breasts which she had let him touch occasionally.

'No, come on. I want to go and dance,' she said impatiently, prancing on the toes of her high-heeled shoes to avoid the cracks in the cobbles. They had cost her an entire week's wages and she longed to show them off.

'Hold on a minute. Can't you wait?' he called after her.

'What's wrong? Let's go,' she threw over her shoulder, impatient to be acknowledged as the girl with Prospero Vallone. He was so handsome with his dark, slicked-back hair and his blue eyes gleaming like cut-glass in the light of the street lamp. She would be the envy of every girl at the wedding party.

He shifted uncomfortably and an embarrassed smile crossed his face. 'Can't you guess the reason? It's you — what you do to me,' he whispered, grabbing her hand.

Anna's eyes flicked to his trousers, and registered the bulge at his groin.

'You shouldn't talk about such things, Prospero. It isn't nice.' Tilting her head, she made a show of being offended, but she couldn't resist looking again.

As they walked, he regained control, and followed her eagerly towards the brightly lit piazza packed with people. Watching her red dress cut a path through the crowd, Prospero wondered hotly how long it would be before she would let him make love to her. Then he suppressed the thought. Girls in Italy guarded their virginity even more carefully than the Italian girls at home in New York. He didn't have a chance; but the challenge made him still more determined.

She waited for him in the moving crowd of dancers near the dais where the red-faced band was playing, aware of eyes upon them — she, the poorest girl in the village and he, the rich man's son from America. The moment he gathered her in his arms a current of desire passed between them. Her skin and hair gave off the scent of crushed summer roses, engulfing him in a wave of sensuality.

Leaning back in his arms, Anna revelled in the hungry looks she caught from the group of young men loitering on the sidelines.

'Do you know, they used to call me "*bastona*",' she whispered, nodding towards them.

'Not any more, though,' he replied, knowing she was probably too proud to admit that the chant of '*bastona*' — the stick

– had often changed to '*bastarda*'. Prospero had heard from his cousins that Anna Gagliani was a bastard orphan when she came to live with her grandfather after the war.

'No, all the boys are much nicer now,' she said with a brazen defiance that passed for self-confidence. 'Do you know, Prospero, your Italian is improving all the time.'

'It's because I have such a wonderful teacher,' he whispered, taking the opportunity to wedge himself against her in the crowd. He relaxed his hold when he saw his mother watching the two of them from the banqueting table.

When Maria Vallone lost sight of her son, she glanced up at the swallows sailing gracefully against the pale evening sky beyond the cathedral. Toying with the strand of real pearls at her neck, she reached for her ivory fan and began to wave it vigorously. She was hot, and her girdle was pinching. The novelty of being the best-dressed woman at her niece's wedding had begun to pall, and the combs that secured the coil of her deep gold hair had given her a headache.

'Can I get you something to drink, Maria? Another glass of spumante, perhaps?' asked Father Giannini, her second cousin by marriage who had officiated at the ceremony and who sat solicitously by her side, an impressive figure in his exquisitely tailored black silk soutane.

'No, thank you, Pietro,' she said, glancing at the young priest, who was the only member of the family to treat her with the respect she believed she deserved. She felt there had been a bond between them since he had paid a brief visit to New York when he was studying in Chicago.

'She's done very well for herself, hasn't she?' he said, nodding towards the pretty, plump bride as she danced past with her beaming father, Maria's brother, her white satin train draped over her arm. As he whirled her round and round to the music, a lock of dark hair escaped from her crown of flowers.

'What a buffoon he's making of himself, trying to outdo the groom,' she said in disgust. 'I guess it's nice for some who can get any husband they want,' she added, nodding towards her brother's wife, a hook-nosed, flat-chested woman. 'That's what you get when you marry a pharmacy instead of a woman.'

Father Giannini tried to think of something tactful to say, but remained silent. Glancing at Maria Vallone's diamond solitaire, her pearls, her clothes – all spoils from her life in America – he knew all the Fontinis would heave a sigh of relief when the Vallones left for Genoa to stay with another branch of the family. They had disturbed the rhythm of life with their money, arousing envy in the village women who felt shabby compared to Maria Vallone, and resentment among the men who couldn't afford to buy their wives and children the luxuries Franco Vallone heaped on his family.

'Don't you ever get tired of this place, Pietro? You can be honest with me.'

He laughed and shook his head. 'You're a city girl, from Genoa. I know how bored you must be here, but you should get out more, go shopping in Florence. As for me, if God wills . . .'

'I don't like to take the bus. At home if I want to go shopping Franco takes me in the car, or I get a taxi. You should see our new apartment in Brooklyn, Pietro. You must come again soon, to America. The boys have their own bedrooms; I have a maid who comes in every day. Franco insists on nothing but the best. He even imported furniture from Trieste when we moved in.' She was in good humour just thinking about home; but glancing around the square her blue eyes narrowed critically.

'Yes, it's a pity Franco couldn't be here tonight. He would have enjoyed it, I think.' As he spoke, Father Giannini wondered why, in fact, Franco hadn't accompanied his wife and children. He was rich enough from his business – importing leather goods – and, apparently, he owned several other businesses as well as property. Franco Vallone was from Sicily, the heart of Cosa Nostra country, and the priest had always suspected that whatever he did wasn't entirely legitimate.

'He wanted to come, but he couldn't. He works very hard, you know.' Worry broke her proud expression. 'Pietro, I haven't heard from him since we arrived.'

He looked at her, surprised at this sudden confidence.

'I'm sure everything is all right,' he soothed. 'You know what the mail is like in Italy. There was a strike not long before you came. I'm sure that's why.' He had already heard from Prospero that Franco was sometimes absent from home for a long time for no apparent reason. This was another such mysterious absence.

'Maybe, but the thing is he was supposed to make arrangements about money before we leave here for Genoa in two weeks. Anyway, I'm sure everything is all right.' She changed the subject, sensing she had been too open.

They were interrupted when Mario Fontini waltzed by with his wife. At the sight of the two of them Maria turned to the priest. 'I see that the American Marchesa didn't come. And yet she,' she nodded towards her sister-in-law, 'was so sure she would be here. Perhaps the Marchesa has a headache.' She gave a triumphant laugh that made the priest positively dislike her.

'She might still come. It's early yet,' he said. He regarded the banqueting table and the remains of roast boar, goat's cheese and wedding cake. There were rings of red wine on the white paper covering the cloth. The speeches were over long ago, and now children were playing hide-and-seek under the tables and stuffing themselves with sugared almonds. He knew the Marchesa di Castello di Montefiore would not come now, and that no doubt there would be an argument later when Maria spitefully mentioned it to her sister-in-law.

'Tell me, who is that girl Prospero keeps dancing with, the one in that cheap red dress? No nice girl would dress like that. I don't remember seeing her before.'

The priest scanned the dancers, easily spotting Prospero and Anna. Her red dress was crushed against his white suit as they danced, close together, like blood against lilies.

'I ask you, what sort of mother would allow her daughter to wear a dress like that?'

'That's Anna Gagliani. Poor Anna doesn't have a mother. She lives with her grandfather in a cottage just outside the village. He has nothing but a few goats and vines. Anna came to live with him after the war when her mother died. She had to quit school and now works for the Marchesa at her villa. In fact, I recommended her for the job.' As he spoke, he knew the story would elicit no compassion whatsoever.

'I don't like Prospero dancing with her. I'll talk to him about it later. Where are Enrico and Roberto, anyway? Enrico – Roberto,' she called sharply.

The priest was still observing Prospero and Anna. His instincts told him they were locked in a dangerous whirlpool of adolescent emotion. Anna was one of the most vulnerable young lambs in his flock for all her precocious womanhood, and he reminded himself to watch that she didn't go astray during the remaining time that Prospero Vallone spent in the village. Prospero's swaggering sophistication bred in the city streets of America was a natural magnet for the blossoming Anna, already the object of gossip in Robbiano. She seemed to revel in the chaos she had created, but who could blame her? In a few short years, life would probably rob her of her youthful beauty.

When the band broke into a rousing tarantella, Prospero whirled the laughing Anna around.

'Pretend we're in New York at a big swell club,' he called in English as she spun under his arm.

'*Comè?*'

He translated. 'You gotta learn English. I'll teach you. We'll start tomorrow.'

'*Si, professore,*' she giggled.

'Come on, let's go sit down and talk.'

They found two chairs behind a pillar near the café. He took her hand and gazed into her eyes. 'Do you know you're gorgeous? You're the most gorgeous girl I've ever seen.'

'Speak in Italian. I can't understand a word you're saying.'

'I said you're beautiful, *bella, bella.*'

'The girls in New York must be very beautiful,' she said doubtfully.

'Not like you. No, I mean it, honest. You know what? You don't belong here and that's the truth. This place is too small for you. New York is where you belong. Every night is a party. You don't have to wait for a celebration. Tonight, for example, you and I would go to the Stork Club or some place like El Morocco,' he bragged.

'America!' she whispered. 'How I would like to go there

one day.' The wistful tone of her voice changed. 'I will go, I'm sure. I've always felt it.'

'Sure you will, sure. Just make it happen. Make it come true. My father did, didn't he?'

'He must be very rich, your father. It's wonderful for you,' she said with unconcealed envy.

He nodded and lit a cigarette. His father was successful and rich, but that success wasn't enough for Prospero. The sight of one of his cousins in the crowd, passive, anonymous, fired Prospero with a sense of urgency that he wanted to communicate to Anna.

'You gotta make it by yourself, you know. It's not enough to have an old man who is rich. I'm going to make it big one day. I got a friend in New York, Tony Fasso. He's twenty-five and he's on the way already. A couple of years, when I'm out of school, we're going to go into business together.' Encouraged by the look in Anna's eyes he added: 'And you know what I'm going to do when I make my pile? Send you a ticket to come over and stay with me first class — on the *Leonardo da Vinci*.'

She laughed incredulously.

'The first thing you're gonna see on the boat coming into the harbour is the Statue of Liberty.' He reminisced about the voyage over to Naples, not mentioning that the Vallones had come second class on the *Leonardo da Vinci*, not first. Even so, he had drunk champagne and bourbon, smoked as much as he wanted, and had a torrid flirtation with a woman ten years older than he was. He confided it all to Anna, who was as impressed as he expected her to be.

'Is it really easy to get rich in America?'

'Dead easy, if you have the right contacts. Just take my father. Suddenly one day when I was about ten we were rich. Bam — just like that, overnight. That's what it's like there. Only, when I do it my way, I'll expand my father's businesses right across the country, or, who knows, try something new. I'll have my own plane, a yacht, a Thunderbird. Maybe even a private island somewhere. And an apartment on Park Avenue. That's the swankiest street in New York. Ever heard of it?'

She shook her head. 'You'll really have those things some day?' It was more a statement than a question.

'Sure. There's no limit if you're smart and work hard. That's the difference between there and here. There, anything's possible.' His serious blue eyes demanded answers that made the blood rush to her cheeks. 'That's why you gotta come. Will you?'

'All right – I'll come. Whenever you ask me.' Her eyes bright, Anna suddenly abandoned the pessimism of her childhood years, when she had known nothing but disaster. Prospero looked godlike at that moment, handsome, strong, afraid of nothing.

'You can stay with us, of course. My mom and dad have a big house. Lots of bedrooms. I'll sneak in and kiss you good-night when they're in bed.' He was burning to slip his hand inside the scooped neckline of her dress, but instead he stood up abruptly saying, 'Come on – let's go dance.'

William Partridge took the Marchesa's hand draped over the faded sofa and turned it tenderly. As he pressed his lips to her palm she reached for his beard to tug him nearer for a kiss.

'I always think that some things are best enjoyed at a distance, don't you?' he whispered in a rich English voice as he cocked his ear to the brash music floating through the open loggia on the warm night air. Glowing lamps cast circles of light in the ancient room, giving it a muted splendour.

'Well, true, but there are some things I prefer to examine rather closely. Just what were you referring to?' Delilah's large eyes were serene, yet inviting.

'You know perfectly well what I mean. You don't really want to troop all the way down to the piazza at this hour? Not seriously?'

'I suppose I'd have to go and change,' she said doubtfully, lifting the embroidered sleeve of her mauve caftan. 'But I did promise. You'll just have to convince me.' Her American voice held the languid slowness reserved for William, her lover of several years.

Nuzzling the nape of her neck, he began to remove the pins from her pale gold chignon, making her laugh.

'All right, all right. You've won.'

William straightened his tie and tugged at the lapels of his blazer before going to refill their brandy glasses. He paused for a moment at the corner of the large room hung with dark old paintings on the burnt umber walls. The gleaming gilt mirrors reflected the richness of faded velvet, the soft textures of aged marble, of silk tapestries and Venetian painted furniture that complemented Delilah's classic beauty. Even approaching fifty, his American mistress stirred his desire as fiercely as his painter's imagination.

'I must do another portrait of you soon. You become more beautiful with every passing year. By the way, I wish you'd remove those photographs to a dark corner somewhere,' he said irritably, nodding to a faded snapshot of the Marchese in a pith helmet, his foot on a tiger's head, which had been taken in India in the thirties.

'Oh William, it's too late to paint me, and you know it. I'm over the hill.' She ignored his scowl at the picture of her late husband. It was a game he enjoyed, pretending to be jealous of a man who had been dead for over ten years. 'Anyway, I'd much rather you remembered me as I was, up there.' She gestured towards a portrait that he had done several years ago, during the first flush of their affair.

'I adore you more with each passing year, I really do, Delilah. When are we going to be married? Just give the word.' He removed her shoe and began nibbling at her toes.

'Dearest, I'm deeply flattered, and I'm sure you mean it, but don't you think we're better off the way we are?'

Their eyes met, and they understood each other. They both knew this was another little ritual.

'I wasn't cut out to freeze in a garret, and neither were you. Why not have all this, and me too? What's the point in marrying if I'd lose the Villa Robbiano? I sometimes wish I had paid more attention to things like wills and trusts when Lino was alive, although I don't suppose it would have turned out differently. He had to pacify his children somehow, I suppose.'

'Of course, you wouldn't be a Marchesa any more, technically speaking,' he said, unfastening her garter and peeling her stocking from her slender leg. 'You'd be just plain Mrs Partridge, unless I got a knighthood, of course.'

'You know all that doesn't matter a bit to me – Lady Partridge, Marchesa di Castello di Montefiori, Mrs Partridge,' she protested, pretending it didn't. But she had grown into the title of Marchesa. It had become as much a part of her as the Villa Robbiano itself.

'Of course, when the Montefiores cut off my allowance we could always go back to New York and live in my apartment there. You could become a society painter. Would you like that? Painting faded dowagers? You could make a killing beautifying all those old trouts.' She gave a peal of laughter.

'Let's discuss this further after we've had time to reflect, shall we?' Stuffing the stocking into his pocket, he slid on to the couch with his brandy and stroked her leg thoughtfully. They had had the same conversation countless times over the years, often as a prelude to their unhurried love-making, but they both understood that marriage would shatter the liaison and detract from the romantic aura upon which they thrived.

'When are you going to the States this year? Have you decided?'

'Oh, probably not until the middle of August. The villa will be packed until then. Maybe you and I could slip away for a week in the south when they've all gone. By the way, I heard today that Nonie and Hector Swope are coming after all.'

'Ah, which reminds me. I understand that young Matthew Swope had arrived yesterday. He is apparently installed in his *pensione* and all is well.'

'Oh, good. I promised Hector and Nonie I'd keep an eye on him. Bring him up to dinner some night after the life class.'

'Which reminds me, I'm going to lose my model in the next couple of weeks which is a damned bore. Any ideas on a replacement?'

'You mean Rosamund, our nubile English rose? Good – I was getting jealous,' she said, tickling him under his chin.

He kissed her absently. 'It's really a nuisance. The first summer I get a really good group together and *presto*, the model disappears.'

'I hope you're charging enough. Their parents can certainly afford it. Why are the rich so tight-fisted?' she mused, reflecting on her own extravagant habits.

'I was thinking about that girl you hired at the beginning of summer. The one I remarked on.'

'You mean Anna?'

'Yes, that's her name. Do you think she'd be willing to pose nude? I'd wager she has a splendid little body.'

'Yes, and you keep your hands off it, do you hear?'

'Well, I think perhaps if you had a discreet word with her, you know, tell her that it's art and that sort of thing. She's just a simple village girl. Or I could talk to her.'

'She'd have all those young American boys gawking at her in the raw, wouldn't she? I mean, it could be delicate, but I know she's very poor and could use the money. Lord knows, she stares at her reflection every chance she gets, so the house-keeper tells me. She might even enjoy the attention.'

'Well, we'll be in my studio in Florence, far from prying eyes. No one in Robbiano need know.'

'That's a thought. I'll arrange it, William. Leave it to me.'

'I don't know what I'd do without you, Delilah,' he whispered, slipping his hand between her thighs.

'You certainly wouldn't be doing that,' she murmured throatily. Her eyes half-closed, she slipped into a reclining position as William slowly undid his trouser buttons.

Trying to ignore the sensation of Anna's breasts crushed to his back as she clung to him on the back of the scooter, Prospero took a corner as fast as he dared, leaving the main road for the isolated dirt track that had taken him two days to discover. It led to an abandoned farm.

'*Ecco*, here we are,' he exclaimed, bringing the scooter to a screeching halt that made Anna laugh. Parking it beyond a crumbling wall, he felt a profound sense of escape now that they were far from prying eyes. Cicadas sang in the long grass, but the birds had fallen silent in the heat of noon. He took the blanket and picnic they had brought with them and turned towards a copse of olive trees completely hidden in the cleft of a hill. Slipping his arm around Anna, Prospero led her to the shadowy thicket of trees. His glance moved from her profile to the wisps of hair beneath her arms revealed by her sleeveless cotton dress, a sight that had at first shocked him, but now sent a strange sensation through him. Luckily he had come to Italy prepared, he thought. His friend Tony Fasso had slipped a packet of condoms into his hand as a joke before he left New York. He'd never bothered to use one before.

'Are you kidding? All the girls there wear chastity belts,' he had replied laughingly to Tony.

'So what? Don't let that stop you,' Tony had replied with a wink.

Now Prospero swallowed hard, wondering if he was going to need them. When he had spread out the blanket they talked for a while, then he lit a cigarette and gave Anna a puff. Dragging too deeply, she began to cough violently which made them both laugh. They talked nervously, and as she sipped a glass of wine he began to toy with her hair and caress her neck. Languid sensuality gleamed in her half-closed eyes as he eased her back on the blanket and pulled her close. The lacy shadows of the trees gave her face a mysterious expression that filled him with an intolerable craving to know every inch of her. To his amazement he felt her hand move along his thigh and gently stroke the outline of his erection. He groaned at her touch. She didn't stop him when he hurriedly unbuttoned her bodice and released her full breasts, stroking her nipples to make them harden. He was like hot iron now, and everything was a blur as he moved his hand under her skirt and into her pants where he found her soft warmth. At his touch she gasped and fumbled with his zipper, making him moan. Breathing hard, he ripped open the condom packet. She was so aroused that her hips were already moving as he wedged himself between her legs. As he paused to drink in the sight of her sprawled beneath him, he forgot all about the condom. Pushing himself gently until he was inside her, the excitement of her response filled him with acute sensation which he struggled to prolong. Drawing back, Anna's sweet smile told him what pleasure had followed the initial pain. When he entered her gently again, Prospero came swiftly, in an explosion that drew the seed from him like a burst of stars in the darkness. Sweating, throbbing, breathing hard, they lay stunned.

'I love you,' he whispered in English, then in Italian, knowing it was expected of him, yet feeling confused by the violence of what had happened. But it had all been so natural. Not a shadow clouded Anna's lovely face as she traced his lips with her fingertips, whispering,

'It was you, Prospero. You were the one . . I'm so glad . . . '

Chapter 8

Dissatisfied with the angle of his easel, Matthew Swope adjusted it yet again, then straightened the sheet of drawing-paper clipped to the board. The ten American students waiting in a horseshoe in William Partridge's studio for the model to arrive were all laughing and talking, but Matthew kept glancing at the majestic view of Florence through the skylight, at the umber-coloured rooftops clustered around the great Duomo. After dreaming for years of coming to study in Florence, he had to keep reminding himself, he was really there. Firenze, Firenze, the name rang in his ears. He half-listened to the chatter of football games, college parties, anything but the life class. Feeling like a fool, Matthew sensed that he was on the brink of discovering something about himself, something he had been unconsciously seeking, a realization he couldn't share with anyone it seemed so wild and out of character. Here he was, thousands of miles away from home, at the heart of civilization. He looked at the charcoal in his hand. It was the divining rod that, in a few moments, would tell him whether or not he possessed real talent. He was galvanized by his first sight of the tall, aristocratic Englishman who strode into the studio.

Matthew gazed at William Partridge, R A, one of England's most distinguished painters. The severity of the handsome Anglo-Saxon face was softened by a clipped grey goatee and moustache that gave him a professorial air. There was a play of amusement about his clear eyes and strong mouth which suggested great humour as well as intelligence, making an instant impression on the students who fell silent. His blue artist's smock worn over cream linen trousers, a pale blue shirt and a yellow tie symbolized the admirable paradox that was William Partridge.

Matthew knew he had broken away from a conventional upbringing as a clergyman's son to attend the Slade School in London, and then the École des Beaux Arts in Paris during the twenties. When Matthew's parents had brought back a catalogue from one of his recent exhibitions in London he had been riveted by the dramatic battle scenes Partridge had painted while on the Italian Front as a British Army war artist. The prospectus for the course said that he had remained in Florence after the war, quoting him as saying that the wine, the light and the people of Italy suited his temperament. It seemed highly appropriate that he now occupied a studio not far from the house where Michelangelo had once lived as a child, an intriguing fact that added to his charisma. The catalogue hadn't mentioned what Matthew already knew – that William's other cogent reason for making his home in Italy was his mistress, Delilah, the Marchesa di Castello di Montefiore. Listening to his parents' tales of their adventures over the years, Matthew had manufactured a romantic aura around the famous painter and the widow of an Italian count who were glamorous fixtures of the expatriate community in Florence. What struck Matthew as he met William's fine grey eyes was his exciting aura of worldliness, which he admired almost as much as William's painting.

William gave the assembled students a benevolent smile.

'Ladies and gentlemen, although some of us have already met, I would like to welcome you formally to the illustrious summer course held annually by William Partridge, R A.'

There were nervous giggles at his flamboyant manner.

'Now, I'm sure many of you have every intention of burning the candle at both ends while you're in Florence, and of not showing up here if you don't feel like it. But I will tolerate no absences for any reason whatsoever. I don't wish to waste my time or your parents' good money. Is that absolutely clear? Right, in that case we're ready to commence. I should like to introduce to you one of God's most magnificent creations, Miss Anna Gagliani, who has kindly consented to model for us.'

Darting round the corner, he returned leading a robed model by the hand with all the grand ceremony of presenting royalty. There was a hush as he looked round at the expectant faces.

'Miss Gagliani, may I present your public, who will try to do justice to your beautiful image,' he said in English, followed by a quick translation into Italian.

Matthew was instantly fascinated by the cloaked model, her eyes still cast down, her arms folded shyly as she clutched the robe that revealed her bare shoulders. Partridge led her to a dais and whispered encouragingly in Italian. Matthew noticed that she blushed faintly as, with obvious reluctance, she let her wrap slip, while Partridge regarded her with the rapt appreciation of a connoisseur.

Matthew was electrified by the sight of her nakedness. The only life class he had attended had had a middle-aged model with an indifferent figure, but here was a young body that was almost too beautiful to draw.

'Wowee,' whispered the boy next to him. His lewd smirk as he stared at Anna made Matthew want to punch him. 'Shut up, you nit,' he breathed.

'No talking or whispering in my class,' said William sharply. 'I think we will hold this pose for ten minutes and then we will ask Miss Gagliani to recline on the chaise longue for a second attempt.'

Picking up his charcoal, Matthew thought for a moment before beginning his drawing. The only sound he could hear was the scratching of charcoal on paper, the occasional shuffle of feet, and these faded as he lost himself in his work.

Anna stood regal and absolutely motionless with all the proud disdain of a naked slave in a market. Swiftly and surely, Matthew began to trace the delicate line of her shoulders dipping to the long line of her neck as she tilted her head forward. His strokes became bolder as he captured her profile, deftly shading her cheekbones and bringing to life the thoughtful, closed expression on her face.

From his easel in the corner, where he sketched with enormous vigour, William said all too soon,

'Two more minutes, ladies and gentlemen.'

When the master dropped his charcoal, he made the rounds to inspect the drawings, arms folded as he studied their efforts critically. It wasn't until he came to Matthew that he paused for more than a few seconds. Nodding, he stepped back, narrowing his eyes beneath the bushy brows. Matthew, who had worked with the fury of a man possessed, felt his heart pounding in dread as he awaited judgement.

'Aha – not bad.'

Coming from the great William Partridge, this faint praise outshone all the acclaim he had received for his drawing at St Paul's School or Yale. For a moment, he was the centre of attention as the other pupils strained to see his work.

William turned to lead the naked Anna to the chaise longue as if she were a duchess cloaked in ermine.

Regarding her sprawled against the rich amber velvet, Matthew wished he were painting in oils. The master's praise still ringing in his ears, he braced himself for another drawing.

Matthew's hand began to move across the paper as if guided by an unconscious force. He felt as if he were drowning in the sensual beauty he was trying to express. Once he paused and lifted his eyes to the sight of the Duomo through the glass skylight, a backdrop that stirred him almost to ecstasy as he set himself back to work.

From his easel in the corner, William observed Matthew, surprised by definite signs of real talent. He had seen it a few times during his career as a master, and when he did he was never wrong. He thought wryly to himself that the gift had appeared in an unlikely candidate, a rich upper-class American boy, product of prep schools and Yale, son of a banker. The pleasing thought that Matthew Swope might have the makings of a real artist renewed his own feverish desire to draw Anna himself.

Climbing the narrow staircase to his uncle's house above the pharmacy, Prospero detected an immediate change in the atmosphere which put him on his guard. Tension gripped him, tension brought on by guilt at the memory of the afternoon he had just spent with Anna. He had just left her on the road to her grandfather's house, with a promise that they would go to the same place on the scooter tomorrow.

When he opened the front door he heard none of the usual clatter of dishes being put on the table for the evening meal, or the chatter of his aunt, his brothers and his cousins. He became even more uneasy as he entered the dark narrow hall. The entire family were assembled around the heavy oak table in the dining-room, their faces illuminated by the harsh lamp overhead. His heart began to pound violently when he saw the dark solemn looks directed at him, and that Father Giannini was sitting at the head of the table. From somewhere inside the house he identified the echo of sobs. It was his mother and his mouth went dry with fear. He approached to face the inquisition, wildly wondering how he and Anna had been found out.

'Prospero, we've been waiting for you. Come and sit down,' Pietro said, rising to greet him.

To Prospero's surprise, his cousin put an arm around him and gave him a hug. When he was seated between his brother Enrico and his uncle he searched the priest's face for a clue to this inexplicable reception.

'Prepare yourself, my son,' murmured Pietro. 'We have just received some terrible news from America. Your father is dead.'

Prospero gasped. There followed a long blurred moment during which his eyes swept around the table, trailed by a bizarre sense of relief that he and Anna hadn't been found out after all. It took a moment for the priest's words to sink in. His aunt was staring stoically at the table and his uncle hung his head.

'He was murdered,' said Pietro. 'We don't know the details yet. We received a telegram from your father's old friend, Dino Cataneo.'

Shaking all over, Prospero leapt to his feet. 'Mamma – where is she?' The sound of her distant sobs was suddenly intolerable.

'The doctor is with her in the bedroom.'

Prospero's eyes darted to his two young brothers, who were staring at him uncomprehendingly with white, pinched faces, their big eyes shadowed by fear. Everyone seemed to be looking to him to shoulder this crushing burden. Struggling to hold back the tears, Prospero felt himself falling, falling into an abyss away from the sunlit patch of ground where he had lain with Anna that afternoon.

Late the following afternoon Prospero was driving back to Robbiano with his uncle in his little Fiat. They hadn't exchanged a word since leaving the post office in Florence, where they had gone to telephone Dino Cataneo in New York. All the beauty of the sun setting over the Tuscan hills was lost on Prospero as he stared numbly out of the window. Finally, he could stand the silence no longer.

'What are we going to do?' he blurted out.

His uncle didn't reply, but only shrugged, and compressed his lips into a thin line.

Prospero was angered by this cold reaction to the catastrophic news they had just received from Dino. His father, Franco Vallone, who had always towered over him like a Titan, had no money at all. The leather import business had been nothing but a shell and the other businesses, the news stands, a billiard parlour, none of them had actually belonged to Franco Vallone. Even the property his father had owned in New Jersey had been mortgaged to the hilt. The apartment that Prospero had always thought belonged to his father had been rented, and Dino had informed them the landlord was already taking steps to seize their personal property. Franco had been up to his eyeballs in debt, playing off one debt against the other every month, and if he hadn't been murdered he would probably have finished in prison, broken and bankrupt. From Dino's garbled conversation with his uncle it was understood that Franco Vallone's precarious empire had collapsed when he failed to honour the most important debt of all, two hundred thousand dollars for the non-performance of a mob favour which he had somehow failed to execute. The details were still sketchy, but when he had heard them from his uncle, Prospero had felt nauseated with horror and shame.

'Tell me, Uncle Mario, please, before we get back home. I have to have something to say to Mamma.' His voice cracked with anxiety and he could feel the fear rising in his throat as if he were stranded on a flagpole in a high wind. In moments he would have to face his grief-stricken mother and his two younger brothers. Even now, as they drove along, everything the Vallones owned in America was being dismantled like a stage set in a darkened theatre.

'Calm down, will you? We have to think,' his uncle replied sharply.

Prospero was acutely aware that during the last twenty-four hours the atmosphere in his uncle's house had changed. His aunt, who had until then controlled her hostility, treated them with open contempt at breakfast, and his uncle was embarrassed and remote. He had heard them arguing the night before above his mother's sobs. It was beginning to dawn on Prospero that their only concern was to get rid of them as soon as possible.

'We must cash in our return tickets on the *Leonardo*,' muttered Prospero, trying to sound businesslike and grown-up. 'We can find a cheaper way home maybe.'

'There are no return tickets.' His uncle's voice was flat.

'What do you mean, no tickets?' His mind had been racing ahead to how they would manage when they got home, how he would have to quit school and get a job. He was completely unprepared for this devastating news.

'Your mother was afraid to tell you. Your father was supposed to wire the money for the return tickets when you got to Genoa.'

Panic engulfed Prospero. 'But we've got to get back to New York. Everything's there. We can't stay here,' he cried, feeling trapped. Reminding himself he was the man in the family now, he said as calmly as he could: 'All right, all right, can you lend us the money then? We'll pay you back as soon as we can.'

His uncle gave a contemptuous laugh. 'Me? I don't have that kind of money.'

'No money? You don't have any money? Jesus,' he muttered under his breath as they reached the village.

'My money is all in the business, in the pharmacy.'

A sharp pause told Prospero that even if his uncle did have the money, he wouldn't be so foolish as to lend it to his sister Maria and her brood.

'Listen, Prospero, you have to grow up. The sooner you face the music the better. You've had a sweet life up until now, and now you've had a hard knock. Take it like a man.'

Prospero was trembling with anger and outraged pride at his uncle's glib dismissal of his shattered existence, but he controlled himself and said nothing.

'And get it out of your head to go back to New York. It's not safe anyway. The hoods who did Franco in might think you're old enough to pay back what he owes them. Your father was a crook. Take it as a lesson and go straight in life. Don't fool around with that kind of stuff or you'll wind up in the gutter like him.'

'I'd rather wind up like him than like you,' retorted Prospero as they entered the piazza. As soon as the car stopped, he leapt out.

'Get out of my sight,' his uncle shouted after him. 'I'll be glad to see the back of all of you.'

As his uncle disappeared into the narrow side street, Prospero stood in the piazza choked with anger. Glancing towards the brightly lit café he knew he could no longer spend the money in his pocket on the pinball machine, on drinks, on cigarettes. What he had left was too precious now. Nor could he spend another lira on Anna. Suddenly he knew he had to pour out his heart to her about what had happened. It was the only thing that could relieve his aching misery.

Moments later he broke into a run along the dark lane outside the village where she lived with her grandfather. He stood at the rusting metal gate at the end of the path and stared at the yellow lights in the window of the small low cottage covered with vines. Then he walked up the path, disturbing the chickens in their coop and a goat tethered to a post. He gave one or two low, distinct whistles to alert Anna that he was there.

After a few tense moments he saw her come out of the

kitchen door and hurry towards him, pulling a shawl over her shoulders. She stopped a few feet away and stared at him, her face illuminated by the light from the house. He knew from the look on her face that she had already heard about his father. The news would have spread like a bushfire throughout the village. He had half-expected, wanted, her to rush to him with open arms and comfort him, but instead her eyes glinted with accusation even in the darkness.

'You know,' he said lamely.

'Everyone knows.' Folding her arms tightly, she led him away from the house. Then she turned on him.

'What are you doing here?'

'What do you mean?'

'How can you embarrass me like this by coming here? Your father is a criminal. Go away from me and don't ever come back. I have to suffer enough now because I have associated with the son of a criminal. You have disgraced me, my family name . . .'

A hurt laugh escaped his throat. 'Your family name?' The idea was ridiculous. 'Hey, wait a minute. I'm the guy that made love to you yesterday. It's me, Prospero Vallone. Anna, Anna, what's the matter with you?' he whispered, reaching out to touch her, but she cringed away.

'Don't touch me,' she warned sharply. 'You no longer have the right. All those big things you told me were just lies, lies. And all the promises about New York, nightclubs, fancy restaurants, you going into business – everything.' She was close to tears, but they were for herself, not for him.

He regarded Anna in mute disbelief, her shoulders hunched, her face distorted by rage. The girl he had loved so passionately was a wax doll melting in a fire. Her hatred seemed more real than her love had been, laying waste all his hopes.

'Have you nothing to say?' she cried.

'Yes, *stronza* – this is what I have to say.' Grabbing her arm violently, he spat into her face, then lurched away down the dark road feeling his heart would break.

As she watched him disappear, Anna began to cry, sobbing quietly into her hands. Rocking herself back and forth she whispered miserably, 'You promised, you promised . . .'

When he was out of sight, Prospero stopped and slumped by a wall. Struggling under the crushing weight of this unexpected loss, he looked up at the bright stars above the row of cypress trees. His chest heaving, he dashed his clenched fist against the rock wall. The searing pain released the boiling misery inside him for a second. He would be rich one day, he vowed; oh yes, he would be filthy, stinking rich. But his wealth would be massive and solid, grounded on unshakable foundations. Some day people would tremble when they heard the name of Prospero Vallone.

In the gloom of the cathedral Anna glanced nervously towards the candlelit altar where a few women were praying, heads bowed. She was relieved that no one else was waiting at the elaborately carved confessional box. She rang the bell and waited for the priest to appear behind the grille, then slipped inside and knelt down on the cushion. When she glanced at the priest's shadowy profile she was unnerved to see that it wasn't the younger priest who usually heard her confession, but Father Giannini, Prospero's cousin. It was too late now to change her mind. What she had to confess had been weighing on her conscience for far too long, and she needed to unburden herself and obtain absolution.

'Bless me, Father, for I have sinned . . .' she whispered hesitantly.

She began her confession with the usual venial sins of neglect, bad temper, laziness, working up gradually to something that made her hesitate.

'And have you anything else to confess, my child?' asked the priest.

'Yes, Father, I have.' Dying inwardly, she blurted out: 'I have committed a mortal sin. I am no longer a virgin, Father.' There was a painful silence before she found the courage to continue.

In the dimness of the confessional, Father Giannini had recognized Anna Gagliani behind the grille. Now he knew for certain that she and Prospero had fallen into temptation and he felt sick at heart. He prepared himself, wondering if there was more to come.

While Anna was whispering her sins in the confessional, Matthew Swope descended the curving stone staircase of the Villa Robbiano, dressed for dinner. As he paused to study a vast tapestry, he could hear his mother's voice coming from the drawing-room.

'It's so wonderful to be back in Italy again, especially here, Delilah. I think your villa is my favourite house in the entire world. Don't you agree, Hector?'

Straightening his bow tie, Matthew entered the drawing-room where a dozen or so people had gathered. The soft glow of the rose-coloured lampshades, the vases filled with summer flowers bewitched his senses. The room made a great impression on him with its pastoral landscapes in heavy gilt frames, fine marquetry furniture, beautiful flowered carpets, all of which looked as if they had been mellowing gently there for centuries. His eyes moved upwards to the ceiling with its faded nymphs and cherubs dancing around the magnificent chandelier looped with chains of crystal. His mother, in her black cocktail dress, her greying page-boy curling about her cheeks, smiled when she caught sight of him.

'Ah, Matthew, there you are,' said Delilah warmly, descending on him in a whirl of Pucci colour. As he kissed her cheek, she inquired, 'Did you have a nice swim?'

'Yes, thank you. I did about forty lengths,' he said proudly. 'Not bad, considering I'm really out of shape.'

'Forty lengths, listen to that. Ah, to be young,' said his mother with a sigh. 'Don't you just love this villa, dear? I was just saying to your father that it's another world, another century. Including the plumbing,' she added.

Matthew accepted a whisky and soda from the white-coated butler as Delilah led him to meet the other guests. He shot a glance at his father who was deep in conversation with William Partridge. Matthew wondered anxiously if they could be talking about him. William had solemnly promised to try and persuade him that he was talented enough to pursue a career as a painter when he left college, but from his father's genial expression Matthew was sure they couldn't possibly be discussing his future.

Later they dined on a candlelit terrace in the loggia overlooking the formal gardens, surrounded by plants spilling from urns and amphorae. The wavering candles cast their shadows on the arches. Matthew, seated between the wife of an Italian banker and an Englishwoman whose title he couldn't remember, looked hungrily at the steaming plate of *fettucini* smothered in cream and *porcini* which the butler set before him.

As the butler filled their glasses, Delilah commented: 'This wine is from our own vineyards.'

'Do you know, I believe it improves every year,' remarked Nonie.

'I'm glad to hear you say so. William keeps promising to design me a pretty label. We're going to call it Bianco di Montefiore.'

'It's going to bring in a fortune,' said William good-humouredly. 'Except, of course, we seem to drink inordinate quantities of it ourselves.'

Matthew laughed, then lost his appetite for a moment as he caught sight of a maid skirting the terrace with a tray. When he received the invitation to join his parents at the villa he had imagined Anna would be there serving dinner. He had become obsessed with making contact with the remote beauty, whose image haunted his days and nights. When he wasn't working or going to museums, he worked feverishly on his Italian, concocting phrases to reel off casually when he finally bumped into her. He was startled from his thoughts when Delilah said:

'Matthew, I wanted to ask you what you think of the model in your life class.'

His heart began to beat loudly, and he was sure anyone would guess how infatuated he was.

'I think she's – uh, fine, excellent. Very effective,' he said lamely.

'I think what Matthew is trying to tell us is that the model currently gracing my life class is the living embodiment of the eternal woman in her most paradoxical form, the madonna–whore,' boomed William with a wink.

Nonie laughed, startled at William's turn of phrase. 'What a witty way to put it.'

Hector Swope added drily, 'I'll keep that in mind when I look at the work Matthew's been doing.'

Matthew felt burning resentment that Anna, his muse, was being discussed so crudely, and William Partridge immediately went down in his estimation as a hypocrite. Behind his model's back, he treated her with none of the flamboyant courtesy that he showed her when in front of his pupils.

'And on that subject,' said Delilah with a nod towards Matthew, 'I was thrilled when William told me on the first day of the class that he thought Matthew has a great gift, that he ought seriously to consider pursuing art as a career . . .'

'Is that so?' said Hector, glancing from William to Matthew, who had laid down his fork.

'In all the years I've known William I've hardly ever heard him praise a pupil. Compliments coming from him are rare indeed. Let's face it, you two, you've got a genius on your hands.'

'Why, I'm absolutely thrilled to hear you say that,' said Nonie. 'I mean, Matthew was always very good in art at school. But to hear this, well, I don't quite know what to say.' She looked at her husband.

Hector said blandly, 'We always knew he had a talent, of course. That's why we were so pleased when this chance came to study with you here in Florence, William. Matthew will always have a pastime, a hobby. In my opinion a man needs to relax. Think of Winston Churchill.'

Matthew cast a guarded look at his father, knowing that this wasn't the time or place to announce that he had made up his mind to become a painter, and that there would be no going back. He knew he would have to face a pitched battle with his parents, but he was ready to make a stand. The conversation switched to Italian politics, and he caught Delilah's sympathetic glance.

'Don't worry,' she whispered. 'We'll wear him down.'

From her conspiratorial smile, Matthew knew he had an ally in the fascinating American Marchesa. She had become legendary among his parents' friends in America and he knew he was lucky to be entertained with such style in her fabled villa.

Looking from William to Delilah, Matthew felt caught in the powerful crossfire of their glance which seemed like a tangible current between them. Matthew's mother had been at finishing school in Paris with Delilah, and she had always kept in touch with her old friend even though their paths had diverged wildly. Nonie had dutifully done what all girls of her class had been expected to do after they had acquired their veneer of European sophistication: she had married a banker and had borne three children. But she had always talked nostalgically of the delightfully eccentric Delilah Cunningham, who had proved herself unconventional even at the age of nineteen by moonlighting as a model for Molyneux. Her long-waisted, slim-hipped figure had proved a natural vehicle for the figure-clinging clothes of the early thirties. By the time that Judge Clifford Cunningham of Philadelphia heard that his only daughter often played truant from lessons in etiquette and French, she was being seen at Longchamps with an impoverished Russian Prince, and dancing until dawn at Bricktop's in Montmartre. Before she was twenty, she had married the French sugar baron Didier de la Courte – DD to his friends. By 1935, she was an established figure in Paris social life, entertaining lavishly at her apartment in the rue des Courcelles and the family château in the heart of the Indre. It had seemed to the friends from her schooldays who admired her from afar that Delilah's star would always shine over Paris until the day that DD was killed in a plane crash while on a spree with his mistress.

Delilah surprised everyone by migrating to Italy where she consoled herself in a palazzo on the Grand Canal in Venice. It was at a ball during the carnival of 1937 that Delilah Cunningham de la Courte acquired her second title by marrying the Marchese Niccolò Castello di Montefiore, a dark wiry widower who had a reputation for conquest. The fifty-five-year-old Marchese astonished himself by falling in love for the first time with a girl from Pennsylvania who possessed all the classic attributes of a New World beauty. He was charmed by her soft-spoken voice, the violet grey eyes and magnolia complexion, but it was her racy wit, her originality of style, and her strength of character that finally won him.

They had travelled the globe together, indulging themselves to the hilt, cruising in the Baltic, big game hunting in Africa, wintering in Luxor. During the war years they were exiled in relative comfort on the Algarve in Portugal and the moment the war was over they returned to Robbiano to put the villa back in order. Though the Marchese's fortunes had suffered along with everyone else's, he and Delilah continued to live as they always had. Matthew had been intrigued at the story of the Marchese's death, which Delilah attributed to a diamond-encrusted seventeenth-century snuffbox she declared had belonged to Marie Antoinette and was therefore unlucky. With the proceeds from the sale of the heirloom, the Marchese, an avid polo player, had bought a thoroughbred from a stud in Deauville. Orion, a glossy brown devil, had thrown him in a tournament in Rome in 1946, killing him instantly.

As he regarded Delilah, whose luminous image had symbolized scandal and glamour for as long as he could remember, Matthew was aware that his conventional family seemed dull by comparison. Now that he had met the Marchesa, he fully understood William Partridge's devotion. The power of the attraction between them was something he had only read about in books or seen at the movies. The very air that they breathed seemed to exude a life-enhancing quality which Matthew suddenly realized was indispensable to his own well-being. If he was going to live life to the full, to explore his talent, he too would have to have a muse as wise and beautiful as Delilah. His mind flew to Anna Gagliani.

When the second course arrived, a roulade of veal, laced with pistachios and fennel, he glanced through the serving doors for some sign of her. He knew he would be looking for Anna everywhere that weekend. He picked up a crystal goblet brimming with red wine. The fragrance of roses came to his nose as he sipped it, half-listening to the conversation against the tinkle of a fountain rising from the depths of the garden. The soft warm Tuscan night enfolded him in an embrace that was almost tangible, summoning the realization that he was in love with life, with Italy.

After dinner, when coffee was served in the drawing-room, Matthew sat restlessly while trying to make polite conversation on the sofa with an English diplomat.

Delilah said tactfully, 'Matthew, you really ought to have a stroll in the village as you haven't seen it yet. The church is spectacular at this time of night and the piazza is full of people making the *passegiata*.'

'Yes, that's a good idea. I think I'll do that, he said, leaping at the suggestion.

With a nod to everyone. he made his escape before his parents could comment.

When Matthew entered the piazza he headed for a brightly lit café. On the way there he had removed his tie, slung his jacket over his shoulder and rolled up his shirtsleeves.

'*Un espresso e una Sambucca, per favore,*' he said to the waiter, feeling very worldly as he reeled off the phrase.

Sitting down, he scanned the crowd passing by: hunched old women in black, old men with weatherbeaten faces smoking hand-rolled cigarettes. Giggling young girls wove by arm in arm, as they glanced obliquely at the swaggering clusters of young men bursting out of tight pants and tapered shirts. Matthew regarded the ebb and flow of street life with fascination. Here new loves began, old feuds were kept alive. He watched the current of people flowing against the backdrop of buildings that pre-dated the Renaissance, with worn stone pediments and scrolls and sloping tiled roofs against the deep blue sky. He narrowed his eyes and thought for a moment how he would interpret it all.

Since studying with William Partridge he had begun to regard the world through an invisible frame as he now observed the cathedral where a girl in a pale summer dress was walking down the steps, untying a scarf from her head to release her brown shoulder-length hair. Stuffing the scarf into her bag, she then slipped her sweater from her shoulders. With a jolt, Matthew realized it was Anna. He knew he had been unconsciously

prepared to sit there all night if necessary to see her, and now
she had appeared as if he had willed it. Without even thinking,
he leapt to his feet as she approached.

'Anna! Anna!'

She turned her head sharply, but didn't seem to recognize
the tall blond foreign boy. When it dawned on her that he
could only be one of the students from the art class she looked
at him coolly.

'Signorina Gagliani – do you remember me? I'm from the
art class,' he said in his best Italian.

'Yes, I know you. What do you want?'

He smiled awkwardly as he realized his mistake. Until that
moment he had never seen her with her clothes on. He realized
that no one in Robbiano knew Anna posed nude for artists in
Florence, or that she would want them to know. In a few
carefully chosen words, he explained what he was doing in the
village.

'I see,' she said, eyeing him up and down.

'And I wonder if you would like to join me for a while?'

She shrugged. 'All right. Why not?'

He pulled out a chair for her and she sat down beside him.
When he ordered the *tartuffo* she had asked for there was a
silence between them. Her arms folded, Anna pretended to be
engrossed in watching people go by. When the iced chocolate
confection arrived, Matthew watched her with fascination: she
curled her tongue around a spoonful of cream, forgetting for
once to hide her imperfect teeth, then popped a cherry into her
mouth. As his eyes dropped to the cleft between her breasts, he
was forcefully reminded of her standing naked in William's
studio.

When she had devoured her ice-cream she turned the full
force of her brown eyes on him. 'Are you staying in the village
for a long time?'

'Only for the weekend.'

As she regarded Matthew, Anna gave no indication that she
had unpacked his bag that afternoon, taking note of every
item. She had set his monogrammed hairbrushes on the dresser
in one of the guest rooms, then quickly examined the contents

of his suitcase from his cuff-links and studs to his shoes and evening clothes. She had noted that everything Matthew Swope owned was very expensive and of the best quality. She had also sneaked a look at his passport and had recognized him as one of the students in William Partridge's class. Arching her back provocatively, she leaned forward and smiled.

'I didn't notice before tonight, but you are really very handsome.'

'Do you think so?' he replied, surprised at her frankness.

'Oh, yes. I suppose I never dared look at you before, but now we're here it's much easier to talk, isn't it?' Anna had just seen Prospero crossing the piazza in the company of his younger brother. She made an instant and unfavourable comparison between Prospero, son of a murdered immigrant, and the rich young American opposite her. Prospero and his family would never have been invited to dine at the Villa Robbiano.

'How old are you?' Matthew asked, after ordering them both coffee and Sambucca.

'Try and guess.'

'I don't know. Seventeen?'

'No, eighteen,' she lied, then launched into an impromptu history of herself. As she talked, she stole glances towards Prospero who she knew must by now have seen her and Matthew.

'. . . and my father was from a very noble family in Lombardy. He was an officer in the Army when he met my mother. She wasn't good enough for his family, and when she was killed in an air raid on the munitions factory where she was working, his family disowned me; and that's how I ended up here with my grandfather. But if my father hadn't died I would be rich now,' she said, almost believing her fantasy.

'That's fascinating,' said Matthew, straining to understand her every word. 'Go on, tell me more.'

Prospero walked jauntily across the piazza, hands in his pockets, with his brother beside him. As he cracked a joke he laughed brashly, and he carried himself with a swagger, aware that people cast pitying glances in his direction. He was immaculately dressed in his best shirt and trousers, and had combed and oiled his hair before leaving his uncle's house.

'You sure you don't want to play cards or something instead of just walking?' asked the thirteen-year-old Enrico uneasily.

'Are you kidding? I don't want to deprive everybody in town of seeing what the sons of a crook look like. You and me aren't cowards. Why should we hole up in the house on our last night? Anyway, Rico, we're a couple of famous guys around here.' Prospero's crooked smile, and his eyes narrowed with defiance, dared anyone to challenge him.

'I have to hand it to you. You got guts.'

'Not as much guts as all these slobs. They probably think we're contaminated. See the looks we're getting?'

His brother echoed his laughter.

'Hey, get a load of that,' whispered Enrico. 'Over there at the café – Anna's there.'

Adrenalin shot through Prospero. Anna wasn't more than a few yards away, strolling out of the café, arm in arm with a tall blond stranger he had never seen before. The sight of them together was like a kick in the stomach.

'That creep looks like he died and gone to heaven,' said Enrico, instantly sensing what his brother was feeling. 'She's nothin' but a tramp. And get a load of him. He looks like a number one square.'

'Yeah, yeah. What do I care, anyway? She's nothin' to me now, nothin'.' He pulled out a cigarette, but his hands shook as he lit it. Prospero waited his ground for them to approach. The real reason he had come to the piazza, apart from showing his face, was that he hoped to see Anna and to apologize for spitting at her that night. Her behaviour still hurt him, but he didn't want to leave it like that. Now, seeing her simpering at someone else, her eyes cast down in that maddening way of hers, he was suffocated with emotion. Prospero stood with his feet planted firmly apart as Anna and the stranger passed a few yards away. He glared at her, and when her eyes slid over him she looked straight through him, then smiled at the boy, driving him mad with jealousy.

'Aw, she's nothin',' muttered Enrico, 'and he's a jerk.'

'Come on, let's get out of this dump. I can't wait to get out permanently,' Prospero cursed. The image of Anna and another man brought tears to his eyes and he didn't want anyone to see.

'What do you care, anyway?'

'Shut up. Just shut the hell up, will you?'

They left the piazza, not with a feeling of pride as Prospero had intended, but slinking away down a dark side street. He was ashamed, disgraced, beaten. Tomorrow night he would be in Genoa with his mother and brothers, where an uncle had offered them two rooms and jobs for the three boys working in a metal foundry.

Chapter 9

Dusk was descending the following day as Matthew stopped the car he had borrowed from Delilah on a side road. He turned to Anna beside him.

Together they looked at the gnarled olive trees on the crest of the hill, silhouetted against the rose-tinged clouds. The cool, earth-scented breeze filled the car, carrying the smell of the Tuscan hills that seemed to compress centuries of civilization.

Folding her arms, Anna leaned back against the window, prompting Matthew to reach out for her hand. The tones of her shoulders, sunblushed roses on olive, would always elude him, he suspected, if he tried to paint her.

'I enjoyed today. *Grazie*, Matthew,' she said sweetly. Even the way she slightly lisped his name excited him.

'Good. I'm glad,' was all he could think to say.

'Will you come to visit the Marchesa again soon?' she asked.

'I'm supposed to come next weekend to go to a ball with her and my parents.'

'How nice for you. It must be very amusing to go to big parties all the time,' she said, her voice half envious, half wistful.

'It sounds fun, but they're often full of older people I don't know, or don't want to know.'

'I don't believe you,' she said with a playful laugh, leaning her head against the window.

As she sat there, he was assailed by pictures of Anna he had seen that day: dipping her head to smell flowers that morning in Fiesole, her uninhibited hunger as she attacked her spaghetti at lunch, her habit of twirling a coil of dark hair around her finger as she talked. 'Can we go out next week when I'm here?'

'You mean you want me to go with you to the party? I don't think I have the right dress to wear . . .' He knew she was teasing him.

'What I was really thinking is that I could leave early. We could meet at the villa. Nobody will be there.'

'I doubt if my grandfather would let me,' she replied vaguely.

The glimmer of her teeth between her full lips sent determination coursing through him. 'Say you'll come, that you'll meet me in the villa by the pool at ten on Saturday night.'

'If the Marchesa found out, I would lose my job. What would I do then?'

He thought of all sorts of wild things, but didn't express them. 'She won't find out. Don't worry. Just trust me.'

'Yes, I trust you,' she whispered, pretending to consider the idea. She was amused and flattered at the tempest of desire her every remark and gesture aroused in Matthew Swope. Her life had been disturbed, changed even, by Prospero Vallone's power over her; but Matthew's transparent desire gave her a pleasurable sense of control. She didn't resist when he pulled her to him. His breath exploded in her ear as she turned her head to avoid his kiss. His lips had found the warm curve between her ear and cheek, causing him to whisper something in English which she didn't understand. When she began laughing he turned her face none too gently and stifled her laughter with a kiss. His hand closed on her breast and she responded for only a moment by digging her fingers into his back before pushing him away.

'Excuse me, Anna,' he muttered, drawing back to look at her. 'You don't even know what you're doing, do you? You're completely innocent. Forgive me.'

Matthew drew his hand across his mouth, reminding himself he had no right even to kiss a young Italian virgin; he was driven with the desire both to protect her innocence and to violate it. When he reluctantly started the car to return to

Robbiano, the expression on Anna's face in the twilight went straight to his heart.

She was thinking of Prospero, who had taken her with unbridled lust, without apology or restraint, Prospero who would never be invited to a ball in Florence, much less leave early just to be with her; nor would he ever have apologized for kissing her.

On Saturday, Matthew drove back at breakneck speed up the winding road to Robbiano. The headlights of the Fiat picked out the forms of cypress trees jutting above rock walls, of vineyards and olive trees as he sped towards his destination. A mile from the village he skidded dangerously, narrowly missing a tree, but he didn't care if it would save him valuable seconds.

He was nearly an hour late when he finally accelerated recklessly down the long drive to the villa, bringing the car to a skidding halt. Jumping out, his only thought was whether Anna was still waiting for him by the pool. In the deep silence, his footsteps resounded on the gravel. He cursed himself that he hadn't dared tell his mother and father that he didn't want to go to the ball. He was twenty, and he could have refused. Bounding through the gates of the walled garden, he raced across the terrace to the pool. He stopped, heart pounding, at the sight of Anna sitting cross-legged, staring into the dark water. Only the distant splashing of the fountain, the timid notes of a single cricket, broke the ancient stillness of the garden, redolent with the scent of jasmine and roses. Overjoyed, Matthew broke into a run.

When she saw him, she leapt up. He had an image of her face and bare arms, luminous, as if she were holding a lamp. 'I was afraid you would leave before I got back.' He grabbed her hands and kissed them.

'Was it a wonderful party?'

'No, not at all. I hated every damn minute of it,' he said in English, searching her eyes.

'All the same, it must have been interesting in a way.' Her voice conveyed satisfaction at having stolen him away from the daughters of the upper-class who she guessed were at the party. As she began to walk along the narrow band of white stone framing the dark water, Matthew trailed after her, his hands in his pockets. She surprised him by saying:

'I think I would like to swim. This might be the only chance.'

'Did you bring your bathing suit?' he said. Then he smiled when she began to laugh at him; it was a stupid question.

'I don't really need one, do I?'

Anna slipped off her dress and tossed it aside without a trace of embarrassment. Even though he had memorized every detail of her exquisite body, Matthew was awed as he gazed at her naked form outlined in the darkness.

Displaying the curve of her breasts, the flare of her hips, she glanced over her shoulder at him.

'No one can see me here, can they?'

Her whisper brought him to his senses. Pulling off his clothes, he followed her to the steps at the edge of the pool. He watched while she waded into the water, arms outstretched, her breasts kissing the surface. When he plunged in to catch up with her, she laughingly eluded his grasp; and then, suddenly out of her depth, she cried out.

He caught her just as her head went under and, when he pulled her above the surface, she spluttered in panic and clung to him.

'Hey, it's all right. You're fine. Don't worry,' he whispered, clasping her to him.

Her breath came in short gasps. 'I was so frightened. I don't know how to swim.'

He laughed. 'Then why did you go in, you gorgeous, you silly . . .'

'I was so frightened. Oh, Matthew.'

A current of excitement shot through Matthew as he realized he was holding Anna naked in his arms. Silvered by the moonlight, she seemed more like a goddess than a woman. Her hair floating on the water was woven with stars of light and her mouth, that incredible mouth, was hungrily parted. He seized her ferociously, tasting the first wet kiss. Feeling him lash firmly against her, she cupped herself to him, her cool wet arms around his neck, her thighs gripping his legs. All his doubts and fears left him as he kissed her again and again, arousing a passion in her that was equal to his own.

With a stabbing motion she thrust her tongue into his mouth, evoking the act of love he had never experienced. His hands explored her hips, her buttocks, as she wedged against him with mounting urgency. Drifting to the shallow end of the pool, he leaned back against the fanning steps as she hovered over him. The water lapping gently around his shoulders, he watched her perfect body straddle him as if in slow motion. He groaned at the stabbing force of his desire as he watched himself disappear between her thighs. As pleasure ripped through him, he reached out desperately for her.

'*Caro, caro,*' she whispered passionately, her wet breasts across his chest. Cradling his face between her hands, she breathed: '*ti amo, ti amo.*'

'Anna, I adore you, I love you,' was his passionate response.

When they climbed out of the pool, he gathered up her clothes and his, and wrapping her in a bath towel, carried her to the staircase that led to his bedroom.

The next morning, when the pale dawn seeped through the shutters, Anna awakened to a chorus of doves and swallows. It took a moment to remember that she was in the villa and that Matthew Swope was lying next to her. She knew she would have to leave soon if she was to avoid discovery, but for a few blissful moments she was content to luxuriate between the cool linen sheets and enjoy the beauty of the dim room. Her eyes moved to the antique armoire, to the mirror that cast a clouded reflection in the soft light, to the vaulted ceiling touched with gilt. She had never really observed the room carefully until now, even though she had cleaned it dozens of times, nor had she appreciated all its fine details.

As Matthew stirred contentedly in his sleep next to her, Anna's thoughts strayed from their repeated love-making during the night. She had already put it out of her mind. When she had made love with Prospero she had given him everything; but with Matthew she had held part of herself back. It was much better that way, she realized. It gave her strength to see things clearly. Yesterday, as a servant she had made the bed she was sleeping in and today, she, a poor Italian nobody, was the mistress of a rich young American who considered her his equal. There were innumerable people who woke up every day of their lives in splendour like this, and Anna decided that, somehow, she would be one of them. If she had the power to become this boy's lover, then surely she could become his wife. Just then his hand moved in search of her. The moment he touched the warm curve of her hip he breathed a sigh of happiness. Turning towards her, Matthew opened his eyes. The look of drowsy enchantment on his face told Anna that he was enslaved by the memory of what had happened the night before.

William Partridge wiped the charcoal from his hands and glanced around the circle of American students working at their easels for what would be the last time. He nodded to Anna, indicating that she could draw her wrap around her.

'Well, ladies and gentlemen, this brings the summer course of fifty-five to a conclusion. I can only express the hope that some of you might return next year. May I also express the sentiment that I hope you have learned from me as I have from you . . .'

He found himself singling out Matthew Swope, whose character had undergone such a transformation during the last weeks. Matthew had arrived as a typical American college student, rather naïve and over-eager. But four weeks in Florence had roused him from his sleep of conformity, awakening him to his own unique identity. William felt a certain pride that he had inspired Matthew's fierce determination to pursue a career as an artist – an ambition that would consume his life if he had the courage to follow it. He gazed from Matthew to Anna, and back again.

'I trust you will remember these halcyon days in Firenze all your lives, where you have walked in the footsteps of Mantegna, Giotto, Masaccio, Botticelli . . .' The names rolled musically off his tongue. 'Some of you no doubt will continue to follow in their steps, not forgetting the warmth of Italian days . . . and nights,' he added pointedly, causing a ripple of laughter. 'Take these images with you: the amber water flowing beneath the Ponte Vecchio, the green-clad Tuscan hills that embrace the Arno . . .'

In his rich actor's voice, William did what he always did best, the glib summing up of the tedious summer period that augmented his income. He found it barely tolerable except for the occasional glimmer of talent that made it worthwhile. This had been one of those rare summers when a particular student had aroused his interest, and he wondered what was going on in Matthew's mind as he saw him gazing at Anna. He told himself he ought to seek him out privately; but William had already mentally abandoned the group of privileged and largely untalented young Americans. By this time tomorrow, William would have locked the door of his studio and he and Delilah would be about to head south for a month, as they had often done in previous years.

'Now, last but not least, I hope all of you will join me here for a humble repast tonight. We will raise a glass or two of noble Tuscan vintage to your future . . .'

He glanced again at Anna. She was staring at the soaring cathedral dome, like the sun fallen to earth, as if she too had closed the door of the summer of fifty-five, aware that things would never be the same again.

That night the studio was filled with the laughter, cigarette smoke and guitar music of the students who sat around balancing bowls of spaghetti on their laps. The drawing-table had been cleared and set with candles and a plentiful supply of Chianti in raffia-covered bottles. William had just passed out copies of the photograph of the entire class taken the week before in front of the Duomo.

Listening to the conversation eddying around him, about football games, sororities, fraternities, the grand tour through Europe, Matthew realized that the other students had already begun their journey home. The high point of their summer would be telling everyone back home about it. He found himself reflecting how quickly the time had gone, how much had happened to him. A hand on his shoulder brought him out of his thoughts.

'Can a friend offer a few words of advice?'

Matthew looked up at William, who was smiling benignly at him. When he beckoned, Matthew followed him to a corner of the room.

'Any fool can tell you've fallen in love with the young Anna,' said William gently.

Matthew knew his silence was an admission.

'I just want to say that as soon as you're back home all this will seem like a dream. Once back at Yale, your life will be in order again, Matthew.'

'I'm coming back here next year. I haven't told anyone yet,' he replied, 'but I've made up my mind that when I finish college I'm going to come back to Florence to paint. I don't care what my family says, what anyone says. I wanted you to know.'

William smiled sympathetically, but his eyes were full of kind disbelief.

'I realize you might find it hard to believe, but the thing is, I have a small income left to me by my grandfather's estate. I think it would be enough to live on if I'm careful. And not only that, but I'm coming back to marry Anna.' Matthew paused. He hadn't intended to reveal himself so frankly, but his eyes burned feverishly.

William's first response was sinking horror. Clichés sprang to his lips about Italian women running to fat, about the un-breachable differences between Anna's and Matthew's back-grounds; but for a moment he envied Matthew's passionate intensity and the singular, flame-like quality that illuminated his face.

'I would rather you didn't mention this, not even to Delilah.'

'No, no, of course not,' William replied, stroking his beard. Through his mind ran depressing visions of all the pupils he would lose from the Ivy League colleges when parents heard that one lamb had been seduced away from the safety of the flock into the fleshpots of bohemian Florence. An American Wasp running away with a poor Italian peasant girl was the stuff cheap novels were made of. He sighed, thinking that Matthew's passionate and rebellious individualism corresponded to his own at the same age. The young American was about to embark on an identical course to the one he had followed thirty-five years earlier.

'I must say I'd like to be a fly on the wall when you break the news to your parents. I don't envy you,' he said thoughtfully. 'But on second thoughts, dammit, I do envy you. Let's be honest.'

Matthew had the impression they were equals, two artists discussing life.

'I've been wondering how I'll make it through the winter without Anna; but more important, how she'll manage. Just thinking of her here all alone, cold, friendless, upsets me. She's illegitimate you know. I'll be all she's got. Her grandfather treats her like a slave, and she said he used to beat her when she was younger. Do you know, she told me once she was glad they didn't have enough coal in the winter so her grandfather's hands got too arthritic to beat her?' Matthew's eyes clouded with anger.

'She's aroused your finest feelings, my boy. It's very noble,' William said tactfully, feeling slightly ashamed of his cynicism about Anna, who, he sensed, was as shrewd as she was beautiful.

'They hardly had a square meal after the war. People in Robbiano used to call her a bastard. She hardly remembers her mother, never knew her father. Imagine what a start she had in life. When I think how she's suffered, yet how gentle, how serene, how good-humoured she is – well, it's a miracle, that's all. Will you keep an eye on her for me?'

'Of course,' nodded William, thinking that Anna was no doubt all the things Matthew saw in her, and more. Remembering the flash of temper he had occasionally seen in her eyes, he knew that underneath her smooth flesh was the steely determination to survive, to conquer, that could only be born of poverty. Anna was a true street urchin, a fact of life Matthew could romanticize but had not lived long enough to understand.

Early November snow flurries drifted past the windows of Matthew's room at Yale as he stared at the leafless trees shaking in the wind. It might have been any Saturday, he thought, glancing at the pile of textbooks on his desk, his papers strewn everywhere. Yet this day was a watershed in his life he knew he would never forget. He looked at the tickets to the Yale–Harvard game he had tacked to his noticeboard. Little had he realized when he bought them, planning to ask a friend, that his whole life would have changed course by then. Next to the tickets was a snapshot he had taken of Anna which had amazed all of his friends; and Matthew Swope had even astonished himself by his conquest of the lovely Italian girl. And now she was pregnant with his child. Even his fear for the future could not conquer a certain pride. His hand trembling, he picked up Anna's letter and re-read it once more, wondering if he had translated it correctly. Fear and joy coursed through him, creating a strange and unexplored blend of emotions. Now he realized there would be no turning back. The more he thought, the more he realized that Anna's pregnancy had given him the conviction he needed to face his parents in the battle to live life on his terms.

Reaching for Anna's photograph, he was suddenly filled with anxiety, knowing how desperate she must be to hear from him. Wasting no time, he sat down at his desk with his Italian dictionary propped open, and began to compose a carefully worded letter to her, expressing his joy and none of his fears. When he had finished, he sealed it and went to the cupboard for his jacket, intending to go straight to the post office. On second thoughts, he took a hundred dollars from his drawer, for a postal order. It was a sobering realization to think he was now responsible for Anna Gagliani, who would be Mrs Matthew Swope by Christmas. He brightened at the thought of the terrific kid he and Anna would have, and what a wonderful wife she would make, how they would look back and laugh some day when the hard times were over. His parents would live down the shame and forgive him when he had become a famous painter. He was just about to leave when his roommate Hank breezed in.

'Hey, man, what the hell has hit you, anyway? You look white as a sheet,' he remarked when he saw the expression on Matthew's face.

Taking a deep breath, Matthew said: 'What do you say we go out and get bombed tonight?' With a crooked smile, he added: 'I've got something to celebrate. I'm going to be a father.'

Chapter 10

Anna came into the huge vaulted kitchen of the Villa Robbiano just as Constanzia was putting the finishing touches on a row of white meringues for a dinner party that evening. It would be the last time the Marchesa entertained before departing for Kashmir, then on to America. The stout middle-aged cook in a white cap and apron moved energetically below a row of polished copper pans suspended from the whitewashed walls. The terracotta tiles on the floor had been mellowed to a deep gleaming ochre by generations of servants walking to and fro. Constanzia eyed the brace of brilliantly plumed pheasants that lay near the stone basin. Her next task would be to pluck and prepare them for roasting over the spit in the huge open hearth where a fire now blazed, warming the entire kitchen.

Turning, she saw Anna eyeing the neat row of perfect meringues.

'They look delicious,' she said, stealing a piece, 'couldn't I have just one?'

'No, you may not,' replied Constanzia, slapping her wrist before turning to remove a cauldron of *bollito misto* that she had prepared for lunch from the fire. The cook gave Anna a sharp glance as she watched her adjust her apron.

'You'll get fat as a sow if you don't watch out. You've gained weight, my girl. You're much too young to be losing your figure, you know.'

'I don't care,' Anna said saucily, popping a crust of bread into her mouth. She felt like saying that soon she would have a cook of her own far away in America when she was Mrs

Matthew Swope. Ever since she had received Matthew's letter a few days earlier, she had gone about her duties at the villa with an aura of serene invincibility. All her hopes for the future had centred on his reply, and when his letter with the postal order had arrived she cried tears of relief. They were to be married at Christmas in the Catholic church. She had already made plans that they would take a honeymoon on Lake Como in one of the big hotels she had seen in a magazine. And then, perhaps, after spending some time in Rome they would return to Robbiano to see the Marchesa, where they would occupy the same room Matthew had stayed in during the summer.

When she saw the butler enter the kitchen bearing the Marchesa's luncheon tray, she smiled to herself at the thought of him serving her breakfast in bed. He had always treated her with such condescension, he and the others, but the day would soon come when he would be obliged to call her Signora Swope.

'But the Marchesa hasn't even touched her lunch,' cried Constanzia, lifting the covered dish. 'What's wrong?'

'The Marchesa isn't hungry,' he replied confidentially, his brow furrowed with concern. 'She just received a telegram from America. Do you remember that young man who was here this summer with his parents?'

'Why yes, of course.'

'He was killed in a car crash in America only yesterday. The Marchesa is devastated by the news.'

'*Santa Maria!*' the cook gasped, crossing herself hurriedly. 'He was so young!'

She and the butler wheeled about in astonishment when a scream pierced the air. Anna had collapsed on the floor.

'*Dio*, it can't be, it can't be,' she sobbed hysterically, as if her heart would break.

A dark November mist shrouded the village, ensnaring the rooftops and the bell tower of the cathedral in Robbiano. locking out the light. In the deserted streets, the shutters were tightly closed against the cold rain that streamed between the black cobbles. Clutching a shawl around her shoulders, Anna hurried towards the Villa Robbiano. On the way she averted her eyes from the house where the village midwife lived, trying to forget her condition. It had cost her several days' wages to buy medicine from the midwife: it was supposed to induce abortion, but had only made her vomit and given her stomach cramps.

When she arrived at the villa through the servants' entrance, the butler ushered her through the long dark corridor leading to the heart of the villa, the Marchesa's private sitting-room. Knocking at the door, he opened it, glancing obliquely at Anna.

'Anna is here, Signora Marchesa,' he said with a subtle condescension that made Anna hold her head high.

Pausing on the threshold of the room, Anna was unnerved by its splendour. She had touched and cleaned each precious object many times, from the scrolled Venetian mirror to the collection of silver boxes and the painted harpsichord. She had plumped up the silk paisley cushions and brushed the oriental carpets by hand; but none of this had given her any lasting familiarity with the Marchesa's treasures, and now she stood alone, exuding the hostility of an unwelcome intruder. To brighten the dullness of the day, all the lamps were lit and a fire crackled in the grate of the marble fireplace. Pink azaleas bloomed in Chinese bowls, creating a blaze of colour against the grey light beyond the tall windows. Delilah was seated at her tulipwood desk in the corner. She was dressed casually in a sweater and skirt and her hand was poised above a sheet of blue vellum. When she had finished the letter she was writing she turned, removing her glasses.

'Anna – Emilio mentioned you wanted to see me. What is it, my dear? Come and sit down over here,' she said, motioning her to a chair beside her desk.

Her mouth compressed with tension, Anna did as she was told. She sat down uneasily, clutching her black shawl.

'Now, tell me what can I do for you?' said Delilah brightly, anticipating that Anna needed money. Seeing how drawn and pale she was, Delilah felt a tug of sympathy.

To her surprise, Anna pulled an envelope from her pocket and slapped it on the desk.

Delilah reached out for it, trying to decipher in Anna's dark eyes what she meant by the gesture. As she sat tensely on the edge of her chair, Delilah found herself reading a letter from Matthew Swope conveying his joy at the news Anna was pregnant, reaffirming his love, stating that he planned to return at Christmas and marry her. The letter was dated a week before his death. An instinct to protect the Swopes seized hold of her, telling her that she ought to tear the letter into a hundred pieces before Anna's eyes. As if she could read Delilah's mind, Anna reached out and snatched the letter back.

'There are other letters, many of them. This is only one of them.'

Delilah sat thoughtfully for a moment, staring out of the rain-streaked window as she pieced together what had happened. She and William had been shattered at the news of Matthew's death. He was so young, and had so much to live for. She had been his champion against his parents and so had William. The awful thought now occurred to her that Matthew had been so upset by Anna's pregnancy that he might have taken the corner at high speed on Thanksgiving weekend, causing the fatal accident. It was a shock to realize that Matthew had been sleeping with Anna while he was in Florence, perhaps under her roof, without her knowledge.

'How old are you, Anna?' she asked, suddenly aware of how potentially delicate the situation was.

'Fourteen years of age, Signora Marchesa.'

Delilah looked at her incredulously. 'I'm sure I thought you were older than that. And what about Matthew? Did he realize how young you were?'

'Why should I deny my age, Signora Marchesa? There were no secrets between us,' Anna replied matter-of-factly.

Delilah put her hand to her temples and thought for a moment. She was horrified by the image of Hector and Nonie Swope receiving such news so soon after Matthew's death. Anna's drawn white face, her hair severely pulled back, made her seem utterly plain. Her youthful freshness seemed tarnished by the black shawl of poverty she clutched around her shoulders.

Delilah sighed. 'And tell me, when is the baby due?'

Anna shrugged. 'I don't know. June, maybe.'

Delilah quickly ran over every possibility in her mind. Italy might be a deeply Catholic country, but abortion was not inconceivable, or the child could be put up for adoption through a convent orphanage. Anna interrupted the thoughts turning over in her mind.

'Matthew Swope is the father of my child. His parents are rich people, important people. I can cause trouble. I could go to the police. I know my rights and it was rape.'

'Just one moment, Anna. Please calm down and don't jump to conclusions,' said Delilah, flushing with anger. Anna's truculence had taken her utterly by surprise.

'I am pregnant, as the letter says. Matthew Swope is the father of the baby, and that is all. I have other letters, as I said. Love letters. And he sent me money. I can make trouble for everybody, and I will if necessary.'

'I don't think it will be necessary at all,' said Delilah calmly, lighting a cigarette.

'You must do something. I want money from Mr and Mrs Swope.' Anna leapt to her feet and began to pace the room. 'I am poor, they are rich, and the baby belongs to their son.'

'Now we've established that, at least,' Delilah said wryly. 'Do you want an abortion?'

Her bluntness startled Anna for a moment. 'No, no,' she shook her head. And it was true. She had heard terrible stories of coat-hangers, of girls bleeding to death and being dumped in ditches. 'No,' she said, struggling to fight back tears.

'All right. You want money, and you want to have the child,' Delilah said crisply, aware of the lack of feeling in her tone; but Anna's volatile mood had made her wary. 'Were you a virgin when you met Matthew?'

Outrage flared in Anna's eyes, touching her cheeks with colour. 'He took my virginity. I had never known a man before. I gave myself to him because he promised me marriage.'

'In that case you can't say you were raped,' Delilah pointed out.

'My honour has been destroyed. I can tell my story to a newspaper. Then everyone would know that the son of a rich American, friend of the Marchesa, seduced a young Italian girl, abandoned her, that the rich people were not willing to help her.'

Delilah cut firmly across her hysteria. 'Anna, the Swopes are good people. They will do the right thing by you, I am sure, and you have no need to fear. Now, please do not threaten me or the Swopes any more. We are not your enemies. You must remember, signorina, that Matthew's parents are mourning their son who has been dead only a short while.'

Proudly drawing herself up, Anna might have been one noblewoman regarding another as she replied, 'And I, Marchesa, am mourning my fiancé.'

NEW YORK

Delilah directed a smile at the doorman of the Plaza Hotel as she went out. Clutching her packages against her mink coat, she paused for a moment to regard the towering Christmas tree illuminated in front of the hotel, and took a gulp of cold air. A light coating of snow had begun to collect on the darkened streets as she walked towards Bergdorf's on Fifth Avenue, ablaze with lights. Caught up by the Christmas atmosphere, she reached into her purse when she saw a Santa Claus ringing a bell on a corner. With a struggle she managed to extract a twenty-dollar bill which she stuffed into his collecting-box.

'Thank you, thank you very much, lady,' called tne astonished Santa after her.

'It's a pleasure. And a very merry Christmas to you, too.'

As she glanced at her watch, she hummed along to the tune of 'Jingle Bells' blaring from a distant speaker. Deciding she had plenty of time to get to her destination, she crossed the street and looked in the windows of FAO Schwartz, piled high with fantastic toys. Feasting her eyes on one enchanting item after another, she wondered what she would pick for an imaginary child. The most enthralling toy of all was a replica of a Victorian doll's house. It was complete, from a nursery under the eaves where a uniformed nurse was bathing a baby, to the basement where a cook was baking pies. The toy family was gathered around a miniature table for Christmas dinner that was complete to the last detail of a tiny turkey. Delilah sighed, thinking what a shame it was that the only little girl she knew was Paige Townsend, daughter of her half-brother Austin Townsend. Paige was already spoiled rotten, and Delilah had never been particularly fond of her mother, Eleanor, Austin's wife. Come to think of it, she wasn't that fond of Austin, either. Why, then, had she bought them all presents?

'Because it's Christmas – the time of peace on earth and good will to all men,' she said cheerfully to herself.

Tearing herself away from the window, it occurred to Delilah that if Anna Gagliani had a little girl, she would give her the doll's house next Christmas, wherever she was. A fleeting image of Anna, now boarding in a convent miles away from Robbiano, came to her mind.

Hailing a cab, she directed the driver to Park Avenue and Seventy Fourth Street where Hector and Nonie Swope lived. On the way there, she brooded about the Swopes, aware that she had avoided thinking of them all day. Delilah was in New York only briefly on her way to Washington to spend Christmas with an old friend, and she had put off seeing Hector and Nonie until the very last moment. As the taxi sped towards her destination, she knew the moment was fast approaching when she would have to tell the Swopes that their late son had left them something to remember him by. As she had done hundreds of times since Anna had told her the news, she wondered uncomfortably how they would react.

All the way to the ninth floor of their apartment block, she tried to suppress the nervous fluttering in her throat. When the doors opened, Nonie was peeking her head around the door of the apartment.

'Delilah, hi, darling. How wonderful to see you,' she cried, throwing her arms open wide. 'My, but don't you look wonderful,' she said with a kiss. 'But then you always do.'

'So do you, Nonie, dearest,' she replied, thinking exactly the opposite.

Nonie laughed. 'You're not serious! I haven't had my hair done for a week,' she exclaimed, leading Delilah into the hall. 'Kathryn and George are in Nassau. They're coming back on Christmas Eve, and I can tell you, I'm worn to a frazzle.' She frowned as the sound of a baby crying came from down the hall.

Delilah slipped off her coat and took two presents from her bag. 'Here you are. A little something to put under the tree.'

'Delilah, you are so thoughtful. How nice to be remembered.' Pecking her on the cheek, she turned as the crying became more insistent. 'He was sound asleep a moment ago . . . Excuse me a minute.'

Just then Hector came into the hall. 'Do I hear voices? Delilah, hello gorgeous. Welcome home.' They threw their arms around each other and exchanged a warm kiss. 'You look great, just great. What's your secret, anyway? Are you ever going to let us in on it?'

She laughed lightly and gave him another hug. It was on the tip of her tongue to say that Italy kept her young, but she caught herself just in time as she thought of young Matthew. She took Hector's hand and studied his face, her grey eyes conveying the sympathy she had not yet expressed in person.

'Hector, how have you been, my dear? I have thought of you innumerable times, both you and Nonie, wishing I could be here to comfort you in some way.'

He shrugged, and said in a low voice thick with emotion: 'Life goes on, doesn't it? Thank you for your thoughtful letter. It was much appreciated. It meant a lot to both of us that Matthew was so fond of you.'

Delilah felt a churning in her stomach as Nonie swept into the hall.

'We are both counting the hours, I can tell you, until we fly to Honolulu the day after Christmas. Come on, you two. Boy, do I need a drink.' Settling on the couch and motioning for Delilah to sit beside her, she said: 'And then guess what we're doing? We've decided to hop aboard a liner and sail into the sunset, to Tahiti!'

'You're not!' exclaimed Delilah.

'Oh yes we are, aren't we, Hector?'

'You bet,' he said with a chuckle, handing them each a Martini.

'That's wonderful news,' said Delilah, gazing at the Christmas tree hung with bows and silver balls. She took a long gulp of one of Hector's perfect Martinis to fortify herself, wondering how she would deliver the news – short and sharp, or with a long rambling explanation. 'I want to hear all about this cruise.'

'Well, I told Hector that it's time we started living. It's now or never, isn't it? Of course, before I always felt we had to stick close to home because of the children, but now Matthew is gone, there's nothing to stay here for, is there?' Her blue eyes clouded over for a moment.

Observing Nonie, Delilah saw the dark circles under her eyes and that her hair was greyer than before. 'It's true. There's nothing like travel to heal wounds.'

'I think I've finally got the travel bug,' said Hector, plopping into a chair. 'Once I started to investigate I began to realize what a big wide world there is out there. You should see the stack of travel brochures I've collected – this thick. I always thought we'd been around, but I realized we've always stuck to the beaten track. There are places in those brochures I've never even heard of.'

'You know Hector. It's all or nothing. Now he's talking about Petra in the spring, then Egypt. Somehow we've got to fit in the fjords of Norway this coming year, too. Oh, and then there are the Maldives – don't forget those,' she said with a laugh.

'You're making me positively jealous,' said Delilah.

'You? You've been everywhere already.'

'Not really. There's South America, for instance . . .'

'Uh-oh,' said Nonie tiredly. 'There the baby goes again.'

'Sit down, honey. He'll cry himself to sleep in a minute.'

Though she knew it was a normal thing to say, and that his patience with his grandson had been tried to the limit, Hector's remark disturbed Delilah.

'I tried to talk Pearl into babysitting tonight so we could all go out, but she wouldn't hear of it, so I'm afraid we'll have to take potluck here, if you don't mind.'

'No, no, I'd really much rather stay here,' said Delilah, wondering how soon she could get away after she had done her duty.

Hector poured another Martini and they began to talk about friends they had in common, and as she regarded the Swopes, Delilah sensed that she had missed the moment to break the news about Anna's baby. The longer she waited, the more brutal it would sound, and the pressure built up inside her as the conversation skimmed over Eisenhower's heart attack, Clare Boothe Luce's Ambassadorial high jinks in Rome and the Woodward murder that had riveted high society. By the time they had supper in the living-room the tension had slackened inside her somehow. Looking around the well-ordered apartment, its polished American antiques, the magazines and books arranged just so, she couldn't envisage the chaos caused by a small child, the child that Anna had decided not to keep, the child that belonged by rights to its grandparents. When it dawned on Delilah that there was no reason whatever to tell Hector and Nonie the truth, the tension eased inside her.

'How are Eleanor and Austin?' said Nonie.

'I went out to spend a night last weekend and we had dinner at the Piping Rock Club. But, to be truthful, it's always a strain. Austin talks about nothing but the stock market, and Eleanor is up to her ears in committee work. I have a soft spot for Biddle, but Paige is a little terror.'

'Don't tell me about little terrors,' said Nonie with a laugh. 'Let's face it, Delilah, we're all too old for this sort of thing.'

Delilah smiled but made no reply, thinking that she didn't feel too old at all.

She left early, which was easy as Nonie was clearly exhausted. They didn't beg her to stay, and when Hector helped her on with her mink coat she retrieved her packages and they hugged each other like old and dear friends who couldn't bear to part. But as the door closed behind her Delilah breathed a sigh of relief that she wouldn't be seeing the Swopes for a very long time, perhaps never again. In the lift, she realized that she had hoped all along this would happen. Her resolve had been weakening fatally for a long time, and she had been looking for any excuse to keep Anna's baby.

It wasn't until Delilah was out in the clear cold night that she allowed her pent-up joy full play. Walking briskly down the street, it was all she could do to keep from dancing a jig and singing a little as an absurd fantasy grabbed hold of her.

'They say it's going down to five below tonight. Watch out for ice on the pavement, lady,' the doorman called after her.

'Thank you for telling me,' she replied with a wave. 'I've got to be particularly careful, you know, as I'm having a baby.'

As her astonishing announcement rang down Seventy Fourth Street, a passing couple looked at her in amazement. She returned their stare with a radiant smile.

TUSCANY

A dark-haired young maid came on to the terrace of the Villa Robbiano bearing a tray of tea just as the cathedral bells struck five. Delilah glanced over the top of her reading glasses from her deck-chair and interrupted the list she had been making.

'Clara, please bring another cup. Signor Partridge is coming, and so is Father Giannini. When he arrives, just tell him to come and join us.'

'Si, Signora Marchesa,' said the maid, arranging the tray on the table in front of her.

When she had gone, Delilah looked at the list she had been composing, a smile of amusement on her lips. It was remarkable the number of things a tiny baby needed. Although she had already been shopping in Florence innumerable times to make sure the baby would have everything from hand-made lace bonnets to tiny little bootees, Delilah couldn't resist indulging herself to the hilt. After all, she told herself, it was her first and only child.

She gazed across the Tuscan hills criss-crossed by vineyards in the hazy distance enjoying the clipped shrubbery of the garden that cast dark scalloped shadows on the green lawn as she basked in the cool evening that swept away the heat of the day. It was a luxury to lean back in a chair and let her eyes wander over the beauty of the setting sun, the geraniums spilling from urns, the wistaria climbing the pergola in lacy confusion. Weaving in and out of her daydreams was the delicious thought of the newborn baby.

Anna had delivered her child at the Convent of Santo Spirito the week before, and the English nanny Delilah had employed had brought the baby back to the villa only two days ago. The feeling of love at first sight had overtaken her instantly. The memory of the small downy head, the delicate fingers, the cooing sounds she made, unleashed a river of tenderness in Delilah that made her exultant and sentimental by turns. It was a completely novel sensation, and something she could share with no one, not even William.

'A penny for them.'

She glanced up to see William regarding her mischievously from beneath his bushy eyebrows. He had rolled up the sleeves of his pale blue shirt and flung his blazer across his shoulder; and his bearded face was in the shadow of his panama hat.

'You caught me,' she said with a laugh, tucking a pin in her chignon with a distracted gesture.

'I can see I've disturbed a very private moment. You didn't even hear me come on to the terrace.'

'I might as well confess. I know it must be written all over my face so there's no use denying it.'

'Denying what?' he asked, flopping into a chair opposite her.

'I'm madly, passionately, in love.'

'Weren't you always? With me, I mean.'

'Ah yes, but you have a rival. And she weighs only seven pounds.'

'Well, I never expected to be competing with a week-old baby. Lord, you are besotted, aren't you? It can only get worse,' he remarked affectionately, seeing her grey eyes mist over.

'I've always been sentimental, I know, but I never expected to feel so deeply,' she said thoughtfully. 'When I couldn't have children and Lino wouldn't hear of adopting – and why should he have, he already had grown children of his own – well, I thought I had killed my desire for children, or at least overcome it by filling my life with so many other things. But it was there all the time, lurking.'

'I don't mind sharing you. If you're happy, I'm happy too. Just don't ask me to change any nappies. Tell me, has Anna left the convent yet?' he said, settling into his chair.

'I heard that she left yesterday.' Delilah couldn't keep the relief from her voice.

She had been so afraid that at the last moment Anna might change her mind and ask to keep the baby. Delilah thought of the day she went with the lawyer to sign the adoption papers. When he had gone she had been alone with Anna in the stark, simply furnished room where she had spent the last months of her pregnancy. She had never once asked to see her daughter, who had been given to a nurse the moment she was born and Delilah felt it was better that way. She sensed that one glimpse of the endearing little creature who had already captured Delilah's heart would be an unbearable cruelty for this child–mother. Delilah had a lingering impression of Anna, her glossy chestnut hair tumbling down one cheek, her hands folded tightly across her flat stomach, a closed expression on her face. She had reached out to accept the thick envelope of notes from Delilah, enough money to start a new life.

'One day when you're older and all this is behind you, it will seem like an unpleasant dream. You'll have a husband to look after you then, you'll have other children . . .'

'I need no advice from you,' she retorted venomously.

Delilah's cheeks burned at the hatred in Anna's eyes, and a wave of helpless concern passed through her as she realized that Anna, with her combination of looks and avarice, would probably become a street-walker in Rome, where she was sure she was headed. It was a harsh but unavoidable judgement. Too much poverty and not enough love had hardened her character irrevocably.

William's voice brought her back to the present.

'No doubt you'll spoil that child rotten, smother her with love. She'll be an impossible and precocious little brat,' he observed. 'It's lucky you've got me to curb your extravagant impulses. I'll have to be the disciplinarian around here.'

'We'll see,' she said, laughing at his earnest expression.

'Have you chosen a name for her yet? Time's running short if you want Father Giannini to christen her next week.'

'I have some ideas,' she said with a secret smile, refilling their teacups. She had more or less decided, but she knew that William wouldn't approve. He would try and dissuade her from the name she had in mind, in favour of something more ordinary. She looked at him affectionately. For all his bohemian exterior, William had a conventional English streak that had always endeared him to her.

'We'll need something stronger than tea to fortify ourselves in a minute,' said William, draining his teacup. 'I've had a hell of a day. The studio was baking hot. I can tell you, this year's students are nothing like the last. Nor is the model. You know,' he said reflectively, 'I still find myself thinking of the two of them – Anna and Matthew.'

Delilah nodded. 'So do I, so do I . . .'

Hearing footsteps, they turned as Father Giannini walked on to the terrace.

'Ah, Pietro, *buona sera*,' said William.

The priest raised his hand and smiled. 'Am I too late for a cup of tea?' he said in the melodious English he had perfected while working for a year in a parish in Chicago.

'Not at all. I'll ring for more hot water,' said Delilah.

'I'm a bit late because there were more people than usual at confession.'

'No doubt it was that Monica Vitti movie playing last week,' commented William wryly. 'Have all the consciences of Robbiano been swept clean, cleared for another week of sin?'

'Clean as a whistle.' He laughed. 'And tell me, where would I be without sin? If it weren't for sin I'd be out of work.'

William opened his mouth to comment, when Delilah said: 'Don't you start, you two. We've been over all that a million times.' Her eyes moved from the confirmed atheist to the man of God, whose face was animated by a devilish smile. She and William had wondered how the handsome, scholarly Giannini could turn his back on worldly pleasures, while both agreed that he was destined for a higher office than Robbiano could offer.

The evening shadows had deepened and nightingales were singing in the depths of the shrubbery. Traces of gold rimmed the horizon, casting a rich amber twilight on the villa and its lush gardens.

When the maid came on to the terrace with a tray of drinks, she was followed by the English nanny, who proudly clasped the week-old baby girl swathed in a white cashmere shawl.

'Here she is, Marchesa. I brought her to you the moment she woke up.'

Delilah's face lit up. 'Bring her to mommy, oh, please do,' she crooned, holding out her arms. 'Here she is, Pietro. This is my darling little girl.'

The priest exchanged an amused glance with William.

'That's right, my precious, have a good yawn,' she said as she held up the infant. Kissing her head, she propped her on her lap. 'Look at her, Pietro, have you ever seen such a beautiful baby?'

'No, never in my life,' he said, throwing up his hands.

'We'll have to keep a check on her, you and I. She'll spoil the little thing to death,' William interjected.

'Ah, but this is an Italian baby. You're English,' said the priest. 'Here we don't worry about such things. A baby by its very nature is born to be spoiled by everyone in the family until it reaches the age of wisdom. Do you mind if I hold her?'

'Please do,' said Delilah, handing her to him.

The priest smiled as he expertly cupped his large hand on the back of her head. Whispering to her in Italian, he was rewarded with a gurgle.

'She understood. Brains as well as beauty. Have you decided on a name for her, Marchesa?'

'Yes, I have,' she replied, catching William's eye. 'I want her to have my mother's family name – Cotton.'

'Cotton? Cotton?' said William, raising his eyebrows. He shook his head with a sigh, knowing that Delilah had made up her mind and nothing could change it.

'Why not something like Amanda or Margaret . . .?'

'Cotton – well, it has a certain distinction, of course,' said Father Giannini. 'She'll need a middle name.'

'I've thought of that already – What about Clotilda? It's Italian and it's her name day.'

'Cotton Clotilda,' repeated the priest, handing the baby back to Delilah as he jotted down the name on a piece of paper. 'Cotton Clotilda Castello di Montefiore. It has a certain something. That's how she'll be christened then. We could do it on Monday, if you like.' He smiled indulgently at the Marchesa's whims.

'Yes, here in the chapel,' she said, nodding towards the Montefiore family chapel that lay on the other side of the villa. 'I still have the christening robes somewhere. Little Cotton could wear those.'

'The name's growing on me,' said William, helping himself to a large tumbler of whisky. 'Can I offer you one, Father?' He cast a glance at Cotton, cradled in Delilah's lap. 'I always think babies have a profound expression, as if they have come from a far wiser world than the one in which they find themselves.'

'And, in her case, into a far more fortunate world than the one to which she was born,' said Father Giannini sagely. 'She's a lucky child and you, Marchesa, are a deeply charitable woman.'

'Oh no, Pietro. The pleasure is all mine, believe me. It's the most selfish thing I've ever done, there's no doubt about it,' she said, suppressing a guilty thought about Hector and Nonie Swope.

Pietro smiled, but he was thinking of Anna whom he had taken the trouble to visit at the convent before she left, to offer any help she might need. She had sat opposite him, eyes lowered, giving polite replies to his questions. He could see from her distant expression that she had already removed herself from her past, and that she had no further need to confide in him. When he had asked if she wanted him to hear her confession, she had shaken her head. His sense of loss and failure at being unable to reach Anna was somewhat lessened by his conviction that her lapse was only temporary. Anna Gagliani was bound to come back to the Church one day, when she needed sanctuary.

'I think it's my turn to hold the baby,' said William gruffly.

'I knew you couldn't resist. Here, take her, and be careful of her head,' said Delilah.

William looked into the squinched-up little face as the baby grimaced and clenched her tiny fists. Bouncing her lightly on his knee he intoned,

'Little Cotton, I wonder what the future holds in store for you. What adventures, what grand designs, what heartbreak and happiness? Tell me, do you know what mountains you'll climb, what rivers you'll cross, what laurels you'll gather? What wishes can your godfather offer you to speed you on your way?' He looked towards the hills beyond the garden. 'Health, wealth and happiness are the traditional assets, I suppose,' he commented, looking at Delilah and the priest. 'But I think I must add something more – the courage to follow your star wherever it may lead you.'

'Amen,' echoed Delilah, touching a finger to one eye to wipe away a tear. 'Just as you said that, William, I looked up. The evening star just appeared.'

William laughed heartily. 'Come out to shine just for baby Cotton, no doubt. My God, aren't we getting sentimental.'

Delilah rose and took the baby. 'If you two will excuse me, I think it's time to take her into the house. Don't want my baby to catch a chill, do we?' Clasping Cotton to her, she crossed the terrace and entered the salon. Catching sight of herself in a looking-glass, she paused, fascinated by her own reflection.

'We look well together, you and I, don't we?' she whispered with a private smile. As the baby curled against her shoulder, she swayed, her eyes closed as she delighted in the smell of this unparalleled infant, and in her soft snuggling movements. Their two lives seemed to be flowing into each other, fast weaving an invisible fabric that would bind them together always.

'We'll have the best times together, you and I,' she

murmured. 'We'll travel the world and you'll be my little companion. Christmas in Kashmir, summer in East Hampton, April in Paris, safaris in Kenya, carnival in Venice. My daughter and I are going to be inseparable.'

Chapter 11

1968

Prospero contained his impatience as he watched his cousin Pietro tugging at his cassock caught between his trouser-legs when he had parked the car off the piazza. Though he struggled not to appear anxious, he felt his heart beating hard at the prospect of returning to Robbiano after all this time.

'It must seem strange for you to come back,' remarked Pietro. His voice was cheerful, but Prospero sensed his cousin understood perfectly the powerful undercurrent of memory coursing through him. His jaw tight with emotion, he waited for Pietro to retrieve the black, red-trimmed hat of a Monsignor from the back seat of the car.

'You're not sorry you came, I hope,' he said as they walked away from the car.

'You kidding?' Prospero said with a cocky smile, narrowing his eyes at the swallows wheeling in the evening sky. As he caught sight of the cathedral, then the piazza, Prospero's nerves wound down slightly. He realized that time and distance had numbed his fear. He tried to remember the confused, angry adolescent who had left Robbiano with a clenched fist to symbolize the end of one life and the beginning of another. Eight years in Genoa, the rest in Rome, had made a man of him.

As they strolled past the shops and houses round the piazza, Prospero had a fleeting sense of the beauty of the village. Years ago he had been blinded by his own misfortune and what seemed the stultifying dullness of Robbiano; but now he saw it as it was. Catching sight of a few adolescent boys loitering near the café, he was strongly reminded of himself. He self-consciously straightened the lapels of the pale blue suit he had bought in Rome, pulling down the cuffs to expose the big blue stones in his cuff-links.

When he had telephoned his cousin to say he would be in Florence on business for a few days, Pietro had suggested he come along to a party given by the Marchesa at her villa. Prospero had rushed out, with money he could ill afford, to buy a new suit, a new blue silk tie, a shirt. At the last moment he had bought a pair of white evening shoes to complete the ensemble. He hoped it would make him feel confident to mingle with important people. It mattered deeply to Prospero that everyone should know he had done well in the intervening years, that he had not been defeated by the tragedy that had struck the Vallone family. His hands were casually in his pockets, but determination flashed in his blue eyes like the fin of a shark breaking water as he strode proudly alongside his cousin, the Monsignor.

'I don't think anyone has recognized me yet in my new finery,' joked Pietro as they walked through the piazza.

'Me neither,' Prospero said, cracking his gum.

Heads turned in their direction and curious glances were cast at the distinguished Monsignor and the flashily dressed young man at his side. Prospero felt a surge of proud affection for this cousin.

'They're probably browned off that you don't come back more often,' said Prospero, breaking into English.

Pietro laughed at the suggestion. 'You could be right. I always meant to come back, but things kept cropping up. It seems like another lifetime that I was here. I miss being close to people, I admit. Power, luxury, position – these things isolate you from what really matters. I always resisted it, as you know, but when I was called I had to accept, even though part of me will always be a simple priest here in Robbiano.'

'Hey, come on, own up,' Prospero said irreverently. 'Admit it – you love the whole thing, the big house, the servants, the car. I'm looking forward to the day when you're made a cardinal, I can tell you. What fringe benefits!'

Pietro laughed and slapped him on the back. 'It's good to see you, Prospero. You help me keep my feet on the ground, do you know that? And I want to help you get ahead. Who knows, perhaps you'll meet some interesting contacts tonight. Pity I'm not in Rome, or I could do much more for you.' He gave a sidelong glance at Prospero's flashy clothes, the oiled hair that would strike a jarring note among the Marchesa's sophisticated guests. But Prospero was young, and in time he would learn the art of self-presentation. In the meantime, his youth and charm would make up for his gaucheness.

'Whenever you come to Florence, you must stay with me.'

'Thanks a lot,' he murmured, thinking he was saving a lot of money; but if he could have afforded it he would have preferred to stay in a hotel rather than in Pietro's fine old Renaissance mansion where the strong smells of soap and polish, the sweep of nuns' habits across the marble floors, made him uncomfortable. He hadn't been inside a church since he went to Mass in Robbiano years ago.

Before they left the piazza to climb the hill to the Marchesa's villa, an old woman came up to Pietro, and Prospero stood apart as he gave her his blessing. Glancing around, he felt nothing at the sight of the café where he used to play pinball with his brother, the pillar where he used to loiter and watch the girls passing by. For a moment Anna Gagliani flickered briefly in his mind. He hadn't thought of her in years.

When the woman had gone, Prospero nodded towards the bright new façade of the pharmacy. 'I see fat Mario Fontini has prospered over the years,' he said, his voice thick with sarcasm. The Robbiano branch of the family was still a sensitive issue and, until now, they had avoided the topic.

'Yes, he's done well. He knocked through to the shop next door.'

Prospero stared darkly at the pharmacy, allowing bitterness to invade his thoughts. For a moment, he thought of his mother and brothers, still living in Genoa where Maria Vallone was no more than a housekeeper to her other brother and his wife. His brothers had remained to work in the foundry when he cut free three years ago. For a moment, he felt himself shrink back into the frustrated adolescent who had been powerless to change their lives.

Seeing him brooding, Pietro put a hand on his shoulder and said, 'Don't let it bother you.'

'Believe me, I don't. I'd rather live in one small room in Rome and work three jobs to make ends meet than be like fat Mario, rich and living in this village. Who wants to be a big shot in a place like this? Not me. In fact in a way he did me a favour. If they hadn't shoved us out, who knows, I might be working behind the counter or something. I could be here just like him, with a wife pushing me around. Instead, I wouldn't be on the brink of making it big in Rome. I wouldn't be opening a restaurant in a month's time. Hey, it's great, isn't it? Me and Gino — our own restaurant.'

'Yes, it is,' said Pietro cautiously. 'But I don't like the idea of your borrowing money on a risky venture.'

'You gotta borrow money to make money. But it's not risky. It's a sure thing. All we have to do is to attract the right clientele. As soon as I have some money together, I'm going to send for Mamma and the boys. You'll see,' he said. He slicked back his hair with a pocket comb as they approached the iron grille and high walls of the Villa Robbiano, gates that Prospero had never dreamed he would enter, even on the coat-tails of his cousin, the Monsignor.

'Tell me about the Marchesa. What's she like?'

'She must be over sixty now, but you'd never know it. She's charming and very generous, but a woman who lives by impulse. I've always kept in touch with her. She was very good to me when I lived here.' He stopped short of saying that the Marchesa's introduction to a cardinal from the Curia had led to his appointment as Monsignor.

'Yeah?' said Prospero. His hands were clenched nervously at his sides as he wondered what kind of people he would meet at her party.

'Don't worry, she's very down to earth. Just be yourself,' said Pietro as they skirted a smoothly clipped hedge lining the drive to the villa, whose golden exterior was visible through the high old trees.

'I like Americans. Well, after all, I am one. I make a point of knowing them in Rome,' said Prospero, exaggerating. 'I'll go back some day, just as soon as I make it big.' He became uncomfortable that his utterances seemed puny and boastful in the atmosphere of centuries upon centuries of wealth and power which was closing around them. The huge urns in the garden seemed to have been placed there by giants, and the imposing house nestling among the cypresses had an air of ancient and impenetrable seclusion.

'You said the Marchesa has a young daughter, didn't you?'

Pietro gave him a glance, realizing that Prospero's question was innocent. Earlier, he had mentioned casually that the Marchesa had an adopted daughter; but he was certain Prospero had no idea Anna Gagliani was her mother.

'Yes, she adopted an orphan from a convent years ago. She's nearly in her teens now.'

'You don't say? An Italian kid?'

'Yes, I assume so. Cotton is charming and she is very precocious, but a bit spoiled. She travels around the world with the Marchesa so she's not a typical teenager.'

'I can see her now,' said Prospero dully.

Pietro was beginning to wonder if Prospero would ever throw his chewing-gum away. The closer they came to the villa, the more doubtful he became about bringing Prospero with him. Everything about him was wrong – the coloured stones in his cuff-links, his tight suit and white shoes, his oiled hair and cocksure expression.

As they passed through the big, heavy doors guarded by a uniformed butler, Prospero stiffened defensively as self-consciousness hit him. He took the gum from his mouth and discreetly tucked it into a jardinière as they faced the crowd at the threshold of the salon. He was suddenly envious of Pietro, who drew his strength and confidence from the trappings of the Church. Straightening his shoulders, he murmured to his cousin:

'You got no worries at all. You're dressed for every occasion.'

Pietro gave Prospero a grin that bolstered his self-confidence.

★

In her bedroom upstairs in the villa, Cotton crossed her bare brown legs and cradled her chin in her hands with a deep sigh. Rolling up the sleeves of the man's shirt that reached to her shorts, she threw back her head and gazed at the pleated canopy over her bed. She knew its every ripple by heart. How many times she had stared at it over the years. She began to count from right to left as she had done when she was little, to keep her mind off the sound of the guests' footsteps crunching on the gravel below the open window. Finally, she could stand it no longer and she jumped from the bed to lean out and have a look. Bracing her hands on the shutters, she knew it was no use pretending she didn't care. She'd been desperate to join the party ever since she had caught a glimpse of the dark-haired young man in a pale blue suit and the flash of black hat piped with red that told her Monsignor Giannini had arrived.

Tears of self-pity welled up in her eyes. Before they could fall she shook herself angrily and crossed the huge dim room to her desk where she picked up her diary. Flinging herself on the bed, she began scribbling as she had done for the past few nights. She rarely wrote in her diary when she was happy.

'Still in Coventry,' she wrote. Then in parenthesis, 'in the doghouse'. She added a sketch of a face with tears and a down-turned mouth.

> Have tried everything to get Delilah to relent. Got up early this morning and went to the village. Spent a big chunk of my savings on flowers. Had them all arranged in vases when she came down. For a minute thought she would smile, but she didn't. It's positively medieval, locking me up like a princess in a tower. Even wrote her a poem that made her laugh at lunch. Everything seemed OK. I impressed her by talking about Jane Austen, so she knows I'm doing my homework, but no dice. She wouldn't budge. Now I can hear the guests arriving one by one. When will this cruel banishment end? The minutes seem like hours, the hours like weeks . . .

She was aroused from her concentration by a knock on the door. Hurriedly, Cotton slammed the diary shut and tucked it under the pillow, then rubbed her eyes to make it look as if she were crying, tousling her long, honey-coloured hair.

'Come in,' she said in a small contrite voice.

'What's this?' William Partridge walked in.

'Oh, William, you're back,' she cried, springing from the bed. Dropping all pretence, she rushed to fling her arms around his neck.

'Of course I'm back. I flew in to Pisa from London this morning,' he said, his beard brushing her cheek as he kissed her warmly.

'You look wonderful,' she enthused, stroking the silk lapel of his green paisley smoking-jacket. 'How did your exhibition go? I wish I could have been there.'

'And I do too, my poppet. It was sold out practically before it opened. Of course I know only too well it's the "Sir" in front of my name now that does it,' he said with a chuckle. 'Perhaps if you and Delilah had been there, this might never have happened.'

Taking her hand, he led her to a chair by the window. 'Now, tell me everything. Your mother said you stayed out all night with a pack of local delinquents. Do you know how worried she was? She even telephoned me in London.'

'I know, I know,' Cotton said, flinging out her arms in despair. 'But it wasn't my fault. We all got carried away, that's all, and forgot what time it was. Then the car broke down on the way back from Florence and we had to walk . . .'

'You weren't allowed to go to Florence in the first place, and you know it. And you'd been drinking and smoking. Those are serious charges,' he said sternly.

'All right, so what if I did have a puff or two of a cigarette and a little drink? I didn't want to seem like a prude, did I? After all, I'm not a child any more.'

William smiled at the truth of her remark. He observed her ripening figure, her tanned legs that were losing their coltish slimness. Beneath her baggy shirt Cotton's swelling breasts were visible. Even when she was small, Cotton's face had escaped the cuteness of childhood. Her stubborn chin and straight nose suggested great character, and her dark eyebrows were in startling contrast to her unruly blonde hair. William had often drawn her, and had found it a challenge to portray the expression on her face. Only now and then had he managed to capture the spirit that animated Cotton, the beguiling uncontainable curiosity in her golden-brown eyes.

'William, please,' she began, grabbing his hand. 'You're the only person in the world who can convince Delilah to change her mind. Oh please, please go downstairs and ask her to let me come to the party, just for a little while. I'll be so good, I promise. It means so much to me to see everybody tonight. I might not see any of them until the autumn, or ever again. Some of them are very old, they might even die . . .' Tears came to her eyes.

William shook his head and laughed.

'It's not funny,' she insisted.

'No, of course it's not funny. But you're putting me in an awkward position. You know I don't want to interfere and that I agree with Delilah. Usually I'm the one trying to persuade her to be more strict with you. But . . .' he paused dramatically, 'as it means so much, perhaps . . .'

'A matter of life and death,' she said hurriedly.

'Now, now, no need to go overboard. Once you've convinced someone, stop there or you may end up falling headfirst into the mess you're trying to avoid. I'll go downstairs and have a word with her.'

Trying to look repentant, Cotton leapt up. It was the first time she had felt anything resembling happiness for days. 'I'll be waiting for you.'

'Don't count on it until you hear from me,' he admonished.

'Of course not,' she whispered, her fingers crossed.

The moment he had gone, she flung open the big Venetian cupboard bulging with clothes and began rummaging through them.

When the summons she expected finally came, Cotton was prepared. She closed the bedroom door behind her and ran down the dimly lit marble staircase at breakneck speed, making her sailor mini-dress dance above her knees. She wished she owned something dark and slinky, but Delilah had had her clothes made to order in Paris that spring.

Her patent pumps clattered on the marble of the entrance

hall as she stopped at the doors of the salon, trying to look contrite. Heads turned as she cut through the crowded room and went straight to Delilah, instantly recognizable by her silvery chignon. She was smoking a cigarette through a long tortoiseshell holder studded with diamonds and her dress of peacock blue Indian silk gave her an air of exotic elegance.

'Thanks so much for allowing me to come down,' Cotton said in a whisper.

At this, Delilah's last resistance crumbled and they hugged each other.

'We won't say any more about it, all right?'

Cotton nodded, relieved to see the tension had left Delilah's face and that she was her old self.

Cotton drifted away, telling herself to behave. She always sneaked a glass of wine at parties and hid it somewhere, and she usually managed to steal a cigarette someone had left in an ashtray. She glanced round at the cardinal from the Abruzzi, who some said might be the next pope, a black American senator, a diva from Milan who was six feet tall, at the groups of interesting American tourists who were mixing with the English expatriates who lived in villas sprinkled throughout the Tuscan hills. Delilah's famous parties had an electric quality. None were alike, yet they were all wonderfully the same. An American publisher had once coaxed her to write a book outlining her flair for entertaining, but even she found that she couldn't define it. The right people, discreet, efficient servants, delicious food and drink and an unrivalled setting were important elements, but none of them fully explained Delilah's success.

Popping a canapé into her mouth, Cotton spotted the famous English actress, Pandora Whitley, a willowy red-haired woman in her forties. Heading straight for her, Cotton hovered impatiently near her elbow as she finished telling a bawdy story.

'Miss Whitley, you probably don't remember me . . .'

'Darling,' said the actress, extending her cheek for a kiss. 'Honesty compels me to admit that I do. You're Delilah's little girl. You came backstage when I opened in *Hedda* last year.'

'Yes, that's right,' said Cotton, joyous that she had made

such an impression. At the time she had desperately wanted to ask her to sign her programme, but it had seemed childish and gauche. Now she wished she had.

'It's nice to see you again, and in much more civilized surroundings. This far surpasses that poky little dressing-room at the Haymarket, doesn't it?'

Cotton glowed as she nodded. She would never forget that evening. The dressing-room had been thronged with admirers drinking champagne. She had met the Oliviers and Paul Scofield and had been stage-struck for months afterwards. Trying not to seem like a tongue-tied child she said:

'I loved your performance. I still think of it, in fact.'

'You're very sweet,' said Pandora, squeezing her hand.

'Are you rehearsing anything at the moment?'

'I've just finished a charming little film in Vienna, and now I'm resting. I've taken a house for the summer not far from here. We're practically neighbours. You must come over soon.'

'I'd love to, I really would. We'll be here until the end of July, when we leave for New York.'

'That's right. You always spend August in America, don't you? Tell me, what do you find to do in East Hampton and places like that?'

'Oh, lots of things. Sailing, tennis, swimming, cycling,' said Cotton, thinking it did not sound very interesting.

'How very strenuous. When I'm reclining under my pergola, gazing at the Tuscan hills, I'll think of you.'

Someone diverted the actress's attention and Cotton moved on, wondering whom to talk to next. A deep voice spoke behind her.

'*Buona sera, piccola Cotton.*'

She turned sharply, annoyed at the word '*piccola*', to see Monsignor Giannini smiling at her. He had been a part of her life at the villa for as long as she could remember.

'Am I still allowed to kiss you now you're a Monsignor?' she said, her eyes dancing mischievously at the handsome priest.

'Of course. I'm not any different. Only my title has changed.'

As she kissed his cheek, she became aware of the dark young man who had accompanied the Monsignor to the party. With one practised glance, Cotton's eyes glossed over Prospero, confirming what he knew already – that the pale blue shantung suit, which the salesman in Rome had sworn was the latest fashion, made him look like a cheap trickster among Delilah's sophisticated guests.

'Allow me to present my cousin, Prospero Vallone. He's visiting me from Rome.'

His posture erect, Prospero reached out for Cotton's hand and brought it abruptly to his lips.

'Signorina,' he said sharply, his eyes daring her to mock him.

For a split second she caught the challenge in his eyes, and felt ashamed and disturbed. Her knees weakened and blood rushed to her cheeks as she drew back. Her hand seemed to be smarting where he had kissed it. She didn't dare look at Prospero again, but politely answered the Monsignor's predictable questions about school and the holidays, while being acutely aware of the younger man's presence. Twisting a lock of hair nervously between her fingers, she shrank back to being a twelve-year-old. She was indescribably relieved when they parted, remarking to herself that the name Prospero was absurdly pretentious.

From the corner of the room where she was standing next to William, Delilah observed Cotton.

'She's smart as a whip, she speaks three languages fluently, plays the piano like an angel and is a devastating little mimic when people's backs are turned. She asks my friends questions with wide-eyed innocence that I wouldn't even dare think of. Sometimes she's just plain obnoxious. Yet I adore her and wouldn't deny her anything,' she added with a sigh. 'What am I going to do with her, William?'

'You're still upset, aren't you?' he asked softly.

'Mmm,' she said, nodding. 'I am. Am I raising some sort of delicious little monster? Oh, I know. Don't say "I told you so." How often I've over-ruled you in these past years – I know, I've spoiled her rotten.'

Her eyes moved away from William and followed his critical gaze across the crowded room, to where Cotton was munching a canapé as she talked flirtatiously with a handsome young Florentine.

'Look at that dress. She insisted on having it that short.'

'And she, little vixen, is perfectly aware of the effect she's having on a thirty-year-old man.'

'Well, what am I going to do now? I can't keep her under lock and key.'

'Of course, there is a perfect solution,' he said, raising an eyebrow. 'You could pack her off to boarding-school.'

'Boarding-school?' she said, aghast. 'You mean in Switzerland?'

'Oh no, nothing as sophisticated as that. I mean a good down-to-earth, no-nonsense English boarding-school.'

Delilah shook her head adamantly. 'I couldn't even think of it. I couldn't bear to part with her, and anyway,' she said, hurrying to justify herself, 'she'd wither and die in a place like that. Why, I mean, the climate for a start. England is so cold and damp. The girls can be such snobs, and they don't learn a thing . . .' She broke off as William looked at her sternly.

'Delilah, you're avoiding the issue. She's growing up much too fast, and we both know it. There's only one solution – to throw her in with other girls of her age. She has to learn to channel that dare-devil energy of hers into achievement, into competition. She's a bit like a hothouse flower that's been allowed to bloom too soon.'

'I know,' said Delilah, defeated. 'And all I wanted was to give her a head start, give her everything I never had.'

'How about starting with a hockey stick?' he said, kissing her cheek.

Delilah shook her head. 'Those schools are so dreary! She'd hate the uniform, the barrack-like bedrooms. I know exactly what they're like. They'd clip her wings.'

'To keep her from flying too high,' he persisted.

'Nonsense. Nobody can fly too high or too fast, in my opinion. Certainly not Cotton. She'll do great things one day, William. She's very gifted.'

'She's also very shapely, and is going to become more so with every passing year. I know you like to think you found her in a cabbage patch, but she actually had a mother and a father, and her mother wasn't a lot older than Cotton when she burst into full bloom. As for the facts of life, I think I ought to have a serious talk with her soon. Otherwise she might try and find out for herself. That incident the other night was a warning.'

'Don't waste your breath. She seems to have been born knowing the facts of life. Where has she gone?' said Delilah, searching the room for Cotton, a worried expression on her unlined face. She looked up to see William regarding her seriously.

'All right, I give in. You win.'

On the terrace in the shadow of the loggia, Cotton took a puff from a stolen cigarette, then held her breath as she heard voices not far away. Peeking around the pillar, she saw she wasn't alone. A sinuous woman in a slinky dress of acid green was leaning her elbows on the balustrade and looking down into the garden. She was Nancy Rogers, an American journalist living in Rome. The light glanced off her bare shoulders and gilded hair. She was the sort of woman whom Cotton admired without necessarily liking. There were many women like her at Delilah's parties – sophisticated, knowing, too preoccupied to notice her.

Cotton's interest quickened when she saw the Monsignor's cousin Prospero step from the shadows to light Nancy's cigarette. He was instantly identifiable by the flash of his blue suit and his aggressive profile. She didn't catch the remark that caused Nancy to laugh and move closer, but Cotton's heart began to pound at the sound of his low voice. Prospero was softly stroking Nancy's arm, and Cotton was aware of adult emotions which bewildered and fascinated her in the same instant.

She watched with rapt attention, wondering what this worldly woman, years older than the Monsignor's cousin, could see in the callow Prospero Vallone, cheaply dressed and wearing too much hair oil. And yet Cotton understood what it was, without being able to put it into words. She could feel his magnetism communicating itself across the terrace, drawing her into a web of conflicting passions. All at once she hated Nancy with her sinuous posture and her husky voice. Dropping the cigarette she held, Cotton crushed it underfoot. The scrape of her shoe on the rough tiles made Prospero look sharply in her direction. Their eyes met, and the impact of his gaze seemed to send feathery sensations up the back of her thighs.

'Excuse me,' she whispered in a choked little voice, and fled. She was crestfallen when she heard him call after her, 'Good riddance, you nosy little brat!'

Chapter 12

LONG ISLAND

Cotton was daydreaming at the gabled window of the attic room overlooking the Long Island Sound when the streak of white on the sloping green lawn caught her attention. It was her cousin Biddle Townsend in his tennis whites strolling jauntily towards his sloop moored to the jetty at the bottom of the garden. Cotton jumped into her dress and searched for her sandals under the bed.

Vigorously brushing her thick sun-streaked hair, she gave herself a critical grimace in the mirror. She had seen very little of her cousin since he'd come back from Maine where he'd been crewing a racing yacht for most of August. She had plodded through a predictable weekend at The Shallows with her Aunt Eleanor and Uncle Austin waiting for him to come back, while Delilah attended the funeral of Hector Swope in Philadelphia. Pleading that she had always wanted to see the Liberty Bell, Cotton had begged to go with her, but Delilah had stood firm.

'You'd hate it, darling. It's so hot and muggy there and I'll be much too busy comforting poor Nonie to take you any-where. Really, you'll be much better off here, my sweet, sailing, swimming, playing tennis.'

From the tone of her voice Cotton knew it was useless to argue. Delilah had never mentioned Hector and Nonie Swope and Cotton wondered why his funeral was so important to her.

Dashing downstairs, Cotton met the fifteen-year-old Paige

Townsend in the hallway. They had always skirted each other warily during the flying visits she and Delilah made to her half-brother and his family whenever they were in New York.

Turning her critical blue eyes on Cotton, Paige said coolly, 'Mother said they'll be ready to leave for Piping Rock at one and to expressly tell you not to be late.'

'Thanks,' Cotton said breezily, casting a quick glance at Paige's piano legs in a kind of private retaliation. She suppressed her violent dislike for her cousin, remembering what Delilah had always said,

'Don't you see, darling? The mere sight of you must make the poor girl seethe with jealousy. Why, you're a beauty and she's the image of her mother. Isn't it tragic? She's already a matron at fifteen. But you, my dove, you are exquisitely made. Every inch of you is sheer perfection.'

Thinking of Delilah's words made Cotton feel pleased with herself. She ran across the grass, her brown legs glinting in the warm September sun. Biddle was just stepping aboard the sloop and as she caught sight of his tanned arms, his sandy hair, she spun a fantasy that he was her fiancé and was preparing the boat for them to run away together.

She came to a halt and languidly strolled the last few yards, self-consciously brushing the hair from her forehead. Watching Biddle remove the mainsail cover, it struck Cotton how unlike the rest of the Townsends he was, and she had an inspired notion that he, like her, must be an adopted child. He was everything the rest of the family wasn't: good-looking, suave, intelligent, kind. He reminded her of Alexander the Great, whose noble head had been immortalized on ancient coins.

Hearing the sound of footsteps on the jetty, he turned.

'Cotton – Hi there.'

'Can I help?'

'Sure. You can stow away the cover if you want.'

She hopped aboard and began to fold the canvas.

'Are you going out later?' she asked hopefully.

One hand shading his eyes, he squinted at the bright blue sky with billowing white clouds chasing each other towards the horizon.

'After I come back from the club I thought I might take a little spin. Want to join me? We could take a farewell sail before you set off for the Sceptred Isle.'

'I'd love to,' she enthused. 'I'll make sure I'm all packed before I go to the club. Are you and your friends having lunch with us?'

'That's the plan, but we could get away as soon as lunch is over. I don't imagine Delilah wants to leave for New York until later.'

Cotton beamed with satisfaction. She would have Biddle all to herself for one last sail on the Sound. She couldn't ask for anything more, she thought, watching his brown hands expertly tie a knot.

'You going to write to me when you get to England?'

His quick smile made her heart lurch. 'I will if you'll be sure and answer,' she retorted, hiding her elation at his unexpected request. None of the other girls at Wycombe Abbey would have a sophomore from Yale writing them letters. Later she would ask him for a photograph which she would place in a silver frame on her chest of drawers. She thought darkly of the dormitory that she and Delilah had seen in August when they had visited the school. The housemistress had assigned her to a huge barrack-like room with iron bedsteads. She had kept her apprehension about boarding-school entirely to herself, telling no one. Suppose all the girls were like Paige? Then what would she do, she wondered. As she trailed beside Biddle back to the house he said, as if sensing what was on her mind:

'Are you looking forward to becoming a proper English schoolgirl?'

'No. The uniform is just awful – a shapeless blazer, a blue pleated skirt, wool socks and even a horrid cloak,' she said, frowning.

'I'm sure on you it will look great, do you know that?'

His compliment instantly lightened her mood. 'You're going to knock them dead over there,' he added. 'Just wait and see. Take a bit of advice from me – these years are going to fly by, so enjoy them while you can. Get good marks so you can get into college.'

'I'm not going to college. I'm going to be an international adventuress instead.'

With a grin he answered: 'That's also a worthy ambition. You could have business-cards printed to that effect: Cotton Castello di Montefiore – adventuress.'

Now he was teasing her, but she didn't mind. 'I'm dropping the last part of my name at school. It's too much of a mouthful.'

'All right, just plain Cotton Castello, then.' As they reached the balustrade skirting the red-brick colonial house, he glanced at his watch. 'I guess I'd better collect my racket. Herron will be here any minute. Oh, by the way, there's something I haven't told you. I've decided to come to Florence next summer.'

'You have? Really?' she exclaimed.

'I've already mentioned it to Delilah, but I thought I ought to ask you if I'd be welcome.'

'Are you kidding? Welcome? I can't wait. I'll show you my Firenze, my Italy,' she said, clapping her hands for joy.

'You know, you look just like Delilah when you do that. You're too much, kiddo,' he said, tousling her hair.

She looked at him with a touch of shyness she rarely revealed.

'If you do write to me, Biddle, I'll have something to look forward to at least.'

He laughed. 'You slay me, Cotton. What do you mean something to look forward to? You and Delilah are meeting William Partridge in India in December, you're going to Gstaad at Easter and now you're on your way to New York for one last fling. If you keep on at this pace there won't be anything left for you to do when you're an adventuress.'

'I suppose I am lucky,' she admitted.

'You sure are, and don't you forget it. Hey, I'd better run or I'll be late. See you later.'

'Me too – Delilah will kill me if she comes back and finds I haven't finished packing yet.'

When they parted she bounded upstairs and began to fill her suitcases with the mountain of clothes she had collected on shopping sprees, while thinking of Biddle's visit to Italy next summer. She studied her own face in the mirror dreamily for a moment. From Biddle her thoughts drifted to Wycombe Abbey, then to India. She spun a daydream of floating palaces in the pink sunset, of elephants, incense and silk. She had stored up so many things to mention to Delilah, and she wondered what she would think when Cotton told her that Biddle had asked her to write. Maybe the four of them, she, Biddle, William and Delilah, could meander south in William's vintage Mercedes in August, stopping at Sorrento and Amalfi.

The deep honk of an expensive car brought her back to reality. Peering out of the window she saw Paige in tennis clothes getting into an open white Thunderbird driven by Herron Easton. Several years older than Biddle, he was dazzlingly handsome in a movie-star way, with shiny smooth hair and a deep tan that contrasted with his polo shirt. Cotton told herself that Biddle easily outclassed him in the charm and intelligence sweepstakes, but none the less her heart lurched when he flashed a smile up at her. When Biddle appeared carrying his racket and jumped into the back seat with a ravishing brunette, Cotton felt a pang of jealousy. When he slid his arm along the seat behind her she was suffocated with envy, but forced herself to smile and wave as they drove away.

Later, Cotton looked down the curving staircase to the hallway where squares of bright afternoon sun poured through the fanlight on to the parquet floor. Eleanor Townsend was looking irritably at her watch. A big-boned woman with a deep suntan, she wore her greying hair clipped short in a style practical for golf. Cotton sensed that Delilah's late arrival had upset her careful planning.

'Really, Austin, I think we ought to go ahead. You know what the club is like on Saturday. If we're late they won't hold our table.'

'What about Delilah?' said the balding Austin, peering over his glasses at his wife.

'What about Delilah? You know your sister has never been on time in her life. I should have known this was going to happen,' she said impatiently. 'It was a stupid arrangement in the first place.'

He shrugged. 'I guess it doesn't matter. When she turns up, Pearl can tell her we're at the club. She probably got held up in weekend traffic.'

'She should have taken the train.'

'Then we would have had to pick her up in Oyster Bay. Then you really would have blown your top,' Austin remarked.

'I am not blowing my top, I am merely pointing out that the whole thing is totally unnecessary.'

Cotton came bounding heavily down the stairs so they would hear her and stop bickering. She hated the way Austin and Eleanor were never able to exchange more than a few words before they broke into an argument. There was a distinct tension running through the household that made Cotton uncomfortable. Her own life with Delilah was dramatically different from this well-ordered house where meals were served exactly on time, all activities were well planned, and there was no room for the spontaneity on which Delilah and Cotton thrived. She was tempted to say she would wait for her mother, but changed her mind, remembering that Biddle and Herron would be at lunch.

'Are you all set?' asked Eleanor. 'My, what a pretty dress. Did you buy it in Paris?'

'Actually, it's from Harrods.'

'Harrods? How nice.'

Eleanor smiled at Cotton, but to her it seemed her compliments were always loaded with disapproval.

'Just think,' said Austin, leading her out the door, 'this time next week you'll be in the heart of merry old England.'

'I still think it's a shame Delilah didn't consider sending you to school in the United States. We have very good schools here, such as Foxcroft and Madeira – any number of them. But then, Delilah loves to be different, doesn't she?' she said with a laugh as Austin went to back the car out of the garage.

'After all, Aunt Eleanor, England is much closer to Italy, and we do live there,' said Cotton in Delilah's defence. Her remark brought a look of intense annoyance to Eleanor's face, but Cotton didn't care. By the end of the day she and Delilah would be gone, and she made up her mind that she was never coming back to the Townsends, no matter what Delilah said.

When they sat down to lunch on the terrace overlooking the golf course of the Piping Rock Club, at a big table shaded by an umbrella, Cotton was sitting exactly where she wanted to be, between Biddle and Herron, looking on hungrily as the waiter set an avocado filled with crab in front of her. The sound of tennis balls coming from the courts beyond the hedge reached them, carried by a sultry breeze. All the tables were beginning to fill up with men in tartan trousers and women in golf and tennis clothes.

'It's awfully muggy today, isn't it?' Eleanor commented.

'I wouldn't be surprised if it rained later,' said Austin, draining the last of his Bloody Mary.

Cotton took a gulp of iced tea and glanced at Herron. She had been observing him obliquely from the moment he came on to the terrace, his hair wet from the shower he had taken after tennis, and he smelt deliciously of bay rum.

'Biddle tells me that you've just finished law school in Georgetown. What are you planning to do with your life now?' she asked.

Cotton missed the disapproving frown Eleanor gave Austin. Paige gave a little snort of disdain, and Biddle raised an eyebrow at her comment.

'That's an interesting question,' said Herron, amused by her boldness. 'I haven't really thought on such a large scale as the rest of my life. But in the immediate future I'll be joining a law firm in Washington.'

'I think that sounds like a perfectly wonderful idea,' she said, nibbling the mint leaf from her iced tea. 'I suppose that means you're going into politics later on?'

'That has crossed my mind,' he said with a laugh, looking more closely at the precocious twelve-year-old, glowing with health and fresh beauty in the soft light cast by the umbrella.

At that moment Eleanor broke in:

'Herron, how is your mother coping? She must miss your

father terribly,' she said, shaking her head sadly. Herron Easton Senior had died of a stroke just before Easter. Cotton could tell by the breathy undertone of her voice that she was trying to play up to Herron, whose family lived in one of the grandest mansions on the North Shore.

'Mother's a tough old bird, really. And thank God for that,' he added with an irreverent smile which dazzled Cotton.

'They say if you fall off a horse the best thing is to get right back on,' Cotton remarked, ignoring Eleanor and Paige whose eyes were on her.

'A totally inane remark,' muttered Paige to Biddle.

Pretending not to hear, Cotton engaged Herron in conversation. As she answered his questions, she became very aware of his hazel eyes studying her curiously. She gestured and tossed her head flirtatiously as they talked about Europe, which he had visited innumerable times. Once she caught Biddle's eye and he gave her a wink which made her want to giggle. She was eager to get him alone to ask the questions about Herron's love life that she didn't quite have the nerve to ask herself.

By the time the cold chicken in aspic arrived, Cotton was enjoying herself enormously. She had forgotten all about the chair at the table that still remained empty. She hardly noticed the waiter who came to tell Austin he was wanted on the telephone. He departed from the table abruptly, and when he returned he called to Eleanor from half-way across the terrace, asking her to join him inside the clubhouse. Cotton was half-aware of their serious faces as they conversed in the doorway.

'What's wrong?' said Paige, turning in her chair.

'I don't know,' replied Biddle, putting down his fork.

By this time they had all stopped eating and were looking in the direction of Eleanor and Austin.

'Why don't they come and tell us what's up?' said Paige irritably. 'Biddle, go see what's happened, will you?'

'Just sit tight. We'll know in a minute.'

When his parents returned, Biddle stood abruptly, looking from their sober faces to Cotton, to the empty chair.

'Cotton, dear,' said Eleanor in a strained voice. Her eyes were blank with shock. 'I think you'd better come with us.'

Cotton leapt to her feet, panic surging up from her toes, invading her stomach, then ending in a hammering sensation in her brain. She was confused when Eleanor gripped her arm and Austin slipped his hand around her shoulder. She had a blurred vision of people turning to stare. At the edge of the terrace, out of earshot of the others, Austin said:

'Cotton, I don't know how to tell you this. Please try and prepare yourself. Delilah – your mother – suffered a massive stroke a few hours ago. Dear, I'm afraid they couldn't save her.'

An invisible fist seemed to be jammed down Cotton's throat, knocking the breath out of her. Tears flooded her eyes, blinding her as she gasped for air and her numb uncoordinated limbs refused to obey her orders. Her vision of the world dwindled suddenly to nothing as the echo of Austin's words tore her apart. In the distance, as if from another room, she heard Eleanor say:

'My God, she's having a fit! What should we do?'

Cotton felt herself locked in a grip from behind as she lost control, screaming a scream that shattered her numbness, turning it into pain. As her frenzied hysteria broke, Biddle ran up from behind. Scooping up her rigid body, he crushed her to him, wrestling with the brute force of her grief. In a lull between sobs, the only thing Cotton comprehended was Biddle's eyes, full of tears as he held her awkwardly to him.

'Cotton, Cotton, it's all right, hush,' he whispered in her hair as he stroked her tenderly. 'Just cry, cling to me, let it all out.' She hugged him desperately as a towering wave of grief swept over her.

Chapter 13

Prospero strolled down the steps of the Uaddan Hotel, accompanied by a darkly suave young Italian, smartly dressed, like Prospero, in a well-cut silk suit. As they waited for the horse-drawn carriage to come to a halt, Prospero gazed at the Mediterranean sunset through the tall palm trees lining the road. When they had climbed into the carriage and the dragoman had cracked his whip, he said:

'I'm going to miss this place. Yeah, I'm really going to miss it,' he remarked as they exchanged a grin acknowledging the satisfaction they both felt.

'Not me. I'll be glad to get back to Rome, I can tell you. I've had enough of Tripoli.'

Prospero laughed expansively and adjusted his cuffs.

'Christ, you don't suppose I meant it, do you? I can already smell Italy coming across the water. It seems like we've been here months instead of weeks.'

'The company is going to be very pleased, I can tell you. I'll always wonder by what margin we beat out Lufanti on the tender. We really had to shave that bid down to the bone.' He stroked his closely shaved chin.

'Not too close to the bone, I hope. You and I have to get our commission, don't we?'

Naldo laughed. 'Sure. There's plenty of fat on this hotel for everybody, believe me. And tonight let's celebrate – let's enjoy ourselves at the Contessa's.' He made a sweeping gesture towards the rugged outline of Barbarossa's castle against the sunset. 'I like you. You're a great guy – more than that, you're shrewd.' Naldo slapped Prospero on the shoulder.

That afternoon, as representatives of an Italian consortium, they had concluded negotiations with the government ministers to build a luxury hotel in Benghazi. It had been a long and tortuous process, but it had taught Prospero a valuable lesson in business methods. He had landed the job that summer, through a contact of Nancy Rogers in Rome, and the trip to Libya was his first big test. Naldo, several years older and more experienced, had proved an able teacher, coaching Prospero in the unorthodox ways that business was done in this still feudal kingdom.

The carriage proceeded along the corniche, where the setting sun cast a pink blush on the surf. Turning off the sea front, they entered the Italian–Arab town, an intricate warren of simple buildings and shabby charm. As they passed through the crowded bazaar, Prospero's eyes followed the white-shrouded figures of women drifting by, his curiosity aroused by the glint of silver bracelets, the flash of dark eyes above a veil, a sinuous hand.

'Naldo, it occurs to me we're wasting our time going to this old bag's party. What do you say we find the best cat house in town? I need a woman.' Prospero lit a cigarette and savoured the thought as he leaned back in the carriage.

'We can always leave early if it's dull but, believe me, the Contessa di Rivaldi knows everybody. You never know – she might introduce us to somebody useful.'

'Business, business, always business,' said Prospero impatiently.

'Business is contacts, first and last. Never miss out on a chance to meet important people – that's my motto.'

'Yeah, I know. I know what you mean,' Prospero replied, interpreting Naldo's comment as a veiled reference to Nancy Rogers. He was uncomfortably aware that if it hadn't been for her he wouldn't have had a hope of earning the generous commission that would help finance his growing taste for luxury.

When the carriage stopped outside a high, weathered wall on the edge of town, there was no sign of the fabulous palace Naldo had described. But as the sound of the carriage faded away he rang a bell above a wooden gate studded with nails, and a robed servant admitted them to another world behind the wall, far from the dusty, crowded town.

Prospero followed Naldo towards the illuminated arches that marked the entrance to the palace beyond a grove of citrus trees rooted in the blue mosaic courtyard filled with the scent of night-blooming jasmine. He began to be intrigued by this lost world where the dim light cast a ghostly pallor on Roman statues among the greenery, making them seem almost real. They skirted a whispering fountain and passed through the pillared archway. Prospero cast Naldo an amused glance that said he hadn't been exaggerating about the splendours of the Contessa's palace. In the huge domed chamber, brass lamps cast coloured light on low settees piled high with silk cushions, brass-topped tables and intricately carved screens. The marble floor was strewn with Persian rugs.

Straightening his shoulders, Prospero felt a surge of adrenalin as he surveyed the room, humming with the fashionable, cosmopolitan crowd assembled by the Contessa.

'There she is. Come on, I'll introduce you,' whispered Naldo.

They approached a tall *grande dame* in a jewelled silver turban and embroidered caftan, her arms weighed down with jangling bracelets. She regarded them through eyes rimmed with kohl as she took a long cigarette-holder from her crimson lips.

'Naldo, how nice to see you,' she said in a reedy English voice.

'Contessa, I'm delighted to be here,' he replied, with a flamboyant bow as he kissed her hand. After flattering her effusively, he turned to Prospero.

'I'd like to present my colleague, Prospero Vallone.'

He took her ring-encrusted hand and brought it to his lips. She gave him an appraising glance.

'Now, who would you like to meet? Come this way. Ah, there you are, Pia. This is my niece and her friend, Ghisela Schmidt.'

Prospero hardly glanced at the Contessa's plump, dark niece, but his heart stopped at the sight of the tall blonde beauty at her side. Ghisela looked coolly at him, and only a flicker in her pale diamond-hard eyes told him that she had registered his presence. Her *haute-couture* cocktail dress of pale blue lace, her jewellery told him that she was rich, and he found her aura of bored self-possession instantly captivating.

'Prospero Vallone,' he murmured, taking her hand to his lips. Her distant expression and immunity to his charm annoyed him. Then and there he made up his mind to seduce her.

'Have you been in Libya long?' she asked politely in German-accented English.

'Obviously not long enough, or we might have met.'

She rewarded his brashness with a vague smile. 'Your English seems very good for an Italian.'

'My Italian is good for an American,' he countered. He had the urge to distinguish himself from Naldo to catch her attention.

'So you're American?'

'With some Italian thrown in for flavour,' he replied, taking two glasses of champagne from a passing waiter. Then he led her away from the crowd to a secluded corner heaped with cushions.

'Tell me about yourself,' she said, curling up on one and inviting Prospero to sit down beside her.

Choosing his words carefully, Prospero painted his background with shadows and highlights that concealed the facts, throwing in a few important names for good measure. He glossed over his origins, his struggles to reach his present position in Rome, and left out the fact that he was now the lover of a rich, well-connected American woman, years older than himself. One thing he had learned from Nancy was that most people were snobs and needed the reassurance of background and connections just as they needed the familiar labels of Cartier or Gucci.

'So you don't live in America, then?'

'No, I live in Rome, but I travel quite a lot. I have an apartment off the Piazza Navona,' he added, neglecting to mention that it belonged to Nancy. His eyes drank in Ghisela Schmidt's pale blonde beauty against the rich cushions.

'And you? Where do you live?'

'I live in Geneva with my father. My mother died two years ago.'

'You're Swiss?'

'Yes.'

'You've always lived in Switzerland?'

'Yes,' she said mildly.

'Where would you like to live?' he persisted, frustrated that he was getting nowhere.

'I don't know – Paris, even Rome perhaps, one day. I would like to travel more.'

'Well, why don't you? There's nothing stopping you, is there?' he said, moving closer.

'It's not as easy as that,' she replied, with an enigmatic smile.

They parried back and forth and Prospero felt he knew little more about Ghisela Schmidt than the moment they met. He couldn't imagine her bursting into uninhibited laughter or tears. He told himself that she was probably young, shy and had led a sheltered life, that her self-possession was only a veneer acquired at an expensive finishing-school.

'Let's take a walk in the garden,' he suggested.

As they rose, she cast a glance over her shoulder in the direction of the Contessa.

'Don't worry. I won't bite your head off.'

For the first time she smiled. They walked through the moon-streaked courtyard for a moment, in silence.

'Tell me, are you having a good time in Libya?'

'Yes, I like it very much. The Contessa has been very kind, and Pia and I have enjoyed our visit.'

He was tempted to say something outrageous to shatter her imperturbable calm, but sensed that it might jeopardize his chances. When he didn't speak for a moment, she herself spoke at last, as if realizing it was her turn to ask a question.

'Where do you ski?'

'Usually Megève,' he replied casually, remembering Nancy had skied there. 'And you?'

'My family always go to St Moritz. It has many fond memories for my father. It's a question of habit, I suppose,' she said with a shrug.

Her pale reflection shimmered on the face of a lily-pond as they strolled by.

'You look like a goddess in the moonlight,' he whispered. 'I find you incredibly beautiful.' When she didn't reply, he said urgently: 'I must see you tomorrow. I'll come for you at eleven and we'll go to the beach.'

'I can't. The Contessa doesn't permit me to go out alone with anyone.'

'Pia and Naldo could come with us if you like.'

'Well, in that case, it might be possible,' she said, refusing to meet his eyes. Folding her arms, she walked away as if avoiding the danger that sparked from him.

Following her towards the house, he said: 'I want to see you every day, to show you the Libya you will never see with the Contessa and her friends: seaside cafés, places in the souk. What about the ruins at Leptis Magna? Have you been there?' He could picture the two of them alone in the wild, remote ruins.

'Aren't you going back to Italy soon?' The way her eyes widened suggested to him she wanted him to stay.

'I was, but some unfinished business remains for me to tie up.'

When, finally, he and Naldo said goodnight to the Contessa, Prospero, determined that nothing would stand in his way, was careful to make the most decorous impression. Returning to the hotel in the open carriage, he brooded in silence, studying the minarets pressed against the star-filled sky. The gentle waves lapping the shore broke the rhythm of the horses' hooves. Lighting a cigarette, he mulled over the impression Ghisela had made on him. Maybe he'd stay on for another week, two or three if necessary. He'd like to shatter that studied composure with a tempest of desire that had no place in her refined upbringing.

'You're wasting your time with Ghisela Schmidt,' commented Naldo. 'You won't get anywhere. Otto Schmidt watches her like a hawk. That's what the Contessa told me.'

'All the more fun — I like a challenge. Anyway, he's not watching her now.'

'True,' said Naldo, with a bored yawn. 'You can never tell with that type. She's probably been having it off with the chauffeur and the butler for years.'

Prospero didn't reply, knowing it would be impossible to learn the truth about Ghisela.

'Who is Otto Schmidt, anyway?'

'Don't tell me you don't know who Otto Schmidt is? He's one of the richest men in Switzerland — maybe in Europe for that matter. Schmidt Pharmaceuticals. You've never heard of them?'

'Oh, that Schmidt,' said Prospero, deeply impressed in spite of himself.

'He's probably already picked out some pedigreed aristocrat for his adored daughter.'

'Tell me more about Schmidt. What's he like?'

'He's entirely self-made. He built up his empire during the war.'

The word 'empire' had a compelling ring in Prospero's ears, and in an instant his intentions raced far beyond seduction. A broad smile spread across his face as he clapped Naldo on the back.

'Hey, Naldo, what do you say we find the best cat house in town, eh? The way I feel tonight I could fuck every whore in the place, you know that?' He gave a rich, triumphant laugh that turned into an impromptu aria, convulsing Naldo with amusement. He sang lustily at the top of his voice, replacing the Italian verses with a graphic description of how he would ravish the first woman he saw.

After several innocent, pleasure-filled days at the beach, Prospero persuaded the Contessa to allow the girls to go to the hotel nightclub. One night he returned to his room in the early hours of the morning, having escorted Ghisela and Pia home. It was too hot to sleep, and discarding his tie and jacket he turned out the lights and went on to the balcony overlooking the waterfront. The phosphorescent waves hissed in the still night, bright with stars. Below his balcony, at the entrance to the hotel, a horse hitched to a carriage nodded sleepily under a palm tree.

His shirtsleeves rolled up, Prospero lit a cigarette and leaned on the rail, remembering how Ghisela had melted against him that evening as they danced to a romantic Italian ballad. The moment he took her in his arms he felt her give way as if something within her had unlocked to his touch. By slow degrees he had metamorphosed the coolly remote goddess into a woman eager for love. His penetrating glances, the sudden silences that broke his easy conversation, had relentlessly conveyed his brooding passion. At first it had been a game to him, but now his thoughts ranged far ahead of this torrid interlude. His desire to seduce Ghisela had crystallized into an obsession to possess everything she stood for. He was driven by the realization that marrying her would transform his life as magically as if he had liberated a genie that could grant him his heart's desire.

As the smoke from his cigarette curled upwards into the still air, his thoughts turned to Nancy. This was the first time he had been tempted to break her hold over him. She wanted him to succeed, but only to the extent that she could still exercise power over him. She sought to trap his energy, channel it for her own ends, creating a vortex of sexuality which he had been unable to resist. But in the end he felt he was no more than her gigolo, indebted to her social power, her influence, her contacts more than her money. Now the pupil had learned all he could from the master and he felt the allure of the greater world offered by Ghisela. He was no longer the brash young man who had walked into Delilah's drawing-room, ashamed of his clothes. As the first halo of dawn tinged the horizon, Prospero still stood on the balcony, lost in thought. As the night lifted from the sky, he felt the last traces of indecision lift from his mind. Today, when he took Ghisela to the ruins of Leptis Magna, he would embrace his destiny.

He collected Ghisela just after seven, in the car he had hired for the day. She bade him good morning as if nothing had happened between them the night before.

In the fresh clear light, she looked serenely beautiful, her flaxen hair neatly coiled into a chignon. He had the urge to reach out and release it like a rope down her back. He met her blue eyes, tranquil as the sea; yet the faint shadows beneath them told Prospero that she too had had a sleepless night. The turned-up collar of her cotton dress framed the hollow of her throat, where he could see the pulse beating. The suggestion of hot blood flowing beneath her marble exterior made his loins quicken with desire.

As he opened the door for her, she glanced at the guide in his long robe and red fez in the back seat.

'So you really did bring a chaperon,' she commented with a faint smile as he closed the door behind her.

'But of course. I gave my word to the Contessa that we wouldn't be alone together,' he replied, closing the door after her. He slipped behind the steering-wheel and started the engine, thinking to himself that the old man would sleep all the way there and back.

She glanced distastefully at the old man, who was smiling ingratiatingly at her.

'Do we have to take him with us? We don't really need a guide, do we?'

Prospero brought the car to an abrupt halt. 'Of course not. I think we can manage very well without him.'

Speaking in Italian, he gestured to the man to get out, and then stuffed a wad of dinar notes into his hand.

'But, signore,' he cried as they sped away.

As he accelerated, Prospero met Ghisela's eyes and they shared a conspiratorial smile.

'How long will it take us to get there?' she asked.

The tremor in her voice conveyed to Prospero that she too had seized destiny on an impulse. She was not even aware of it, but she had offered herself to him as clearly as if she had disrobed.

They drove along the road that traced the jagged, deserted coastline, speeding through small flat hamlets built of baked earth. Children, chickens and scrawny dogs were lost in the dust they left behind. As the morning wore on, a hot desert wind filled the car, loosening tendrils of hair from Ghisela's neat chignon. Prospero glanced at her face, flushed with heat and what he sensed was mounting desire, but he made no attempt to touch her, aware that her eyes moved to his bronzed arm every time he changed gear. Though they didn't exchange more than a few words of polite conversation, the atmosphere became charged with sexual desire. Just outside Leptis Magna, he lit two cigarettes and passed her one. As their fingers touched a spark seemed to leap between them.

He parked the car on the crest of a hill overlooking the sea and they walked towards the shimmering ruins. The time-battered arches of Leptis Magna caught the gleam of the sun in the drifts of wind-rippled sand. The city that had once teemed with life lay deserted before them and they wandered among piles of gnarled stone and columns which thrust into the blue sky. An eerie, wind-whipped silence pervaded the ruins, and a few stray goats tugged at tufts of grass in the shadows.

They crossed the market square that in the distant past had echoed with chariot wheels, their footsteps hollow in the void left by time. The crumbling ruins, scoured clean by the desert winds, seemed inhabited by ghosts of Greeks, Turks, Phoenicians and nomads. Now only spears of naked sunlight glinting off the white stone suggested the gold and silver filigree prized by Roman women; the zithering of the wind imitated the babble of Sanskrit, Aramaic and Latin, and the rich aroma of perfumes and spices loved by the Romans had been thrown to the four corners of the earth by the storms of centuries. The bones of Nubian slaves with velvety dark skin and tapering eyes had sunk into the sand without trace, along with those of the alabaster-skinned Circassians captured in battle.

They passed into the Temple of Jupiter, where the open space beyond a window to the sea beckoned them towards the white-capped blue water. Prospero pushed Ghisela roughly against a pillar and crushed his mouth to hers. She capitulated immediately, weakened by sleepless nights and tormented days of suppressed desire. Tilting back her head, she emitted groans of pleasure as his hands raked her body. Drawing back, he looked into her eyes, blank with lust. Her mouth open and waiting, she was drugged with the promise of love-making. Her eagerness surprised him and made him doubt her virginity. In one fluid motion, he released her hair about her shoulders and it fell like a weight. It was a symbol of conquest. Her pure city was falling, stone by stone, to his sweet corruption.

Pushing her skirt above her hips, he muttered: 'I want you – here, now.'

She nodded and grabbing his hand she thrust it between her thighs. She began to unbutton his trousers with hot impatience. Easing her back in a cleft of marble he encountered no resistance and entered her in one smooth, forceful thrust. Her head thrown back in ecstasy, she breathed a passionate cry of response. As he watched her rise and fall to the power of his movements, he plundered Ghisela's golden splendour like a hidden treasure. His commanding virility brought her to a shuddering orgasm. Gasping, he held her close to him, overtaken by the almost pagan sexuality of her response. Welding her mouth to his in an impassioned kiss, he felt himself hardening anew within her.

'Marry me, Ghisela,' he whispered, pinning her hands on the cold rock.

'Yes, Prospero, yes,' she uttered, feeling him still stirring within her.

'Here, in Tripoli. Next week.'

'Yes, yes, I will. Anything, yes,' she assented, moving her hips once more in exquisite rhythm.

CAP D'ANTIBES, FRANCE

Five weeks later Prospero was standing beside his new father-in-law in the lush garden of the Villa Mimosa, just as a journalist managed to climb the high spiked fence that protected the house from intruders.

'If the fence was electrified we would have *journaliste en brochette*.' Otto Schmidt laughed at his witticism.

Prospero gave a dry laugh, then glanced across the lawn at the *haut monde* of Europe, gathered to celebrate the marriage of the Swiss magnate's only daughter to a nobody. Cars that had passed the security guards at the formidable iron gates were still driving up to the rose-coloured Provençal mansion with its deep overhanging verandahs that gave on to the plush lawn spreading between banks of verdant shrubbery. The reception for 200 guests had been in progress since Prospero and Ghisela had arrived in a white Mercedes limousine accompanied by the party of friends and family who had attended the ceremony in an old stone church on the Cap, their second wedding within the month.

The Italian paparazzi fought with reporters from *Newsweek*, *Paris-Match*, *Stern* and *Oggi*, who remained outside the impregnable fence that sealed off Otto Schmidt's world from theirs. Prospero had not yet told his family about the marriage, intending to break the news as soon as the honeymoon was over. He dreaded facing his mother who he knew would be deeply hurt that she had not been invited to the wedding, but it seemed better that way.

'We're going to slip away at about four,' Prospero told his father-in-law. He couldn't conceal his satisfaction at stealing Schmidt's prize possession from him. An eighty-foot yacht had been chartered to take Prospero and Ghisela on a private cruise of the Greek islands, and it waited in the limpid blue water beneath Stavros Niarchos's clifftop mansion, just yards away from Schmidt's. The handsome, fabulously wealthy Greek, owner of a shipping line, was standing not far away. Prospero recalled their conversation earlier with tingling amazement. His instant entrée into such exalted circles was one of the benefits that went with the job of being Schmidt's son-in-law.

'When you come back next month, I want you and Ghisela to come directly to Geneva,' said Schmidt, narrowing his small eyes. They were set deep in a strongly made head that sat squarely atop his stocky body. 'You can start right away, learning the pharmaceutical business from the bottom up. I've bought you a comfortable villa, not far from mine. It has a pleasant garden that runs down to the lake, with plenty of room for children,' he said pointedly.

'And then what?' inquired Prospero.

'And then we'll see. You might become involved in one of the many subsidiaries that comprise Schmidt International. Who knows, southern Europe, England, or perhaps Germany.'

'What about the States? That's where I would be most useful.'

Schmidt gave a sharp laugh. 'In ten years or more, maybe. Learn to walk before you run.'

'I can run already,' Prospero retorted. 'I'm set to run, and I will, and it won't take me ten years either.'

Disbelief glinted in Schmidt's shrewd eyes.

'Excuse me a moment. I'll just go and find Ghisela,' said Prospero abruptly.

'Don't be long. Someone has just arrived whom I want you to meet.'

Prospero nodded courteously, but inwardly he seethed with resentment that had begun the moment he had come face-to-face with his father-in-law in the Schmidt stronghold on Lake Geneva. As he walked through the crowd of guests, nodding to people he didn't know, he could feel Schmidt's eyes on him. The dangerous sweep of his glance had struck Prospero the moment he and Ghisela had returned from Libya to present him with a *fait accompli*. Ghisela had sent a telegram with news of their marriage, to give her father time to simmer down; but Prospero had felt his blood run cold when he realized that his new wife was amused at the impending confrontation between her powerful father and the interloper who had stolen her affections.

The two men had disliked each other at first glance, this solidly built little man and the son-in-law whom he regarded as an obvious fortune-hunter. But, after his anger had cooled, Schmidt began to recognize that he might put Prospero to good use. Threats and bribes had failed to persuade him to abandon Ghisela, so Schmidt set about assessing his aptitude for business, recognizing at the same time that Prospero's sexual rapport with his daughter might produce a generation of sons to command the Schmidt business empire. That sexuality had been the dowry which Prospero had brought to this marriage of opposites, but he was aware he would be on trial every moment. This lavish reception was a signal to the world that Schmidt blessed his daughter's union, a face-saving formula he had adopted when his vanity had got the better of his outraged pride. Prospero sensed that many of the guests were looking at him with polite condescension mixed with surprise.

Handsomely dressed in a morning coat, he strode among the guests on the velvety lawn of the sumptuous villa, ignoring the coquettish glances of pretty women beneath their elaborate hats. He knew they were regarding him as they would a prize bull.

The circle surrounding Ghisela parted as he approached. The guests comprised rich industrialists and members of the moneyed European aristocracy, shoring up the aura of social invincibility so indispensable to a self-made man. Knowing that Otto Schmidt had come from nothing himself helped Prospero to understand him.

Ghisela smiled serenely when she saw her bridegroom. They were linked by a look that excluded everyone, witness to the passion that flowed between them. She wore a bridal gown of priceless Valenciennes lace, and baby orchids were woven through her flaxen hair. At her throat was a rose diamond necklace that had once belonged to the Empress Elizabeth of Austria. Faces that Prospero recognized from the newspapers looked on as he kissed his bride's neck, and he found their admiration more heady than the vintage champagne passed around unceasingly by the waiters.

'Oh, look, here comes Daddy with one of our dearest friends,' Ghisela whispered into his ear.

Prospero found himself staring at the famous face of the American film star who had married into one of Europe's royal families. Dazzled, he watched the Princess kiss his wife on both cheeks. He was so awed by her incandescent beauty that he scarcely heard her glowing compliments. When he was introduced, he bowed correctly.

'Your Serene Highness,' he murmured, raising her hand to his lips.

'I'm so happy for both of you,' she said warmly, appraising him in one glance.

Chatting with the Princess for a few moments, he mentioned his honeymoon plans.

'It sounds utterly idyllic, slipping away to the Greek islands at this time of the year.'

'I wish I could rechristen the yacht the *True Love*,' he said.

'What a charming thought,' she replied, with a polite smile.

Prospero felt pleased at his own cleverness. Pipe-dreams sprang to his mind like the plumed white clouds he and Ghisela would chase across the horizon to Greece. He would make her happy and get rich in his own right.

Later, when a few reporters were admitted to take photographs of the bride and groom on the steps of the terrace, flanked by celebrities, it crossed Prospero's mind that his great moment would be splashed over all the gossip magazines in Rome the following week. It gave him a sweet sense of triumph to imagine the astonished looks on the faces of people who had thought he would never amount to anything.

Chapter 14

LONG ISLAND

A sharp October wind blew off the dark water of the Long Island Sound, bringing with it cold air and angry skies. Following dry leaves chased by the wind, Cotton walked up the shrub-lined drive of The Shallows, skimming her hand against the serpentine privet hedge that bordered a monkey puzzle tree, its twisted branches shaking against the sky. Usually she walked along the shore, but today she had rambled for an entire morning through the wet woods and emerald pastures dividing the estates of Long Island's north shore. Skirting the east wing of the house, Cotton passed through a gate that led to the back door. The stamp of her feet on the mat outside alerted the black maid who was in the kitchen preparing lunch.

'Is Paige having lunch at home?' Cotton asked cautiously, intending to say she wasn't hungry if she was.

'No, she's gone out and won't be back till later, and Mr and Mrs Townsend are having their lunch on a tray in the library,' Pearl replied.

'Do you have any idea if Biddle is coming home today?' Cotton asked, an anxious note creeping into her voice.

'Nobody tells me anything. I just work here,' Pearl said cheerfully.

'Thanks,' Cotton mumbled, avoiding her eyes that always seemed full of pity. Pearl had tried to be friendly, but Cotton had kept her distance, sealing herself off from everyone but Biddle, who was back at Yale.

She took a chicken sandwich and went up the back stairs to her room under the eaves, pausing at the window to look at the grey water of the Sound. At the end of the garden she could make out the mast of Biddle's sloop, *Odyssey*. He had said on the telephone the week before that he might come home that weekend to batten his boat down for the winter.

Eating her sandwich, Cotton propped herself up on the bed to read Jane Austen, but her ear was cocked for the sound of Biddle's voice drifting up from the hall, or the noise of a door slamming. Biddle, and Biddle alone, had seen her through the nightmare that had descended on her.

Cotton's memory of the week following Delilah's death was vague and confused. She had been plunged into a state of shock, and through the wall of sedation Biddle had sat with her, talking in a soft reassuring voice about anything he thought would distract her. He had been her mainstay at the funeral in the Episcopal church in Cold Spring Harbor, which was thronged with friends of Delilah's who heaped sympathy on the twelve-year-old girl.

Telling herself that Delilah would have expected her to behave with dignity, Cotton had somehow managed to survive. The only person in the world she felt close to, apart from Biddle, was William, and word had reached him in the remote province of India where he was painting far too late for him to attend the funeral. He had written her a long, grief-stricken letter, hinting that he would probably stay in India for some time to distract himself from his loss. But he had consoled Cotton by saying that he would always be there if she needed him.

Whenever Cotton asked the Townsends what was going to happen to her, she was met with evasive replies. The void left by Delilah's death had left her in limbo, waiting to hear when she could go home to Italy.

During the weeks that followed Delilah's death, she had lots of time on her hands to think, and she had written a long letter to William pouring out her heart and suggesting that when he came back to Florence the two of them could live in his studio, or even at the villa if he could arrange it. Every day she became more restless to leave The Shallows, which was made all the more unbearable by Paige's frostiness and Eleanor's crisp orders delivered with a chilly smile.

Putting her book aside, Cotton's eyes strayed to the suitcase in the corner. She had steadfastly refused to unpack it again, removing clothes as she needed them, then closing it. She was comforted by the sight of the packed bag, ready to go at a moment's notice if necessary. When the summons came from William, she would be ready like a horse at the starting-gate. When she was thinking clearly, and not merely daydreaming, she found a flaw in her plan, realizing that Delilah would have wanted her to go to boarding-school in England. She worried that she might be too late to catch up at Wycombe Abbey, and worried what would become of the uniform which was waiting at Harrods.

Sighing restlessly as the afternoon ticked by with maddening slowness, Cotton's mind drifted thousands of miles eastwards, to the Villa Robbiano. Thinking of the head gardener, Giuseppe, she remembered how every year Delilah had made it her business to oversee the clipping of the shrubbery, a delicate job that needed supervision. Now there was no one to do it, unless William came back early. It seemed essential to Cotton that she should get back as soon as she could.

Her thoughts had wandered, and now as she returned from her daydream of the past she met the cold, empty present. Staring at the door, she couldn't believe Delilah would never come back to rescue her the way she always had, like the time she was lost in Paris, an episode she had dreamed about repeatedly during the last weeks. How to comprehend that the indestructible Delilah, the immortal Delilah, was no longer there?

Hearing footsteps on the stairs, Cotton jumped off the bed, waiting for Biddle to appear. She felt a sinking disappointment when Pearl put her head round the door.

'Mr and Mrs Townsend want to see you in the library, honey,' she said.

'What about? Did they say?' she asked warily.

'I don't know. They just said to come right down.'

Cotton braced herself as she walked downstairs, wondering if the summons she had been waiting for had finally come. Crossing the polished floor of the hall, she wondered with a pounding heart what was to become of her.

Austin was standing somewhat ill at ease near the bookshelves, and Eleanor was sitting in a wing-backed chair with a sheaf of papers in front of her. She took off her reading glasses and set them on the pile.

'Come on in, Cotton, and sit down, won't you?'

The minute she faced them she felt the tension in the air as if it were a tangible force.

'I'd rather stand up if you don't mind.'

'No,' said Eleanor firmly. 'I'd rather you sit here, opposite me. There are some things we have to discuss.'

Cotton did as she was told, suppressing a shiver. She sensed that imaginary knives were being sharpened against her somewhere.

Eleanor bit her lip. 'Well now, I really don't know where to begin.' She looked up at Austin, who smiled reassuringly.

Cotton filled the silence. 'I hope you called me down to tell me when I can leave for my school in England. I'd like to be off as soon as possible because I've missed so much already . . .' Her confident voice hid the grief and fears that had gripped her these last weeks. She met Eleanor's impatient expression with composure, fiercely determined to maintain her fragile dignity.

'Well, in that case, I think we'd better come straight to the point as you seem to have made up your mind exactly what you want. I think,' she added to Austin, 'she should be told the truth.'

'What we have to tell you may come as a bit of a surprise,' said Austin, seeming embarrassed by Eleanor's brusqueness. 'The fact of the matter is that you will not be attending school in England, Cotton. You'll be going to the local high school in Oyster Bay.'

It was as if the breath had been knocked out of her. 'What do you mean? That's not what Delilah would want me to do.' Her voice broke.

'I'll explain it all to you slowly, so you understand the situation precisely,' said Eleanor wearily. She picked up a sheet of paper. 'This is an itemized list of all Delilah's outstanding bills, at least the ones we know about. We suspect there may be quite a few that haven't come in yet. Already the amount owed exceeds the funds Delilah left on her death. This means, Cotton, that there is no money for boarding-school, not here and certainly not in England. Put simply, Delilah lived beyond her means all her life. That's why there's no money for school fees. You must try and get that into your head.'

Cotton struggled to contain the hurt, the shock, the resentment that rose inside her. 'That can't be true,' she cried. 'What about our house in Italy, the apartment in New York?' she heard herself saying in a trembling voice.

'I was coming to that.' Eleanor put on her glasses and sorted through the papers in front of her. 'This is a letter from Delilah's lawyers in Italy. I'm afraid that her main income, apart from her small trust, came from the Marchese's family estate. It now reverts to the Marchese's grown-up children by his first marriage. You never met his children, I take it?'

Cotton shook her head numbly.

'And as for the villa, under the terms of the Marchese's will it too reverts to his heirs. That was always understood. Delilah knew perfectly well that she could live in the Villa Robbiano only during her lifetime. You look so surprised, Cotton. Surely she told you that?'

'No – I mean, I didn't know.' Her chin held high, Cotton looked unflinchingly into Eleanor's expressionless eyes.

'Now, as for the apartment in New York, she bought a long lease years ago with the money she inherited from Austin's father. The fact that she rented it this summer, which was unusual for her, must have been an obvious sign that she was short of money. At any rate, we were shocked to discover that she re-mortgaged it years ago and so, by the time the bills are paid, with the funeral expenses and the lawyers' fees, there will be next to nothing left, if anything at all.'

'I don't believe all that. We never had money problems. Delilah was rich,' Cotton blurted out.

'Rich?' said Eleanor with a snort. She shook her head, glaring at Austin. 'Cotton – the truth is cruel, but you must face it. Anyone else would have put money aside to provide for the future, but not Delilah. She always lived to the hilt and never denied herself, or probably you, anything your hearts desired. I'm sorry to be the bearer of bad tidings, but sooner or later the piper must be paid, and in this case it will be Austin and myself who will foot those bills the estate can't cover. You must face the fact that you are left with nothing.'

Nothing. Nothing. The word spun around her brain. She saw herself running towards the villa on a darkening horizon; the faster she ran, the further away it seemed.

'But what about me? I've got to get back to Italy, back to school,' she cried, her frustration veering towards anger.

Eleanor gave her a wan smile. 'Have you been listening to me? It would appear not. You'll have to learn to control yourself, Cotton. This has been a difficult time for us as well as you. There's no need to raise your voice.'

'I wasn't, I wasn't . . .' she persisted, perilously close to tears.

'It would appear, as you have no other relatives to take you in, that you're stuck with us. And we're stuck with you, so I suggest we all make the best of it. I'm afraid, as there's no money, you'll have to go to Oyster Bay High. I'm sorry, but it's the best we can do.'

Cotton looked from Austin to Eleanor in speechless disbelief. Suddenly she lost control. 'No, I won't stay here with you and I don't care what you say. I hate it here, I always have. We only came here to be polite. We never wanted to come. And now Delilah's dead you're taking her money instead of giving it to me. You never liked her. You were jealous of Delilah. She always said you were boring, frumpy . . .' the words spilled out.

Austin's perturbed voice cut through her hysteria. 'Now that will be just about enough, Cotton.'

'I mean it, I mean it, and I'll say it again and again . . .'

Eleanor gasped and stood up rigidly. 'How dare you speak to me in this way!' Her rage mounting, she spat out the words. 'Just who are you, anyway? Why, you're nothing but a stray cat Delilah picked up off the street. We've treated you as a member of the family, and this is all the gratitude we get.'

'Eleanor, please,' pleaded Austin.

Eleanor whirled round on him. 'If I don't say it now I'll never say it. We're taking in this little piece of flotsam out of the goodness of our hearts and this is how we're repaid – she tells us they've been laughing behind our backs all these years. But they weren't too good to accept our hospitality every goddam summer, were they? I never liked Delilah. I put up with her because she was your half-sister. She was a vain, shallow, silly woman who lived entirely for her own pleasure. I only wish to God I'd told her to her face what she was, nothing but an international gadabout infatuated with cheap café society.'

Rage exploded in Cotton. She rushed at Eleanor, flailing her arms in her face as she shrieked,

'Don't you say that about her. Don't you say that about my mother, or I'll kill you.'

'Cotton!' cried Austin. Lunging at her, he grabbed her and pushed her against a chair.

'Have you gone out of your mind? Now stop it, stop it, do you hear?' His face was flushed with indignation.

'Get her out of here,' Eleanor gasped. 'I'm going upstairs, and when I come down I don't want to see her here. I want her out, out! I don't care what happens to her. Just get rid of her.'

Austin grabbed Cotton by the arm and pushed her from the library. 'Go upstairs and stay in your room until you're told,' he mumbled. 'What's the matter with you, anyway? Have you gone mad?'

Cotton's hatred for Eleanor overflowed as she stared at the innocuous Austin. There was nothing wrong with her that running away from The Shallows wouldn't cure. As she climbed the stairs, he called after her:

'When you've calmed down I'm going to come up and talk some sense into you, young lady.'

She broke into a run, paying no attention. By the time Austin came upstairs she would be gone.

The house was quiet an hour later when Cotton crept down the stairs with an overnight bag and quietly closed the door behind her. Her windbreaker tied round her shoulders, she hurried down the drive without looking back. Once she reached the shrub-lined avenue that led to the main road she breathed easier, knowing she was out of sight. Tiers of crimson and yellow had appeared almost overnight on the surrounding countryside, and as she headed for the bus stop down the road she kicked at the drifts of bright leaves.

She had stuffed only a few necessities into her overnight bag: a change of clothes, two favourite books, toothpaste, soap, her diary and her passport. With over a hundred dollars of savings in her purse, she planned to head for New York where she would hide out until she could get in touch with William and ask him to send her the money to get back to Italy. Now that it had finally sunk in that she would never return to the Villa Robbiano, she was placing all her hopes on William, who would surely let her live with him in his studio.

Every time a car passed her on the main road she resisted the instinct to turn her head, deciding that if anyone came to look for her she would refuse to go back to The Shallows. She was completely on her own now, and glad to be free. It crossed her mind that Eleanor and Austin had let her stay because they were plotting to get control of Delilah's money. Preoccupied with her thoughts, she was quite unaware of the car that had stopped a few feet away.

'Hi there, want a lift?'

Jerking her head around in surprise, she saw Biddle looking at her from behind the wheel of his car.

'No thanks,' she gulped, tears springing to her eyes.

'Mind telling me where you're going?'

She thought for a minute, weighing up the situation. Biddle was her friend but she couldn't be sure whose side he would be on if he knew what had happened.

'You may as well know,' she said with a sigh. 'I've decided to leave. I'm going back to Italy.'

'Wish I could come with you,' he replied with a grin, turning off the engine. 'It's still summer over there, isn't it?'

She nodded and swallowed the sudden urge to confide in him that left a rawness in her throat. She looked anxiously down the road at the bus stop not far away, calculating it might be some time before the bus came.

'Have you had lunch yet?'

'I had a sandwich.'

'Just a sandwich? Come on, get in. I'll buy you a hamburger in Oyster Bay as a send-off. Then I'll drive you wherever you want to go.'

The word 'hamburger' gave her an unexpected pang of hunger. Hesitating for only a moment, she got into the car.

Half-an-hour later they were sitting across from each other at a picnic table near the harbour. Cotton felt completely rejuvenated after a cheeseburger, french fries and chocolate malt. She wiped her mouth with a napkin and gave Biddle a philosophical smile.

'Never leave home on an empty stomach. I learned that lesson a long time ago,' he said.

'Did you ever run away from home?' she asked, surprised.

'Sure I did. More than once.'

'The difference is, it's not home to me, I guess.'

'Maybe not, but it's the next best thing, isn't it?'

'You haven't heard what happened,' she replied sombrely, brushing her wind-whipped hair from her face. She watched the wake of a boat disappearing into the bright blue horizon.

'Why don't you tell me all about it?' he said sympathetically.

As she looked at him, Cotton recalled that Delilah had always said Biddle was a character straight out of Henry James.

'Well, we had a sort of an argument. I don't really think I want to discuss it.'

'Okay. It's up to you.'

She was expecting him to coax or admonish her, but his indifference took the wind out of her sails.

'Are you still hungry, by any chance?' He narrowed his eyes and smiled mischievously. 'How about blueberry pie *à la mode*?

You can't get that where you're going. Better have some while you can.'

When they had finished their pie he said: 'You know, it seems a shame, really. I came home hoping you'd come with me to take the *Odyssey* out for one last tour around the Sound before I put her up for the winter. We couldn't ask for a better day.'

She realized it was true. The sky had cleared and it was one of those perfect Indian summer days when the sun seems suspended in the clear air. A strong gust of wind slapping her face made Cotton ache to sail again with Biddle, one last time.

'What do you say – can you spare an hour or two?'

She looked at him with questioning eyes, biting her lip, then looked away again. Cotton knew that if he as much as touched her shoulder she would burst into tears, and he seemed to sense exactly what she was feeling. Ever since that day when he had carried her screaming from the Piping Rock Club they had shared a bond of affection that she could feel now, tugging her back to earth and away from her plan. She fought with herself for a moment, losing ground as he looked at her. The only other person in her life who could help her was William Partridge, but he was thousands of miles away.

'All right, I'll come,' she murmured.

Before they went to the car they passed a phone box.

'I think I ought to give Ma and Pa a call. They were expecting me to be home by now, and they might be wondering where you are, too,' he added.

Her eyes flared angrily. Was this betrayal?

'Don't worry,' he soothed. 'I'll leave the door open so you can hear what I say.'

She waited, arms folded tensely across her chest as she leaned against the phone booth.

'Hello, Dad? Hi – yes, I'm on my way. Listen, I bumped into Cotton . . . yes, she's here with me. We just had something to eat. Hang on, let me explain. We're going to take the sloop out for a while. No, no, she already told me what happened. Yes, I know, I know . . .'

She studied Biddle's face intently for signs of what was

being said on the other end of the line. He caught her glance and winked.

'We're going to have a little talk. Yes, don't worry. Look, don't expect me until later tonight – or even in the morning.'

When he had hung up he said, 'Ready to go?'

She wasn't but when he put his arm around her her resistance melted.

An hour later they were moving across the gleaming water with Cotton at the tiller of *Odyssey*, as Biddle had taught her the previous summer. When he hoisted the mainsail and the jib a gust of wind filled the canvas and sent the sloop skimming smoothly across the blue water of the Sound. Biddle nodded to Cotton to guide them at close-quarter to the wind. He had changed into a heavy sweater, jeans and topsiders, and Cotton had rummaged through her bag for her thick Aran sweater. For a while they said nothing, enjoying the freedom of being pushed by the wind past the jigsaw of the shoreline, where banks of multi-coloured trees sheltered the big mansions of Long Island.

When Biddle slid beside her and took over the tiller he said: 'Do you want to tell me what happened this afternoon? I want to hear your side of the story.'

Taking a deep breath, she told him what had taken place in the library. When she finished she said softly: 'I said some terrible things, but I had to get them off my chest.'

'Did you ever have any idea that Delilah might have money problems?'

Cotton thought hard, examining her conscience. Though she was too proud to admit it, there seemed no way to avoid the truth. She had always known there were problems, but Delilah's sunny attitude to life made them easy to ignore. She had heard the servants grumbling sometimes about not being paid. There were incidents of shopkeepers coming to the villa to demand that overdue bills be settled on the spot. Delilah often traded on her charm, using her gifts of persuasion to make people forget she owed them money. Cotton had always been aware of various little economies, like turning off the heat and closing down parts of the villa that weren't used, and hiring servants temporarily when guests arrived. But when Delilah entertained all the lights blazed, the heat went on, the silver came out and the table groaned with delicacies like wild strawberries, asparagus out of season, white truffles or saddle of lamb. There was always imported Scotch and brandy, even though they were outrageously expensive in Italy. Wherever she and Cotton went, they always travelled first class, though they stayed in the luxurious apartments and houses of friends in Paris or London. Delilah had made it a tradition to attend the Paris couture collections, but later she would turn up in copies of Balmain or Chanel made up by her own dressmaker in Florence.

As Cotton searched for an answer to Biddle's question, she knew that life with Delilah had been a delicate balancing act, performed with artistry and flair, but which had caught up with Cotton now that Delilah was no longer there. Cotton had painful memories of Delilah selling choice pieces of jewellery now and then, vowing she didn't like them anyway. She recalled an unpleasant row with the Marchese's family when a valuable painting disappeared from the villa and turned up at an auction at Sotheby's. It was discreetly withdrawn, and never mentioned again.

'Nobody's perfect, I guess, are they?' said Cotton. The defeat in her eyes said it all.

Biddle shook his head. 'No, nobody's perfect.'

She brushed her hair from her eyes, avoiding Biddle's penetrating gaze. Eleanor and Austin had spoken the truth, and she had been unable to accept it. She had lashed out in anger, but while part of her wanted to apologize the other half didn't.

'I guess I said some things I didn't mean.'

'Dad mentioned that on the phone. But I think you said those things because you're still angry at losing Delilah. You said you hated Mom because at the moment you needed to lash out at someone.'

'I said more than that. I told your mother she was dumpy and boring. And I said Delilah had never liked her, and that she was just jealous of Delilah.' Cotton looked into the far distance, seeking solace in the biting wind that stung her cheeks.

'Well, let's face it, I suppose my family, compared to the

kind of people you're used to, are pretty dull. But they can't help it. My mother probably *has* been jealous of Delilah all these years. But who wouldn't be jealous of Delilah? Everybody loved her. She drew fascinating people to her, and you were a very lucky girl to have her as your mother for the first twelve years of your life. Look at the head start you've got, how high it's made you set your sights. At twelve you've done more than most people, including me. You've been all over Europe, you speak three languages.'

Her fists clenched, Cotton tried to close her ears to Biddle's words, but she couldn't evade their implications. With all her might she tried to hang on to what she wanted, to stick to her own plans.

'Pride is a funny thing,' he said perceptively. 'It can make or break you. So, you've had a rough time. Use it. Make it work for you. Don't let it ruin your life. You say you're going back to Italy. Okay, let's assume you do make it back to Italy. What then?'

'I was planning to look after William. He'll come back from India sooner or later. Now that Delilah's gone he'll need me.'

He gave her a doubtful look. Biddle knew all about William, the flamboyant English artist who lived in a big draughty studio, the man who had been the love of Delilah's life.

'I know what you're thinking,' she hastened to say. 'You think there's no place for me there. But if that doesn't work out then I'll do something else, that's all.' The moment she spoke, Cotton realized she had painted herself into a corner. Not trusting herself to speak, she scrambled to tack over the sail when he gestured. She shouted over her shoulder:

'I can't go back to your house after what I said to Eleanor and Austin. They don't want me anyway. They just feel they have to take me in.'

'I want you to stay. I'm the one who is asking. Will you do it for me?'

Cotton met his clear eyes that reflected the water, as bright as if a cloud had lifted from the sun. The salty air, the broad horizons ahead made her wish they could keep on sailing and never stop. They could travel the world together like two vagabonds, trusting to fortune. But as soon as the idea formed in her mind, Cotton knew this was just another fantasy.

She slid alongside him and sighed. 'What can I do?'

'That's no problem, believe me. Just two little words. That's all it takes.'

Chapter 15

Waking up in a darkened bedroom, Prospero took a moment to remember he was in a girlfriend's apartment. He reached for his watch on the bedside table and, seeing it was nearly five o'clock, leapt from the bed just as Elaine stirred languorously and reached out for him.

'Where you going? Hey, come back here,' murmured the young model sleepily. She stretched her long naked limbs and opened her arms. 'We've just got started,' she purred at the sight of his muscular nude body disappearing into the bathroom.

Moments later he came to the bedside, rubbing his face vigorously with a towel.

'I've got a cocktail party at six.'

'What?' She threw back the covers. 'You didn't say anything to me about a cocktail party. Are you coming back?'

'No. After that my wife and I are having dinner with clients.'

She stared at him incredulously. 'I turned down a job to be with you today, you know that. And after Christmas I'm off to Mexico and we won't see each other for at least three weeks.'

'The time will fly by very quickly, I assure you,' he said, jumping into his clothes.

'Shit – shit and damnation,' Elaine wailed, sinking back on to the bed. 'You're a bastard, that's what you are, a rotten bastard.' Her abuse dissolved into tears. 'Why the hell do I put up with you, anyway?' she sobbed.

'No one is asking you to put up with me, *cara*,' he said, hurriedly tying his tie. Digging in his pocket, he brought out a wad of money. He peeled off two hundred dollars and put the bills on the dressing-table. 'Go out and buy yourself something nice. I'll call you when you get back.'

'I can't believe you, I really can't.' As she regarded him through her tears, Elaine found it hard to comprehend that this cold, preoccupied man was the Prospero who had made passionate love to her all afternoon.

'*Ciao, bella,*' he called from the doorway. 'Have a good time in Mexico.'

With that, Prospero snatched up his briefcase and left the apartment. Pulling on his trench coat, he took the lift to street level where he waited for a taxi. Everything he wore was of the finest quality, from his custom-made shirt to his grey tweed suit. His immaculately styled hair, his manicured hands, were hallmarks of a rich and cosmopolitan man. When he hailed the taxi, he leapt in and directed the driver to take him to East Seventy Second Street, off Park Avenue.

On the way home Prospero thought about Elaine, his third affair within a year. She was beautiful, she was desirable, but like the others she spoiled everything by her possessiveness. He had taken her to glamorous restaurants, given her a number of expensive presents, and he had made passionate love to her, but her hysteria a moment ago had ruined their relationship and he had no desire to see her again. He felt a twinge of conscience at his behaviour, but quickly dismissed it from his mind.

Arriving at East Seventy Second Street, he looked up at the towering apartment block where he lived and which he would once have described as 'swank'. It never failed to give him pleasure to see the uniformed doorman standing to attention outside the plate-glass doors beyond which was a gushing fountain surrounded by palms and pink azaleas.

It had been over six years since he and Ghisela had come to New York after spending three long years in Geneva. While under his father-in-law's thumb, he had applied himself relentlessly to learning the mechanics of the pharmaceutical industry and the complexities of international business. Otto Schmidt had finally been forced to acknowledge Prospero's prodigious capacity for hard work and his natural business acumen, which could never have been acquired at the Harvard Business School. Finally recognizing Prospero's potential, Schmidt had grudgingly agreed to making him a vice-president of his American operations. Prospero had soon concluded that he would be satisfied with nothing less than his father-in-law's position, an ambition which appeared futile while Otto Schmidt remained in his prime. Soon after his arrival in the United States, Prospero had decided that he would have to cultivate other pastures discreetly if he was ever going to acquire independence.

The doors of the mirrored lift that took him to the fourteenth floor slid open and Prospero walked down the thickly carpeted hallway to the door of the apartment. As it swung open he was greeted by the elegant vista of the drawing-room furnished in Louis-Philippe style at the end of which a large Flemish winter landscape glowed above a white marble fireplace. He set his briefcase down by a console table decorated by a crystal vase filled with white lilies and tulips.

At the sound of his entrance, his daughters, eight-year-old Sophia and five-year-old Elysia, came running towards him.

'Papa, Papa,' they chorused.

'Come and give your papa big hugs and kisses,' he said, opening his arms. He kissed them and smoothed their blonde hair as he spoke in Italian. Glancing up, he smiled at Ghisela who regarded them sombrely. She wore a beautifully tailored gaberdine suit, and a rope of pearls rested on her Hermès scarf. The shining blonde hair he had once loved to uncoil was elegantly swirled into a chignon held in place with ivory combs.

'Hadn't you better go and change? I told the driver to be here before six. Why aren't you ready?' he said, trying to interpret the expression in her eyes.

'I assumed you wouldn't come back at all tonight,' she replied in a tight voice.

He became wary. 'And what did you mean to imply by that remark?'

'I called the office today. You weren't there.'

'So what?' he said, with a shrug. 'I had a meeting. Do I have to account for every moment of my time? What is this, anyway, an inquisition? I'm already treated like an errand boy at Schmidt. Do you want me to punch a clock too?' He was saying too much, but anger boiled up inside him. Looking at his remotely beautiful wife, he found it hard to imagine he had ever made love to her on the steps of a Roman temple.

She replied in a staccato voice: 'I spoke to my father this afternoon. He is waiting for us at the Palace in St Moritz. All the arrangements have been made. A limousine will be here in a few moments to take us to the airport.'

Just then the maid brought suitcases into the hall, followed by the nanny with the children's coats.

He stared at her dumbfounded. 'It's out of the question. You know I can't leave New York. I have too much to do.'

'The invitation does not include you.' The coldness in her tone completely dismissed him.

'I don't want you to go,' he replied flatly, keeping his emotions in check. 'There are lots of important parties around Christmas, and I want you by my side.'

They fell silent until the nanny, the maid and the children were out of earshot. Prospero fixed Ghisela with a penetrating gaze, trying to read her mind. Although her passion no longer matched his, even now one of his greatest pleasures was walking into a prestigious gathering with her on his arm. For years they had danced a polite minuet, and only occasionally did the curtain fall away to reveal the emptiness of their lives, a void he was confident he could fill once he had amassed a fortune of his own. But living without her had never entered his mind.

'Christmas is a family occasion, Ghisela. I don't want to be separated from the children, from you — surely you know that,' he said in a gentle tone.

'Ah yes. Christmas is a family occasion,' she said mockingly. 'But my family is in Switzerland, where I wish to be as well.'

Her eyes had a look that he could never remember seeing there before. It was not the usual coldness she adopted when they argued, but a challenge.

'How long do you plan to be away?'

'We shall see,' she replied, revealing nothing of her thoughts.

Prospero had a sudden terrible vision of being flung down from the summit to which he had climbed. Fear rolled over him in shock waves: she had found out about Elaine, perhaps about his other affairs as well, maybe even his deals on the side. Or more likely, one of Otto Schmidt's flunkeys had been spying on him. A hot rush of angry pride kept him silent, and he cautioned himself that an ultimatum would only alienate Ghisela further.

She slipped into her pale mink coat as he watched helplessly; then she nodded at the doorman who had arrived to collect the baggage.

'Don't you at least want me to come with you to the airport?'

'No thank you. That won't be necessary.'

When the nanny had buttoned up the children's velvet-collared coats, Ghisela said: 'Go and kiss your papa goodbye, Sophia, Elysia.'

Feeling their lips brush his cheek, he came alive for a moment and crushed them to him roughly, making them giggle in surprise. Ghisela was regarding him as if revolted by his display of emotion.

When the door closed behind them, he stood for a moment in a state of numb incomprehension. The voice of the maid brought him to his senses.

'Will there be anything else, sir?'

'No. No, you can go home.'

'In that case, Merry Christmas and Happy New Year. I won't be coming back until the New Year.'

'Goodnight,' he said tersely.

Prospero poured himself a drink from the first bottle that came to hand, then slumped in a chair. He was alone. It was Christmas. His wife had left him. As his mind swirled in confusion, the real reason began to penetrate his thoughts. Realizing that someone must have blown the whistle on him and Tony Fasso, Prospero broke out in a cold sweat. The more he thought about it the more convinced he became, recalling that on several occasions he had suspected he was being watched at the office. Little things like an unexplained click on the telephone, an embarrassed silence when he entered a room full of Schmidt executives, pointed to the truth. He knew he had to do something fast. If he didn't, he stood to lose everything.

It was almost dark when Cotton drove through the high gates of The Shallows bordered by the dark shapes of rhododendrons coated with the snow that had been falling lightly all day. She drove past the house, which was ablaze with lights, and parked her old Mustang near the rambling garage. Turning off the Christmas music on the radio, she got out, taking her bag from the back seat.

The windows of the house beckoned invitingly in the darkness and the fir trees near the door, draped with red and green lights, made The Shallows appear as cheerfully idyllic as a Christmas card. Walking up the gravelled forecourt, Cotton reflected that a stranger could easily believe this house was inhabited by a large, happy family.

She had welcomed the chance to get away from her Master's thesis and Columbia for the holidays, but as she faced the colonial house where she had once lived, Cotton almost wished she hadn't come. Brushing the snowflakes from her navy trench coat, she rang the bell which was answered by Pearl, who greeted her with a welcoming smile.

'Hi there, honey. Been expecting you. Come in out of that cold. Lotta traffic on the turnpike?'

'Hello, Pearl. How are you?' she said warmly. 'It wasn't too bad tonight, considering. Where is everybody?' She glanced up the curving staircase draped with pine branches and red ribbons, and took in the familiar details: the Adam chest with a gilt mirror above it, the polished parquet floor, the chandelier hanging from a brass chain.

'Mr and Mrs Townsend are upstairs getting ready for the party. Paige is arriving any minute with her husband, and Biddle is upstairs, of course. He says to be sure and tell you to come straight up when you get here.'

Climbing the stairs, Cotton was seized with anxiety as she thought of Biddle. Even though she had known for months, she found it impossible to think that this might be his last Christmas.

'Are a lot of people coming tonight?' she called down.

'About eighty. Mrs Townsend said to put you in your old room as usual. Just go on up. It's all ready.'

Cotton dropped her bag on the landing, intending to go to Biddle's room first. As she walked down the hall, Eleanor came out of her bedroom clipping a pearl earring to her ear.

'I thought I heard voices,' she said brightly. Pecking Cotton on the cheek she added: 'My, but don't you look attractive? I like your hair like that, Cotton. You've had it cut since you were last here in October.'

'Yes, I have. It was very kind of you to ask me for Christmas, Eleanor,' she said with characteristic formality.

'Well, it's lovely to have you.' Eleanor's smile was brittle.

Cotton smiled back, knowing that neither of them would acknowledge the real reason for her visit the entire time she was there. They would tactfully skirt the truth and pretend to have a happy family Christmas, forgetting the past and Biddle's condition. But behind Eleanor's brusque manner Cotton sensed acute pain, and her pity was aroused.

'Well, I'm glad you're here safe and sound. Was the traffic just awful?'

'Pretty bad. I thought I could beat the rush hour, but I was late picking up something from my typist before I came,' she said by way of conversation, impatient to bring the strained welcome ritual to an end.

'Austin and I can't wait to hear all your news. Now you're here you can forget graduate school and relax. Kick up your heels a bit.'

Cotton was compelled to say: 'How is Biddle, Eleanor?'

'Oh Biddle's fine, just fine. He'll be so pleased to see you,' she replied, glossing over her concern. 'I'd better run down and see that the caterers have everything under control. We were just having a few people in for egg nog, and then before I knew it the party just grew like Topsy. Come down as soon as you're ready.'

Before entering Biddle's room, Cotton paused for a moment. Though they had talked often on the phone, she felt guilty for not coming to see him more often. She dreaded the change she knew she would find in him, but whatever she might feel she was determined not to let it show.

'Biddle?' she said, putting her head round the door. 'Anybody home?'

'Hey, hi there, kiddo. Come on in,' he called cheerfully. He was propped up in bed, with a uniformed nurse tucking in a blanket at the bottom of his bed.

Swallowing the lump in her throat, Cotton put her arms around him and hugged him tenderly for a moment. She blinked to keep the tears back as she felt how wasted his body was.

'I don't think you've met the incomparable Carol, have you? My latest flame. She's everything a man could wish for, and more,' he said with an amused smile as he leaned back on the pillows.

'You ought to realize by now that flattery will get you anywhere,' Carol retorted with a wink to Cotton. 'I have to keep my wits about me with him, you know.'

'Persistence pays. You'll see, Carol.'

'Well, you've already got me where you want me. I'm going to leave you now, but I'll be back later,' said the nurse, leaving the room.

Cotton pulled up a chair by the bedside and reached for Biddle's hand. She was heartsick to see the change in him in a few short weeks, and as always it took her several minutes to reconcile his shrunken sallow form with the vibrant athletic young man she loved. The illness that had overtaken him two years before had raced through his body with frightening speed, yet his bright eyes seemed to burn with an inner incandescence, reminding her of the unconquerable spirit that had so strongly influenced her life.

'I want to hear everything that's been going on,' he said, fixing on her with curiosity.

'Not much, I can tell you, except work, work and more work.'

She was always tempted to paint her life in drab, dreary

terms even though she knew she wasn't fooling him. As always, the unspoken question nagged at her mind: Why him? Why Biddle, who loved life so much, who had so many plans, so much energy, so much talent? It made her deeply bitter at times. His own anger had long since been smothered by the resignation that had taken its place.

'How's the thesis coming on? Uncover any links between drugs and big business since we last talked?'

'Nothing new, I'm afraid. But don't worry, I have plenty of material. Now all I have to do is glue this masterpiece of investigative reporting together.'

'I think you should get a bodyguard. I don't like the sound of that stuff you were telling me on the phone.'

'Oh yeah, I can really afford one on the shoestring I live on.'

'As soon as your thesis is finished you'll have publishers eating out of your hand. It's going to read like a thriller.'

'Okay – I'll forget the Pulitzer and go for a bestseller.'

'You're a born rabble-rouser,' he said with a touch of pride.

'And who's to blame? You made me what I am today,' she replied, kissing him on the cheek.

'Me? What did I do? You did it all yourself – Northwestern, Magna cum Laude, Phi Beta Kappa, then Columbia, the Marguerite Higgins Fellowship. You showed everybody – you really did.'

'That's the only thing I could do. I had to channel that bottled-up anger and resentment somehow.' Reflecting how much she owed to Biddle, she felt herself getting dangerously sentimental. 'Anyway, one thing is for sure. I'm not going to start my career writing obituaries.' The minute she spoke, she could have bitten her tongue at her thoughtlessness.

At the look of pain that crossed her face, he reached out and brushed her cheek with cool fingers.

'Come on, Cotton. Everybody around here avoids the subject of death like the plague, pretending I'll be entering the Olympics this summer. I don't want you to feel like that too.'

'Right. Will do,' she said, trying to smile.

'Of course the only thing that bothers me is that the footprints I leave in the sands of time won't be deep enough to make the newspapers. Better luck next time around. I think I might have done it, though, if I had had a few more years.'

'You would have,' she agreed. 'Explorer, world traveller, genius, man for all seasons. And I love you very much,' she said in a whisper.

They were overtaken by a poignant silence as the dark future pressed in on them. Biddle broke the atmosphere by picking up the remote control and turning on the television.

'Speaking of crime, there's a great old George Raft movie on at nine. Maybe you can sneak up and watch it with me if you can tear yourself away from the *beau monde* of the North Shore.'

'That won't be too difficult. I'll just put in an appearance, then slip away. Why don't I order a pizza from Mario's with everything on it? Do you think we can get away with it a second time?'

'We'll have to sneak it past Carol. She watches me like a hawk. Speak of the devil,' he said with a laugh as she came through the door.

'Did I hear my name mentioned? Say, I hate to break this up, but we have a little chore to perform here.'

'I thought you weren't coming back till much later,' said Biddle.

'It's that soft dreamy voice and those dreamy eyes of yours. You make me forget what I'm doing,' she cracked.

'I'll be on my way,' said Cotton hastily, seeing a bedpan and sponge and other paraphernalia in her hand. She was suddenly reminded of the indignities of illness, which Biddle bore with such stoicism.

Taking a backward glance, Cotton remarked to herself that he had more style, more grace, even when dying, than any other human being she had ever known. Every man she had ever dated she measured against her cousin, and she couldn't imagine life without him, which would be like an empty room with the lights turned out. He was her touchstone, her anchor. She had always tested her mettle against his probing intelligence, and there was no one to replace him.

When Cotton took her suitcase up to her old room under

the eaves she decided she wasn't in the mood to dress up for the party. She glanced round at the familiar yet impersonal bedroom she had occupied for six years before leaving for Northwestern to major in Communications, and it crossed her mind that this might be the last time she would ever stay there. When Biddle died she wouldn't want to come back. There would be nothing to come back for.

She experienced a wave of fear mixed with dread at the prospect of his death as its inevitability hit her forcefully. She knew there was no escape from the truth she had evaded for the last two years and she wondered how they would get through Christmas, she and Biddle, without breaking down. Would his sense of humour carry them through, or had they gone beyond that? She had looked forward desperately to Christmas in one sense, imagining they would have long profound conversations about the meaning of life as they used to have years ago. She hadn't realized until that moment that the spectre of immediate death rendered such philosophical conversations cruel and meaningless.

Pausing only to run a comb through her hair, she went to the landing above the entrance hall to watch people coming through the front door, their coats and hair sparkling with snow. A butler collected their coats, while a waitress in a black uniform and white apron stood by with a tray of drinks. Cotton quickly identified Paige's blonde blunt-cut hair held back by a black velvet band. She was wearing a choirboy maternity dress with a big red bow and she was talking to Herron Easton. Her eyes narrowed when she saw Cotton coming down the stairs.

'Hello, Cotton. Merry Christmas.' Paige's voice was distantly polite.

'Merry Christmas to you too, Paige,' she said, smiling.

The flicker of disapproval on her face told Cotton she thought her skirt and sweater were inappropriate for a cocktail party.

'Hello, Herron, nice to see you,' she said with a nod. One glance told Cotton he was as handsome and smooth as ever.

'Cotton, what a nice surprise. I didn't know you would be here,' he said, kissing her on the cheek. 'Merry Christmas – it's been a long time since we've seen each other.'

'Yes, it's been ages. I've kept up with your career, though. Biddle tells me that things are going very well for you in Washington. I was very impressed to hear you're working for the Justice Department.'

'That's right, and loving every minute of it.'

Paige, who had been listening, impatiently said: 'Excuse me.'

As she walked away, Cotton realized she should have asked her polite questions about her stockbroker husband and the baby she was expecting. The two of them had avoided each other over the years, and now they had nothing in common. Cotton made a mental note to try and be more friendly to Paige. After all, it was Christmas – maybe Biddle's last – and this was no time for rekindling old grievances. She looked up to see Herron watching her with a thoughtful smile. There was an appealing directness in his eyes that she had all but forgotten.

'How long has it been since we last saw each other? I've been trying to remember,' Herron asked.

'Let's see. It will be three years next summer. I know it was the summer Biddle became ill.'

'That's right. We all went sailing together. You were at Northwestern then. I remember I thought you looked damned cute in a pair of shorts and a Snoopy T-shirt. You made a fetching sight, suntanned and sunstreaked, as you hoisted the mainsail.'

Cotton gave a startled laugh at the recollection. There was no mistaking the interest in Herron's eyes and it took her by surprise. 'What a prodigious memory you have,' she murmured, taking a drink from a tray. Herron Easton was very rich, ten years older than she, and going places; they lived in different worlds, and they always had.

'Yes, those were wonderful, carefree days. I sometimes think of them. We didn't know how lucky we were, did we?' There was feeling in his voice.

Though neither of them said it, they both knew they were thinking of Biddle.

'How is he, anyway? I haven't seen him since last summer,'

said Herron quietly. 'I've been meaning to get in touch, but I just haven't done it. I feel guilty for not coming over before.'

'His condition seems stable, but prepare yourself. He's deteriorated a lot since you saw him. He still has that amazing sense of humour, though.'

'I was thinking of popping up later to say hello, but I didn't want to upset him, or intrude.'

'He'd love to see you, Herron, he really would. And don't worry,' she added, sensing his uncertainty. 'He'll put you at ease. You can come up with me in a while if you want to. I was going to order a pizza. Would you like to join us?' she said, sure he wouldn't. The Townsend living-room was filling up with people and she would have understood if he'd wanted to stay and mingle with old friends. He surprised her by saying,

'Thanks. There's nothing I'd like better than to be with Biddle – and with you.'

On the way to Little Italy in a taxi, Prospero found himself brooding about his first meeting with Tony Fasso. He had avoided all the other people he knew in his youth, but he had sought out Tony not long after he and Ghisela had arrived in New York. They had got together now and then like two old friends who had little in common but who enjoyed each other's company. One day Tony had proposed a deal that proved to be the answer to all Prospero's prayers. When the arrangement had been set up, it ran like clockwork. Some time that month another shipment of drugs whose shelf life had expired would disappear without trace from the Schmidt warehouse in New Jersey and be on its way to Third World countries, relabelled, unrecognizable, via mob channels. After making a few strategic payoffs, their operation was pure profit and Prospero's share was quietly accumulating in a Swiss bank.

He told the cab driver to stop at the corner of Mercer and Spring, intending to walk the rest of the way to the restaurant while he rehearsed in his mind what he intended to say to Tony. It was a cold, overcast night with snow threatening to fall. Catching sight of a clock, Prospero realized that Ghisela and the children would soon be boarding the plane for Geneva. He wiped the thought of her from his mind, intending to deal with the crisis in his marriage later. Walking down a narrow, brightly lit street, he came to an abrupt halt at a grocery store with a striped awning, where he stared at the light reflecting in the gutter. Franco Vallone had been murdered on that very spot nearly twenty-five years ago. Could it really be that long? Prospero had a cruel vision of his father lying in a pool of blood, face down. Usually, if he couldn't avoid passing the spot, he blanked the memory from his mind, but tonight he shuddered involuntarily.

Tony was waiting in a booth at the back of the restaurant, talking to the thin, bald 'Gloves' Amato. The minute he saw Prospero, Tony signalled for Gloves to leave. Prospero nodded to them both, then slipped into the booth across from Tony.

All the way there, Prospero had weighed up the wisdom of confiding his personal problems to Tony before going into the real reason he was there. As he looked at his friend's darkly ringed eyes and his sallow, lined face, Prospero felt uneasy. He had once worshipped Tony, who had been like his big brother; but he suddenly became aware of the gulf between them.

'What did you want to see me about so urgently?' Tony asked in a friendly tone.

His shoulders hunched forward, Prospero said flatly: 'My wife left me tonight. She took the kids and went back to Switzerland.'

'Say, that's rough. Right before Christmas? Sorry to hear it, Prospero. Why don't you come out and spend Christmas with me and Jeanette and the kids?'

'Thanks for the offer, but I want to be alone to think things over. You know how it is.'

The waiter brought drinks and Prospero watched Tony's big hands as he lit a cigarette.

Prospero shifted restlessly. 'You know, Tony, I've been thinking about everything on the way down here. I've been kidding myself. Ghisela has never been happy in New York. She misses Europe, her father. And I'm on a treadmill at Schmidt. I'm nothing but a figurehead. I've got to get back to Geneva where the power centre of the company is.'

'Hey, wait a minute, what's all this talk?' said Tony, his face darkening. 'When we started this thing you always said how you wanted to make your pile and then cut out. And that's just what you're doing. You've got money in the bank to prove it, haven't you? And there's a lot more to come, especially when we go ahead with this new thing. Everything's all set up. We're just waiting for the word "go".'

'I know, I know,' said Prospero. He swallowed nervously. For months Tony had been pressing him to get out of the relatively harmless area of repackaging and move up into hard drugs where the big money was.

'Prospero, hey, I can see you're panicking,' said Tony, fixing him with accusing eyes. 'This thing with your wife has thrown you. Why not forget about it for a few days?'

'That's just the thing. If I don't get this cleared up with Ghisela, then I'll be out on my ear with the company.'

Tony's look of veiled contempt conveyed that he thought Prospero was hiding behind his wife; that he was soft, spoiled by the good life. He was suddenly filled with self-loathing at his own weakness, his phoneyness, his lack of substance.

'I should level with you, Tony. Ghisela's not the only thing.' His voice dropped. 'I don't know if it's my imagination, but I think somebody is fishing around at Schmidt. There have been a couple of phone calls, a guy from the purchasing department asking questions – that auditor who was so nosy. We could even be under surveillance by the Feds.'

'That's bad,' said Tony. 'I better talk to a few people, do a bit of snooping myself. Yeah, you let me take care of it. I'll get to the bottom of it. You got enough on your mind. You should concentrate on your wife and kids. Go after her. Convince her to come back.'

Relief flooded Prospero at Tony's nonchalance. He had half-expected anger, even threats, knowing it meant a huge loss of easy money for Tony, even though he had projects all over the East Coast. Tony had never met Ghisela, an admission that shamed Prospero, though neither of them ever referred to it. Prospero always wondered if Tony held it against him, felt

Prospero thought he wasn't good enough to socialize with his beautiful, aristocratic wife.

'You're a great guy, do you know that?' Prospero muttered.

'Don't mention it. I know what women are like. When you're on top of things at Schmidt again, give me a call and we'll do something. You don't have to be living here in New York. In fact your being in Geneva might be an advantage in some ways. We'll talk about it.'

Prospero tried to smile, but he couldn't hide his relief. He knew they would never talk about it. In fact, once he had left Tony he never wanted to see him again.

'Can you hang on just a minute? There's something that I've got to tell Gloves. I'll order another round of drinks. Same?'

Prospero nodded.

After half-an-hour of friendly conversation they parted with a handshake, and as Prospero walked through the restaurant he had the illusion of struggling from a quagmire one difficult step at a time.

In the taxi on the way back home he began to feel much better now the meeting with Tony was behind him. He decided to take the first flight to Geneva next morning. He would interrupt Ghisela's cosy reunion with her father and reclaim her as his wife. He would win her all over again, promise her heaven and earth if she would come back to him. They would move to Europe if it pleased her. He would use the money he had made with Tony as a capital base to build his own fortune. And, he told himself, he would quit being unfaithful. He would devote all his spare time and attention to Ghisela and they would have another baby, a son this time.

By the time he had arrived back at the apartment he was impatient for the next day so that he could put all his new resolutions into action and secure a second chance for his family. Tipping the cab driver generously, he walked towards the entrance, stopping in his tracks when he heard a voice utter his name. Turning, he saw a man step from the shadows. Prospero got a quick glimpse of a gun fitted with a silencer.

'Tony says "Merry Christmas",' muttered Gloves as he pumped three shots into him.

Cotton's eyes met Herron's over the box of pizza.

'Want another slice?'

He shook his head. 'What about you, Biddle?' she asked, even though she noticed he had only picked at the piece on his bedside table.

He shook his head. 'No thanks. Don't want to get Carol in a bad temper. She's going to scold me as it is.' His smile was mischievous.

'In that case, Herron and I will polish off the last of it. Come on, Herron, how about it?'

'If you absolutely insist, all right. I didn't realize how hungry I was until I had the first bite.'

'It beats that rabbit food mother serves at her cocktail parties,' commented Biddle. 'If they heard downstairs there was pizza going up here there would a stampede.'

Cotton swirled a strand of mozzarella into her mouth and glanced at the television. George Raft, his hat pulled down, had just slipped a gun from his trench coat. There was a close-up of his face as he fired three times at his assailant. The picture faded and a commercial came on.

'Life was simple in those days, wasn't it?' remarked Herron. 'There were good guys, and bad guys.'

He had removed his jacket and rolled up his shirtsleeves, revealing muscular tanned forearms. Every now and then Cotton found her attention straying from the movie to Herron. While he chatted to Biddle, displaying none of the awkwardness some people felt in his presence, Cotton was forced to reconsider the impression she had had of him all these years. She had always thought of him as a typical ambitious Wasp on the make, a man too handsome to be taken seriously, too rich to have real ambitions; but now she realized she had misjudged him. Just then she became aware of a news flash on the television: 'Son-in-law of Swiss pharmaceutical magnate Otto Schmidt, Prospero Vallone, vice-president of Schmidt, was shot and critically wounded outside his apartment off Park Avenue and is now in intensive care in Bellevue General Hospital. Vallone's own father was shot in the fifties, in the rising tide of gangland violence, and it remains to be seen whether the vice-president of Schmidt has any underworld connections.'

Cotton noticed Herron's face had gone serious as he stared at the television. 'Vallone's one of the guys I've been trying to nail for ages. If I could get him to crack, we could put quite a few people behind bars,' he said with bitterness.

'You mean he's a criminal?' said Cotton with a start. 'That's juicy,' she added, her mind ticking over.

'This is right up Cotton's street,' said Biddle.

'Do you know the guy?' asked Herron, seeing the look of surprise on Cotton's face.

'Oh no, I don't know him,' she said, shaking her head. As she spoke she wondered if there could be two men in the world with a name like Prospero Vallone. She had never forgotten meeting Cardinal Giannini's cousin at the Villa Robbiano that last happy summer before Delilah died. Later, William Partridge had written that Prospero had married an heiress and that his dazzling success had become the talk of Robbiano.

'Tell me more about this Vallone guy. I'm really interested,' said Cotton.

'He's not your stereotyped mobster. He comes from a family with mob connections, though. He's very slick, very smooth and moves in high circles. I think he's got the perfect front for a drugs racket.'

'The greed of some people makes me sick. Doesn't he have enough money?'

'I don't know. Maybe he wants more. Anyway, it's his wife who is loaded to the eyeballs, not him. Listen, you two, this is all confidential. It has to be kept under wraps until our investigation is concluded. But mark my words, I'll nail Vallone one day.'

'Surely he's just small fry,' Cotton commented disparagingly.

'Confucius say: If you want to catch barracuda, use small minnow,' remarked Herron, causing Biddle and Cotton to laugh.

'Yeah, Sheriff Easton always gets his man,' cracked Biddle.

After the laughter died down Cotton became aware that Biddle's brief burst of energy had left him exhausted and that Carol would be in soon to prepare him for the night. Rising, she said:

'I'm sorry to break this up, but I'm heading for bed.'

Herron said: 'Yes, I've got to get going too. I told mother I'd be home for a late supper. We've got a house full of relatives for the holiday.'

Cotton had never been to the famous Easton estate, The Lindens, but she had often passed the stone griffins that marked the vast property. The house was reputed to be one of the most magnificent on the North Shore.

'Goodbye, Biddle,' said Herron. 'Nice to see you, old buddy. I'll be over to see you again before I go back to Washington.' He touched Biddle's shoulder affectionately with his fist.

'It's been great talking to you, Herron. Let's have a couple of games of chess some time soon. I'll see if I can still beat you.'

'There's no doubt of that, I can tell you.'

Cotton leaned to kiss Biddle.

'Nighty night, Kiddo. I'll be along to see you in the morning.'

'Sweet dreams,' Biddle whispered in reply, his eyes drooping.

The wan smile on his ravaged face broke Cotton's heart. When she and Herron stood outside the door she pressed her lips together, trying not to cry.

'You were great,' he murmured, slipping his arm around her shoulder.

'So were you – so is he.' For an instant he held her fast, and she allowed herself to lean against his strength. When he released her she felt much better. 'Why him? Why?' she whispered, shaking her head.

'I wish I knew,' he replied. 'Jesus, Cotton – you've had a rough time. First your mother when you were a kid, and now this. I remember that day so well,' his voice trailed off. 'To lose two people you care deeply about a few years apart is a devastating blow. I know how close you are to Biddle. If there's anything I can do . . .'

'Thanks, Herron. Watching his face light up told me how much your being here tonight has meant to him,' she murmured, wiping her eyes.

She accompanied him to the landing where they watched waiters carrying trays of empty glasses from the living-room. Voices told them that the party was still in progress.

'Are you going down to join the fray?' he said.

'No, I don't think so.' A crazy idea had been forming in her mind and she wanted to be alone.

'Well, goodnight, Cotton,' said Herron as if reluctantly. He turned on the stairs. 'Say, are you going to be around New Year's Eve?'

'I'm planning to be back at Columbia by then.'

'The reason I asked is because my sister is giving a party at The Lindens. A few of my friends are coming up from Washington and there will be a lot of people from around here as well. You might bump into people you haven't seen for years.'

'I doubt that, Herron,' she said simply. 'Don't forget that I didn't go to Madeira or Foxcroft like Paige and your sister. I went to Oyster Bay High.' She smiled, not wanting him to think she had a chip on her shoulder.

'That doesn't matter. I mean, you might also meet some good contacts for later, people who could be useful to you.'

Catching the embarrassment in his voice, she was surprised that the mighty Herron was on shaky ground. His habitual smoothness had deserted him and he was searching for words. As the barriers dropped for an instant, she felt a little spark pass between them.

'It would be a lot of fun,' she said, wavering. 'The thing is, my room-mate and I had planned to go out on the town together.'

'Is the room-mate male or female?'

'Female, of course.'

'By all means bring her along. The more the merrier.'

'Thanks. I'm sure Chiquita would love it. In fact we both would.'

The moment she said goodbye to Herron, Cotton hurried upstairs to her room. Facing herself critically in the mirror, she said aloud:

'Is this the craziest idea you've ever had, or what?' But as she spoke she knew she had to do it. Her curiosity had been aroused by the news flash about Prospero Vallone, and she had a hunch that it would make a sensational story. Grabbing her coat and bag, she sprinted from the house down the back staircase.

She drove like a madwoman. Less than half-an-hour later she walked through the doors of Bellevue General Hospital's emergency ward. She had been there before and knew what to expect. It was always chaotic, no matter what time of day or night. Ambulances were continually screeching to a halt before the doors, their sirens screaming as desperate cases were rushed inside. The starkly lit rooms echoed with urgent voices and the rumbling of stretchers being pushed up and down the corridors by the porters. Cotton glanced from right to left at the less urgent cases slouched in chairs with bandages on their heads or hands. Children cried and anxious relatives paced the floor awaiting news from nurses and doctors coming up and down the corridors.

Adjusting the scarf she had tied over her head, Cotton approached the desk to await her turn. As she faced the matron, her face stricken, she said with the trace of an accent:

'I'm Mrs Prospero Vallone. I have come to see my husband.' As she spoke she prayed that the real Mrs Vallone hadn't yet appeared. Something about Cotton's dignified bearing seemed to keep the nurse from questioning her further.

'Mrs Vallone? Just a moment,' she replied, glancing down a roster. 'Your husband is in intensive care. His condition is listed as stable. He's come out of surgery and is in the recovery room now; but as soon as he's out I imagine the doctor will allow you to be at his side.' Her voice dropped as two men approached the desk. 'Those men are from the papers. Why don't you come with me and I'll get you out of here.'

The nurse was so solicitous that Cotton felt a pang of guilt. She took her to a private waiting-room and handed her a cup of coffee. After a while she returned.

'Mrs Vallone, your husband is in his room now and the doctor would like to have a word with you.'

She followed the nurse down a corridor where a doctor was waiting.

'How do you do, Mrs Vallone,' he said with a nod. 'Your husband is still in danger, but we're confident he'll pull through. He was shot three times in the chest and he's lucky to be alive. One bullet just missed his aorta.'

The nurse and doctor were regarding her intently.

'But who ...? Why ...?' Cotton choked with apparent emotion as she spoke.

'It seems they have no idea yet, but when we tell the police you're here they'll probably want to talk to you after you've seen your husband.'

'Oh, please, not tonight. I left the children alone – with a neighbour,' she said worriedly, wondering wildly if Prospero had any children.

'Don't worry. I'm sure they won't keep you any longer than necessary. Why don't you go in now?'

They admitted her to the room and closed the door quietly behind her. The figure of a powerfully built, dark-haired man attached to a life-support machine lay stretched out on the bed.

Certain it must be a criminal offence to impersonate the wife of a victim of attempted murder, Cotton slipped into a chair at Prospero's bedside, estimating she had five minutes or less to get the hottest story in New York.

It was the same Prospero Vallone, she realized, looking down at his muscular brown shoulders, his hairy chest half-concealed by a bandage that crossed one shoulder. He was on a drip, and a tube attached to his chest fed in blood from a bottle attached to the bed.

'Prospero – Prospero,' she whispered urgently, studying his face for signs of consciousness. Perspiration had collected on his upper lip and his breathing was uneven. At the sound of her voice he turned his head slightly.

'Prospero,' she repeated. 'Wake up. You're in Bellevue Hospital and somebody tried to kill you. Do you know who it was? Try and remember what happened.'

After a few seconds his lips began to move and he started to murmur incoherently.

'It was Tony . . . Tony. Can't believe . . .'

'Tony who? Who?'

'Fasso . . .' he said at last, forming the word with difficulty. His forehead creased in frustration, or was it anger? 'Gloves pulled the trigger. He did it . . .'

'Who is Gloves?' she said, amazed.

'Does Tony's work.' He peered in her direction with half-closed eyes without seeming to see.

'But why? Why did he do it, Prospero?'

'No dice . . . I said. No more deals. No good – the thing's too hot. It's over . . . finished.' He winced in pain.

'What deals? Tell me.' When he didn't answer she said: 'Who is Tony Fasso?' She reached out and enclosed Prospero's hand in hers for encouragement.

'My best friend. We used to shoot pool. Sorry – Elaine, sorry. I didn't call. He shot me – Gloves. Ghisela left me tonight. Sorry Elaine,' he repeated.

As he gripped her hand, Cotton realized Prospero thought she was someone else. If Ghisela was his wife, she figured Elaine was his girlfriend.

'I'll take you some place nice, later – okay?' he whispered.

'Sure you will, sure you will,' she replied, leaning closer. She succumbed to the urge to stroke his forehead and it seemed to soothe him. Her train of concentration was momentarily broken by his vulnerability. For a minute she forgot why she was there and was seized by tenderness for this man who was all but a stranger. As he clung to her hand in an almost childlike way a current of sympathy seemed to pass between them. Cotton was touched by the poignant irony that their lives had crossed a second time and that he would probably have no recollection of it.

'Is Tony with the mob, Prospero?'

Eyes closed, Prospero swallowed and coughed before replying, mumbling an affirmative.

'So you knew too much. Is that why they did it?'

Prospero began to breathe heavily as he struggled to reply. Uneasy, Cotton sat back sensing that his moment of lucidity had come and gone and that she was taking a big risk by staying any longer. Reluctantly she stood up, but before she left his bedside she impulsively leaned to kiss him on the cheek.

'Good luck – you're going to need it.' With that she walked to the door, pausing only to glance back at the unconscious Prospero.

Entering the hallway, Cotton looked obliquely to the right

and left as porters rushed past with patients in wheelchairs. She counted herself lucky that no one noticed her as she slipped past the desk and out of the door just as the victim of a traffic accident was wheeled in. The sight of so much blood made her feel physically ill for a few seconds, but the sharp night air brought her back to life.

'Mrs Vallone?' a voice called.

She was startled when a flashbulb popped in her face.

'*Daily News*,' said the photographer.

'Oh shit,' she murmured, hurrying on.

Not wanting to think what the consequences would be when her picture appeared in tomorrow's paper as Vallone's wife, she put her mind to the job ahead. She was already mentally sifting the scant information she had prised from Prospero into a substantial article, relying on the elements of research she had gathered for her thesis to fill in all the gaps. She ran towards her car, calculating that her story could make tomorrow's edition of *The New York Times*. It was a piece of news they were bound to print, she told herself, ripping the scarf from her head and fumbling for the car keys. She had good contacts at the newspaper, since writing a story about a fire in a big apartment block on Riverside Drive, and if the night editor balked she would talk him into it.

As she drove too quickly through the cold, dark streets, she recalled the night she had first met Prospero with startling clarity. The memory was tinged with the nostalgia that only loss and time can give. She rarely allowed herself to dwell sentimentally about her childhood, but for a moment she gave in. Those years had been her own Eden, and Delilah's death had marked the closing of the gates. The blast of Prospero's blue eyes as he had looked at her that night had imprinted Cotton with her first awareness of desire. Prospero had coloured her adolescent mind with its first erotic image, and now, years later, she was present as he hovered between life and death in a hospital.

When the image flickered and died, she deliberately swept all her emotion away, fully aware that from tomorrow morning she would become Prospero Vallone's enemy.

Chapter 16

On New Year's Eve, Cotton drove her Mustang slowly along Piping Rock Road, which was bordered by high walls protecting large estates.

'I think The Lindens is just around the next bend, though I haven't been along here in years,' she remarked to Chiquita, who gave a slow whistle.

'This sure is big bucks country.'

At the rustle of Chiquita's gold lamé and velvet dress, Cotton gave her room-mate a wry smile. 'I don't need headlights with that glitter you're wearing. The North Shore won't know what's hit it when you walk through the door.'

Chiquita giggled. 'Have I overdone the glitz?'

'You can't possibly overdo it as far as I'm concerned. But I'm afraid it will be wasted on the dried-up old fogies who are bound to be there. You deserve something better.'

'Ah, come on, you're depressing me. It can't be that bad, can it? I want a young preppie to dance me off my feet.'

'Live in hope, that's all I can say. Herron will be there, anyway, and he must have invited some halfway decent guys from Washington. If it's a disaster we can cut out early and find a disco back in town.'

'Old fogies, huh? In that case, why are you wearing your drop-dead-I'm-too-beautiful-for-you number?' Chiquita asked.

Cotton was wearing a shocking-pink dress with a chartreuse bow on one shoulder.

'I better warn you — you and I are going to stand out like a couple of Christmas tree ornaments. No doubt the women will all be in basic black or in long skirts and sweaters. And they won't wear any make-up or jewellery either – just a few discreet pearls.'

'Now you tell me,' groaned Chiquita with a mischievous grin. 'I couldn't help noticing your aunt tonight. Cotton, my old lady wouldn't be caught dead wearing a dress like that. She wouldn't have worn it twenty years ago, even. No wonder the rich get so filthy rich. They never spend a dime on themselves.'

'I remember my mother always used to say that just as youth is wasted on the young, so money is wasted on the rich. Truer words were never spoken.'

'Now I'm a nervous wreck,' said Chiquita. 'I mean, I like to make a splash, but I don't want to sink.'

'You? Sink? Believe me, you'll be the belle of the ball.' Cotton recalled the expression on Eleanor's face when Chiquita, her twenty-five-year-old Hispanic room-mate at Columbia, had arrived to stay the night at The Shallows. When they found themselves alone for a moment, Eleanor said with icy condescension:

'I don't know what you think you're trying to prove, Cotton. You never learn, do you? Always the rebel. Your friend will only be uncomfortable at The Lindens. Of course everyone there will be perfectly nice to her, but the poor girl will feel completely out of place. It's a cruel, tasteless joke on your part. What if she happens to be taken for a member of the cabaret?'

Cotton had suppressed her anger, saying nothing, a habit she had cultivated during her years with Eleanor. One of these days, she promised herself, she would cut loose and tell her aunt exactly what she thought of her just as she had done once before. The trouble was, she always came up with the perfect retort an hour later, after she had simmered down.

Austin had looked surprised when she had introduced the vivacious, dark Chiquita, but he had been polite. Biddle was the only well-bred member of the family. They had spent an hour with him before he was settled for the night, and he and Chiquita had hit it off immediately. For a while Biddle had seemed his old sparkly self. Cotton knew that if things had been different he should have been going with them to The Lindens to see in the New Year.

'I think I just passed it,' Cotton said, backing up a few feet. She turned the car through the open gates and followed the tail lights of a Mercedes up the private road. Her beat-up Mustang looked absurdly out of place among the line of expensive cars cruising towards the house.

'At least mine's paid for,' she remarked.

'Honey, so are theirs, don't worry,' Chiquita responded, and they both laughed. 'Nobody, but nobody is going to have as much fun as you and me tonight, and I mean it,' she vowed, catching sight of mink-covered shoulders in the car ahead. 'But what a drag I didn't have time to get my sable out of cold storage.'

The two of them howled with laughter as they crawled along the private road bordered with snow, past the spreading oaks and sycamores. The house came into view as they rounded a shrubbery.

'Wowee!' exclaimed Chiquita. 'Why didn't you tell me the *Queen Mary* was in dry dock on Long Island?'

'It's quite a sight, isn't it?'

The vast house rested like an ocean liner at sea in the spacious gardens, its tiers of illuminated windows like beacons in the clear, star-filled night. But, beautiful and grand as it was, Cotton felt The Lindens represented a world that had shut her out years ago. During her childhood as Delilah's adopted daughter, she had always been confident anywhere, but her rude awakening after Delilah's death had sent her in the opposite direction from the Herron Eastons of the world.

During all the years with the Townsends she had never lost the sense of being a poor relation, marking time until she was self-sufficient. It was strangely ironic, she thought as she watched the big cars discharging their passengers, that her childhood had been more glamorous and cosmopolitan than, perhaps, those of any of the women now climbing the wide staircase to the Easton house. Though Eleanor didn't realize it herself, Cotton knew she had as little in common with the Eastons' friends as Chiquita had.

When they entered the house, Cotton glanced at the crowd in the hall, but didn't see anyone she knew. She and Chiquita gave their coats to the English butler and paused for a moment in the huge pillared entrance hall echoing with voices. Cotton's gaze swept the floor, a mosaic of coloured marble as large as a skating rink and rose to take in the massive oak staircase which branched at the foot of a marble statue of Aphrodite. Lifting her eyes to the glass dome overhead, she could imagine light showering down in the daytime on the huge Chinese urns filled with blue hydrangeas on pedestals each side of the staircase.

'Let's go find the powder room,' Chiquita whispered, her stiletto heels clicking loudly on the marble.

'That's chickening out, and you know it,' replied Cotton, guiding her towards a pair of massive open doors.

'Okay, but here goes nothing,' Chiquita murmured as they paused at the threshold of the drawing-room where several dozen people had already gathered for drinks. There wasn't a sequin or rhinestone in sight, just a ripple of sombre colours, smooth pageboy haircuts, pearls and covered shoulders.

Cotton caught the startled looks on a few faces as she and Chiquita made their entrance. It was worth coming all the way out to the North Shore, she thought, just to feel like a parrot among penguins. Adopting a confident air, Cotton had to admit to herself that Eleanor was right: she was a bit of a rebel.

As soon as they had taken a glass of champagne from the waiter, Herron spotted them and threaded his way through the crowd. Cotton was struck again by how absurdly good-looking he was, especially in a dinner jacket.

'Cotton – it's wonderful to see you,' he said warmly, kissing her on the cheek. 'And this must be Chiquita. I'm delighted you could make it.'

'I'm delighted to be here,' she replied, shaking his hand. 'You live in a remarkable house, Mr Easton.'

'Please call me Herron, that is, if I can call you Chiquita.'

'Sure you can,' she said, with a big smile.

'Otherwise, Mr President or just plain Senator will do for him,' Cotton remarked to Herron's amusement. He at least showed only pleasure at seeing them.

As they joined the crowd, Cotton could see Chiquita blooming like a hothouse orchid. Not a man in the room was unaware of her lithe figure draped in gold lamé, her dark flashing eyes and her coffee-coloured shoulders gleaming in the soft lamplight. Cotton knew the two of them made a striking pair as she caught sight of their reflection in a mirror. Her own wheat-coloured hair was brushed rakishly to one side, revealing crystal heart earrings tied with pink bows; and she realized her own dress was the same riotous shade as the azaleas banked on the marquetry commodes. Looking up at the beautiful room full of people, she was suddenly pleased they had come. She had given Herron good marks for his warm welcome, and when his back was turned Chiquita caught her eye, casting a wink of approval in his direction.

Herron turned to them. 'I'd like you both to meet an old friend of mine – one of the brightest guys in Washington. He's just come back from Greece where he was political officer at the Embassy. Now he's been posted back here, which is a great boon as far as I'm concerned.'

'Hey, Herron, slow down – you're not running until 1990,' said Archie, with an infectious laugh.

Cotton was immediately taken by the balding, bespectacled Archie Bowles, who had a pleasant face and an engaging manner.

'You two should have a lot to talk about,' commented Cotton when they had all shaken hands. 'Chiquita's doing her PhD in Economics.' And, indeed, Chiquita and Archie were soon absorbed in conversation. Cotton found that she and Herron were studying one another.

'Well, well,' he said as their eyes locked. 'If it isn't that ace reporter, Miss Cotton Castello.'

She had to think for a moment. 'Oh, that. It all seems ages ago,' she said disparagingly, but secretly pleased. He must be referring to her story which had made the front page of *The New York Times* just before Christmas.

She looked at him innocently. 'Believe me, Herron, no one was more surprised than me to see my picture in the *Daily News* as Mrs Prospero Vallone. They were so keen to get their story out that they didn't even bother to check with their picture department, which didn't hurt me or my article – just the opposite.'

'Did you get a retraction?'

'I didn't ask for one,' she said with a shrug of her bare shoulders. 'There probably was one buried somewhere in the paper, I imagine. The real Mrs Vallone would have seen to that.'

'You cunning little fox,' he whispered, squeezing her elbow. 'You must have raced out of the house the minute I left the party and driven like hell into the city. You really had me hoodwinked about how tired you were – yawning and feigning exhaustion.'

'I was only doing my job, or what I hope will be my job. I thought I should start as I mean to go on. Journalism isn't like medical school where you have to wait until you get a diploma to do surgery.'

'No women's page for you, then? No gossip column or fashion?'

She looked at him witheringly.

'Forget that remark. It was very condescending.'

'Don't worry – you don't have to do any campaigning with me,' she replied with a knowing smile. 'I'm aiming for that big wide world out there. Think of all those far-flung postings, from China to Chad, just waiting to be filled.'

'The wide world is where she came from, and that's where she's bound for,' he said thoughtfully, his eyes moving over her.

'Who said that?' she asked, sipping her champagne.

'I did. America will be very sorry to lose you, Cotton.'

He was flirting outrageously and Cotton's eyes never left his face. 'How very nice of you to say so,' she responded, meaning it.

When Herron's attention was diverted, she took the chance to study the room with its huge chandelier. The gleaming parquet floor laid with Chinese carpets and the rose silk walls made a luxurious backdrop for velvet sofas. Priceless porcelain was on display in antique French cabinets and on console tables.

But most astonishing of all was the collection of Impressionist paintings hung around the room. Their gauzy light and the shattered brilliance of their colours took her breath away. Looking at them made her recall going with Delilah to the Jeu de Paume in Paris in the old days.

'I had no idea you had such a collection,' she nodded towards the paintings when Herron came back to her.

'Gramps bought them when they were affordable. It was quite thoughtful of him, don't you think?'

'I should say so.'

'Yes, old Percy was no dummy. He also had the shrewdness to marry the most beautiful girl in Pittsburgh, Florence Caldwell. It was a great match. She had breeding and beauty, he had the dough.'

The way his eyes rested on her made Cotton wonder for one wild moment if he was making some sort of subtle suggestion. 'Now I think of it, I don't believe I've seen a collection like this in a private house since I lived in Florence,' she remarked.

'You're a woman of many parts, aren't you, Cotton? I'm impressed. One minute you're dicing with death with the mob, the next you're regarding pictures with the eyes of a connoisseur.' Fixing his eyes on her sternly, he said: 'What you did at Bellevue was very dangerous in more ways than one. You know that, don't you? Somebody might have bumped you off.'

'Unlikely.'

'Maybe, but be careful. Or don't you like being careful? No, I suspect you don't. You obviously thrive on excitement.'

'It gives me a kick. I guess I have the need to be first, that's all.'

'Were you always like that?'

'No, I don't think I was,' she replied thoughtfully. 'I fell to the bottom of the heap once in my life and now I rather enjoy climbing back up on my own.'

'A sentiment I share. I want the top job in Washington.'

'So I've heard. Can I have your first interview when you're elected?'

'That's a deal. I never forget a promise.'

'Fine. I'll keep you to it. By the way, I thought you might be interested to know that Prospero Vallone is threatening to sue me. I got a letter from his lawyers.'

'He didn't waste any time, did he? I'll bet he was in a rage when he found out what happened. Watch out he doesn't put out a contract on you.'

'He'd rather kill my bank balance. I'm afraid he won't get very far. Maybe I should apologize.' There was a mischievous gleam in her eye.

'Don't bother. I'll have him behind bars soon.'

'I wouldn't be too hard on him. From what he told me when he was delirious, I'm sure he's innocent.'

'Like hell,' he retorted, with a determined set of his jaw.

She had a quick, powerful image of Prospero lying helplessly at the Bellevue General Hospital, then swallowed her absurd plea for mercy. She didn't feel like his enemy, but like a friend he didn't know he had.

'We'll talk about this some other time,' she said.

'Yes, ma'am,' Herron replied, touching his hand to his forehead. 'Come on,' he continued, taking her hand. 'I want to introduce you to my mother and sister.'

Later they passed on to the dining-room where the long table draped in damask and lace was set for thirty-six people invited for dinner before the dance began. Here was unabashed luxury, Cotton reflected, curling her hands around a Chippendale chair when she had found her place card. Pink camellias bloomed richly between an artillery of silver and porcelain. The glasses were of crystal and a gold-embossed menu lay beside every place. Delilah had instilled a love of fine things in her which Cotton had all but forgotten these past years and, as she soaked up the heady atmosphere in the sumptuous dining-room, she felt her appreciation spring involuntarily to life again. Cotton's eyes fastened on the portraits of women which hung on the deep green walls, obviously former chatelaines of The Lindens. In their ballgowns and jewels, they looked as if they inhabited a world created solely for their amusement. For an instant she wondered what it would have been like to be one of them.

Near midnight, Cotton was dancing with Archie Bowles to a combo in the gilded ballroom lined with mirrors.

'What are your plans after Columbia?' he asked, as a trumpet crooned 'Cheek to Cheek'.

'There's the small matter of finding a job.'

'I don't know if you'd be interested, but my uncle owns the *Washington Herald*.'

'Only mildly interested,' she said, deeply impressed. 'You're *that* Bowles, are you?'

'That's right. I'll have a word with unc if you want me to,' he said cheerily.

'Wouldn't that be going out on a limb?' she teased. 'After all, you hardly know anything about me.'

'I know a thing or two. I know you're gorgeous, and that you have a mind like a steel trap.'

She laughed uninhibitedly. 'Where did you get that idea?'

'Herron. He and I have been talking about your escapade last week. I was mightily impressed, and I think my uncle would blow his stack if I didn't do a bit of private recruiting for the family business now I've got the chance.'

'You're serious, aren't you? You really mean it,' she said, amazed.

'You got it. I'm serious. I'm also mildly inebriated and completely infatuated with that gorgeous girlfriend of yours over there,' he said, nodding towards Chiquita who came dancing by with Herron.

'Hey, it's nearly midnight,' called Herron over his shoulder. 'What do you say we change partners?'

Cotton found herself in Herron's arms. By the look on Chiquita's face, Cotton realized she was just as smitten as Archie was. The crowd parted as they began to jitterbug madly.

'I don't believe it,' said Cotton. 'It's Tina Turner meets Arthur Schlesinger.'

He threw back his head and laughed. 'Right – you got it!' he exclaimed, whirling her around.

As the orchestra broke into 'Auld Lang Syne' a huge net of balloons was released from the ceiling.

'What a way to begin the eighties,' cried Cotton, reaching out to grab a balloon.

'And what a way to begin a relationship,' Herron countered, as he pulled her close.

Chapter 17

On a rainy April day Prospero stared from the speeding limousine at the blossoming cherry trees lining the Potomac as he listened to the droning voice of his lawyer.

'The main thing is to keep your replies short and sweet. If you remember that you won't have a problem,' said Walter Lowe. 'I feel good about the whole thing, really. We've played every card, and now we can't stall any further, so just relax and enjoy the show, okay?'

Prospero caught the reflection of Walter's bald head and fleshy face in the window. He had never liked his lawyer personally, but something in his shrewd dark eyes and aggressive manner inspired confidence. During the last few months the two of them had spent uncounted hours conferring together, building his case. Walter now knew almost everything about him as he battled to stave off a subpoena from the investigation committee in Washington.

'Heard from Ghisela?'

'She called me this morning from Geneva to wish me luck.'

'Did she? That's great. She's a real credit to you, Prospero. She's a lady, and that image can only do you good. Believe me, some of the broads my clients hook up with – I'd do anything to keep them out of sight. I'm glad you two patched up everything finally. Sometimes it takes a crisis like this to knit a relationship back together.'

Prospero sat in stony silence, resenting his familiarity. Walter

Lowe presumed to know the truth about his marriage, but in fact he knew absolutely nothing.

When he had come out of hospital, Ghisela had returned to New York, ostensibly to pack up and then go back to Switzerland. She had been deeply awed by the ten-inch scar on his chest, and he found it strangely ironic that the violence which nearly cost him his life had changed her mind about separation and divorce. He had responded by making love to her with a fierce new passion, which in retrospect he knew was a reaffirmation of his will to live. He was determined to reknit their relationship the way it was in the beginning. During the process of reconciliation he acquired the habit of holding back part of himself, realizing that Ghisela didn't want, didn't need the warm and tender side of his nature which he longed to express. After his brush with death and nearly losing Ghisela, the brute edge of his character had reasserted itself. He had been like that in the old days, he now realized; tough, sure of himself, uncompromising; and he would be that way from now on.

'So, you're going back to the old country,' Walter said. 'Can't say I blame you. You can raise your kids there with no drugs, no violence. Life is less competitive. I envy you, really.'

'There's smog in Rome and Milan, and there are drugs. And life is all about competition,' replied Prospero contradicting Walter's notion of the mandolin-playing, spaghetti-eating Italians. He was impatient to arrive as he caught sight of the Capitol etched against the grey sky ahead. 'By the way,' he said abruptly, 'I'm resigning from Schmidt as soon as all this is over.'

'Good. Glad to hear it. But take my advice and wait until this whole thing dies down a bit, or it might look funny.'

'If it does die down,' Prospero pointed out. He didn't share Walter's buoyant optimism.

'Sure it will die down. You're not what they're after. They put out a wide net and the small fish got through the holes. When Herron Easton has flexed his muscles so all the potential voters can see what a hero he is, then it'll blow over.' Walter patted his briefcase. 'That cv looks pretty good. It spells out how you've been giving to all those charities for years – Boys'

Club in Brooklyn, the Italian earthquake fund, that Catholic charity. That's not to mention the individual incidences of generosity we were able to cite. I laid it on thick about your widowed mother living in Italy, your two brothers and their families you help to support. It's lucky you kept your private life clean. If Herron Easton tries character assassination, he'll have a tough time.'

'It might make it look as if you're trying too hard to paint me as some sort of humanitarian, which I'm not.'

'Sure you are – you're more of a humanitarian than any of those guys on the committee. Before you're through they'll give you the Presidential Medal of Freedom.' Walter gave a chuckle.

'Well, I won't be here to collect it. I'll be in Rome by then,' Prospero observed drily.

'We'll just have to make sure this whole thing is cleared up in one session so you can get on with your life. If we run into trouble you can always turn State's evidence.'

'Forget it,' Prospero responded vehemently. He thought of Tony Fasso, now in gaol for an offence unrelated to attempted murder or drugs and still able to move people like pawns if he chose to do so.

'Okay, okay, so what do we have to worry about, anyway?' said Walter jovially.

Prospero had never felt so alone in his life as in the moment when he got out of the car and faced the entrance to the Justice Building. Walter forged ahead, holding up his hand to fend off a few reporters outside the door. There was a scuffle as the newsmen fired questions at Prospero.

'No comment,' said Walter, hustling his client through the door.

They were ushered down an echoing hallway, and Prospero's face registered contempt as he identified Herron Easton standing outside the door of the hearing room in conference with another member of the committee.

'That's Easton,' muttered Walter through his teeth.

Prospero felt his stomach twist at the sight of Herron's unmistakably patrician bearing. Everything about him suggested privilege, power and confidence.

Prospero and Walter walked into the hearing room and took their places in the arena of chairs around a big table on which stood several microphones. Prospero suddenly thought of Cotton Castello, the muckraker who had barged into his hospital room when he was fighting for his life. He had heard only the week before that she was engaged to marry Herron Easton which, he reflected with bitter irony, was a perfect match.

'I want you to step up the suit against that Castello woman,' he muttered to Walter.

'Let's get this over with first.'

Herron seated himself at the table, followed by his aides. He brushed back his shock of brown hair, a self-important gesture which irritated Prospero. The craving for vengeance ignited in him. Some day, he promised himself, he would confront Cotton Castello and ask her what she and her boyfriend had against him; and if he ever had the chance he would punch that smug bastard Easton on the nose.

He waited impatiently for nearly an hour until the preliminaries of the hearing had been completed. By the time he was called to speak, Prospero was beginning to look forward to crossing swords with Herron Easton. Squaring his shoulders, he made his way unhurriedly to the chair, knowing he looked good in a dark suit, a white shirt and a conservative tie. He was acutely aware of the stares of men who had all the power of the government behind them; but it was Herron's unclouded gaze he sought out. Folding his hands on the table in front of him, Prospero waited for Herron to begin.

'Mr Vallone, do you know Gus Moretti?'

'No.'

'You mean you've never met him or heard of him?'

'No, I haven't,' he reaffirmed. His thoughtful expression gave no clue that he knew Gus was a friend of Tony's in the Teamsters' Union, who had squared off everything with the drivers in the warehouses.

'Let me mention a few other names of people you might have met, or at least who might be familiar to you: Solomon Linsky, for example.'

'No, it doesn't ring a bell.'

'What about Jug d'Amato?'

He shook his head. 'No, never heard of him.'

Herron's brow puckered in a frown. 'You must have heard of Bill Bonomo. He is a well-known member of a Mafia family, and this committee would find it very hard to believe you've never heard of him.'

'I might have seen his name in the papers.'

'But you've never met Bill Bonomo in person?'

'As I said, I read about him maybe in the papers.'

'What did you read about him?'

'I can't recall.' His eyes automatically sought out Walter, whose face was blotted out by blinding overhead lights.

'Do you know anybody who is a member of Cosa Nostra, or a member of what is called "the mob", or the Mafia?'

'No. At least, not to my knowledge.' Prospero's pulse was racing and he could feel pinpricks of anxiety at the back of his neck as Herron pressed harder.

'But you do know what the Mafia is. You are of Italian descent, Mr Vallone, and the committee is aware of that.'

'I've heard of it, sure. Who hasn't?'

'Strange, your father is reputed to have been killed by the Mafia, and yet you don't know much about it!'

'That was never proved. There is no evidence of who murdered my father,' he replied angrily. At the mention of his father, hatred ripped through his composure.

'All right, let's try another name. What about Tony Fasso? I think you know him.'

'Yes, I know him. We grew up in the same neighbourhood.'

Herron leaned across the table. 'You know that Tony Fasso is in gaol?'

'So I heard.'

'This committee wants to interview Tony Fasso about several matters in connection with drug trafficking. He has been arrested several times in the past for related offences.'

'He was never convicted.'

'That is true.'

'I'm a personal friend of his. I know nothing about his

business interests,' replied Prospero evenly, determined to hold his ground.

'When you first came back to New York after a prolonged absence from this country you didn't see Tony Fasso for at least eighteen months and yet you say you're a friend. What made you resume contact with him?'

Prospero shrugged. 'I can't remember. I must have run into him somewhere. I have no recollection of how we got together.'

'And yet, this committee has been informed that there was a disappearance of a large quantity of pharmaceuticals from your company, mainly outdated antibiotics, not long after our sources say you resumed contact with Fasso. Don't you think that is a strange coincidence?'

'I don't see why,' Prospero replied, his mind racing ahead. The news about the discovery of the missing drugs came as a shock.

'This committee has evidence that Tony Fasso, via mob channels, was involved in the theft of outdated drugs that were repackaged and then sold to Third World countries.'

Prospero remained silent, his brow knitted. He had the sensation of falling, but got a grip on himself. He braced himself for the next question.

'Do you know anything about the disappearance of drugs worth millions from the Schmidt warehouses in Brooklyn?'

'I know nothing. This is the first time I've heard of it,' he said. His ignorance appeared genuine.

'Our evidence comes directly from company sources. And yet, you are an executive vice-president at Schmidt, answering directly to your father-in-law, Otto Schmidt, the major stockholder who lives in Switzerland. It's hard to believe you're unaware of this, unless you are remiss in your job.'

Prospero thought quickly. 'I doubt the veracity of what you have just said. All expired drugs are destroyed as a matter of routine.'

'Should be destroyed, but not if they are stolen.'

Herron reached for his notes. 'At this time, I'd like to bring to the committee's attention the damage done by this kind of trafficking in outdated drugs in Third World countries. The human suffering it causes sick people who are duped into thinking they are getting effective treatment is difficult to exaggerate. The proud name of a great international industry, of the United States itself, is being dirtied by practices which have enriched a few unscrupulous people.'

Prospero listened, his fingers locked, his eyes blank. He was forced to sit in uneasy silence as Herron passed oblique judgement, knowing he would have no right of reply. He wanted to say that the expiry date on drugs was grossly extended, that they were effective long beyond their shelf life; that these drugs were better than no drugs at all; that people got them cheaper because the brand name was effaced; that they went through swift black market channels much of the time, avoiding corrupt bureaucracy in poor nations. His self-justification stuck in his throat as Herron hammered away.

Prospero felt only contempt for Herron Easton's arrogance. He had been born into a privileged family where struggle was unknown. He could afford to devote his life to the ego-building pastime of politics, and he had conveniently forgotten the origins of the Easton fortune which had been founded on trade monopolies and the exploitation of immigrant labour. Prospero told himself that all he had done was to put out his foot to tilt a fortune his way. To do otherwise would have been foolish.

Later, Prospero and Walter left the hearing and hurried to the waiting limousine to avoid reporters. As they drove away, Walter sighed with relief.

'I think it went off very well, don't you? You really behaved yourself, Prospero. Congratulations. I don't think they'll get anywhere. You kept your cool completely under fire – especially that bombshell about the missing drugs. Wonder who tipped them off? I think a complete denial was the only answer. Which is what you did – good work.'

'I don't know who's behind it, but I'll find out,' Prospero said, a dangerous edge to his voice. And yet, as he spoke, he knew he would avoid the issue. All he wanted now was to leave New York behind him, to start life again.

'You know, for a minute there when Easton was interrogating you about your father I thought you'd spring across the table and get him by the throat,' Walter chuckled.

Prospero stared ahead as the limousine sped past the famous monuments of Washington. In the aftermath of the hearing, he felt no release from the tension coiled inside him.

'When all this mess is cleared up you can start again. You're a born fighter, a winner. You can't keep a good guy down, and anyway, success is the best revenge.'

Prospero thought to himself that he wasn't so sure.

'In the meantime, I want you to sue the pants off Miss Cotton Castello.'

Chapter 18

NICARAGUA

'I see Jim is catching a well-earned catnap in the back seat,' remarked the *Newsweek* correspondent, Mitch Halverson, to Cotton. He glanced at Jim in the rearview mirror, but his eyes darted everywhere, looking for danger in the sleepy village through which they were passing.

Cotton, who was sitting beside Mitch, stirred and glanced over her shoulder.

'Poor guy. He's exhausted,' she said, stifling a yawn herself.

'You'd think he was the one who was hung over! Hey, you're missing some great scenery, Jimbo. We're passing another banana plantation,' called Mitch.

'Hush – don't wake him up. He needs to be bright-eyed and bushy-tailed when we get to Matagalpa.' The hot air pouring through the vents of the old Chevrolet made her eyes droop, and she blinked to stay alert.

'You should have come with us to that club last night,' said Mitch. 'It's a great place. I'll take you there when we get back.'

'I'm glad I played it smart if looking at you two is anything to go by,' she said with a sidelong smile. Mitch's eyes were bloodshot and he had cut his chin shaving.

'Do I look that bad?' he said, squinting at his reflection in the rearview mirror.

'You look even worse. I hate to tell you . . .'

'But you have to be brutally honest,' Mitch added, and they

laughed. 'Well, you don't look rough. You look as if you slept like a baby.'

He cast her a complimentary glance. In a T-shirt and canvas trousers, her hair caught in a pony-tail, she looked like a teenager. 'Let's make a date now for tomorrow night. How about it?'

'If you let me read your stories before you file them, then it's a deal.'

'I'm going to hold you to it,' he warned.

'I can't wait.'

They changed the subject to the latest skirmishes between government troops and the guerrillas as they passed through another village lined with low stucco houses painted in bright colours, their doorways edged in white. Mitch slowed the car down as a sow and a litter of piglets crossed the road. Dogs barked, children scattered and women turned to stare as they drove through the town.

'How much further?' murmured Jim sleepily.

'About another hour. Man, I need a beer, I can tell you.'

When Cotton pushed open the side window she was rewarded by a blast of hot air on her face, which was already covered in a film of perspiration though it wasn't yet ten o'clock. As she observed the rich green countryside rolling towards a ridge of blue hills, she twiddled the engagement ring she wore on a chain round her neck. She hadn't wanted to leave it behind in Washington, so she took it with her on her first assignment for the *Herald*; but the heirloom solitaire would have looked ridiculous with jeans and a T-shirt. It had all happened so fast that at times the ring seemed the only tangible proof that she was engaged to Herron Easton. They had conducted their romance in high gear in the same way they pursued their careers, jetting between Washington and New York whenever their commitments allowed.

'It will get cooler as we start to climb,' Mitch remarked.

'If you want, I'll drive next time we stop. Then the two of you can catch up on your sleep.'

'I won't say no. I'll stop in a few more miles when we reach the next village. Okay?'

'Sure,' she agreed, conscious that on her first assignment she didn't want anyone to think she wasn't pulling her weight. If she wanted to be one of the boys among journalists, she couldn't allow anyone to buy her drinks or carry her bags, or open doors without returning the favour. After trying to turn up human interest stories in the capital, she had welcomed the chance to get out of Managua with Jim and Mitch to gather hard news about the civil war between the Somoza government and the Sandinista rebels. Cotton was acutely aware she would be under the scrutiny of two old pros during the journey. She kept quiet most of the time, content to absorb their fund of information.

She had gone to great lengths to conceal her engagement to Herron Easton, whose name was bound to be familiar. She knew instinctively that some of the other journalists there to cover the outbreaks of violence might not take her seriously if they knew. She risked being labelled as a rich man's future wife, there to amuse herself until the big day when she became Mrs Easton. She was also very careful to keep it quiet that Archie Bowles had pulled strings with his uncle to land her a job on the *Herald*, information that wouldn't go down well with seasoned correspondents who had climbed up the hard way. It was her intention to write a series of bracing articles highlighting the disastrous consequences of US involvement in Nicaragua, and to earn quick recognition for herself. Only when she had won her stripes in a battle zone would she claim to be a correspondent.

Later, Cotton was at the wheel of the Chevrolet as they approached Matagalpa. Jim and Mitch stopped their wisecracks, and they all fell silent as they passed through the town, its houses and buildings marked by shelling. The streets were nearly deserted and the shutters of the houses were tightly closed. No one said it, but Cotton knew they were all thinking of the A B C correspondent who had been shot in Managua the week before. Entering a dense tunnel of trees, Cotton braked suddenly when she saw a group of government soldiers.

Mitch sat up abruptly. 'Is that a roadblock ahead?'

'No, it looks as if there's been a skirmish,' said Jim, leaning forward to peer through the windscreen as he cocked his camera.

'They're waving us on,' said Cotton. 'Should I stop and pretend I don't understand?'

'Not unless you want a sten gun shoved in your face. Just cruise by as slowly as you can while I get some pictures.'

Suddenly they were in the thick of frenzied activity. Soldiers, who were dragging bodies from the road and into a truck, turned as the car flying a white flag and painted with 'PRENSA' drove by. The road was streaked with blood pouring from five dead men, none of them over twenty.

'Look –' Cotton cried. 'Red bandanas – they're wearing red bandanas. Those boys are Sandinistas.' The camera clicked repeatedly in her ear as Mitch waved the flag out of the window to distract the commandant who was angrily gesturing them on.

She watched the soldiers disappear from the rearview mirror as she accelerated slowly. Her knees had gone weak and she realized she was shaking in spite of herself. It was the first time she had seen bloodshed since her arrival in the country – or anywhere, for that matter, and the sickening brutality of war hit her forcefully.

'How many bodies did you count, Jim?' asked Mitch. 'I reckon there must have been seven or eight of them. I think I spotted a couple in the truck.'

'I don't want to be here when this whole thing blows sky high, I can tell you. And it's going to blow up any minute. I can smell it,' he muttered, wiping the sweat from his face.

'Even the trees seem to have eyes,' Mitch said with a hollow laugh, as he glanced at the lush, tangled landscape through which they were travelling. 'I'll be glad to get to Matagalpa.'

They continued for a few more miles until the brilliant sun flashing through the shadows became almost hypnotic.

'Uh-oh, roadblock ahead,' announced Cotton, gripping the wheel so tightly her knuckles went white. 'I'll have to stop.'

'Just don't stop too close. They get upset,' Jim muttered. 'Get that flag out of the window, quick. They're bound to be trigger happy after what happened down the road.'

Cotton brought the car to a halt ten yards or so away from the truck where a dozen armed soldiers were waiting for them.

'Give me your press cards,' muttered Mitch.

'I'm going with you,' said Jim. 'Safety in numbers.'

'In that case, we'll all go,' said Cotton.

'No, you stay behind the wheel, so you can start up the car the minute they've checked our ID.'

As Cotton watched Jim and Mitch walk towards the road-block with their hands up they appeared perfectly at ease, but she knew that the death of the ABC correspondent the week before, in similar circumstances, was on their minds. Sweat trickled down her neck and back and her heartbeat sounded in her ears. She watched anxiously while Jim and Mitch lowered their hands and gave their passports and press cards to the soldiers who then frisked them. Her eyes moved over the soldiers for any signs of a gun being raised while the one in charge fired questions at Mitch in Spanish. She saw him shrug and smile, gesturing to the press car. Her heart sank as it began to look as though they would have to give up and return to the capital. Finally Cotton could stand it no longer, and got out of the car. Her Spanish was much better than either Jim's or Mitch's, and if there was a problem she thought she might have a better chance of straightening it out. She had only taken a couple of tentative steps forward when she saw a movement out of the corner of her eye. Then one of the soldiers swivelled his gun as if bracing himself for attack. She experienced the next few seconds in flashes of colour as a violent explosion rent the air. Green for the trees, red for blood, blue, the colour of the sky as she fell, cut by a quick image of Jim and Mitch thrown into the air like rag dolls. Screaming soldiers fell forward within a swirling cloud of smoke as a curtain of darkness engulfed her.

NEW YORK

The muted echo of Park Avenue traffic seeped through the double windows, reaching Prospero in his study where, casually dressed in a white polo shirt and light trousers, he sat at a makeshift table piled with papers. He could sense the punishing heat of July that held the city in its grip as he glanced at the wedge of yellowish-blue sky between two buildings. The unmistakable colour presaged a heatwave and reminded him vividly of growing up in Brooklyn. It was going to be the kind of scorcher when women would sit on the stoops of the apartment houses fanning themselves as they gossiped. Closing his eyes, Prospero could imagine himself walking through waves of heat past buildings with all the windows flung open to admit the slightest breeze. The air would smell of melting asphalt and faintly of rotting rubbish and exhaust, and the sounds of boys playing ball games would bounce off the buildings. He could see himself walking towards the entrance of the family's apartment, looking forward to the coolness as he opened the oak and glass doors to a lobby that gave off the inviting aroma of polish mixed with the suggestion of supper cooking somewhere. On the way in he would have caught sight of the fire-escape where he and his brothers dragged their bedding on nights when it was too hot to sleep indoors. He still remembered the pleasure of those hot nights, whispering with his brothers when they should have been asleep.

The muted whine of a siren brought him back to the present, and Prospero found he was smiling. His nostalgia faded as he tapped his pencil thoughtfully on the pad of paper in front of him. He jotted down some notes, adding to those already crowding the paper. Tearing off the sheet, he started with a fresh page, intending to distil all he had written that morning into the simply worded principles that would govern his life for the next year. Number one, the baseline from which the rest would be accomplished, was to move from the flat on Park Avenue, and the bare study was evidence that this had nearly been accomplished. The packers had been there for several days and all that remained in the flat were the bare essentials and cartons containing items too precious to send to Geneva by sea, such as Ghisela's collection of jade figures, the Limoges porcelain, the silver and the paintings.

Prospero jotted down the second item on his list with an

aggressive flourish, his resignation from Schmidt. After the hearings in Washington, Otto Schmidt had threatened to fire his son-in-law rather than allow him to resign, even suggesting he would press criminal charges. Ghisela's pleading had been useless, and Otto Schmidt had remained adamant until several weeks later when Ghisela announced she was pregnant. Unable to express the impotent rage he felt against Schmidt, Prospero consoled himself with the fact that to protect his daughters, and to ensure his reconciliation with Ghisela, he had to submit with good grace, but the humiliation had taught him a lesson and he renewed his determination to win his independence at any cost.

As he concentrated, Prospero's mind worked on two levels. Whenever he thought of the baby Ghisela was expecting joy leapt inside him. He glanced at his watch, acutely aware that at any moment she would come through the door of the apartment bearing the results of the scan she had had earlier in the week. With increasing anxiety, Prospero realized that he would soon know whether their child would be healthy, and if it was the son he had longed for, conceived during the catharsis he had experienced after his brush with death.

Forcing himself back to work, he applied his energy to finishing the simple diagram that had occupied the morning. The prospect of a son had filled him with the determination to strike out on his own, and this led him to the next item on his list. With a sure stroke he noted the intention to sell his block of shares in Schmidt, something he had vowed he would never do. The shares were part of his son Alessandro's patrimony – he had decided to call his son Alessandro after two heroes: Alexander the Great, and his father, Franco Alessandro Vallone, who had conquered his fears and emigrated to America to start a new life. There would be new worlds for Alessandro Vallone to conquer, and anyway, Prospero reasoned, one day the boy would inherit his mother's money and interest in Schmidt so that he would never miss the shares his father might have given him.

He had chafed at first at having had to buy Schmidt shares as all vice-presidents were required to do, but now he was grateful. They had appreciated many times over and with the proceeds he planned to invest in Dalby computers, shares which were expected to soar when an acquisition bid was announced within a month. Once he had bought the shares in Dalby and reaped the profits of a quick resale, he would have substantial capital to cushion him while he established his foothold in Europe. It wasn't much of a gamble, he calculated, certain the tip he had received on Dalby was from an impeccable source.

The next step in his strategy, Prospero could define in one word: gold. When he got to Geneva where he and Ghisela were planning to spend August with the girls, he intended to invest all the money he had earned with Tony Fasso in the gold market, make a quick killing and get out. Risky and unpredictable as the market was, the temptation was too strong to resist, and it could net him a lot of money fast.

Leaning back in his chair, Prospero bit his pencil thoughtfully before making the final entries on his list. When he had survived the first three hurdles he would be ready to think big. That would be the moment to invest in London property, tipped to soar within the next few years, and then to set himself up in Italy. The first step would be a summit meeting with his two brothers, Roberto and Enrico, both poised to join him in the company that would be known as Vallone Enterprises. They had already chosen their first venture – a small container company with a huge growth potential where Enrico had worked as an accountant, and which the owners were offering at a vastly undervalued price. Roberto, whom Prospero had financed while he studied international law, would be a vital link in the chain. Together, the three brothers would build a business empire, arms linked, backs touching, their eyes trained outwards. The image appealed to Prospero and he had already incorporated the idea of their partnership into a logo for Vallone Enterprises, a triangle with an interlocking circle.

After he had finished mapping out his plans, Prospero remained in deep thought, his hands locked behind his head as he regarded a shaft of sunlight, illuminating the wall of the study. The plan he had composed in his bold handwriting seemed deceptively simple, but it was the distilled essence of all his successes and failures and represented a blueprint for his future independence. He was both proud and daunted as he thought how absurdly simple it had been to reduce all his ambitions to a few taut phrases, but he regarded it as a way of proving to himself that his plan was realizable. He told himself that he didn't need to be a graduate of Harvard Business School to see that the key to any successful enterprise was to reduce it to its manageable components. Now, here before him lay the theoretical outline of everything he dreamed of. All it took to implement his plan was a bit of luck, and the courage that he knew he possessed.

When he detected the sound of a key turning in the front door, Prospero rose quickly from his chair.

'Ghisela, is that you?' he called, striding down the hall.

'Yes, it's me,' she replied, depositing a Sak's bag on the marble tiles.

In spite of the wilting heat she appeared cool in a pale blue cotton dress trimmed in white piqué, her waist encircled by a wide belt and showing no sign she was four months' pregnant. Only the faintest trace of perspiration shone on her upper lip and her blonde hair was coiled in an immaculate chignon that revealed the nape of her neck which he kissed lightly. At his touch she moved away, brushing her hand tiredly over her forehead.

'Well? What did the doctor say?' Prospero asked anxiously, following her into the empty living-room piled with cartons and boxes.

When she saw them, Ghisela said irritably, 'Haven't the packers come for the air freight yet?'

'No – they called and said the inventory wasn't completed for the insurance papers that I have to sign. When it's ready this afternoon they'll bring it with them to save time. Anyway, who cares about that – ' he said abruptly. Sensing she was teasing him he smiled and caught her wrist. 'Come on and tell me what the doctor said.' His face darkened when she didn't reply. 'There's nothing wrong, is there?'

A little cat-like smile softened her face as she arched her back in a stretch. 'It's so hot and the traffic was terrible. It's nice and cool in here. I'll close the curtains against the glare.'

As she moved away he was close on her heels. 'Ghisela, what are you trying to do, drive me crazy? Are you all right? Is the baby all right? Tell me, *cara*, before I explode!' He threw his hands up in exasperation as he watched her methodically close the filmy sage green curtains, pleasantly dimming the room. Looking over her shoulder, Ghisela said laconically,

'Calm down, will you? Give me a chance to speak. Yes, the doctor said that everything is fine. I'm fine, the baby is fine. It looks like he might be a Christmas baby.'

Elation shot through Prospero. 'He? Did you say he? Is it definitely a boy?'

'Of course. There's no mistake. It will be a boy,' she said with a satisfied smile, amused at the expression on his face.

With a howl of joy, Prospero dashed towards Ghisela and scooped her up in his arms. Galvanized by the almost super-human strength her news had given him, he whirled her round exuberantly. When he stopped he clasped her to him, his elation dissolving to tenderness as he kissed her repeatedly. He was filled with renewed strength to face the difficult months ahead.

'A son – you're giving me a son, my precious wife,' he murmured. 'This is the happiest day of my life.'

She gave a little laugh, allowing him to smother her with affection for a moment, though not reciprocating his emotion. None the less, she seemed to be enjoying his adula-tion. For an instant she looked as happy as he had ever seen her, a realization that prompted him to dance her around the room.

'Stop, stop,' she cried breathlessly. 'Please, I'm feeling dizzy.' With a laugh she added, 'You'd think that no one had ever given birth to a son before!'

He let her go. 'I'm sorry, I guess I went crazy,' he said, amused at himself. 'I didn't hurt you, did I?'

'No, no,' she said over her shoulder as she walked from the room.

'Come and sit down for a while and let's talk. What's your hurry? I'll get you something cold to drink.' As the thought of the baby hit him again he pounded one fist into the other in jubilation.

'I told the driver to wait downstairs. I've decided to go out to The Hamptons early to avoid the weekend traffic.'

'No – wait, I've got a much better idea. Why not stay in town tonight and drive out with me tomorrow morning? Sophia and Elysia are fine with the nanny. One night won't make any difference, will it? Tonight is very special. I want us to be alone. We'll go out somewhere to celebrate. Say you will,' he added when he sensed her wavering. The power within his blue eyes told her what it meant to him.

What Prospero wanted more than anything was to lie for hours holding her next to him, to stroke her swelling stomach, though he would never have suggested it, knowing Ghisela would, as always, shun the outpouring of Latin warmth so alien to her Nordic temperament. Yet he yearned to feel, to hear, his son's faint heartbeat, to trace Ghisela's blue-veined, pale skin with his fingers as he dreamed what the child would be like. He wanted the two of them to forget the rest of the world while they spun plans and dreams for their future.

'No, Prospero,' she replied firmly. 'I can't stay. I've already made plans and I don't want to change them now.' The tone of her voice dismissed him.

He nodded, manfully swallowing his disappointment; her abrupt denial of his need to be close to her that night crushed all his elation. Loneliness filled the void where love should have been as he helplessly watched her walk from the room.

The *maître d'hôtel* gave Cotton a friendly smile as she entered the chic little restaurant near Capitol Hill where she and Herron were regulars.

'It's a scorcher today, isn't it?' he remarked.

'It sure is,' she agreed, brushing the beads of perspiration from her forehead. To herself she added, almost as hot as Nicaragua. Looking cool and collected in a belted summer dress, she followed the *maître d'hôtel* down the centre of the packed restaurant buzzing with the conversation of Washingtonians at the pink-clothed tables set with flowers. When he saw her, Herron stood to greet her with a kiss on the cheek.

'Hello, gorgeous,' he whispered.

'Sorry I'm a bit late, but there was a mix-up at the last minute about my itinerary for Rome, and then Judd called me in for a chat.'

'It doesn't matter. I haven't been here long.'

When they sat down across from each other they held one another's eyes for a long moment. They had parted at midnight when Herron left her apartment for his house in Georgetown.

'I hate the way I have to leave you every night. I'm glad that's all going to end soon,' he said, toying with her fingertips.

'I was thinking exactly the same thing,' she admitted. 'Just think – you won't have to worry about the Moral Majority when you put a ring on my finger. I mean a wedding ring,' she corrected, catching sight of her huge engagement ring that was now back on her left hand. She had been surprised to find it still round her neck when she had woken up in a mission hospital in Nicaragua.

'Well, only one more month until countdown,' Herron said triumphantly as the waiter filled their glasses with wine. 'Here's to us.'

'To us, again?'

'And again, and again, and again,' he said happily, clicking his glass to hers. 'By the way, how are you feeling today?'

'I'm fine – much better.' She noticed his eyes straying to the blue marks from shrapnel lodged beneath the skin of her arms. 'It's too hot to wear long sleeves now,' she said, touching the marks self-consciously. 'Your battered bride,' she quipped. '"And do you, Herron Easton, take this woman, shrapnel and all?"'

'I do, indeed. You don't have to be ashamed of them, you know. You should be proud.'

She smiled ruefully. 'It's just that I'm so damn vain. A guy at the office calls them my tribal scars. He says journalists are the lost tribe condemned to wander the earth.'

Herron laughed, then his face went serious. 'When I think of it . . . It still gives me a shiver.'

'Well, don't think of it,' she chided.

'If those headaches don't go away soon, I really think you ought to see a specialist.'

'I will,' she promised, glad when the waiter came to take their order. Even now she didn't like talking about her brush with death. Beneath Herron's concern she sensed the doubts about her chosen profession that she herself had brooded over all the time she lay in the hospital. Until now she had avoided frank discussion. Her first foreign assignment had nearly killed her and had made her witness to the deaths of five other people, including Mitch. She had done endless soul-searching in Nicaragua and later in Washington, but she was beginning to realize that Herron didn't understand how strongly the tragedy had bound her to her profession.

'Wipe that worried expression off your brow,' she teased. 'From now on I'm invincible. I've proved it.'

'Cotton, you mustn't say things like that,' he said, taken aback.

'I didn't realize you were superstitious,' she said, aware she had touched a raw nerve.

'No, not superstitious – just cautious.'

Herron had done everything he could to make her forget Nicaragua, taking her sailing at Cape Cod and Martha's Vineyard in August. But just as she thought she had put it all behind her, Biddle died, and no amount of prior knowledge could have prepared her for the loss. Herron had been there for her to cling to, and together they mourned Biddle, and would always mourn him. But Cotton's salvation had been her job at the *Herald* and she had insisted on going back at the beginning of September to prove something to herself and to blot out all the grief and terror in her mind.

'By the way, I meant to tell you,' Herron said as the first course arrived. 'You won't have to worry about that hood Vallone any more.'

'No? Why not?' she said, raising an eyebrow. He had been the least of her problems during the summer and she had all but forgotten the threatening letters she periodically received through her lawyer.

'Apparently he packed up and went back to Europe where he belongs. His big lawsuit was just a puff of smoke, like I always said.'

She had a quick image of Prospero lying in his hospital bed, prompting her to say: 'Maybe he heard what happened to me in Nicaragua and thought that was enough of a come-uppance.'

As she spoke, Cotton had a hunch it was true, though it sounded far-fetched. Her destiny had been stamped by violence in the same way his had been, and it might have softened his heart.

'Men like him would kill their own grandmothers. Anyway, we got the big fish we're after, Tony Fasso and his cronies,' he said, smiling with satisfaction. 'That's all I care about.'

Cotton dispelled the image of the handsome Vallone swaddled in bandages in Bellevue. It seemed cruelly ironic that she was lying bandaged in a hospital in Nicaragua only a few months later.

After they had talked about the last-minute preparations for the wedding in the Episcopal Church in Cold Spring Harbor, there was a pause. Breaking a roll in two, Cotton said:

'Herron, something is on your mind. I can tell.'

'You know me pretty well by now, don't you?'

It was a question she had often asked herself during their frenetic courtship from New Year's Eve to Easter, when he had proposed to her beneath the chandelier in the ballroom at The Lindens. She had been deep in her thesis, and he in the investigations that led to the questioning of key Mafia figures in Washington. Herron refilled her glass as he considered his words.

'Cotton – after I left you I drove home and sat downstairs until the wee hours of the morning . . .'

'I hope you're not getting cold feet at the last moment,' she couldn't help saying. 'They say it's normal.'

He smiled. 'No, that isn't it. I came to a decision that I've been mulling over for some time; but I'll need you to back me up.'

'What is it? What's the big mystery?' She touched his sleeve affectionately.

'You know that Senator Farley's seat will be empty next year? Well, I'm going to go for it.' He paused to let his words sink in. 'It's a safe Republican seat. Carter will never be re-elected, and I guarantee you that Reagan will get in and we'll have a Republican Congress. Why wait four more years? The long and short of it is, I need you, Cotton – I need you by my side.' When she stared at him without saying a word, he added: 'This comes as a big surprise, I know.'

She nodded and smiled. She thought she knew and under-stood Herron by now, but she hadn't expected this. 'I'm abso-lutely thrilled for you, Herron. Of course I'll back you all the way – you know that.' Leaning across the table, she kissed him. 'If I seem at a loss for words, it's because I never imagined you'd run so soon.'

'But you do see the sense of it, don't you?'

'Yes, of course I do. It's what the old cliché calls a golden opportunity.' She was aware she was trying to inject enthusiasm into her voice.

'Look, I know you've been through a lot these past months, but by spring life will be back to normal and we'll be settled in the house. It's months away.'

She sighed and played with her wine glass. 'It's not going to be easy, juggling my assignments abroad with your campaign, but I guess we'll manage somehow.'

He sighed impatiently. 'I guess I'm not stating my case very well. Look, you're a sensational asset, Cotton, and I want you with me full-time, not only lobbying to get the spot on the ticket, but during the campaign. That old saying is true now more than ever, that behind every great man there's a great woman. You've got to be there every step of the way with me – kissing babies, eating chicken dinners . . .'

She bit her lip and frowned. 'It's just that when we always talked about your running for the Senate it seemed umpteen years away. Give me a minute to try and get used to the idea,' she said gently.

'It was always umpteen years away, like having a family, you mean?'

'Yes, well, since you put it that way – like having a family.' There was a defensive edge to her voice.

She was distracted by the seafood salad the waiter set in

front of her, beautifully arranged on a Chinese plate. As she stared unseeingly, memories of Herron during the last few months flickered through her mind, ending with Biddle's funeral when she had cried her heart out in his arms. Remembering how close they had been then, she was frightened by the gulf widening between them. She knew if she didn't speak her mind now, she would have to remain silent for ever.

He said, 'What I was really trying to say, I guess, is that I hoped you got something out of your system in Nicaragua. I thought that what happened down there would have convinced you what a rough profession you picked. How do you think I felt when I knew you were somewhere in Central America half-dead, maybe dying . . . I don't want to go through that every time you go off on an assignment, and I don't want you to either.' His voice was indulgent, dismissive. He had allowed her to sow her wild oats, but now she must conform.

'So that's it,' she murmured, dropping her eyes for a moment. When she looked up she gave his strong features a long, searching study. How could they have made such a disastrous mistake, she wondered? They weren't children. But as she formed the words to herself, the reason hit her. Biddle's illness had acted as an emotional catalyst, disguising fundamental differences that could not be breached. In a fatal second Cotton comprehended that the spark which had ignited between them at Biddle's bedside during Christmas had died shortly after he had. During the long pause between them she tried to interpret misgivings flickering in Herron's eyes, but she had to be the one to say it:

'I don't want this to sound melodramatic because, believe me, I'm not saying it for effect; but let's face it, Herron. It's not going to work.'

She half-expected him to leap up and protest, try and brush away her doubts and his own as well, but he merely regarded her in shocked silence. In Herron Easton's world, an engagement and all the accompanying formalities of photographs in major newspapers, parties to introduce the bride to the family, the shopping, setting up house, meant that it became tantamount to marriage.

'I simply don't know what to say,' he uttered in disbelief. He blinked, as if trying to wake up from a bad dream. 'Jesus,' he muttered, putting his hand to his head for a moment. 'How did this all start, anyway? How did it happen?'

'We're two people going in different directions, that's all. Thank our lucky stars we discovered it in time.' Cotton felt numb and anxious all at once, but her voice was steady.

'But what a hell of a time to find out, a month before the wedding when the invitations have been sent, when the presents have started arriving. It's a nightmare.'

'Herron – none of that matters. You know that as well as I do.'

He regarded her with shocked disbelief. 'I can't believe what I'm hearing,' he muttered in a controlled voice, but she could see by the sharpness in his eyes he was holding his anger in check. 'It may not matter to you what people think, but it matters a great deal to me. I'm in the public eye – I have a career to consider, apart from anything else,' he added, glancing obliquely around to see if anyone had overheard their conversation.

For a moment Cotton wondered what to say, bewildered not just by the violent and unexpected rupture that had changed the course of her life, but by the intimation that Herron was more concerned with the social embarrassment than the thought of their break-up. She felt sad but strangely relieved as she looked at him, seeing him for the first time as he really was. Shrugging she said,

'The only thing I can say is that under the circumstances it would have been rash for us to go ahead and get married anyway. I had to be honest, Herron.'

'You're right there,' he replied, his mouth twisting in a sardonic smile. 'What you're telling me is that I should thank my lucky stars, is that it? I guess it beats waking up the day after the wedding and discovering the truth.'

She didn't reply. Thoughts about the consequences of calling off the wedding began to buzz in her head. She must let William know right away. There was no time for a letter and she knew that he was already involved in a flurry of preparations to come to the United States for the wedding. Everyone would say she was crazy to ditch Herron Easton almost at the altar. In so many ways he seemed the ideal man but Cotton realized with a jolt that she wasn't truly in love with him and probably never had been.

'Life won't be the same without you,' she remarked, meeting Herron's accusing eyes. At all costs she was determined to maintain some sort of dignity at their parting and not return his sudden hostility with anger of her own.

'Same here,' he replied, rising abruptly. 'Come on, let's get out of here. I'll pay on the way out.'

Leaving their food unfinished, they left the restaurant. Cotton was glad to be out of earshot of the nearby tables. When they were in the vestibule Herron hesitated, looking around uneasily. For a second Cotton almost wished she could turn the clock back to an hour earlier, when her entire life had seemed to be moving smoothly on golden rails. But it was too late; neither of them could go back now, and they both knew it.

'I really don't know what to do in a situation like this,' said Herron with a hollow laugh.

'Neither do I, but I suppose the first thing that must be done is for me to go back to Long Island this weekend and tell everybody — Eleanor and Austin, your mother . . .'

'I'll call Mother tonight to pave the way. I think that would be better. It's going to come as quite a shock to her, but I guess she'll weather this storm like she has so many others.'

'I'm sure,' she said, thinking of Bess Easton. Her instinct told her that in spite of all the upheaval it would cause, Herron's mother would be relieved. She had never felt fully accepted by Bess Easton, who had asked probing questions about her background and her political views. It was she, Cotton suspected, who was behind a prenuptial agreement that Herron had asked her to sign. Cotton had shrugged it off at the time as being normal and businesslike; but the implications that she might be after Herron's money were clear.

'The next thing that's in order is this,' she said, suddenly conscious of the engagement ring which belonged to the Easton family. She slipped it off and put it into Herron's hand. It sparkled in the spotlight for a moment as he quickly wrapped it in a handkerchief and stuffed it into his pocket.

'Come on – I'll walk you to your car.'

Waves of heat came up from the pavement as they went slowly down the tree-lined street towards Cotton's Mustang. Only the week before they had ordered a shiny new car to replace it.

'About the car – it's already been ordered. Why don't you just keep it when it's delivered? I'd like you to have it as a present from me,' he said with a magnanimous smile.

It was a generous offer and for a moment she was almost tempted, but she knew she had to walk out of the relationship with a clear conscience.

'The thing is,' she said, 'I have an idea that I'll be spending a lot of time out of the country. After all, wanderlust is in my blood.'

'Yes, it must be. Funny, but I guess I didn't understand that.'

Taking her by the shoulders, he kissed her formally on both cheeks. She responded by hugging him briefly, trying to summon up a semblance of affection as she realized they might never see each other again.

'Take care of yourself. And remember, if you're ever in trouble, if you ever need me, just call.' From the heartiness in his voice, she might have been a stranger.

'Thanks for the offer. I have a premonition that I'm going to get in lots of trouble. I can't seem to help it,' she replied, remembering to smile.

He shook his head and kicked a pebble at his feet before turning with a wave. She watched him until he had disappeared from sight.

'You what?' gasped Eleanor.

'I said, Herron and I have decided not to get married. We're cancelling the wedding.'

Austin practically dropped the bottle of bourbon he was holding. When Cotton had arrived at The Shallows from Washington that evening she had found the Townsends sitting in the library having a drink.

'Have you taken leave of your senses?' muttered Austin blankly.

Eleanor let out a shrill little laugh of disbelief.

'Don't be silly, Cotton. The two of you have just got cold feet, that's all. Every bride and groom feel exactly the same way at the last moment, don't they, Austin? The same thing happened to us. Why, he called me on the eve of the wedding and said – I'll never forget it – "Eleanor, are you sure you want to go through with it?" Can you believe it? Of course he didn't mean it.'

Austin forced a smile but he was regarding Cotton intently, his normally expressionless face dark with concern.

'I really don't know how to convince the two of you that our decision is irrevocable, but I assure you it is,' she began quietly, with all the sincerity she could muster. All the way she had held her emotions tightly in check, refusing to give in to the sudden weightlessness that came over her whenever she comprehended that the future – the future that had been so full and bright – was now a blank. She had poised herself for the long detailed explanation the Townsends would expect, but she was thrown off-course when she realized their astonishment was laced with deadly hostility. She faced them squarely, knowing it had been a mistake to count on their sympathy in the first place.

Eleanor struggled for a moment, still unable to grasp what Cotton had said. 'Why just look at you, you're exhausted. It's all the fault of that slave driver Judd Marshall at the paper. He knows you're getting married and he's made you work until the last moment anyway. No wonder you're such a wreck. You don't even know what you're saying. A hot bath and a good night's sleep and you'll feel differently. You and Herron have had a little spat, that's all. It will blow over.' She gave Cotton a strained smile but her eyes were forbidding.

Cotton watched Austin refill their glasses, noting that he neglected to offer her a drink.

'I'm sorry to say that it's really nothing to do with last-minute jitters. I wish it were, really, but what happened is much more serious. We didn't have a fight; Herron and I simply came to the same conclusion over lunch today in Washington and I thought it was my duty to fly straight here and tell you about it. Please don't think for one minute that this is any easier for me than it is for you, because it isn't.'

'I'm so glad you thought it was your duty,' retorted Eleanor, unable to keep the sarcasm from her voice. She shot a look at Austin, who said,

'Cotton, it seems to me that you haven't given any thought about what this is going to do to the two families concerned. Your manner indicates to me that you have no conception of the social disgrace involved in cancelling a wedding of this magnitude so soon before the event. Quite frankly I'm flabbergasted that you would even consider it. Are you aware of the expense and trouble that Eleanor and I have gone to on your behalf?'

'Austin,' she began, exasperation creeping into her voice, 'I am aware, believe me, of all you both have done but wouldn't it be a bit pointless for me, for Herron, to get married just to please everybody? And you keep saying *me*, yet I've tried to explain to you that it was a mutual decision, Herron's and mine.' At the glowering disbelief that crossed his face she blurted out, 'For God's sake, Austin, it's my life! I have to think of myself!'

An angry malevolence distorted Eleanor's face. 'Did you hear that, Austin? Think of herself,' she cried. Rising from her chair she confronted Cotton. 'I don't believe for one minute that Herron Easton had any part in this. No – it was you who were the cause of this whole thing. I don't know what you did, or why, but right now he's probably reeling from the shock in Washington while you have the gall to stand here and say you have to think of yourself so coolly, as if butter wouldn't melt in your mouth.'

Cotton's eyes widened, but she marshalled all her will-power to keep her temper in check. She felt as helpless as a boat in a storm but she steadied herself to see the ordeal through until she could make her exit.

'If you don't believe me,' she said, 'I suggest you call Herron right now.'

'Call Herron? I wouldn't dream of it,' she snapped. 'It would only upset him further. And anyway, what would that prove? He's such a gentleman I have no doubt he would take the blame to save you any embarrassment because he's a fine, noble, outstanding young man.'

And rich, Cotton thought to herself; not to mention socially impeccable. If Herron weren't so incredibly wealthy, so socially prominent, Eleanor wouldn't be defending him with such ferocity. Feeling sick she said mildly,

'There is no blame, as you put it, Eleanor. As I've been trying to tell you, it was a mutual decision. We both realized that we had rushed into things, and that we weren't really compatible.'

'Oh, shut up,' screamed Eleanor, as the venom that had been collecting for years began pouring out of her. 'After all we've done for you, this is how you repay us. We've fed you, clothed you, raised you – struggled to make the best of the mess Delilah left behind. Why, there's not even a drop of Townsend blood in you, and yet we took you in out of the goodness of our hearts knowing that your mother was probably some local Italian tramp. Well, you're a guttersnipe just like she was. Blood will out, oh yes, it will. How dare you stand there with that smug expression on your face after wantonly destroying the happiness of one of the finest young men who ever lived – as if he wasn't good enough for you! You little bitch – you make me want to puke.' Her arm shot out and the drink in her hand splattered across Cotton's face.

Cotton turned her head just in time, but the bourbon dripped down her blouse. A blind anger churned up inside her rupturing the deep channel of grievance that had never healed in all the years she had lived with the Townsends. The degrading spectacle of Eleanor's own loss of dignity was mirrored in her mind, strengthening her resolve not to lose control. In moments she would walk out of their lives, never to see them again and she wanted to leave an impression of flinty indifference behind her proving that, no matter what, she was untouchable. Quelling her urge to flee the room, Cotton stood her ground knowing that this foul abuse was the price she had to pay for untangling herself from the ties that had been dragging her down for so long. She watched as Eleanor collapsed into a chair and began to moan.

'The florist, the caterer, the church – all the money we've spent – a small fortune. And the presents that will have to be returned, invitations cancelled,' she wailed. 'Oh, the humiliation of it. We're ruined. What will we do? How are we ever going to hold up our heads again?' At this litany of horrors she regarded Cotton, panic-stricken. 'No, we can't let it happen,' she cried, rising awkwardly from her chair. She grabbed Cotton's arm. 'Please, I beg you, Cotton, change your mind. Oh, forgive me for all those awful things I said a minute ago. I didn't mean it. I'll do anything if you'll just change your mind . . .'

'Eleanor, for God's sake, stop it,' interrupted Austin sharply, an embarrassed flush crossing his face.

'Please, Eleanor, don't,' muttered Cotton, breaking away. 'I'm very sorry it has all turned out this way. That's all I can say at the moment. Let's just leave it at that.'

When Eleanor collapsed sobbing into her chair, Austin walked menacingly towards Cotton. For one moment she thought he was going to strike her, but she was too stunned to move away.

'Do you know what you are? You're sick, that's what. Deeply, seriously sick. You need a psychiatrist.' He was almost apoplectic with rage as he hissed the words. 'You're a twisted scheming little parasite, that's what. I'm glad you're not going to marry Herron Easton, he's too good for you. Now get out. I want you out of here, or I'll throw you out.'

The suppressed misery of the past years seemed to uncoil within her as she regarded him with withering contempt. 'That won't be necessary, Austin. I'm going upstairs now to collect my things and then I'm going to do what I would have done years ago if it hadn't been for Biddle: I'm going – for good.'

~Book Three~

Chapter 19

The morning following her meeting with Prospero, Cotton drove a rented Fiat along the Via Appia Antica to keep an eleven o'clock appointment with Chiara Galla.

She had stormed out of Prospero's office the previous day and had fumed all the way back to Parioli where she had poured out her feelings to Chiquita. When she had calmed down and taken stock of the situation, she realized what a mistake she had made in her interpretation of Prospero's mood and character. With wry self-deprecation, she understood that the arrogant Vallone was the last person she should have approached to contribute to a worthy cause.

Her mind was elsewhere as she drove through the heavy traffic along the wide boulevard lined with old houses behind walls and shielded by dense shrubbery. She found herself combing over every detail of her meeting with Prospero, with an impatience that was threatening to boil over again. He seemed to her immature, childish, harbouring a grudge against her after all these years. For a man who appeared so suave and sophisticated, he had the mentality of an adolescent. He was, she decided, spoiled, corrupted by money and power. Though she might once have been the pampered daughter of the Marchesa di Castello di Montefiore, she had spent the last two decades coming to terms with the real world as well as with herself, which was more than Prospero could claim. He, on the contrary, was a classic megalomaniac who had forgotten where he had come from.

She sighed, and blared her horn impatiently at the car ahead. Driving through the long pools of shadow cast by the umbrella pines overhead, Cotton concluded that at least her ill-fated meeting with Prospero had served a good purpose: it had given her a trial run for more serious attempts to raise money for Seamus. The imbroglio with Prospero had inspired her to approach his intriguing mistress who was, after all, in the film business.

Parking her car in the shade near a bed of fragrant lilies, Cotton got out and hitched her bag over her shoulder. A wicked smile spread across her face at the thought of Prospero Vallone's expression when he heard that she had persuaded Chiara Galla to contribute to Seamus's film. Cotton had read in a gossip column that they were temporarily estranged after a lovers' quarrel, and she knew now was the time to act before they were back in each other's arms again. Ringing the polished brass bell in the villa's entrance, she told herself it would be the coup of the year if she walked away from Chiara's residence with the promise of financial backing.

The moment the butler admitted her to the cool marbled hallway, Cotton came down to earth. She wondered if she had made yet another mistake as she caught a glimpse of herself reflected in a scrolled Venetian mirror. The gold leaf on the ceiling, the curving staircase with a wrought-iron balustrade overlooking the palatial hall, had the impersonal grandeur of a hotel lobby in Cotton's eyes. When she took a peek through the doors of the salon, one glimpse of the ornate living-room revealed volumes about the personality of Chiara Galla. The heavy tapestries, over-sized lamps thick with silk fringe, the velvet upholstered furniture and gilt tables reminded her of the set for an Italian 'B' movie. Even on a beautiful June day, the brocade drapes were half-closed and the lamps illuminated. Cotton observed that in all her years in America, Chiara had clearly never lost her love for the rococo.

After an interminable wait, during which Cotton had begun to wonder if they had forgotten about her, she heard a door close and the sound of brisk footsteps coming down the corridor. A young woman, peeking through a gigantic floral arrangement, called breathlessly:

'Hello, I'm Diane Saunders, Miss Galla's secretary. Sorry to keep you waiting, but I just had to unwrap these.'

Cotton watched as she teetered to a console table and deposited the flower arrangement. As an afterthought, she detached the card and slipped it into her pocket. Cotton couldn't help wondering if the sprays of pale roses and long-stemmed freesias were from Prospero.

The petite blonde smiled sweetly at her.

'If you'd like to come with me, Miss Galla will see you shortly,' she said in a breathy voice that suggested she regarded her employer with awe. Cotton realized she was expected to feel privileged to see the busy star at such short notice.

Feeling a slow burn of impatience, Cotton followed the chattering secretary down the hall, guessing that the meeting would be a waste of time. They emerged from the dimness of the house on to a balcony overlooking a rectangular pool where Chiara was swimming, sheltered by high trees that filtered the midday sun. She was instantly recognizable, even though she wore big dark glasses and her hair was piled on top of her head and tucked into a towelling band. Chiara didn't acknowledge her friendly wave as Cotton skirted the pool with the secretary and joined a white-coated masseuse in a gazebo overlooking the water. When no one acknowledged her presence, Cotton slid her bag from her shoulder and pulled up a deck-chair. She crossed her legs and prepared to wait, unable to shift her eyes from Chiara's head and bronzed shoulders rippling through the turquoise water. The only sounds in the quiet garden came from Chiara as she inhaled and exhaled in controlled gasps that made Cotton impatient.

After ten minutes, when Cotton looked pointedly at her watch, the secretary said in a hushed voice:

'Miss Galla will be finished with her swim in a few moments. I'm afraid she'll only be able to give you an interview of twenty minutes or so as she has a luncheon engagement.'

'Thank you,' said Cotton, realizing with a start that the girl had assumed she was there to interview Chiara for the *Herald*.

When she had called the previous day to ask for an appointment, she had mentioned she was from the *Washington Herald* as an entrée, adding that she was a friend of Senator Easton's to place herself in Chiara's memory; but she had made no mention of an interview. It was going to be difficult to explain her gaffe, and seeing Chiara's swim was nearly at an end she was tempted to go through the charade of an interview; but she instantly dismissed the idea. She didn't know the first thing about Chiara Galla – who would see right through her if she tried to fake it. Reminding herself that she hadn't come to grovel, Cotton had the feeling that Chiara was regarding her critically from behind the dark glasses, even though she pretended not to be aware of Cotton's presence.

It was another ten minutes before Chiara emerged from the water, her perfect body encased in a parrot green swim suit that clung to her like a second skin. The water rolled off her gleaming shoulders and down the long, shapely thighs, accentuated by the deep cut of her bathing suit. From a distance Cotton couldn't detect a single flaw in Chiara Galla. Even her golden skin seemed cast with a burnished perfection that defied nature.

Cotton reflected how many long hours of self-absorption must be required to create and maintain such a flawless image. She watched in amazement as the well-spoken and presumably intelligent young secretary hovered at the edge of the pool, holding up a towelling dressing-gown that Chiara could easily have fetched for herself. She slipped into the dressing-gown with an unhurried languor that suggested she enjoyed being the centre of attention.

'Miss Galla, some flowers came for you while you were swimming. Here's the card,' said the secretary, taking it from her pocket.

Cotton watched as Chiara read the card, a secret little smile stealing over her face; then she tucked it into her pocket. Only after that did she acknowledge Cotton's presence.

Cotton stood up as Chiara strode towards the gazebo with a gracious smile, the click of her leather mules echoing on the stone.

'Miss Castello,' she said, extending her hand.

As their fingers touched, Cotton said in friendly tone: 'We met at the American Embassy earlier in the week.'

'Oh, yes, I remember now,' Chiara replied, narrowing her brown eyes. 'How nice to see you again. Won't you please take a chair.'

The tone of her voice gave no hint that she recalled the embarrassing scene that had taken place between Herron and Prospero. As the two of them sat down, Chiara's eyes glanced off Cotton in a practised study, noting from her direct gaze and unruffled manner that she had an inborn confidence. When their eyes met, Chiara could understand why Prospero had been attracted to her, if only fleetingly. Her rather serious face dominated by large amber eyes narrowly missed being beautiful; but her body was firm with youth and she projected a self-possession beyond her years. She had a well-modulated, lowish voice that told Chiara she had had training in broadcasting, probably television. Her nonchalant elegance could come only from an upper-crust background, which, Chiara knew, could not be counterfeited. As they faced each other, it was Chiara who felt on the defensive as her eyes challenged the young journalist to speak.

'I think I'd better come straight to the point, Miss Galla. I have to tell you straight away there's been a misunderstanding. I didn't come here to interview you,' she said with a wry smile.

'Not to interview me? Why have you come, then?' Chiara asked warily.

Cotton gave a helpless laugh. 'I really have to apologize. I'd love to do a piece on you, but interviews with Hollywood celebrities are not actually my beat. I write hard news. I'm a foreign correspondent for the *Herald* and I've just returned from Ethiopia.'

She paused, weighing up her chances when she saw the perturbed expression on Chiara's face. But it occurred to Cotton that the promise of publicity might possibly stir her interest in Seamus's film, and she launched into her spirited sales pitch. As Chiara's expression hardened she realized she had come up against the same indifference she had met in

Prospero. She ended her speech by saying: 'And so, while I'm here I'm approaching a number of people who are in a unique position to show they care.'

Chiara crossed her legs and knitted her beautifully manicured hands together. 'Have you talked to other people about this?'

'No, as a matter of fact, not yet. I've only been in Rome a few days, and I thought I'd start at the top of my list,' she added quickly, gambling that Prospero hadn't mentioned her visit. 'I'll be contacting the American Ambassador, and Senator Easton before he leaves Rome, to name a few.'

The swift change in Chiara's expression suggested Cotton's flattery had worked. 'I'm very honoured you have thought of me first, Miss Castello. My late husband and I always welcomed a chance to contribute to a worthy cause. Diane, bring me my chequebook – the Citibank account,' she called.

'Yes, Miss Galla,' responded the secretary, hurrying towards the house.

'Now, what was it I wanted to say to you?' said Chiara, pressing her hand to her temples. 'Ah yes, I know. You're a friend of Senator Easton's. Did the two of you meet at a press conference or something?' she added, unable to contain her curiosity.

'Oh, no. I've known Herron since I was a teenager growing up on Long Island. He's a family friend,' she added, wondering how much Chiara was going to contribute to the cause. She sensed that behind the pleasant mask lay a burning curiosity to ask more questions about Herron, which she fended off by asking one of her own.

'Speaking of Herron, I'm reminded of the other night at the party. I guess you could say, literally speaking, that Prospero Vallone was the hit of the party. Didn't you think so?' she said mischievously.

An indulgent smile crossed Chiara's face at the mention of his name. 'Ah yes, Prospero is very possessive, very hot-headed. He can't control his emotions.' Her voice conveyed a certain proud satisfaction. She gave no hint to Cotton of how deeply hurt she was that Prospero hadn't called her since the reception, and that he had refused to answer her messages.

Cotton was telling herself that Prospero and this beautiful, spoiled woman were meant for each other. The violent scene that had exploded at the Embassy seemed to have no more importance than a strip of celluloid in Chiara's memory. It was obvious that she didn't know or care why Prospero had punched Herron, assuming that it came from barbaric possessiveness which she found deeply flattering.

Still, there was something beguilingly childish about Chiara, Cotton thought, regarding the wistful smile that played about the corners of her pretty, full mouth. She seemed to be inventing herself, inventing life as she went along, which contradicted her underlying shrewdness. And yet, self-absorbed as she was, she couldn't quite conceal an inner vulnerability. Cotton could only conclude that this quality, coupled with her surface charm, held people like Diane and Prospero in her thrall.

By the time the secretary rushed breathlessly down the stairs, waving the chequebook in her hand, Cotton was anxious to get away. She curbed her impatience as the secretary went through the ritual of preparing a leather blotter laid out with chequebook and pen, then handed Chiara her tortoiseshell glasses transforming her into the consummate businesswoman Cotton guessed she really was. Looking pensive, Chiara suspended the pen over the cheque, sucking in her cheeks.

'Who should I make this out to?'

'Seamus Mahoney, please.'

'Would you spell it?'

When she had written in the name, Chiara hesitated, the pen hovering over the box for the amount. Her first impulse was to write one hundred dollars, the lowest possible figure she could think of without appearing to be niggardly. She prudently added another zero, realizing that it would be money well-spent where it concerned the press.

'There you are,' she said, folding the cheque. 'I hope this helps you achieve your goal.' Her fingers uncurled from the cheque in an elegant gesture as she handed it to Cotton.

'And if there's any chance that you think Wolfe Productions might like to back the idea, I'd appreciate a call,' reminded Cotton.

'Oh, yes. Make a note of that, Diane. I'll look into it.'

As she spoke, Cotton knew she wouldn't.

'Miss Galla, excuse me, but I think it's time . . .' prodded the secretary gently.

'Yes, Diane.' Rising in elegant symmetry, Chiara put on her dark glasses. 'Yes, would you excuse me, Miss . . .'

'Castello.'

'Are you Italian?'

'Of Italian descent.' There was no time to say more as the interview was obviously over.

'*Arrivederla,*' murmured Chiara, extending her hand.

'Thank you very much, Miss Galla,' Cotton replied.

But Chiara had already forgotten her. When Cotton followed the secretary back into the house, she slipped her hand into the pocket of her robe and withdrew the card that had accompanied the flowers sent that morning, re-reading it with satisfaction.

'*Ciao* . . . from a Senator . . . Herron Easton.' Chiara was already thinking of all the things she would say to him when he arrived for lunch that afternoon.

As she followed Diane up the stairs, Cotton glanced at the cheque to see the amount, recalling how Chiara had hesitated when filling it in. She was disappointed that it was for only a thousand dollars. Glancing up at the biscuit-coloured villa, its dark green shutters closed against the sun, she calculated that it must cost a fortune to rent. A thousand dollars wouldn't have covered more than a few days' rental. But, she thought, at least it was a start, with the five she herself had pledged and the money Chiquita and Archie had promised.

Cotton was glad to leave the luxurious villa cocooned in verdant seclusion. Driving away, she couldn't help but think of Prospero Vallone in his fortress on the Via Aurora. Catching one last glimpse of Chiara's domain in the rearview mirror, she told herself each had found the perfect mate.

The following week, when Prospero came back to the office after lunch, he impatiently shooed his secretary from the room.

'Come back later with those leasing contracts, Paola. I have some important phone calls to make, and I don't want to be disturbed.'

The young woman gave him a sympathetic glance, shrugging off his curt manner. She thought it was due to the death of his father-in-law the previous week and all the attendant family problems which would be weighing on his mind.

When he was alone, Prospero picked up the telephone, then put it down again. It was just after three o'clock, and he was in a dilemma about whether to call Chiquita Bowles again. He had already telephoned her flat twice, on Tuesday and Wednesday. Now, on Thursday, he had successfully resisted the compulsion to call again, making a concentrated effort to keep his mind off Cotton Castello, wherever she was. Cotton's friend Chiquita was friendly, but non-committal about her whereabouts, and he was beginning to wonder if she was telling the truth when she claimed not to know where she had gone for a week in the sun. It irritated him beyond measure that he had to accept Chiquita's explanation with good grace when he was obsessed to know what had become of the elusive Miss Castello. Would he, he wondered, follow Cotton back to London on some pretext or other if she had slipped away discreetly? If Chiquita Bowles was lying and Cotton had left Rome for good, he would have to find another way to get in touch with her, knowing that after their disastrous meeting she wouldn't make it easy.

Otto Schmidt had died on the day following the Embassy reception, and Prospero had flown immediately to Geneva. The funeral had been a huge affair in the village church in Rolle followed by a long meeting with Ghisela and her lawyers to discuss her inheritance, which brought with it a host of new responsibilities and problems. In spite of the emotionally charged atmosphere between them, Ghisela had leaned on him for support and guidance, and Prospero had surprised himself by mentioning divorce. The subject had slipped out inadvertently, causing the corners of Ghisela's mouth to tighten as they sat in the wood-panelled library of the Schmidt château on Lake Geneva. Pale and starkly elegant in black, she gazed at him with cool disapproval making him feel just as vulgar and coarse as he had on the day they had met in Tripoli seventeen years before.

'As always, your timing is superb, Prospero,' she said, displaying her usual maddening self-possession.

'Unfortunately, there is never a right time for such a thing. Maybe I shouldn't have brought it up so soon after the funeral.'

He had broken off his apology when she turned on him contemptuously, her face illuminated by the light filtering through the lace curtains. 'In the circumstances, I thought it might be the honourable thing to do. After all, you're now coming into your inheritance . . .'

'It would seem you're planning to marry that woman from Hollywood,' she interjected. 'I find it very amusing, though you have a fortune of your own you still feel compelled to seek out women of means.'

He had promised himself that he wouldn't allow Ghisela to make him lose his self-control. In an even voice he said:

'No, as a matter of fact the woman from Hollywood, as you call her, and I are no longer seeing each other. Our divorce has nothing to do with her.'

He felt himself go cold all over at her icily beautiful image that had dominated such a large part of his life. As he rose to leave she said tartly:

'I suppose she's had enough of fortune-hunters after all.'

Pinning her with a deadly glance, he said flatly, 'As a matter of fact, I've had enough of heiresses.'

With that he had walked out, aware that something inside himself, caged for many years, was now free.

On the way from Geneva to Rome his mind had strayed to Cotton Castello. Since she had disappeared, he had had a premonition that they had missed their chance and that his own life was trailing slowly yet inexorably in the wrong direction. As the plane cruised over the Alps, he pondered deeply, trying to discover what there was about a girl he knew so little that attracted him.

For years he had lived with the notion that Cotton Castello was just another ritzy débutante riddled with snobbery and crass ambition. He had been convinced that she was a journalist of the worst type, who destroyed people's reputations to enhance her own. But, when they met in the garden of the Embassy, she had struck a deeply responsive chord in him. He found her desirable in an offbeat way that he had never encountered before, oddly but familiarly beautiful, as if she had been stamped in his mind years ago. She was pure northern Italian, with her hair the colour of wheat in August, her strong classical features; her serious eyes opened the world to him as he looked at her.

He had liked at once the humour lurking behind her expression, her generous laughing mouth, the proportions of her body. And the day she had entered his office, he had been touched, in spite of his rage, by her zeal and idealism, qualities he had never met in a woman before. He had seen through to the gentleness beneath her tough façade. The idea of pursuing her was tempting, but she was highly intelligent and knew her own worth, a challenge that made him consider her with care.

Though Prospero had read prodigiously over the years to make up for leaving school at fifteen, he wondered if he could engage Cotton's mind as effortlessly as he knew he could make love to her; but he was intrigued by the prospect. As the thought circled in his head, his misgivings were over-ruled by his questing, stubborn nature. It whispered that anything was possible if only he was willing to take the chance.

As the plane approached Rome, Prospero ironically recalled his mother's comment on his brother's wife whom he had found only two streets away. In a way, Cotton Castello had also been living only two streets away. They had passed each other more than once, but had not been fully aware of each other's existence until the day she came to his office. He had arrived home from Geneva shadowed by suspense, wondering if his pursuit of this exciting woman would lead to another meaningless unmasking of two strangers bound for separate destinations, or if fate promised something more.

Now, as he stared at the telephone, feeling himself fluctuate between reluctance and eagerness, he knew he had to talk to

Cotton, to see her. He told himself that if he possessed her for a night, for a weekend, he might break the obsession that had disturbed the rhythm of his life. As he reached for the telephone, Prospero knew there was no guarantee that she would speak to him if he found her, and he wondered what he would say to her if she did.

When Cotton pushed the doorbell of the Bowles's flat in Parioli, the click of heels behind the door told her that Chiquita was there to greet her.

'You're back,' she enthused. 'But I thought you were going to stay in Sabaudia until tomorrow at least. For heaven's sake, come in. Am I glad to see you!' she said, with a mischievous gleam in her eye. Cotton was standing on the threshold in shorts and a T-shirt, her hair tied up loosely.

Dropping her suitcase in the hallway, Cotton said: 'I guess I missed the big city. I hope you don't mind, but I made a last-minute decision and didn't even stop on the autostrada to call you. Isn't it lovely and cool in here,' she said, enjoying the waves of cool air coming from the darkened flat closed against the afternoon heat.

'So, you've had enough of solitude and clean living. I must say, you look great, tanned to a crisp.'

'I confess,' she said with a laugh. 'As beautiful as the Baia d'Argento was, when I started talking to myself on the beach I decided it was time to come back.'

Though she pretended to joke, she knew it was true. The previous weekend she had driven down to Sabaudia seeking a retreat; but she was genuinely glad to be back in the Bowles's pleasantly cluttered flat. Hadrian came crawling across the terrace towards her and she scooped him up in her arms and kissed him.

'Hi, fatty. Watcha been doing?' She looked up to see Chiquita regarding her with unsuppressed excitement.

'Get a load of what came for you while you were away,' she announced, gesturing towards an enormous arrangement of summer flowers whose perfume filled the room. Putting down the baby, Cotton walked towards it with a mystified expression, touching the profusion of cornflowers, lilacs, fat pink roses and tulips.

She gave a snort of laughter. 'What's this, my consolation prize from Herron because he couldn't see me before he left Rome? Only he could think of something so wildly lavish, so . . .' she searched for a word, 'so melodramatic. On the other hand, I don't suppose they could be from, say, Mike, could they? Come on, Chickie, out with it,' she coaxed searching for the card.

'Not Herron, not Mike. Guess again.'

'Who else would send me flowers?' Try as she would, she couldn't imagine. Chiquita handed her the card. There was no message, only the name: 'Prospero Vallone'. 'I don't believe it,' she said, with a quick intake of breath. 'He's going to be sadly disappointed when he hears there hasn't been a funeral.'

'And not only that,' Chiquita squealed, 'but he's called Tuesday, Wednesday, Thursday. I was very vague about where you were because I didn't know what you wanted me to say. But I know what I wanted to say. He's obviously out of his mind wondering where you are. I confess that when he called this morning I broke down and told him that I expected you any time, praying you would come home. I didn't want the whole thing to fizzle out. It must be ESP your showing up today.' Chiquita stopped breathlessly as she interpreted Cotton's expression.

'What the hell could he want, anyway?' said Cotton, pretending to be perturbed. Inwardly she was stunned by his extravagant and inexplicable gesture.

'What do you mean, what could he want? What a question! You've obviously made quite an impression on him. Don't tell me you didn't notice when you were in his office last week that he found you devastatingly attractive. Boy, did you read him wrong. I thought you said he was fuming. Some fuming, that's all I can say.'

'I did,' she said. 'I mean, he was.'

'I get it. He likes them with a feisty temper. Well, he's met his match in you.'

Cotton thought for a minute, unable to admit to Chiquita

that all those days on the beach, as the waves of heat washed over her, the image of Prospero would suddenly fill her mind. She kept thinking of the line of his jaw against his white collar, the shock of blue-black hair brushed back from his suntanned face and those blue eyes that had churned up a rippling attraction in her when they ran into each other at the Embassy. She tried to banish the thought of him, but when she opened her eyes to be met with the deep blue sky and the dark pines, she was sent back again and again to the haunting feeling of a missed chance, a train not taken, a destination unexplored. But now here was evidence that Prospero Vallone had had the same inexplicable change of heart. Though Cotton's heart was pounding with excitement, she told herself to keep her head, postponing judgement until she knew what he really wanted. She saw Chiquita looking at her with a look of sisterly wisdom.

'Just wipe that look right off your face, Chiquita Bowles. I wouldn't go out with him if he were the . . .'

'The last man on earth, right?'

'Right!' she said, then broke into laughter. 'So if he calls again make some excuse. Tell him I've gone back to London or something, I don't know.' She realized her voice lacked conviction. She was filled with panic. She told herself she preferred to remember him as he was that day in his office, arrogant, cold, rude. And yet she could not dispel the notion that the two of them couldn't let the situation rest without exploring it further.

Chiquita's dark eyes went serious. 'Cotton,' she began, resting her hand on her arm. 'Why are you running?'

She thought for a moment. 'I don't know,' she admitted.

Later that afternoon Cotton was reading a magazine when the phone rang. As soon as she heard it she realized that she had been edgy, waiting for Prospero to call. She listened in suspense when she heard Chiquita pick it up.

'*Pronto?* Oh, Cotton, it's for you,' she called in an artificially cheerful voice that told Cotton it could only be Prospero.

As Cotton took the phone they exchanged a glance. Instead of the sultry tone she intended to use, her voice cracked.

'Hello?'

'Cotton?' came Prospero's low urgent voice, like a summons.

'Prospero —' as she spoke his name she felt an inexplicable relief. Her heart was still pounding, but with pleasure rather than tension. 'Thank you for the flowers you sent. They're beautiful . . .' Chiquita was grinning from ear to ear at the softness that had crept into her voice.

'I'm glad you like them. Listen, I'm very sorry about what happened last week. Sometimes I have a terrible temper. I was wrong, and I apologize . . .'

As he spoke, she had a vivid picture of him that brought a smile to her lips. Behind his little speech she sensed a sincerity that melted her doubts completely. She could imagine the apology must have cost him dearly, conveying what she had always known, that apologies didn't come easily to Prospero Vallone — any easier than they came to her. Now that he had plunged in first, she must follow.

'On the contrary,' she found herself saying. 'I'm the one who should apologize to you. It was very presumptuous of me to barge into your office like that and expect you to be interested in what I had to say, after I hadn't even bothered to make amends for all the trouble I caused you years ago. So believe me, you were perfectly within your rights . . .'

'No, no, no,' he insisted. 'I was boorish, insensitive . . .'

She burst out laughing. 'Are we going to have another argument about who's right?'

She had never heard him laugh, and when the gust of his rich humour came over the phone she could picture the becoming lines around his mouth and eyes. When there was a pause on the other end of the line, she wondered if he would let it go at that and say goodbye. Still, when he said what she was hoping to hear she was unprepared.

'The reason I called is that I was wondering if you would have dinner with me tonight?'

Chapter 20

At nine that evening they were settled in a corner table on the crowded terrace of Sabatini's on the Piazza Santa Maria in Trastevere. The famous mosaic-fronted church on the edge of the square was dramatically outlined against the deep azure sky, and the whisper of the fountain was in counterpoint to the buzz of conversation around them. Regarding Prospero over the top of her menu as he consulted with the waiter, Cotton sensed his undercurrent of impatience to dispense with the formalities so they could talk in earnest. All the way to Trastevere they had engaged in stilted small talk, saying none of the things that were on their minds.

The first sight of him at the door, casually dressed and handsomer than she remembered in summer slacks and a silk jacket, had sent a tremor of approval through her; and now she found herself noting all the details that she hadn't registered before. She liked his strong square hands, the touch of black hair bordering the starched cuffs. His somewhat flashy good looks contrasted with the serious expression in his eyes, those eyes that kept meeting hers as he talked to the waiter. She found herself following the deep laughter lines at the corners of his good strong mouth, the way his dark eyebrows knitted together in concentration as he chose the wine. When he suddenly snapped the wine list shut and smiled, she felt a hollow sensation at the pit of her stomach, which might or might not have been hunger. He regarded her for a long moment with an undisguised pleasure that made her acutely aware of every detail about herself.

She had spent far too much time that afternoon agonizing over what image to strike – glamorous, businesslike, sexy, demure. In the end she had settled for a loose white shirt and a slim grey skirt with a wide belt inlaid with silver. Around her neck hung the Coptic necklace Seamus had given her, and silver bracelets she had bought in Ethiopia gleamed on her brown arms.

When the waiter had gone, Cotton opened a packet of *grissini* and handed him one as she shook her head incredulously.

'Who would have ever thought that you and I would be sitting in Rome having dinner together,' she said, with a disbelieving smile.

'There's something I should get out of the way. I'll have to be honest with you and say I'm not sorry for punching Easton, even though I know he's a friend of yours.'

'Oh, he's not that good a friend. When you interrupted us, he and I hadn't seen each other for years.'

'I'm very glad to hear that. It's less awkward if I can be honest with you, and quite frankly I hate his guts.'

'That's your privilege, and I understand why you feel that way. But Herron's not a bad sort really. Now we've got that settled, tell me, how is Miss Galla taking all of this? Did you see the pictures of them together in *Oggi*, by the way, after the party? They were sensational.' Nibbling *grissini*, she waited for his answer.

He nodded. 'Yeah, I saw them. You know, after I stormed out of the party, Chiara and I had a big fight and now it's all over between us.'

'Oh,' she said, more pleased than she liked to admit. 'No wonder you hate Herron. Now you've got cause for a new grudge. He ruined your love life,' she suggested humorously.

'No, that's where you're wrong. What happened between Chiara and me has been on the cards for some time now. The fight with Easton was just the straw that broke the camel's back.'

'Who's the camel?'

He gave her a shrewd, laughing appraisal. 'I'll leave that for you to decide. Look, I want to apologize for the way I treated you when you were in my office the other day . . .'

Oh no, please,' she interrupted, holding up her hand.

'I just want to get it off my chest. Like I said, I lost my temper. But there's no excuse. None whatsoever.'

'I'll tell you what, after I've said my piece, let's never mention it again. You know, while I was in Sabaudia I had a lot of time to think, and if I'm honest with myself I'll have to admit you nudged my conscience. What I did years ago was a callous invasion of your privacy. I was a young, brash reporter following a lead like a bloodhound. I didn't even stop to think of what pain it might cause. And looking back, I think I did it partly for escape, rushing off to Bellevue like that. You see, it was a terrible Christmas for me that year.' She told him about Biddle.

'Christ, no wonder,' he said sympathetically. 'If that was the worst Christmas of your life, it was certainly mine. I spent it in intensive care and my wife had just left me.' He filled her in on what had happened to him.

'I didn't know what you were going through,' she said, shaking her head wistfully. 'You're separated from your wife again now, aren't you?'

'Yes, but this time it's permanent; we're going ahead with a divorce. There's something I've always wondered,' he began. 'Did you know who I was when you decided to pursue that story?'

'I had a strong hunch. As I said the other day, I'd never forgotten meeting you when I was twelve.'

'I hope I've changed a bit,' he said, with a deprecating grin.

'I hope I have, too. I was an obnoxious brat,' she said, returning his smile. 'When I heard your name on the television that night I acted on impulse I said to myself, how many Prospero Vallones can there be in this world? So I went for it. Then I thought the world was mine to exploit, but now I feel differently. That sort of thing is gutter press and I don't want any part in it.'

'Well, that's an honest admission. You and I both got our start in an unconventional way. There's something we have in common.'

Their eyes locked, and she knew he was thinking of the

Mafia. Some day, she sensed, they would talk about it – when they knew each other better.

'I'll never forget how you looked that night at the hospital,' she said to change the subject.

'Bad, huh?'

'No – pale and very, very ill. Don't think I've got ice water in my veins. I felt very sorry for you. I really did.'

His eyes caressed her. 'The humour of it was lost on me at the time, but now we're here I realize that it took a lot of guts to do what you did. You're a gutsy broad, aren't you?'

She shrugged her shoulders disparagingly and laughed. 'You should have seen me that night. I did a whole number. I put a kerchief on my head and did my best Ellis Island accent, pleading I left the *bambini* at home and the spaghetti sauce on the stove.'

He laughed appreciatively. 'I had a lot of explaining to do when Ghisela heard about the picture in the paper. I mean, she was thousands of miles away at the time. She was sure you were a girlfriend of mine who had talked her way into the hospital under false pretences. The truth is that I'm not always a good boy, but that time for once, I was innocent.'

As they talked and sipped wine, Cotton had to keep reminding herself that she and Prospero were still no more than strangers. Beneath his surface charm glinted a thirst for life, a drive that she sensed had remained unchanged since he was a young man in his twenties.

'When I got out of the hospital I was hell-bent on making you pay for what you'd done to me. I tried to trump up a suit on any grounds I could find, but when I cooled down that summer I dropped the idea.'

'You could have ruined me if you had wanted to, do you know that?'

'And you know what? I'm glad I didn't. It would have taken me a lot more than a bunch of flowers to get you to come out to dinner with me if I had.'

His eyes glittered, making his meaning clear as forcefully as if he had pressed his mouth to hers.

'There was a time that summer when I was sure you had dropped the suit because you felt sorry for me,' she confessed.

'Sorry for you? I might have secretly admired your guts, but I was never sorry for you. What made you think that?'

'I thought you might have decided I'd been through so much that you ought to let me off easily.' She told him about her first assignment for the *Herald* in Nicaragua that had brought her close to death and had won her her spurs as a correspondent.

'I didn't know anything about it,' he replied, with a shake of his head. 'Just think, you and I both came close to pushing up daisies in 1980 after that lousy Christmas . . .'

The disturbing memory of sudden violence reverberated in the distance, far from the civilized atmosphere of the Piazza Santa Maria in Trastevere. For a moment they were intimately bound by the spectre of annihilation which made time seem precious. Life was reduced to the simplest of sensations: the taste of the chilled wine, the murmur of conversation, the beauty of the distant church. Their hands touched across the table, sealing the moment.

When the waiter set the *tortellini* in front of them, Cotton was talking about Herron again.

'I was bowled over when you called me Mrs Easton.'

'So was I when you said you never had been.' Herron Easton had been the one thing about Cotton he couldn't explain away, but now he was satisfied. 'I have to tell you I don't think that smug bastard is your type,' said Prospero, taking up his fork.

'Now, now,' she chided, pretending annoyance, but she was still put out that Herron hadn't even telephoned as he had promised, after they had necked in the back seat of Archie's car. 'We seemed to be ideally suited at the time, though. We met because of Biddle, and it was his death that brought us so close.'

'Your cousin Biddle was like a big brother to you, I guess.'

'He was, and if it hadn't been for him I might have ended up another teenage runaway who became a drug statistic. He made me believe in myself, because he loved me. I loved him more than anyone in the world, except perhaps Delilah.'

Cotton's honesty sparked off a moment of introspection in Prospero. Who did he love, he asked himself? He loved his family, his children, especially Alessandro, but that love was mixed with guilt, rage, frustration that nothing about his life would ever be normal.

When Cotton told him about the circumstances of Delilah's death, he registered yet another coincidence between them – the emotional centre of both their lives had been destroyed in adolescence.

'So that must mean you're completely alone in the world, that you don't have anybody?' Realizing she had been orphaned not just once, but twice, he warmed to her resilience of spirit. In their way, both of them were street fighters.

Matter-of-factly she said, 'Yes, I guess I am all alone. It's not something I dwell on. But you, you're lucky to come from a big family.' She couldn't disguise a certain envy in her voice.

'Families – don't mention them,' he said disparagingly. 'Believe me, there are days when I wish I lived all alone on a desert island. One wants this, one wants that. They call you repeatedly, asking for favours, advice, loans. It never ends.'

He pretended to be annoyed at the responsibility, but Cotton detected pride at being the patriarch of the vigorous, successful Vallone clan.

'You shouldn't say that. Being part of a big happy family is everybody's dream.'

'Who says it's always happy?'

'All right, happy sometimes.'

'Sometimes,' he agreed, and they both smiled.

'It sounds like fun if you ask me. Don't forget, I'm Italian, too, and part of me will always yearn for a family life. Just part of me, mind you. I'm a confirmed career girl,' she said, wanting to make it clear.

'You can judge for yourself whether you like it when you meet my family.'

'I'd like that,' she said with enthusiasm.

'Then it's a promise.'

Turning her head, she drank in the sight of the lamplit piazza. 'I haven't been to Sabatini's in years. I always half-expect everyone to suddenly burst into song – the piazza is just like an opera set.' She nodded towards the church in the distance, its mosaic a field of gold glowing in the evening sky.

'That reminds me. you and I have still to discuss your film.' When she looked surprised he added: 'I think I've worked out something with a production company I've just bought into. I contacted a producer of documentaries I'm working with to ask his advice and he thinks we could do something if Seamus is on the level. The Italian colonial history of the country has a strong appeal, apparently, and, well, you know, it seems perfectly feasible.'

Cotton beamed at him. It was more than she had ever expected.

'I suppose I shouldn't say this, but you're not doing it for me, are you? Because really, if you are . . .'

He shook his head. 'No, as a matter of fact. I'm not doing it for you. Let's call it an old debt that I want to repay. And, anyway, if what you say is true, it ought to be a good deal.'

At his mention of old debts her mind leapt back to the hearings in Washington, the scandal at Schmidt that had led to his resignation, all of which she had consumed eagerly in the papers. What Prospero was confiding to her now, in thinly veiled terms, was that he had been guilty and that he wanted to pay for his crime in the best way he knew. This strangely unexpected revelation was like turning a corner, kindling in her an eagerness to make up for lost time, to fill in the gaps of the twenty years that their lives had been running parallel.

As she talked, Prospero tried to remember what Cotton had looked like all those years ago; but only the briefest impression remained of a gangly adolescent with an impudent expression on her upturned face. He tried to reconcile it with the woman before him, gifted with such warmth and intelligence. He gazed at the line of her cheekbone, the delicacy of her collarbones, the fine hands that belied the strength of a body brimming with an exciting vitality, vitality that communicated itself in a wave across the table as he met her gaze.

Prospero suppressed an impulse to pick up her lean brown hand, kiss it and replace it on the table, a gesture which would have made his intentions clear at once, too clear. He had become aware already that he wanted Cotton Castello far too much to move hastily.

After dinner, as they crossed the piazza, Cotton looked up at the sky.

'You don't really notice the stars in the city. You should see the stars in Ethiopia. I think they're the brightest I've ever seen.'

'I'd like to see them very much,' he said, lightly guiding her by the elbow. 'But in the meantime, I could show you the stars from the terrace of my apartment. It's not quite the same thing, but I'll throw in a view of the hills of Rome at night for good measure. What do you say?'

She hesitated, but only for a split second. 'Yes, why not?' All night he hadn't made a pass at her, but she suspected he meant to now. As they approached his sleek white Mercedes convertible parked near the edge of the piazza she decided she ought to refuse him, but the idea of a little fling before she returned to London tempted her.

It was after eleven as they crossed the Tiber and drove through the streets of Rome alive with bright lights and the noise of traffic. Whenever Prospero caught her eye, Cotton responded with an amused grin. There seemed something absurdly glamorous and clichéd about driving through Rome on a summer night with a smooth, handsome Italian in a white convertible. It was an escapade that was out of character for her, but slowly she felt herself give way to the novelty of it all.

When they reached the villa, Prospero opened the locked gates with a remote-control device. There was a guard in the courtyard who greeted them and took over the car.

A small side entrance led to a stone corridor where they entered the lift. When the doors had closed and they were standing close together in the confined space, Cotton felt a fluttering in her stomach at the realization they had locked the rest of the world away and anything might happen. All the way up he didn't say a word, but he was watching her intently as the doors to his private domain opened.

Stepping out on the tiled floor she was greeted with a collection of cartoons and drawings on a white wall lit by overhead spotlights. As she followed Prospero down the hallway, she noted every detail with interest.

'So, this is home, is it?' she said as they entered an impressive rectangular room overlooking a verdant terrace, from which there was a spectacular view of the city.

'What can I get you to drink?'

'I'd love an Amaretto.'

He crossed the room to a lacquered cabinet where the drinks were kept, leaving her free to look around. What struck her at once was the apartment's uncluttered simplicity, in contrast to the coldly ostentatious office on the floors below. The soft terracotta tiles were strewn with a few kelim rugs and the stone-coloured leather chairs and sofas were modern and comfortable, yet not stark. The ceiling had been bordered with a classical frieze echoed by Roman statues in niches flanking a fireplace with a simple marble mantel. There were one or two pieces of good antique furniture and a few bronze sculptures on pedestals. Cotton liked the big ceramic lamps with pale shades, the bushy plants in urns, the soft abstracts on the walls that gave the spacious room an open aspect. It was, she decided, the retreat of a man who favoured space and simplicity, a man with good taste and the means to buy what pleased him. And she was intrigued by the vast collection of books – something she hadn't expected to find. Approaching the library to browse, she assessed the titles, seeking clues to the man who had proved he was full of surprises. She was impressed by the range and depth of his reading, reversing the image she had had of him moments ago at the wheel of a flashy car.

She turned to take another sweeping glance at the surroundings in which Prospero lived, forced to re-examine her persistent misconceptions. Some time in the distant past the idea had taken root in her that Prospero Vallone was a peasant at heart, charming maybe, but vulgar; but as he approached her, two glasses in hand, she realized that the years of sophisticated living had given him a polish that no one, certainly not she, could fault. Thinking of her own somewhat shabby flat in London, she felt like congratulating him, but she knew he would think she was being patronizing. Remembering the night the gauche young man had come to the Villa Robbiano, she acknowledged it was her turn to be taken down a peg and she realized how it must have pleased him to have come so far in life.

'I love your apartment,' she said as she took the glass of Amaretto. She felt an unaccustomed shyness as their eyes met. She couldn't help wondering if he still felt a deep pride in all that money could buy, or if after so many years of being rich the novelty had worn off. She suspected, hoped, that even Prospero Vallone wasn't a man who had everything.

'I've always lived here alone, never with my family or my wife.' He held her gaze for a long moment before he said abruptly, 'I'd better keep my promise.'

'Promise?'

'The stars with the hills thrown in,' he said, sliding open the door of the terrace and gesturing for her to follow.

A warm breeze ruffled their hair as they leaned over the balustrade and looked down on the roof gardens of the surrounding villas sloping towards light-studded streets that threw up the murmur of traffic.

'There's something I wanted to ask you. How long has it been since you went back to Robbiano?' said Prospero.

She knew she had been skirting the subject all evening, longing to ask him about it. The knowledge that he had actually been to the villa had always set him apart from other people in her mind and she felt a craving to talk about it.

'I haven't been back since the summer when you came to the villa, but I'm often there in my dreams. Part of me still lives there, as if my life ended abruptly that summer, and a new one began. I didn't know when I met you for the first time that my childhood was nearly over. Oh, I've kept in touch with my godfather William Partridge – he's a painter and lives in Florence. I keep meaning to go back, if only to see him.'

'Do you mean you haven't gone back since that summer?' he asked, surprised.

'I suppose I must be afraid of what I might find,' she admitted.

For a moment Cotton sank into the shadows that came over her whenever she thought too long or too hard about

Robbiano. She could conjure up every detail of that last grand party before she and Delilah left for America. Glancing at Prospero's profile edged in light, she realized that his journey away from Robbiano had been much more remarkable than hers.

'And you haven't been back either?' Her mind raced towards the possibility that they might go back together.

'No, but I had no reason to go. My reasons for staying away are different from yours. I don't have any happy memories to keep intact. My memories are all unhappy ones.'

'Because of your father, you mean?'

'Come on, let's go inside. You're shivering,' he said, leading her indoors.

When they had sat down he said cautiously, 'How do you know about my father?'

Sensing he thought she might be condemning him, she hastened to say: 'I must have heard it from Delilah years ago. Why don't you tell me about it?' For a moment she thought she had offended him, but he had only paused to think.

'My father,' he said with a nostalgic shrug. 'As it turns out I'm a lot more like him than I ever imagined.' Prospero reflected that no one had ever asked him about Franco Vallone before.

Cotton was impressed at the honesty of his admission.

'You could say he wanted too much too fast.' Prospero resisted the painful moment of truth inside himself. Meeting Cotton's eyes he wished he could tell her that he still felt himself to be a criminal, though he guessed she already knew. He had told no one about the deals he had done with Tony Fasso, but those deals had laid the foundations of his present wealth, an ugly reality that diminished his achievements in his own mind – that and his marriage to Ghisela. But as much as he desired a release to confide in Cotton, as much as he sought the escape from isolation such intimacy would bring, pride held him back. Sipping his brandy, he contented himself with the knowledge that they were partners in a sense, now he had given his support to her film project. Prospero would never know whether his lucrative deals with Tony in the late seventies had snuffed out lives – he preferred not to dwell on it. But the film on Ethiopia seemed a way to try and repay the debt that weighed on his conscience. He could never tell Cotton that was partly why he had put up the money – he wouldn't have to. She would know. It crossed his mind to wonder if they became closer, whether she would forgive his past and all the things he wasn't proud of.

He began to reminisce about his father, how he had escaped Sicily where he had been born the son of a poor farmer, by going north to Genoa in the late twenties. His instinct for survival had been sharpened by the deep prejudice against southerners he encountered, and when he fell in love with Maria Fontini, the golden-haired, blue-eyed daughter of his boss in the foundry, he was laughed at. Vowing to win the beautiful Maria, he emigrated to New York. For eight years he worked unremittingly to earn enough money to support her in the style her father demanded before he would accede to the marriage. Finally, in 1938 when Franco Vallone could call himself a success, Maria's family capitulated.

Though he didn't allude to it, Cotton realized it was then that Prospero's father must have begun his contacts with the underworld which had ended his life nearly twenty years later.

'You know, for a long time I was ashamed of my father when he died, before I understood what he was trying to do. He just wanted to be somebody, that's all. He was smart enough, ambitious enough to have made it on his own. It would have taken time, that's all, and he didn't have time to wait. I didn't either. I was in a hurry. The same thing happened to me, only I was luckier than my father. The bullet missed my heart.'

He told her of the summer before she was born that changed his life, when he was sentenced to years of working for his uncle in Genoa where the once-proud Maria Vallone became a disgraced and shadowy figure in her brother's household.

'I should hate the guy, and my uncle Mario, too, the fat pharmacist, but after Zio Giorgio died I realized how much I owed the bastard,' said Prospero with a laugh. 'If he hadn't taught me how to work I wouldn't have had the guts to get

out. If he were alive today, I would shake his hand and thank
him for it.'

Then Cotton began to talk about her past, and the look of
disbelief on Prospero's face when she told him she had grown
up in the Townsend family as a poor, unwelcome relation
gave her a sense of wry amusement.

'Well, after all, I was the illegitimate daughter of some peasant girl that Delilah rescued and took in like a . . .' she resisted
the words, 'stray cat'. Eleanor Townsend's stinging insult was
still lodged in her mind after all these years. 'It turned out that
Delilah didn't have a penny, so they were stuck with me. To
tell you the truth, they would have liked to dump me in an
orphanage, but it wouldn't have looked very good. Looking
back now, I don't blame them. I was such a precocious brat.
Snobbish and rude. Oh, I was really impossible, I can tell you,'
she said with a laugh, warming to the subject.

'To think that you went through the same thing as I did,' he
said with amazement. 'I was wrong about you, Cotton.'

'And I was wrong about you.'

When Prospero went to fetch them another drink, Cotton
saw it was after one, but she didn't care. Their conversation
had shaken her awake and she didn't want the evening to end.
She couldn't remember feeling so at ease with another human
being since Biddle had died. Prospero was talking about the
night when he had come to the villa, laughing at the memory.

'So here I was, mixing with high society, and one look from
a twelve-year-old kid reduces my self-confidence to smith-
ereens.'

'Me? Did I do that?'

'You know damn well you did,' he said, narrowing his eyes
appreciatively.

He told her about throwing away the suit, which had cost
him his savings, adding with a gust of laughter: 'And my cuff-
links – you probably don't remember them. They were blue
polished stones set in silver plate. They cost me five thousand
lire. I hung on to them after I chucked the clothes and the next
day when I drove to Rome with Nancy I couldn't bear to part
with them because they had cost so much. Yet I knew they

were all wrong. Just north of Orvieto they started burning a hole in my pocket. I took them out and threw them on the roadside.'

Cotton thought of Prospero in the company of the glamorous Nancy Rogers, whom she still remembered.

'I made you do that? It's unforgivable.'

'No, you didn't make me. You only made me aware of what I already suspected.'

As they reminisced, Cotton told Prospero about the post-mortem on the party the next day at lunch with William and Delilah. She said with relish: 'I can still almost hear Delilah crying "Scandal has erupted! Have you heard that a temptress has absconded to Rome with the Monsignor's nephew?"'

Prospero laughed indulgently. 'I was so green in those days.' When he saw the sceptical look in Cotton's eyes he added: 'But not so naïve that I didn't recognize an opportunity when I saw it. I owe a lot to Nancy, I know. The trouble is, I never had a chance to thank her. I treated her badly because I was young and on the make.'

When she asked him about Pietro Giannini, now a cardinal, he said, 'Pietro and I are still very close, even though I'm not in his flock.'

'What a combination the two of you make, one an angel, the other a devil.'

'Like you and me, you mean?' he retorted.

'I'm no angel, if that's what you're thinking,' she said wryly. 'He christened me you know, your cousin.'

'Did he? I didn't know. We'll have to have dinner soon, the three of us. How long are you staying?'

'I'm not sure,' she replied evasively. In her mind Cotton had already decided to beg for extended leave from her London boss, sure they could spare her for a bit longer.

'It makes me so happy to know you're related to Giannini. I don't know why, but it does,' she added, with satisfaction.

Cotton had kicked off her shoes and pulled her feet up on the leather couch, and Prospero moved closer, drawn by their growing intimacy.

Absently toying with a strand of her hair, Cotton thought

of the sun-filled days of her childhood, memories that had been incomplete until now. Locked away in her mind was all the physical beauty of the past, but she had almost forgotten the joy of living that had formed her character until she was twelve. For years she had suppressed it, as if afraid she would never find it again. The time had now come to revive all the goodness of those years and lay away the sad ghosts that had lingered. It arrived without warning on a warm summer evening in Rome and she wondered if she had left it too late to communicate with the rich legacy that she had allowed to wither.

Trying to guess her thoughts as she looked absently into the distance, Prospero realized that his original idea of pursuing Cotton Castello in a whirlwind affair, of wooing her and bedding her, seemed laughably simplistic. He was overtaken by an unexpected vision of the unravelling of time, a luxury that belonged only to love. His instincts told him that it was already too late to pretend that their meeting would lead to a casual liaison, a pleasant interlude that would end when she went back to London. At two o'clock in the morning, he became aware of the host of unexplored emotions that lay before them.

They looked at each other. All the time he had been talking, Cotton had been aware that Prospero was stirring up the suppressed memories of years. Now she understood that even though he seemed so strong and sure of himself he still felt a smouldering dissatisfaction. It was this, she guessed, which fuelled his vaulting ambition. Sensing that when he loved, he would love fully and recklessly, she wondered what it would be like to love him back.

Prospero drove her back to Parioli and stopped the car on the street near the Bowles's apartment building. Leaning back with one hand on the steering wheel, he reached for Cotton's wrist. At his touch she felt a wave of desire, stirring an impatience she had held in check all evening. When they were sitting on the sofa in his apartment she had longed for him to kiss her, but something had held him back. It wasn't her habit to make the first move, but it was all she could do, watching his profile in the half-darkness, to restrain herself from reaching out to him. When she sighed, he picked up on her mood.

'Whatever you're thinking, I'm thinking the same thing. Whatever this thing is that hit us, I don't want to spoil it.'

She was deeply stirred. Releasing her hand he whispered,

'As much as I want to, I'm not going to kiss you goodnight because if I do, I won't be able to stop.'

Chapter 21

Sandy Vincent stirred his espresso irritably and gestured towards the cathedral in Robbiano, frowning at Chiara as he tapped his watch, then glancing to Diane and the locations director, Renato.

'Just look at that. It's nearly eleven. Look at that piazza. It's still deep in shadow.' His mouth set as he waited for Chiara's reaction.

But she was only half-listening. Her eyes hidden by huge sunglasses, she pretended to be observing the swallows wheeling above the tower set against the deep blue sky. At the same time she was acutely conscious of the oblique glances of the local people, their curiosity aroused by the glamorous, well-dressed strangers – obviously movie people.

Trying to keep the impatience from his voice, Renato said:

'Sandy's right. One glance will tell you that this isn't the place. It's no good at all. Look at it – Kodak signs, dry cleaners, the telephone kiosk, even an Agip station. I don't know why we're wasting our time here. San Treviano has the atmosphere we need – if anything, we've got to update it.'

'Another thing is that there isn't really a suitable place for the crew to stay,' said Diane helpfully.

'She's right,' said Sandy. 'And we've already talked the guy in the hotel in San Treviano into a good deal. This is the way you go over budget, Chiara, by wasting time. Now be reasonable,' he said when she still remained silent.

They all looked at each other uneasily, knowing that when Chiara wanted to, she could shut out everyone. She did that now, ignoring the three of them although she was aware they were waiting for her to speak. Until the moment they had walked into the piazza, Chiara had been convinced that Robbiano would make a perfect location for the opening sequences of *Village in the Sun*. But now, as she scanned the centre of the town where the action was supposed to take place, she knew how wrong she had been. She would, however, take her time in admitting it.

'Sandy, order some *aqua minerale*,' she said, not bothering to sweeten her words with a smile. As the balding waiter hurried to the table, Diane said diplomatically:

'The church is beautiful really, and the upper storeys of those houses across the piazza are quite lovely. It's a shame they spoiled them with all those modern shop fronts.'

'*Prego, signor?*' said the waiter.

'How many mineral waters? *Due, tre*? Make that four,' Sandy said sourly.

'*Americani, no? Parlate italiano?*' said the waiter, trying to be friendly.

'*Poco,*' spoke up Diane with a bright smile which triggered off an enthusiastic description of Robbiano.

'This is a beautiful village, one of the finest in Tuscany. We have the best of everything here, the modern, yet the old. If you haven't seen it yet, you should look inside the cathedral. There are frescoes there by . . .'

'Just bring us the *aqua minerale*,' said Sandy under his breath.

A cold look from Renato silenced the waiter. Sandy gave a shrug and Diane looked uncomfortable as she regarded the chauffeur loitering near the car that had brought them there. Chiara stood up suddenly, gathering her scarf and bag.

'I'm sorry to have inconvenienced you, gentlemen,' she said regally. 'You were right. This is not the best place. Let's go, shall we?'

'But what about the water?' said Diane.

'I've changed my mind. And anyway, Sandy and Renato are obviously in a big hurry. Come on, Diane. Let's go to the car.' She stalked away from the café.

Sandy rose angrily and went inside the café, followed by

Renato, to pay for the water the waiter had already opened. As he slapped the money on the bar, Renato said:

'What's wrong with Chiara, anyway? She's been like this all the way here.'

'One call from Prospero Vallone and she'd be all smiles. He's been messing her around. Love – it's for the birds. I'm glad I'm fat and over fifty, and that I have a wife and four kids and don't play around.'

'Oh, so that's it. I should have guessed. Did they split up?'

'Don't you read the papers? Anyway, who knows?' said Sandy with a shrug. 'Just brace yourself. It's going to be hell until his replacement comes along.' He gave the handsome Renato the once-over, as if a thought had just occurred to him.

'Don't look at me! Once I might have jumped at the idea, but not now, oh no, not now . . .' he said, with a shake of his head. 'Maybe they'll get back together.'

'The answer to my prayers. Maybe they will,' conceded Sandy as they left the café.

Just when Cotton thought time was passing much too quickly, Prospero had asked her to accompany him to Florence. They had been spending as much time as possible together since their dinner at Sabatini's and that day he had picked her up directly from his office at noon, throwing her overnight bag into the boot alongside his.

'I see you like to travel light, just like me.'

'All my life I've tried to avoid excess baggage,' she had responded, sliding into the car. He was dressed in a polo shirt and jeans, and she wore a chocolate linen shift, making her feel they were just like any other weekenders getting out of the city. Yet she had slept badly the night before, lying awake analysing the underlying significance of their weekend together. As they drove off, she couldn't dispel the strange cocktail of emotions coursing inside her. The last thing she had done was to telephone William Partridge to let him know she was coming and would at last honour her promise to visit him in Florence.

She and Prospero were both eager to reach their destination, and they had agreed to bypass such inviting stops as Orvieto perched on its dramatic butte of black rock overgrown with greenery.

'Keep your eyes peeled for a pair of white winkle-picker shoes and a blue suit last seen in the sixties,' he commented as they passed the city.

'Some day they'll be a national monument, you can bet,' Cotton said, laughing.

As the miles of dark road swept by, Cotton reached in her bag and brought out some sandwiches she had made that morning.

'You think of everything, don't you?' he said appreciatively.

It occurred to her that seldom, if ever, had the flamboyant playboy Prospero Vallone had a woman make him a ham and cheese sandwich. Leaning back in her seat she took a bite, warding off an acute attack of butterflies as her mind raced ahead.

'You're a great cook,' he called above the wind, taking another sandwich when she offered it.

Cotton ate without appetite. The sight of Prospero's arm propped on the steering-wheel was a disturbing reminder of why she was there. He had booked a hotel, and neither of them had said anything about separate rooms, even though he hadn't so much as kissed her until now. As the miles disappeared behind them, Prospero's presence overshadowed her anticipation at returning to Robbiano and she began to wonder if it was a mistake to mix pleasure with nostalgia. She hadn't slept with a man for nearly six months, having vowed that the next relationship she entered would have to be lasting. Lasting, she thought to herself: she had to be back in London in ten days.

A moment later, when he reached out and clasped her hand tightly, Cotton knew how transparent she must seem. It was a gesture of warmth, reassurance, not passion, that conveyed his understanding of her confused emotions. The empathy flowed between them until he moved his hand to change gear, leaving the impression that he had been thinking about her as much as she about him in the past week. He had gently prised loose her reserve, bringing her closer to the enigma that was Prospero Vallone. The hours they had snatched together that week had to stand for days, weeks, in their crowded, demanding lives as they began the long process of exchanging hopes and dreams and fears. She had talked a lot about her work, including the kidnapping, and he had confided the tragedy of his son Alessandro, now six, who had been born deaf.

The only explanation the doctors could offer when they diagnosed his affliction at the age of seven months was it might have been caused by a seemingly harmless tranquillizer that Ghisela had taken during the tension-ridden days of the hearing in Washington. For years Prospero had suffered from guilt and remorse. Not only had he been directly responsible for Ghisela's anxiety in early pregnancy, but also the drug she had taken had been manufactured by Schmidt Pharmaceuticals.

She was met with a glimpse of a tortured dark corner of his life, churned up with bitterness. Another barrier between them had fallen, making her readier to trust him.

It was as if a stranger had cast a protective cloak over her to help her through what lay ahead. Fate had joined them in order to take this momentous journey together. She looked away, conscious of little ripples of anticipation as she registered everything about him, the way he squinted at the sun through his glasses, the way the wind tousled his black hair which, she now noticed, was beginning to go grey just above the ears. For the rest of the journey, she tried not to think too far ahead. Soon after they skirted Siena, the landscape of the Tuscan hills took on a poignant familiarity.

As they approached Florence, Cotton realized with a jolt that they had arrived. Cruising down the wide, tree-lined avenue that led through the Boboli Gardens, Prospero put on a tape of Italian ballads and as they drove down the serpentine road lined with grand old villas set in big gardens it seemed as though they were like any other pair of lovers.

She opened her mouth to speak when she saw the Villa Cora, the hotel where they were booked for the night, fly by. Looking over her shoulder, she caught the gleam of determination in Prospero's eyes that told her he had seen the hotel and that he wasn't going to stop until they had reached a more important destination.

'Now? You're going to Robbiano now?' she said, covering her surprise with a laugh. Suddenly, it closed in on her that she couldn't put off her return to the villa any longer.

'Now is as good a time as any, isn't it?'

'Sure, why not?' she replied off-handedly, but she knew she wasn't ready to go back, and probably never would be.

With unexpected suddenness the sweep of Florence came into view as they skirted the Piazzale Michelangelo crowded with cars and tourist buses. The burnt-orange Duomo, the fulcrum on which the city turned, rose above the collage of red-tiled rooftops. She had a heart-stopping glimpse of the crenellated bell tower of the Piazza della Signoria and Giotto's tower near William's studio, familiar landmarks from her childhood. The sound of motor scooters like the buzzing of giant bees filled the air, a sound so evocative of Italy in summer. The cool air washed over Cotton's face and she detected the ancient earthy aroma emanating from the gardens they passed. Florence had been Delilah's city, William's city and hers, and she reached out to embrace its unique atmosphere.

When they crossed the bridge spanning the Arno, Prospero slowed down the car so she could get a better view of the Ponte Vecchio casting its reflected arches into the bronzed water.

They linked with the chaotic traffic circling the ancient northern gateway of the city, then crossed the canal where there were signs indicating Bologna, the first leg of the real journey back to Robbiano. From there on Cotton found herself retracing every mile of the way, thinking she remembered faded signboards, cafés or offices that gave way to mellowing old villas surrounded by gardens; but she wasn't sure. Gradually they too died away and the land opened up to vineyards and groves of shimmering olive trees planted on steep terraces, themselves crowned by clusters of umbrella pines and cypresses that sheltered huge villas in earth colours of sepia, gold, burnt umber.

As the last few kilometres went by, Cotton warded off a

sense of last-minute panic at the prospect of the crossroads she was powerless to avoid. The first sight of Robbiano atop its hill reduced her to a state of pure inarticulate emotion. The village lay on the blue horizon as it had since the thirteenth century, shored up, safe and secure above the terraces of olives and vines. The view was lost when they passed through a glade of trees and across a small stone bridge that spanned a narrow stream of rushing water that she remembered dried out in July. Then the village appeared again, closer now.

Prospero drove the last mile slowly, sensing that she wanted to absorb every detail of the landscape.

'What a good memory you have,' she remarked when he took a small short-cut she had forgotten.

'I'm sure yours is better.'

'We'll see,' she replied.

When he took the turning to the unpaved road that led to the villa, Cotton blinked back tears that she was determined not to let fall. The cicadas singing in the dry grass beneath the lacy shade of ilex trees cast a gentle spell over the ripe afternoon. She leaned forward, disturbed at the neglected state of the approach to the villa's private road. Ahead she could see the high wall set with an iron grille securely locked by a padlock and chain.

'What's going on?' she whispered as Prospero stopped the car on the quiet, shady lane and turned off the ignition. For a moment they listened to the birds that filled the silence.

'It seems to be locked up. Wouldn't you like to get out and have a look?' he asked, seeing Cotton hesitate.

She nodded, stung by disappointment at the sight of the big rusting padlock and chain at the gate which struck an uneasy chord within her. With a jolt it came home to her that her memory was nothing but a well-worn track, and that somehow she had deceived herself into imagining that the villa had been lying intact, sleeping in the Tuscan hills all these years, waiting for her to come back. What she had subconsciously hoped to experience in returning there at last was a trip through time where she could re-create every sensation of coming home exactly as it had been when she lived at the villa with Delilah.

In the picture of the past she cherished, there was no place for a locked gate and all it implied.

They got out of the car and walked along the path to the gate. Cotton braced herself for the changes she would find, but in spite of all the promises she had made to herself, in spite of all the imaginary journeys she had made to the gardens of her childhood, nothing could have prepared her for the haunting neglect that she found when she peered through the iron bars. The pebbled drive that had once been so immaculate was overgrown with brambles. Box hedges that bordered the path had grown wildly out of shape and the tall dark cypresses had an unkempt look, robbing them of their ancient dignity. One giant urn that Cotton remembered had shattered and was lying in pieces, and a statue of Apollo she used to believe was a man turned to stone had fallen off its pedestal and its head rolled away.

'I can't believe it,' she whispered, suddenly remembering Prospero.

'Just look at it,' he muttered as he observed the devastation that neglect had wrought.

She stared into the garden, trying to reconcile what she saw with what she remembered. Throughout the years when she had nothing permanent to cling to, the image of the villa, unchanged for hundreds of years before she had been born, had become her own private symbol of continuity. And even if she comprehended as an adult that she couldn't re-create the happiness of those years, she would have been consoled by the fact that someone lived there as the guardian of its beauty and tranquillity. It was like looking into an open grave and seeing the decaying corpse of a person she had once loved. A sudden vivid memory of Delilah came back to her and she found herself choking back the tears.

'Come on, let's go – I've seen enough.'

Prospero grabbed her arm. 'No, not yet. It's criminal the way they let this place go to ruin. Now we're here we've got to get to the bottom of it. I intend to find out who the hell is responsible. What kind of barbarian would let a fine property like this become derelict?' His voice was harsh with anger, his face darkly serious.

'I don't know,' she replied, shaking her head. All Cotton wanted to do was to leave. She was about to suggest they abandon the idea of staying in Florence and return to Rome that evening, but the angry determination written on Prospero's face brought her to her senses.

'No, of course you're right,' she said.

'We didn't come all this way to go back without knowing why this thing has happened. Come on – there must be another entrance to this place. Maybe there's a caretaker.'

'It's possible,' she admitted. As she looked again at the neglected garden, anger unexpectedly negated her sense of desolation. She wondered if he was thinking the same thing she was when they caught sight of the weathered 'For Sale' sign at the top of the gate. 'There must be someone around who can tell us what's going on. We've got to see this through, to find out, Cotton. Don't you realize that I too care about this place? It means a lot to me. If I had never come here with Pietro that day I might not be here now with you.' His hands gripping her shoulders, he conveyed his steely determination. From that moment on they were two people bound together by a common cause, the riddle they needed to solve. Cotton thought for a moment.

'There is a back entrance to the property. If a caretaker is here, that's where he would be living.' Looking down the overgrown road that skirted the wall she said doubtfully, 'The road looks bad, though. You might scratch your car or get a flat tyre.' There was a glint of humour in her eyes.

'I don't give a damn,' he said with a shrug. 'Come on, let's go.' Grabbing her hand, he pulled her back to the car.

As they drove along the track that skirted the wall, the suspense became unbearable.

'That intent expression on your face – you look just like Sherlock Holmes,' she said with a laugh.

'Thanks. You don't bear much resemblance to Watson I'm glad to say,' he retorted.

When they passed a gap where the ancient stone had given way, Prospero braked while Cotton peered through.

'It's like a jungle in there,' she said in bewilderment. Cotton strained to see ahead.

'Look,' she cried as they turned the last corner. 'The back gate is open. That's where the gardener's cottage is.'

'See? What did I tell you?' cried Prospero triumphantly.

The moment he stopped the car Cotton leapt out and ran towards the iron gate. It creaked as she touched it. Her heart beating wildly, she looked inside. At a glance she saw that the cottage was inhabited and that the vegetable garden surrounding it was well tended. Relief flooded through her at the signs of habitation, the washing on the line, the garden chairs under the adjoining pergola.

'Is anybody living there?' said Prospero behind her.

'Yes, thank God,' she said. 'You were right,' she added, squeezing his hand as she led the way inside. 'Is anybody home?' she called in Italian.

A man in faded overalls, his face in the shadow cast by a straw hat, emerged from behind the bean poles.

'*Buon giorno,*' Cotton called hesitantly. 'I'm sorry to disturb you, signor, but I used to live here when I was a child – in the villa,' she gestured. 'I'm the daughter of the Marchesa di Castello di Montefiore, widow of Niccolò . . .'

The old man stared at her blankly for a second, then a smile spread across his weathered face. Taking off his hat, he revealed a shock of grey hair.

'Signorina Cotton! It's Giuseppe the gardener, remember me? Remember?' he cried.

'Giuseppe?'

The old man with a stubbled chin, his hands and face leathery from countless seasons of Tuscan sun, bore little resemblance to the vigorous dark-haired head gardener she remembered. Eighteen years had changed him into an old man. 'Giuseppe!' she cried, rushing forward to embrace him.

Patting her on the back, he laughed heartily.

'*Piccola* Cotton, I don't believe you've come back after all these years. *Dio*, it's good to see you.'

'It's about time, isn't it?' she said, trying to laugh away her deep disbelief that Giuseppe was still there. 'It's so good to see you, so good.' Suddenly remembering Prospero, she turned to him. 'Giuseppe, this is Prospero Vallone, a friend of mine.'

'*Buon giorno*,' said Prospero with a friendly smile, extending his hand. Giuseppe had begun to weep when he saw Cotton's eyes fill with tears.

They fell silent as Cotton regarded the walled corner of the estate, constructing from memory the long-forgotten details of her childhood paradise. Where two acres of surrounding land had once been cultivated to provide produce for Constanzia's kitchen and Delilah's table, now only a small plot remained, like an island carved out of an encroaching wilderness. Cotton searched for signs of the asparagus beds, remembering how the sharp green spears had poked their heads through the straw in spring, but there was no trace of them. She did recognize the purple heads of artichokes raised in the distance above jagged silver leaves, glossy aubergines ripening in the sun and ruddy-cheeked tomatoes supported by bamboo poles. All that was left of the fine greenhouses that had provided grapes and white peaches for the table was a collapsed frame obscured by a tangle of vines. But the sound of insects still filled this far corner of the property and she caught the heady bouquet of oregano and garlic mingling with the smell of freshly watered earth, a nostalgic reminder of the herb garden that had once been Delilah's pride and joy. She turned to see Giuseppe regarding her with unabashed sentimentality. He squinted at the sun, trying to reconcile this tall young woman with the child in pigtails he remembered.

'This one,' he said to Prospero, 'she was a real devil. Remember the time you cut all my prize roses?' He shook his head and laughed.

Cotton grinned. She had all but forgotten the incident. 'You chased me, but you didn't catch me. I remember that.'

'I was so angry,' he said, clenching his fist at the thought. 'She climbed a tree and sat there looking like a cat. I went straight to tell the Marchesa, remember? I said: "This child needs to learn a lesson." But she didn't do anything. This one got her way, always.' He chuckled fondly.

'Something tells me she hasn't changed much,' said Prospero with amusement.

Cotton shot him a warm smile, feeling a rush of gratitude

that he was there with her. The look in his eyes told her he had understood, that she didn't have to explain anything. He too knew what it was like to be exiled from a place he loved, knew about partings and reunions.

The gardener threw up his hands. 'I've offered you nothing at all after you've journeyed all this way. What is the matter with me? I'm not used to having guests – what a fool! Come, come and sit down,' he insisted, leading them to the vine-covered pergola. He motioned to them to sit in the rickety chairs he pulled up round a table. 'I still make the best *vin santo* in Italy, and I've got a special bottle I've been saving.'

Before they could protest, he disappeared into the house. He returned with a bottle and glasses, a tin box under his arm.

Beaming, Giuseppe filled the glasses to the brim with deep amber liquid, the same mellow shade as the pools of late afternoon sun that lay at their feet.

'The vineyards – what happened to the vineyards?' Cotton was prompted to ask.

'The vineyards, that's another story,' Giuseppe said with a sigh. 'But first we must drink a toast to you, Cotton, who has come home again.'

As Cotton raised her glass to her lips, the rich perfume of the wine opened another floodgate of memory. She had been allowed a small glass of the aromatic *vin santo* bottled on the estate as a treat from the time she was small. Giuseppe opened the tin and presented the amaretto biscuits. She took one, and dipped it into her glass. As she bit into the wine-soaked biscuit its almond flavour brought back a lost picture of the dining-room in the villa. She could almost feel the coolness of the blue panelled room at the height of summer, illuminated by a green filtered light coming through the open doors that led to the garden. She could see the flowers on the table, the white cut-work cloth that was spread with the remains of lunch served on the old crested Cremona plates. The hand-blown Venetian goblets were emptying rapidly, to be filled again with wine that made the conversation and laughter flow. The murmur of voices evoked the faces they belonged to, people who were either dead or dispersed to the corners of the earth. The memories came back thick and fast as Cotton stared into the verdant garden; but now she was becoming aware that she welcomed them whole-heartedly, that she was no longer trying to forget.

'Now,' said Prospero, settling back into his chair. 'Tell us, Giuseppe, how this villa fell into such a state.'

While he and Cotton listened, Giuseppe began a long, emotional account of what had happened since Delilah's death. He confirmed what Cotton already knew from William, that the Marchese's eldest son and heir had immediately taken over the villa when he heard of Delilah's death. He had fired most of the servants, except for Giuseppe and one maid, and had closed down the villa. He himself was living in Rome, where he worked as a functionary in the government. Giuseppe had no idea what had become of all Delilah's personal belongings, her jewellery, her clothes, all the *objets d'art* she had collected during her travels over the years, that should by right have belonged to her adopted daughter. Cotton had heard years ago from William that when he had returned from India the Marchese refused to relinquish any of Delilah's possessions to him, even for sentimental reasons, including the gifts he himself had given her over the years. Giuseppe reported that one by one, many of the paintings and antiques had been removed from the villa and were never seen again.

Then, when the Marchese's eldest son, now the Marchese di Castello di Montefiore, failed to move into the villa, there were rumours that his brother and sister had legally contested his inheritance in court. This, thought Giuseppe, was the main reason for the decline of the Villa Robbiano. During the intervening years the villa, its rooms now emptied, had fallen into disrepair. Eventually, after years of dispute, the estate was settled and the Marchese put the villa up for sale. Giuseppe believed this was forced on him, to settle the suit against him.

'And the villa is up for sale now?' asked Cotton, scarcely able to believe what she heard. 'But this house has been in the family for hundreds of years.'

'Even the mighty fall, Signorina Cotton,' said Giuseppe sagely. 'But in fact, he's asking too much for the place. He'll never sell it. He's crazy, the Marchese,' he said, touching a finger to his head. 'He might ask for that kind of money if the villa was in good condition, the frescoes restored, the vineyards producing wine, the gardens full of roses like they used to be . . .'

'How much is he asking, do you know?' said Prospero.

The gardener shrugged. 'I'm not sure. A fortune, though, believe me. You can inquire at the Notaro Perini in Florence. He handles the Marchese's affairs.'

'And how long has it been on the market?' inquired Cotton.

'Eighteen months, two years – I don't remember exactly. He's crazy, that man,' he repeated. 'Me, I don't get anything from him. I'm just allowed to live here and grow vegetables in exchange for having somebody on the property. But what do I care? I have my pension, my garden, and it's not a bad life. Why worry about the future?' He filled their glasses again.

'Let us drink to the Marchesa, shall we?' His rheumy eyes filled with sentiment as he raised his glass.

As he evoked Delilah, Cotton shivered, filled with bittersweet recollections. Deep peace stole over her as the shadows of evening lengthened, darkening the corners of the garden. If there was such a thing as immortality, Cotton wanted to believe that Delilah's spirit lingered there. A warm breeze moved the curtains of memory for a moment and Cotton pictured her strolling down the path in her garden hat, a basket over her arm full of angelica, bleeding hearts, and the fat peonies she loved to arrange in the house. The echo of her voice as she called Cotton's name still seemed to hang in the air, waiting for a response. Part of Cotton, as if disembodied, rose to answer the call from a shady corner overgrown with ferns, where she had been playing with one of the tortoiseshell cats who had bred at the villa since time immemorial. She still remembered their names: Moghul, Mud, Twinkle, Pinkey and Soho.

Prospero rose and said: 'I think we ought to take a walk around the property before it gets too late. Do you have the keys in your possession, Giuseppe?'

'Yes. Yes, I do,' he replied. His mind had been far away, nudged by several glasses of the strong wine. Prospero and Cotton exchanged a thoughtful glance as he went inside the house. When he returned, he was jangling a ring of keys.

'I'll come with you and open it,' said the gardener, leading them down the path. 'It sticks, and is hard to open.'

When they passed the swimming pool marked by tall cypress trees, Cotton saw it was cracked and peeling and its bottom was filled with seasons of dead leaves.

'For a while I tried to keep it clean,' mumbled Giuseppe, seeing the look of dismay on her face. 'But it was impossible. I'm much too old to do everything.'

But Cotton wasn't listening. They were walking down the path, weeds sprouting beneath the paving stones, towards the arcaded back of the villa in cool shadow. Once there had been rose gardens between the clipped yew hedges, but weeds now choked the earth. The basin of the fountain that had once emitted a soft gurgle to serenade guests on the terrace skirting the loggia was dry and strewn with debris, its cracks sprouting grass, its pouting bronze cupid tarnished and silent.

'It will come as a shock to you when you see the interior I'm afraid, signorina.' Rattling the keys, he went up the steps.

'My friend,' interjected Prospero, 'if you will just be good enough to open the door, then we will look around and lock it after we're finished.' He waited beside the gardener who was struggling with the enormous key he had slotted in the grilled door, its opaque glass cracked in several places.

'Some vandals broke in one night and did some damage,' Giuseppe remarked with a shake of his head.

'Probably some of those young ruffians from the village,' said Prospero, giving Cotton a wry smile which recalled that he had once been one of them.

When Prospero swung open the door and stepped aside for her to enter, Cotton overcame her sudden reluctance and stepped over the threshold. A musty smell filled her nostrils as she peered into the dimness, Prospero's footsteps echoing behind her. The shutters of the upper windows had been locked, casting a sepulchral dimness into the hall. They walked down the wide corridor, their footsteps resounding coldly on the flagstones. She found herself confronted with a shell laid waste by the years. Cotton led the way to the drawing-room, but when she tried to open the double doors they were warped and wouldn't budge.

'Here, let me do that,' muttered Prospero. 'You never could open a door, could you?'

A laugh escaped her throat, soothing the ache within her. At that moment she loved him for what he had just said. She watched as he forced open the door with his shoulder, then stepped inside. Prospero went to unfasten one of the long shutters while Cotton waited in the centre of the spacious room for the light, feeling as if she were in a tomb.

A shaft of sunlight sped across the marble floor stripped bare of all its precious carpets. The room had been raped of every treasure. Nothing remained of the elegant, welcoming drawing-room where Delilah had lavished hospitality on her friends over several decades. Cotton went to the wall and touched her finger to the tattered heliotrope silk that had been hung only months before Delilah's death. The unusual and beautiful shade evoked something precious as it tore beneath her finger. The colour was pure Delilah, a colour echoed in a few hybrid roses still struggling to survive in an overgrown bed outside the windows. Cotton scanned the walls marked with lighter patches where paintings had once hung.

'The ceiling frescoes have been damaged, but they could be restored,' Prospero commented, hands on his hips as he searched the ceiling.

Cotton followed his eyes, half-expecting to see the huge chandelier of Bohemian glass that used to tinkle faintly when a breeze stole through the loggia on warm summer evenings. There was only a hook to suggest it had ever been there.

They wandered into the dining-room, the library and the other small sitting-room where she and Delilah used to have tea or read on winter evenings in front of the fire. Things she hadn't thought of in years came back to Cotton, even though there was so little left to remind her. She remembered Delilah and William playing heated games of gin rummy, arguing over every point while she was curled up in a chair immersed in *Anna Karenina*. And yet, as Cotton sadly observed the destruction wrought by time, in spite of the fact that the villa had been stripped of all the beautiful things that had embellished it in its heyday, it still had a dignity which she knew it would retain until it had fallen to the ground. The cold, hollow rooms had retained a suggestion of former splendour that Cotton would always associate with her own private paradise. She had never known anything to compare with it, and she never would.

They wandered into the entrance hall and paused at the foot of the wide stone staircase. Cotton looked hesitantly at Prospero. A deep twilight had fallen on the landing and the slanting sun invaded the shutters, casting bars of gold on the peeling walls.

'Do you want to go up?' he whispered.

She shook her head. She didn't know why, but she didn't want to see her old room.

'Some other time, maybe.' Her voice echoed up the stairs.

When they returned down the corridor she took a deep breath, trying to dispel the heaviness that filled her but knowing she was only postponing the moment when she would give in to it. She wouldn't cry in front of Prospero, but some time when she was alone she would have to release the accumulated grief, and then perhaps the healing process could be complete.

'Thank you for coming with me, Prospero. I can't tell you how glad I am that I'm not here on my own. I'm truly grateful to you. In fact, I know now that if you hadn't urged me to come, I would have put it off until doomsday.' She gave him a quick smile, wishing she could adequately express what his support had meant to her. His reply was to encircle her shoulder with his arm.

When he had relocked the door, they went to the front of the house where the sense of decline lingered. The golden layers of paint were peeling off in long strips and the plaster had been invaded by mould. Swelling roots had burst urns and pots, and weeds had proliferated in the cracks between the stones underfoot. They wandered to the side loggia that overlooked a small rose garden where a few stray roses still bloomed. As Cotton looked into the vista of unkempt shrubbery she felt her knees go weak at the sight of the pergola at the bottom of the garden, heavy with a lacy profusion of pale mauve wistaria. This magnificent vine was thriving in riotous disregard of the devastation all around it. It was as if the pergola, where Cotton had spent so many hours daydreaming, had lived its own secret life all these years, growing stronger and more vigorous just as the rest of the property declined. With amazement, Cotton regarded the pale blaze. It was the spirit of the Villa Robbiano, risen from the ashes.

She could no longer stop the tears from coursing down her face. All she could do was to look helplessly at Prospero, who gathered her in his arms. As sobs shook her, he murmured softly in Italian, beautiful words that soothed the grief imprisoned inside her for so long. She clung to his strength, losing herself in his arms. The harder she cried the more tightly he held her, harnessing the pain and transforming it into a torrent of pure feeling that welded them together. When she had exhausted her tears, Cotton gave a shuddering sigh. They stood together for several moments, locked together. When she tilted back her head and looked at Prospero, he gently kissed her eyelids.

He kissed her lips chastely at first, but almost the moment their mouths met they were lost. The world evaporated as they clung in the shadow of the loggia, forged together by a living warmth that blotted out all the coldness of loss and death. In Prospero's embrace, Cotton found herself responding hungrily to kiss after kiss, each one peeling away a layer of deception, of illusion, until their hearts were laid bare. A burgeoning desire, rooted in time and place, entwined around them, destroying the last vestiges of strangeness.

When they broke apart, Cotton was aware as she looked into Prospero's face, transfigured with longing, that something extraordinary had happened to both of them that afternoon. He was regarding her with a powerful tenderness woven through with a passionate need which made her feel she was watching her own life change. The deeply sensuous lines of his mouth, the shadowy fire in his eyes, told her he felt the same way as she did. She had been right to trust him, she knew. They were not standing there in the ruins of the past, having both survived so much, simply to play with each other's emotions. A clear serenity blew around them, carrying with it the suggestion of gardens that were yet to bloom. As he brushed her face with a sense of wonder, they seemed to be saying all they would ever say, in one long glance. She had come there reluctantly to face the past, but as they stood in the pool of amber light that rose beyond the roof of the villa, Cotton knew she had found a future which would take greater courage to explore. The emptiness inside her had been filled with a sense of rediscovered values. Just how precious it was came home to her as she regarded the man who had been a part of her consciousness since she was twelve.

'Here we are, back where it all started,' he said, moved by the emotions crossing her face.

'Not quite,' she said with a mysterious smile.

'What's that supposed to mean?'

'Just take a few steps back,' she gestured. 'Near the balustrade.'

He obeyed. 'Is this where you want me?'

'Yes – don't move.'

He was standing in the exact spot where she had first seen him with Nancy Rogers. There was nothing about Prospero that resembled the brash young man she remembered – or was there? For a minute she recalled what it was like to be twelve again, experiencing the same innocent expectation as a twelve-year-old in a white dress, moved by her first sexual feelings.

'Come here, you nosy little brat,' he murmured. He gathered her in his arms again.

She laughed. 'So you did remember after all. That day in your office you said you didn't.'

'I was too proud to admit it. But this time, you're not going to get away so easily, Cotton Castello. And now I've caught you I'm going to . . .'

'Spank me?'

'No, I'm going to love you . . .'

Wedging her against the stone, he kissed her until they were aching with desire that had quickened in the sudden and unexpected intimacy of an afternoon.

When they were walking back to the gardener's cottage, their arms around each other, they stopped for one last look at the villa bathed in a golden light that was spilling over the hills, burnishing everything it touched. Like a dove set free, Cotton's nostalgic longing to return had run its true course, dispelling a darkness inside her.

'It's the strangest thing,' she admitted, 'but the villa doesn't look nearly as forlorn as it did when we came.'

'Maybe it's because for a little while, anyway, there's been some life here again.'

Clasping his arm around Cotton, Prospero gave the crumbling exterior of the villa a quick study, calculating how many millions of lire it would cost to restore it. Probably everything was wrong with it, he thought, after so many years of neglect inside and out. A team of master artisans and craftsmen would be needed to refurbish every inch of the Villa Robbiano, but then Florence was the place to find them. He viewed the weathered façade with an experienced eye, mentally rebuilding its decaying lines, restoring them to their former splendour. He could envisage the paths swept clean, the gardens tended once more, the roof replaced, the plaster restored – there was no end to it.

While Prospero was thinking, Cotton speculated along the same lines. She was seized with a rush of energy to bring the overgrown garden back to what it had once been. In her mind's eye she wove a little fantasy, imagining Giuseppe on a ladder, clipping the yews back into shape, removing dead branches from the straggling magnolia trees, planting roses between the privet hedges in the French fashion that Delilah had admired. She could hear the water in the fountain rushing again and caught its mossy scent on the breeze at evening. She could envisage the pebbled path swept clean of leaves, creating an avenue worthy of the villa that had been carefully restored. Mentally she replaced the peeling green shutters tilting on their hinges. She would see that window panes were mended, broken flagstones replaced, statues put back on their pedestals. And when everything was done she would set a stone table under the loggia beneath the grand weathered arches resting on pillars, just where a late sun now brushed the old tiles. It was a table for two set with the majolica ware she loved, and hand-blown

Venetian glass, with a bouquet of sweet peas and pansies from the garden. To make it complete, she pictured Prospero with her, idling away the summer evening and admiring the amazing transformation she had wrought. As the sky melted to crimson and deep blue overhead, they would share a bottle of wine from the vineyards that were once again producing their own robust wine, laid down in the cool cellars beneath the house. As Cotton embroidered one detail after another on to her dream she felt it flicker hesitantly in her mind. She had neither the means nor the need to ever own the Villa Robbiano. The thought of owning it was a child's dream, but one she allowed herself to cling to, even if only for a little while.

When they had returned the keys to Giuseppe, promising to come again, they drove through the hills back to Florence. As they crossed the Arno, the Ponte Vecchio was silhouetted against the flaming sky and the river was washed with pink. Cool evening air whipped their faces as the car climbed the hill through the Boboli Gardens where the road was marked by a bracelet of street lights.

They drove through the gates of the Villa Cora just as the sky turned to pale lemon between the umbrella pines. Prospero stopped the car beneath the floodlit portico and a uniformed doorman jumped to unload the luggage and park the car while they entered the lobby.

As they went through the formalities of checking in, the act of watching Prospero move a pen across paper was enough to send nervous expectation ripping through Cotton with a force that weakened her knees. Pretending to study the huge Venetian chandelier overhead, she counted the seconds until they could be alone.

'Signor Vallone, you are in the Pauline Borghese suite.'

'Yeah? Thanks,' he said in English, shooting an impatient glance at the porter who took the keys from the receptionist.

In the lift, Cotton hardly dared look at him for fear she would burst into nervous laughter – anything to defuse the tension in the air, that coiled around them like a rope, pulling them together until their hands touched.

The porter admitted them to the vast frescoed room, magnificently restored and furnished, its parquet floor gleaming like glass. As the porter busied himself with turning on lights, opening the huge long windows, she and Prospero exchanged a look of thinly veiled tolerance. Finally, when he could stand it no longer, Prospero dug his hand into his pocket.

'That's fine, fine, that's enough,' he said tersely, slapping a wad of notes into the man's hand without bothering to count it. 'If we need anything, we'll ring.'

When the door had closed they regarded each other for a long moment. She watched Prospero unbutton the shirt which she had stained with her tears that afternoon in the sunlit garden. Trembling in a second innocence, she could still see the flickering shadows of the Villa Robbiano pass over her closed eyes as he moved towards her, then tasted her lips with his tongue. Her body heavy with desire, she caressed his brown shoulders, absorbing their strength. Discovering the hollows and curves of his body for the first time, she was overcome with the need to press her breasts against his sinewy chest, marked with dark hair that concealed the deep scars from the shooting. When their clothes lay in a pile at their feet, his face was alight with pleasure at his first sight of her body. The passionate endearments he murmured as his hands moved down her shoulders, over her hips and brushed the golden down between her thighs impaled her with longing. He drew her to him, and as their naked skins touched she whispered, casting sensuous ripples of pleasure in the air. Flames began leaping in her abdomen, and down the insides of her thighs. His every muscle was steeled with urgency as he held her. Dipping his tongue repeatedly between her lips he stabbed his erection against her, calling forth longing that cried out to be freed. They fell back on the bed, flung there by the force of their desire. As his wide shoulders crushed hers and their legs entwined, they moved against each other in urgent rhythm. Then his tongue travelled the path between her breasts to the hollow of her navel, making a wet furrow until he tasted the bud of flesh buried in the tangle of golden hair. He kissed her reverently, sweetly, trying to convey with his lips all that he felt in his heart. A languishing softness blunted his heated need to be inside her, a gentleness and patience he had felt with no other woman. As he explored the beauty of her, he transcended his own need which seemed almost sated by the mystical rite of first discovery. He strove to give what he had received, glorying in her glistening form against the coverlet, her throaty murmur, the musky taste of her. With smouldering restraint his mouth sought every secret of her body, claiming her, possessing her, until she was his by right of passion.

Caught in the torrent of sensations that Prospero aroused in her, Cotton seemed to recognize all the sight, the taste, the smell of him, even before he himself had filled her. The sight of his potency sent arrows of longing through her abdomen and she ached to receive him. In the dimness his eyes shadowed hers as she finally gave herself up to his first thrust.

'Prospero – *caro*,' she grasped for the syllables.

'*Ti amo, per sempre ti amo . . . sei cuore mia, sempre,*' he whispered blindly, burying his lips in her hair as they were joined together.

They lay together united by one breath that fuelled the next thrust, stronger and yet more urgent. Trembling on the brink of an uncharted fulfilment, Cotton sought to hold back. Her eyes were glazed with love as she clutched Prospero's head in her hands, willing him to penetrate to her very soul, lying undiscovered at the depths of her being. Gathering his hands beneath her he bore down and they began to move again in a powerful arabesque, seared by the heat of their ripening senses. At last the gates opened and they shot through as helpless as driftwood into a thundering channel. Locked together, gasping, whispering, they flew free in a moment's immortality.

The next morning the first sensation that seeped into Cotton's consciousness was the smell of perfumed soap mingling with the aroma of coffee. She stirred in the tumble of linen sheets. Turning her head she smiled, her eyes still closed, as the memory of the night before came back to her. As she stretched her legs she luxuriated in the sated sensation her movements aroused. Opening her eyes, she saw in the shadowy dimness a streak of white, a trolley draped in damask and set for breakfast.

A soft rasping made her turn her head on the pillow and she saw Prospero standing naked a few feet away, rubbing his wet hair with a towel.

'Hi,' she murmured.

As she spoke her eyes dropped to his erection springing from a mass of dark hair, a discovery that sent a concentration of desire through her half-slumbering body.

The beauty of Cotton sprawled in abandon on the rumpled bed had brought Prospero to an instant state of arousal. Dropping his towel in a heap, he smoothed back his hair and came closer. He smiled when he saw her languorous expression of morning desire, a contrast to their violent need for each other the night before.

'See what you've done to him,' he said with a laugh.

Prospero traced her classically beautiful pose against the snowy sheets. Her linear perfection rose and fell in infinitely desirable curves like the sweep of a sand dune, seizing him with a need to possess her body all over again.

'Your body is made for love,' he said in a whisper.

'You've already proved that,' she murmured with an inviting smile, brushing a lock of hair from her forehead.

'May I be allowed to prove it again, *bellissima*?'

She gave a gurgling little laugh as he kneeled on the bed and, parting her legs, made a path of biting kisses along her stomach, ending at her abdomen. He drew back and watched the pulse quicken in the hollow of her belly, betraying the wanton impatience caused by the sight and touch of him. Still pulsating from the night before, Cotton sucked in her breath at the agonizing pleasure of his virility. For a second they lay there, their eyes liquid with desire. His first movement inside her sent a surge of unfathomable wanting and she went with it, pushing hard against him down a chute of pleasure.

Later, Prospero handed her a cup of coffee as she sat up in bed, propped on a pile of pillows. Their eyes met in recognition of all that had happened during the last twenty-four hours. Cotton knew she was in love. The paradoxical lightness, and yet the feeling of landing on solid ground, had come to her unbidden.

It was nothing to do with sexual exhilaration, and yet that had expressed everything she felt for Prospero Vallone. They were more than just lovers waking up the morning after; they were soulmates whose lives now merged each in the other. As she sipped the strong milky coffee, Cotton was gripped by the contradiction of belonging utterly to a stranger in a strange place. All the tempestuous changes of fate that had governed her life until that moment had led her to that sunlit Florentine morning, the bed, the man, whose name and image seemed to have been grafted upon her before she had taken her first step or uttered her first word.

There were problems, so many problems, to overcome, she realized as he kissed her and handed her a roll and butter.

'Jam?' he asked, with a smile, as if reading her mind.

'I feel like I've had all the jam I have a right to in the figurative sense,' she was moved to say.

As she watched him dip a silver spoon into the jam pot, it seemed to Cotton that their union of opposites had the power either to destroy them or exalt them. Last night they had both given their trust, whispering promises that had already begun to send feelers into their future. Yesterday was different from today and all the cataclysmic changes it implied, because they had found each other.

Chapter 22

Instead of returning to her chauffeured car after paying a fleeting visit to the rusting gates of the Villa Robbiano, Chiara had impulsively taken a deserted track that triggered a memory. As she forged through the thick foliage, the scent of dust and wild flowers set her on edge. The sound of her own footsteps on the uneven path thudded emptily in her ears and she hugged her arms to her sides to avoid the thorns and branches that leapt out to ensnare her. Now and then a bird struck a strident note breaking the soothing rhythm of cicadas that rose from the sunbleached grass. When the undergrowth thinned out suddenly, she stopped, a cool sharp blade of recognition cleaving her in two. For a moment she could go neither forward nor back, but stood fixed, impaled by a misery that she hadn't felt in years. Nothing she had achieved, bad or good, over the past three decades could overpower the anguish that she felt as she regarded the road that appeared ahead, carved by generations of cart tracks rolling over the hardened clay. Behind her the undergrowth seemed to close in, barring her way. There was no choice but to go forward, down the abandoned cul-de-sac.

At last she saw the house, perched precariously on a ragged slope engulfed by the surrounding landscape and made smaller by the passage of time. She walked towards it, as if in a dream, commanded by the power of her heart beating wildly in her chest. She could see from a distance that the cottage still stood in the middle of a vineyard that shimmered blue-green in the morning sun. Weed-choked and derelict, the house was obviously abandoned, with the roof tiles caved in exposing the beams beneath, the yellow plaster all but worn away. She stood mesmerized for an instant before drifting trance-like down the overgrown path. When she reached the end, she gently pushed the rusty gate that creaked as it opened. Chiara's eyes moved slowly, gathering every half-forgotten detail that had lain at the back of her mind all these years. She identified the rainwater barrel which had burst and was lying in pieces near the pergola where a trumpet-vine ran riot; she noted the broken dirty windows, the front door tilting on its hinges. Impassively she examined the empty shell where her life had begun, like a dry chrysalis long since discarded.

Chiara's eyes glazed over and her breath came heavily as she fell into the pit of memory summoned by the ghostly wail of a train whistle reverberating in her ears. On the platform of the station in Florence, passers-by moved around her like bundles in their winter clothes, their breath clouding in the blue, misty air. A small, battered suitcase in her hand, she was hurrying desperately after the hunched old man with dirty fingernails and an unshaven face who had come to collect his five-year-old granddaughter in the year the Americans had landed at Palermo. She was crying and shivering because her coat, warm enough for Naples, was too thin for the north in winter. The scowling old man had just ripped off her identity tag so carefully attached to her coat lapel by her dead mother's friend Nina, when she had put her on the train in Naples.

'Don't lose it, whatever you do. Don't lose it, do you hear?' the tall, pretty brunette smelling of perfume, her red mouth carefully painted, had cautioned her. 'It's the only way he'll know who you are . . .' The voice was full of kindness and pity. Nina had come to the apartment to rescue her when her mother didn't return home after the munitions factory where she worked had been bombed. After two days with Nina, she had discovered her mother was dead.

'Don't lose it, do you hear?' The words echoed in Chiara's mind.

When at last she had caught up with the old man with white beetling eyebrows over suspicious black eyes she screamed at him, tears running down her cheeks. 'Give it back to me, give it back, that's for my grandfather, not you.'

Whirling around, he glowered at her angrily, squeezing the back of her neck until it hurt. He bore down on her with fierce dark eyes set in a hardened face.

'Stop that bawling, do you hear? I *am* your grandfather.'

She shrank back, her tears drying on her face, as he crumpled her identity tag in his clenched fist, then threw it on the ground. Taking her roughly by the hand, he pulled her through the crowd. As she stumbled along she strained to look backwards, to see the paper lying crushed on the pavement, stamped underfoot by passers-by. It bore her destination, Firenze, and her name, Anna Gagliani.

Chiara came back to the present as she gazed at the house where she had spent the cruel years that had tempered her character. She imagined the young Anna coming out of the door to feed the chickens and give water to the goat. Nobody knew what had become of Anna, not even Chiara, as she tried to resurrect the child she had once been. It seemed she had died on that first day in Rome when Chiara Galla was born, inspired by the cross between a film star Anna had seen in a magazine, and a smart leather goods shop on the Corso.

Perspiring from heat and dread, Chiara forced herself to approach the house. She felt sick to her stomach when she peered through a broken window at the wooden table near the blackened hearth where she used to eat in silence with her grandfather. She could hardly bear to look at the open door that led to her squalid bedroom with the iron bedstead. She was revolted by a collection of decaying fruit in green bottles near the sink, the yellowed newspapers scattered on the floor, and shrank back with a gasp when she saw a huge spider suspended on a web near the kitchen window. A tattered mattress tossed on the floor reminded her that her grandfather had probably died there, alone and miserable; but she felt no pity when she thought of his barking commands, his eyes bloodshot from drink. She stepped back unsteadily and let out a little moan that was swallowed by the silence. Wiping away the perspiration on her forehead, she recalled how her own summer had finally come. With the sudden glory of spring forcing winter to release its grip on the land, her season had arrived, that startling moment when she had become an object of desire, astonishing everyone in the village, even herself.

When Chiara hurried back down the path by the way she had come she had no further desire to look back for any lingering traces of Anna Gagliani. She had done what morbid curiosity had compelled her to do, and now she concentrated on shutting it out of her mind. But as she went back down the lane, passing a short cut that led to the village, she almost imagined she heard the sharp echo of a child's taunt.

'*La bastona, la bastona,*' the laughing voice whispered again and again, slurring the words to '*la bastarda*'. The insidious voice hissed the words with a teasing slyness she could never forget, twisting the vague memory of her mother into something sinister. She had never quite been able to remember her mother's features – only her heavy golden hair that she had loved to brush – the blonde hair of a northern Italian that she always wished she had inherited. Chiara rejected the memory, not wanting to feel anything but resentment for her mother who had left her a bitter legacy of illegitimacy and poverty, then deserted her by dying. '*Bastarda, bastarda*', the words still cut deep when she passed the spot where a mob of children had pushed her and pulled her hair. She recalled with gratitude how the village priest had come upon them, how he had angrily broken up the chanting circle and put his arm protectively around her as he whispered kind words. For a long time she had cherished the memory of his hand on her shoulder, the kindly smile that illuminated his handsome face. For years she had harboured a passion for Father Pietro Giannini, until that summer when she had bloomed into a woman and had rashly given herself to his cousin, Prospero Vallone, and then to the American, Matthew Swope.

Regarding the spot at the end of the lane where Prospero used to drop her on his Vespa, she recalled the evening of his cousin's wedding, in the piazza, when she was young and confident and he was strong and feared nothing. It amazed her that that glory still survived all that had happened, but now she swept her mind clear of sentiment. She thought instead of the man Prospero had become, the man she loved. Yes, she loved him. Why else should she feel this restlessness since they had quarrelled, this compulsion to do something as unpleasant as returning to Robbiano?

When she had learned that the boy who had taken her virginity, only to disappear overnight in a cloud of scandal, had become a rich and powerful man, she had been fascinated and intrigued by the similarity of their destinies. When she realized Sandy Vincent was a mutual friend, she had avoided meeting him again; terrified that he would recognize her and expose the carefully constructed background she had invented for herself. But when it became obvious that Prospero had no idea of her real identity, that she had changed beyond recognition, she began to relax. As time went on she started toying with the idea that she would tell him the truth some day.

It had been thirty years since the passionate summer that had changed her life, and Prospero Vallone was the only man to whom she had given herself with no other motive than young, hungry desire. The time was wrong for them thirty years ago, but now they were ready to belong to each other.

When she came back to the short-cut to the Marchesa's house, she was unable to resist following it again. She plunged into the undergrowth as if trying to flee the unhappy past that seemed intent on poisoning the present.

'Prospero, Prospero,' she whispered his name aloud as she climbed, wondering why he was still punishing her. Her mind clouded over, blotting out the possibility that he might not come back.

For years she had toyed with the idea of coming back; the more she achieved in life, the more she relished the fantasy of walking into the Villa Robbiano as a rich and famous woman. Armed with wealth and fame, nothing could touch her. The idea should have meant less over the years but somehow that had never happened and now all that she had wrested from life seemed diminished in value if she couldn't prove how far she had come. All she wanted was one moment of triumph and then she would be satisfied. She had never been able to relinquish the pipe-dream of showing the formidable Marchesa what she had made of herself, against all odds, of meeting her on an equal footing. And now it was too late. Time had cheated her, robbed her of the chance to meet the Marchesa again and to ask what had happened to her daughter. Her heart thudded as the word invaded her mind without warning. 'Daughter' – she hadn't spoken the word, not even to herself, in years. She pushed away the unpleasant thought that, wherever she was, her child would be nearly thirty by now.

A few moments later when she arrived at the back entrance of the villa she saw the open gate to the gardener's cottage, where as a young girl she had stolen strawberries, pears and blackcurrants.

She was just trying to gather her courage to enter the gate when she turned to see an old man approaching, wheeling a bicycle.

'*Buon giorno, signora,*' he said, inclining his head. 'May I help you?' Taking a bag of groceries from the bicycle, he smiled at her.

'*Buon giorno,*' she replied in a startled voice, remembering to smile back. Seeing the man trying to stare behind her sunglasses she reluctantly took them off.

'I used to be a friend of the Marchesa's years ago,' she began. 'That is, my mother was.' She gestured towards the abandoned property. 'Is she . . .?'

'Yes, she's dead,' he replied, shaking his head mournfully, then identifying himself.

When she realized that this was Giuseppe the gardener, Chiara suppressed her shock at how cruelly he had aged. He gave no sign that he knew who she was, as he regarded her politely. She extracted from him the story of the Marchesa's death and the decline of the Castello di Montefiore family fortunes.

'And now the house is finally up for sale, which means that from one month to the next I don't know whether I have a roof over my head, signora,' said Giuseppe with a philosophical shrug.

He was just about to mention that the Marchesa's adopted

daughter had come back only yesterday, when she interrupted him.

'I would like to see the villa again, for sentimental reasons. That is, if it's not too much trouble.'

The stunning news that the villa was for sale galvanized Chiara.

'Si, signora, of course,' Giuseppe replied, hurrying to fetch the keys. When he returned, he said:

'Who did you say your mother was, signora?'

Ignoring him, she asked: 'Do you know who is handling the sale of the villa?'

'Yes, yes. When you've finished looking I'll give you the address. A notary named Perini. He never comes here, and neither does the Marchese,' he said, leading her down the path.

Later, Chiara passed through the back gate of the villa, closing it thoughtfully behind her. In one hand she clutched the paper on which Giuseppe had written the address of the notary in Florence. She paused for a moment, turning over images of the derelict house in her mind. She shrugged off the penetrating coldness of those bare rooms, the smell of damp that seemed to linger in her nostrils. Her every hollow footstep as she wandered throughout the villa had been shadowed by a kind of horror as she remembered what it had been like to be young, friendless and poor. When she had passed the swimming pool now filled with leaves, she had recalled the night she first made love there with Matthew Swope – the satisfaction of that small triumph had long since faded. The months she had worked for the Marchesa had been coloured by an acute sense of exclusion that she had never forgotten. She had existed only as a shadowy presence as a servant to the Marchesa, and for her lover, Signor Partridge, for whose students she had posed – she had been a mere object, a slave. Only Matthew Swope had loved her for herself, but he had died too soon to change her life. Now, thirty years later, the tide had turned and she was in a position to right the wrong they had all done her.

Arriving back at the car, she slipped on to the back seat as the driver held open the door.

'Take me back to Firenze,' she ordered. 'First to the hotel.'

Leaning back as the driver headed down the hill, Chiara's mind ticked over as she resolved to buy the Villa Robbiano, no matter what it cost.

In the heart of Florence, Prospero blocked the traffic on the narrow Borgo dei Greci with his Mercedes as he stopped to let Cotton out. Before she could leap out, he gathered her in his arms for a last passionate kiss, oblivious of the honks and shouts of protest behind him.

'So, we rendezvous at the corner of Tornabuoni and Strozzi, then, say four?' he said, looking up at her as she leapt flustered from the car. He gave her a dazzling smile of appreciation as she self-consciously brushed back her hair.

'I could meet you earlier if William is busy,' she replied hopefully, ashamed to admit that she didn't want to let him out of her sight.

'*Vaffanculo, stronzi!*' boomed Prospero over his shoulder at the concertina of traffic, unable to keep from breaking into laughter. 'The thing is, I'm having a meeting in the Via Strozzi and I'm not sure what time I'll finish, so I'd better see you then, okay? *Bella*,' he called with a wave as he pressed on the accelerator.

She watched him disappear down the narrow street. As she walked along, the line of cars streamed past her, their fury dissolved by the sight of the willowy blonde who had caused all the chaos. She proceeded along the narrow pavement, compliments ringing in her ears.

'*Bellissima! Che bella!*'

She sailed proudly along, playing the moment for all it was worth. The compulsion to share her happiness was bubbling inside her and she found herself smiling at perfect strangers as she crossed the Piazza della Signoria. An inner incandescence propelled her along the street she hadn't visited in years, and as she threaded her way among the pigeons and tourists crowding the ancient uneven cobbles, her eyes moved upwards past the magnificent statues sheltered in the loggia, to the great bell tower that watched over the ancient square.

On the corner of the piazza she stopped on impulse to buy a bouquet of flowers, suddenly aware that she was approaching William's studio empty-handed. When she passed a confectioner's shop near the Piazza Santa Croce, she bought a big box of chocolates, remembering how much he liked them.

Walking down the busy street flooded with morning sun, Cotton reflected that it had taken her nearly twenty years to retrace the route to William's studio, a walk she and Delilah had made countless times when they were shopping in the city.

After Delilah's death, William had prolonged his stay in India, meant to last only a few months, into two years, since there was nothing for him in Florence. Over the years he and Cotton had exchanged letters, some brief, some long and moving, but gradually time and distance had lengthened between them. They had met only once, while Cotton was at Columbia. William had had a one-man show in New York, in a gallery on Fifty Seventh Street. Their reunion had been cut short by the crowd, and when they lunched together the next day Cotton had been sorrowful about the change in him. It wasn't just that he had aged greatly in the decade that had elapsed, but that a distance had come between them. At the time she had been hurt and puzzled at the way William treated her as if she was an acquaintance he was pleased, but not overjoyed, to see. Now, with the maturity of adulthood, Cotton realized poignantly that the spark must have gone out of William's life when Delilah died so suddenly. She had represented the golden age of his life, the flowering of his talent and, with her passing, part of him had ceased to exist. Cotton guessed that for years William had confined her adopted daughter to the past, that meeting her in New York had churned up deeply painful memories he had preferred to avoid. At the time she had been stung by his behaviour, but now she understood.

When Cotton passed through the big old doors gnarled with age, between two shop fronts, she paused at the brass where William's name was engraved: Sir William Partridge, 4th Floor. Yet another door in her consciousness swung open as she approached the wide stone staircase with its worn balustrade. Even the ancient smell rising from the building brought back memories of the times she and Delilah called in, laden with bags and boxes from Ferragamo and Pucci. They had always arrived at the top of the stairs out of breath, and Cotton recalled Delilah furiously dabbing her nose with powder and applying lipstick before she would let her ring the bell.

Now, as Cotton stood on the dark landing hearing footsteps beyond the door, she was eager to see William again. This time the moment seemed right. Would he have aged unrecognizably? A glance over her shoulder at the flight of stairs she had just climbed told her he must still be fit at eighty if he could manage them twice a day. Was it really possible he was eighty, she asked herself?

When the door flew open she was blinded for a moment by sunlight flooding through the skylight above. She saw a bushy white beard, and William's ruddy face lit by a radiant smile.

'Cotton – Cotton, my dear child,' he cried, clutching her by the shoulders.

'William, I can't believe it!' She laughed joyously, delighted at the strength of the hands that gripped her shoulders. She was reassured to notice how dapper he looked in a blue denim shirt, a yellow cravat and grey flannel trousers.

'Here, these are for you,' she said, delivering the chocolates and flowers into his arms.

'How kind you are, how very kind,' he murmured, setting them on a chair and then regarding her with deep blue eyes under bristling white brows.

Tears sprang to Cotton's eyes as she encircled him with her arms and hugged him warmly. They clung to each other for a moment. She looked up to see that his eyes, too, were glistening with tears.

'Well, well, well, it's about time, isn't it?' he murmured.

'The last time we met didn't really seem to count.'

'No, it didn't. You're right,' he replied with a shake of his head.

Looking at William now, Cotton realized she had never come to terms with losing him as a mentor, a father figure, any more than she had been able to come to terms with Delilah's death. They had wasted so much time when they could have meant something to each other, as they grieved thousands of miles apart.

William regarded her with his brow furrowed in thought.

'You look radiant, Cotton. You've bloomed.'

'I have?' she said, touched that he had picked up on what she was feeling, but noticing a blush of surprise rise to her cheeks.

'It's finally happened, hasn't it? I can see that you've fallen in love.'

She gave a startled laugh at the shrewdness of his observation. 'Is it really that obvious?'

He chortled with pleasure. 'Oh yes, oh yes. You have the unmistakable and compelling aura of a woman whose affections have been profoundly engaged.'

She hugged him, recalling that he had never talked down to her, even when she was a little girl. Since she had first been able to talk, he had spoken to her with the same flamboyant language that had nurtured in her an early love of words.

'I'll say this, William – it feels simply wonderful. I've never known anything like it.' She was trying to sound calm and rational, but her euphoria broke through.

'Now tell me, who is this paragon who has stolen your heart? Does he deserve you?' queried William. His arm on her shoulder, he led her into the airy, spacious studio crammed with easels, boxes of paints and canvases stacked everywhere. The glass skylight gave a sweeping view of the tiled rooftops of Florence.

'William, wait until I tell you,' she began. 'That last summer, he came to a party at the villa, the one I nearly missed because I had been misbehaving, remember? He came with Pietro Giannini, his cousin, who had just been made a Monsignor. His name is Prospero Vallone. His mother is the sister of fat Fontini who used to run the pharmacy.'

William laughed heartily at the recollection. 'Of course I remember him. How could I forget? He was the young stud who shocked us all by absconding with the redoubtable Nancy Rogers, umpteen years his senior, wasn't he?' Stroking his beard, he looked at her doubtfully.

'Oh, I know what you must be thinking,' she hastened to reassure him. It had occurred to her that William might not approve of this black sheep who had now made good, and to put his mind at ease she said: 'It's true that Prospero may have done things in his life he's not proud of, but haven't we all? That doesn't change the fact that he's the most marvellous man I've ever met. He's intelligent, warm-hearted, sensitive. I've never known anyone quite like him. Do you know something, William, he's made me realize that I've never really been in love with any man until I met him.'

'This sounds serious.'

'I'm hoping it will be.' She laughed at herself. 'Hoping, I say. No, better than that. I know this is it for me.'

'My, my, this does come as a surprise. Cotton in love. How long has this been going on? You didn't mention it in your card from Ethiopia.'

Knowing how absurd it sounded she said: 'About two weeks. We met in Rome. He's here with me, and we want to take you to dinner tonight.'

William shook his head and remarked with a chuckle: 'Two weeks? As long as that, really?'

She gave him a sheepish smile. 'I know it must sound ridiculous in a way, and I guess it is all a bit mad, but that's just the way it happened.'

William said cautiously: 'I would be less than honest if I pretended I hadn't heard about Prospero Vallone over the years.'

William was thinking not only of his indiscretion with Nancy Rogers, but his marriage to a rich woman, his run in with the law, the doubtful shadow cast by his father's murder and the attempt against his own life, reputedly by the Mafia.

'But how would you know about Prospero?'

'Through Pietro Giannini.'

'Yes, of course. I should have known you were still in touch with the Cardinal.' She was gratified to discover yet another link between herself and Prospero, drawing their net of intimacy even closer.

'Pietro has confided in me now and then over the years. And

there were times when he was worried about Prospero. He has a tendency to over-reach himself – he always has had.'

'A quality that I adore,' she said, her eyes shining.

'He has a way with women, apparently.' William gave her a cautionary glance.

'I guess that's how he won me over,' she replied, undaunted.

She told him how they had met, how their lives seemed to have been running parallel over the years. The way William was regarding her affectionately told her she had almost convinced him.

'Don't listen to a stuffy old man's objections. I wouldn't cloud your happiness for anything in the world,' he said, kissing her forehead. 'I only want the best for you. You do understand?'

'He is the best,' she said simply.

'But just one thing – don't you think you're rushing things a bit?'

'Dear William, we're in such a terrible hurry. We've got so much time to make up for.'

'Ah, yes, time ... Yes, I know all about that,' he said nostalgically.

'I can't wait for you to meet him. We'll take you to Enoteca Pinchiorri. Remember? The last time was my birthday that summer ...'

'That would be simply splendid,' said William. As their eyes met, Cotton had a sudden glimpse of the pain submerged so many years after Delilah's death.

'Come, let me fix you a cup of coffee,' he said, adopting a cheerful expression.

She followed him into the small room off the studio that served as a kitchen and washroom, where she instantly recognized a familiar row of blue painters' smocks below a collection of hats – a Homburg for his trips to London, a straw hat she remembered he wore when he painted during the summer, a vintage top hat and a yellowing panama. A canvas topi reminded her of his sojourn in India after Delilah's death that had marked his passage from a renowned painter of Tuscan landscapes and society portraits to an artist of greater scope and depth. Those were the years when he had been as inconsolable as Cotton.

As he fussed with the espresso pot, Cotton studied the neat rows of spotless paintbrushes carefully stored in stone jars, a reminder that William had always been meticulous in his habits.

'I was wondering if I might see some of your work from the India years?'

He gave her a poignant smile, his face brightening.

'I thought you might ask that. When you called and said you were coming I dug out the catalogue for you, among other things,' he added with a secretive twinkle in his blue eyes.

When he had set the china cups on a painted Florentine tray she was upset to notice his hands trembling. She quelled the impulse to reach out and touch a gnarled, freckled hand in a gesture of affirmation of her love for him, love that she was sure must have nurtured some lasting good in her.

They went back into the studio and William ceremoniously set the coffee on the table and pulled up two chairs.

'Excuse me for one moment while I call down for a titbit to accompany this powerful brew,' he said with a wink.

As Cotton studied the rooftops of Florence clustered around the Duomo, he cupped his hands and bellowed into the court-yard below.

'Immaculata, Immaculata – *per favore* – would you fetch two almond pastries from the bakery, please?'

A sonorous feminine voice responded to his call.

William counted some lire notes into a tattered basket tied to a rope and lowered it into the courtyard, re-enacting one of the favourite little rituals that Cotton had all but forgotten. Moments later there was a tug on the rope, accompanied by a shout, and he drew up the basket. Carefully removing the pastries dusted with sugar, he set them before her on a plate.

'Here, try these. They are pure sin.'

'But I've just had breakfast,' she said feebly.

'Don't be fooled into thinking you can live on love, because you can't, you know. And believe it or not, I remember what it was like.'

With a pang Cotton remembered Delilah with William all those years. William, too, had felt the tug of their loss for a moment, and rose briskly to his feet to fetch the catalogue of his Indian period to camouflage his emotions. Neither of them wanted their happy reunion to dissolve into grief, though they had left so much unsaid.

While they drank their coffee, Cotton browsed through the exhibition catalogue. Turning the pages, she was struck by the milestone the pictures represented in the life of Sir William Partridge R A. Tragedy had transfigured his work, infusing it with a searing imagery, the like of which she had never seen. Until then, Cotton had had no real perception of the depth of William's talent, nor the acutely personal impact that the first sight of his Indian pictures would have on her. Despair had stripped his talent to the bone, and his work exhibited compassion and humanity. She studied portraits of the people of India's teeming cities, their faces filled with stoic indifference, and the moving, graceful images of toiling peasants, the sweeping landscapes of Punjab, the lushness of Assam, the beaches of the Coromandel coast and the rugged faces of its fishermen.

'William, these are wonderful. I'm speechless with admiration,' she said at last.

'Keep the catalogue if you like. I have others.'

'Thank you. I'll always treasure it.'

'I thought you'd also like to see this,' he said, handing her a catalogue of the exhibition of British Twentieth-Century Art at the Royal Academy, scheduled for the following year.

She thumbed through the catalogue representing William's peers, Lucian Freud, Stanley Spencer, Francis Bacon. William's inclusion put him firmly in the select group of prestigious painters who had indelibly represented their age.

'Let's see, I think I'm on page eighty-five. There are six drawings and six paintings which they've managed to gather from the ends of the earth.' His face lit up with anticipation as he waited for her reaction.

She looked up in disbelief when she came to the reproduction of the portrait he had painted of Delilah when he first came to Florence. It had disappeared when the Marchese's son had taken over the house, emptying it of all Delilah's personal possessions. It had watched over the salon like a latter-day madonna. As she gazed at Delilah's provocative face set with large grey eyes, it seemed to Cotton that she was about to speak. William had caught her at the peak of her beauty, smiling at the observer over one polished shoulder like a pale tulip, her lithe figure almost alive beneath a gown of creamy rose satin. The humour in her face suggested that the artist had just said something outrageous but amusing, bringing Delilah's personality to life so vividly that she seemed to be in the same room.

Cotton looked up to see William watching her thoughtfully, his mind obviously suffused with the memory of his happiness with Delilah.

'Weren't we lucky to know her, to love her?' he inquired.

Cotton nodded.

'There's never been anyone else for me, you know. Not before, and not since. How could there be? Just look at her – so radiant, so alive. She was an enchantress, a goddess. And that – that is how I'll always remember her.'

'I can't wait to see the picture in London. But it will seem very strange to see it hanging in the Royal Academy.'

'You must come to the private view. And when the exhibition is over, you'll have to collect it.'

'Of course, I'd be happy to.'

'What I mean is that it's yours. I've been keeping it as a surprise. In fact, I'm going to amend the proofs of the catalogue to read: "In the collection of Miss Cotton Castello".' Taking the catalogue from her, he pencilled in the correction.

Cotton looked at him, stunned with gratitude. 'William, I don't know what to say. This portrait means everything in the world to me. How can I ever thank you?' She rose and put her arms around him for a moment. 'But tell me, how did you discover it? Where has the portrait been hiding all these years?'

'Well, one day last winter my spies in London telephoned to tell me that it had come up for auction at Sotheby's. Since it hung in the Villa Robbiano it's had an interesting history – travelling first to Texas, then to Vienna, until it found its way back to London. I'm pleased to say that in the meantime the amount the Marchese got for it was greatly increased. So, when I found out it was for sale, I told a friend of mine to buy it back. I said I didn't care what it cost – I wanted it to be back where it belonged. Now at least, Cotton dear, you'll have something of the Villa Robbiano and Delilah.'

'Not just something. The one thing in the world I would have chosen out of all the things there.'

The only mementoes Cotton possessed were the few pieces of jewellery that Delilah was travelling with at the time of her death, and a number of photographs she had been able to collect from friends over the years.

While William fetched another cup of coffee, Cotton continued to study his drawings and pictures in the catalogue.

'William – what's this drawing, the one labelled "Study of Anna"? I see it was done in fifty-five, the year before I was born. Do you still have it, or is it already in London?'

'No, I haven't sent anything yet. I suppose it's around here somewhere,' he said. His face was unreadable for a second.

Detecting his discomfort at her mention of the drawing, Cotton concluded that the beautiful and mysterious Anna had been more than a model to William. She was burning with curiosity but held her tongue, feeling it was none of her business. William interpreted the look on her face.

'I know what you're thinking,' he said defensively. 'Believe me, there was never another woman in my life from the moment I met Delilah. You mustn't even contemplate . . .' His voice rose to an angry tremor.

Cotton flushed with embarrassment. 'Forgive me, William. I didn't know I was so transparent, but quite honestly I wouldn't blame you if you had been attracted to her. I'm not a child any more, and I would understand.'

'None the less,' he said vehemently, wagging his finger, 'I'd be mortified if you even thought such a thing. She was just a young girl who happened to be working at the villa at the time I needed a model for my class of American students.'

'By the way, do you have a group coming this year?' she said, her mind still on the mysterious Anna. William's face had reddened, and his blustering denial aroused her curiosity.

'Yes, as a matter of fact. I've got a group coming in July. Small, but quite promising . . .'

As he talked, Cotton could sense William was greatly relieved by the change of subject, but she wasn't willing to let it go at that. When he thought she had forgotten the subject, she said casually: 'What do you suppose has become of Anna? Where do you think she went? I can't help wondering.'

William gestured vaguely. 'No doubt she's sitting in a doorway somewhere, in a village, swathed in black, gossiping, gone to fat, probably sporting a moustache and surrounded by grandchildren.'

Cotton sat back and folded her arms, regarding his flustered expression as her mind ticked over. It had long been her stock in trade to interpret the look in a person's eye, the undercurrent in a voice, to probe between the lines. In the way some people could divine water with a forked stick, or farmers could predict if it was going to rain by sniffing the air, Cotton had always had an instinct for ferreting out the truth when she wanted to. Prospero had been right to call her a nosy little brat all those years ago; it was a quality that had taken her to the top of her profession. She calculated how she might unravel the secret behind the woman in the drawing.

After lunch in a nearby trattoria they came back to the studio. They began talking of the Villa Robbiano, and of her visit there the day before.

'Ah,' he said wistfully. 'Would that you or I had enough money to buy it.'

'That crossed my mind, I must confess,' she said. For a moment the tempting possibility flickered between them. 'But you know, William, it isn't just the money needed to buy and restore it. You have to fill a house with so much more than paintings or furniture.' What was also needed was the sound of music and laughter, children running down the stairs, friends filling the empty chairs in the dining-room.

'Wisely said, my dear. And are you glad you went back?' He searched her eyes, clouded with the thousand memories they had in common.

'Very glad. I left it far too long because I was afraid to face it. I know now it was silly of me, but I couldn't stand the pain. So many things came back to me – some sad, but some wonderful things, too, that I'd forgotten; and that was good. Even seeing the place in that deplorable state, I realized how lucky I was to grow up there. Tell me, William – there's something I want to ask you now I'm here. I never knew all the details of my adoption, how Delilah came to adopt me out of all the children she might have chosen. I've grown more curious about my background over the years and I was hoping you could throw some more light on it.'

He shifted his eyes to the horizon. 'Let me see, it's all so long ago that I can hardly remember. But it seems to me that Delilah knew the Mother Superior of the convent, you know, Santo Spirito – about twenty kilometres from Robbiano. She happened to mention that she was looking for a home for an abandoned baby girl. Well, you know Delilah. She got carried away by the idea of adopting the baby herself, and thank heavens she did,' he said with a laugh.

He met her eyes for only a second, then looked away, clearing his throat nervously in a manner that betrayed him. Cotton was struck with the sense that she was on the brink of unearthing something acutely important about herself. For a second she said nothing, and when William remained silent, pretending to brush crumbs from the table, she knew she had to pursue the clue he had unwittingly dropped. She felt that she had to choose whether to close the box she had discovered by chance, and shut everything safely away again, or drag it out into the light. And like Pandora, she had to know.

Hazarding a wild guess, she said: 'It isn't anything to do with . . . Anna, is it?'

She felt her heart pound as William lifted his eyes, focusing on her with a tender expression that told her so much. He gave a sigh that made his shoulders droop and seemed to sap him of energy for a moment. Then he began to speak in a soft voice full of resignation.

'Nearly thirty years ago I made a solemn promise to Delilah that I would never, never reveal to you who your parents were. It was for a very good reason at the time. Yes, Cotton.

Your mother was Anna.' His eyes fell on the drawing that she still had in front of her. 'Delilah lived in fear for years that perhaps one day Anna might return and claim you. She feared that if she were childless, or full of remorse, she would come back searching for the child she left behind. Then there were times Delilah was afraid Anna had prospered and would want to make up for her youthful indiscretion. But for whatever reason, it was a very real fear that shadowed Delilah's life. I don't think she could ever quite believe her luck in having adopted you.'

'And the convent? What has that got to do with me? Anything?' she asked in a whisper.

'That's where you were born. Delilah told you part of the truth, at least as much as she thought you ought to know.'

'My God,' murmured Cotton. She sank into her chair and sat listlessly for a moment, stunned by what she had heard.

William stroked his beard pensively and watched her, determined to conceal another reason for Delilah's desperate desire to hide Anna's identity from Cotton. He wouldn't have been at all surprised to discover her plying the trade Delilah always said she was born for, in the red-light district of Rome or some other city. But this was, after all, only speculation, and he had no intention of shaking Cotton's self-esteem. In his mind he sifted through the facts, picking out the ones he thought she needed to know. Her clear, questioning eyes were fixed on him.

'And my father? Do you have any idea who he was?'

'Yes, and I'll tell you about him. You see, the responsibility for your existence can be placed at my door, so to speak,' he began. Cotton's face was a study in confusion and he laughed when he guessed what she was thinking. 'Now don't jump to any conclusions. Let me explain.

'If it hadn't been for that art course attended by Matthew Swope, son of Hector and Nonie Swope, none of it might ever have happened. But I'm getting ahead of myself. Let me start from the beginning. That summer, that halcyon summer, one of so many I spent with Delilah, I suddenly needed a model for my life classes and I thought of Anna Gagliani who was working at the villa. She was one of the most arresting girls I think I have ever seen . . .' In a sonorous voice full of emotion, he began his story.

When he had finished, Cotton said thoughtfully: 'Matthew Swope, son of Hector and Nonie. I remember wondering at the time why Delilah wouldn't take me to Hector's funeral. She was so adamant about me not going to Philadelphia that summer, and yet she assured me Nonie was one of her best friends. Imagine – he was my grandfather,' she said incredulously.

'It might seem peculiar that she never told them about you, or vice versa, but I'll never forget when she came back from New York the December before you were born, where she had gone with every intention of telling Hector and Nonie.' With a chuckle he said, 'In her opinion they seemed far too old and impatient to raise a child, and Delilah concluded that fate had decreed you remain with her. She'd always wanted children, and she thought it was God's amusing little way of blessing her with one. You remember what funny ideas she had about God.'

'Yes, I do,' Cotton agreed, sharing his laughter. She shook her head, then picked up Anna's portrait and stared at it again.

'Think of how frightened, how miserable she must have been, and how alone at fourteen. It must have been a nightmare for her, William. Do you suppose there's any way I could get in touch with her? I mean, how would I begin?'

He shook his head and suppressed his earlier vision. 'I'd be very careful about that, Cotton. She is probably married with other children. I know how keen you must feel to meet her, but it's often a big mistake to dig up the past. My advice is to let things rest. I understand your motives, but you needn't feel any guilt or responsibility over what happened. Believe me, Delilah saw that Anna was very well looked after when she gave her enough money to start over again, something Anna was only too happy to do. So you see, what could have been a tragedy ended happily for us all.'

'To start a new life,' she repeated, trying to imagine what kind of new life it would have been.

Her arms folded across her chest, Cotton stared at the drawing, a sense of unreality creeping over her.

'I don't look anything like her, do I?'

'Yes, in a way,' he said, studying her face. 'There is something about the eyes, and you have her chin. Yes, there's no doubt about it,' said William, tracing the drawing with his finger, then lightly touching Cotton's chin. 'Just a minute . . .' he exclaimed, with a sudden recollection. He went to a cupboard, brought out a large envelope full of photographs, and began sorting through them.

'I keep meaning to put these in an album,' he muttered, 'but I never seem to get around to it.'

'You can do that in your old age,' she said affectionately. Her curiosity aroused, she crossed the room to look over his shoulder.

'Ah-ah – here they are. I knew they were here all along,' he cried. Triumphantly, he handed her two photographs, his face flushed with satisfaction. 'That's your father. That's Matthew, second from the left in this portrait of the class of fifty-five I snapped in front of the Duomo. And that's him again in this snapshot I took of the class *in situ*.'

Cotton studied intently the two images of Matthew Swope, her father, trying hard to find something of herself in the wide sweep of his eyebrows, his fair colouring and his determined expression. She stared at the photograph, which was too small to convey much, but the sight of it moved her deeply.

'What colour were his eyes?'

'Oh, I can't remember, but I'm sure they must have been blue or blue-green with his fair colouring.' He gazed into her eyes. 'Your mother had brown eyes, which I remember even to this day. But yours – they have a unique colour, as if they were cast from two beakers of liquid, brown and hazel, poured into luminous pools of golden cognac.'

Cotton smiled at his fanciful image.

With a painter's eye he gave her a shrewd appraisal. 'But I'll say this, you seem to have been blessed with all your mother's curves in the right places. She had the most astonishing figure, even at the age of fourteen.'

Seeing that Cotton was eager for more details, William touched on aspects of Anna's character, consciously avoiding any reference to her darker side. Instead he painted her avarice, her ambition, in positive terms that would imprint a loving image in Cotton's heart, consoling himself that they would never meet and that it didn't matter. Better that Cotton should revere the mother she had never met, remaining ignorant of her shortcomings.

As the afternoon light cast a violet shadow over the rough-hewn table splashed with age after age of paint, he tried to convey what he remembered of Matthew.

'No, he wasn't like the other boys. I've never had another student like him. His talent was genuine, pure, undeveloped, yes, but who knows what he might have made of it if he had had a chance. Of course the Swopes were horrified that their son might become an artist. If he had, he would have made them proud. They expected him to become a banker or stock-broker, naturally – anything more suitable to his upper-class background. He was cut down so tragically, before he could enter the battle with his parents about his future, a battle I have no doubt he would have won. He wrote to Anna to say he would return to Robbiano at Christmas to marry her, when she told him she was pregnant. That should tell you what kind of young man he was – honourable to a strict degree. Nobody would have blamed him if he had simply taken a realistic attitude and supported Anna without marrying her. But he loved her. He told me so before he left Florence, before he even knew she was pregnant. I should mention, he didn't know how young she was. She had lied about her age to Delilah because she needed the job. When Matthew confided in me what had happened, I was horrified, but I'll admit I was a little envious. Here was a young man possessed of remarkable talent and in love with the delicious Anna. At that moment he seemed like a young god who possessed everything.'

When he told her about Matthew's death, Cotton speculated for a moment how a patch of ice on a road, coupled with Matthew's burning impatience to get to his destination, had altered her entire life.

William said: 'I suppose in time you might want to contact the Swope family.'

'That's something I'll have to think about,' Cotton answered.

'Well, Matthew had an older sister. But I'm certain Nonie died some time ago. I seem to recall that someone wrote to me about it.'

Looking at her watch, Cotton realized the time had come to leave. Rousing herself, she said: 'I told Prospero I'd meet him at four. I'd really like to sit here and talk to you all afternoon, William dear.' She hugged him affectionately.

His arm over her shoulder, he led her to the door of the studio. Seeing his brow furrow in thought Cotton said:

'I hope you don't regret breaking your promise to Delilah.'

He shook his head. 'No, you mustn't think that. Even Delilah couldn't foresee everything and I think the time had come for you to be told. Everyone has the right to know about their beginnings.

'Little Cotton . . .' he murmured, his eyes full of sentiment as his own words came stealing back to him: '"What does the future hold in store for you? What adventures, heartbreak, what happiness, what grand design? And what wishes can your godfather offer to speed you on your way? Health, wealth and happiness, I suppose. But more than that, I must add a wish that you have the courage to follow your star . . ." or at least something like that. I seem to recall saying that to Delilah after you were born, on one of those rare moments that are as clear to me as if it were yesterday, when the nanny brought you to us as we were sitting with Father Giannini on the terrace. But forgive an old fool for being sentimental.'

'Thank you for the beautiful legacy. I'll cherish it always,' she said, brushing his beard with her cheek. 'I'll never forget this day, William, never,' she whispered as he patted her on the back. 'You've given me so much to think about, so much.'

'Goodbye, dearest Cotton. Until tonight, then.' He stood in the shadow of the door so she couldn't see the tears in his eyes. 'I'm looking forward to meeting this handsome swain of yours.'

'We'll come by for you about eight-thirty at your apartment, all right?' she called from the landing.

'Fine, fine.'

When he had closed the door, Cotton walked slowly down the stairs, her footsteps echoing in the stairwell flooded by a shaft of light from above. In her bag she carried the photograph of her father which she was anxious to show to Prospero. She suddenly realized that he would probably remember her mother, and perhaps even Matthew, from the summer before she was born in Robbiano. He was bound to remember the most beautiful girl in the village: Anna Gagliani.

Chapter 23

In a small book-lined office off the Via Strozzi, Prospero leaned back pensively in his chair and drummed his fingers impatiently on the leather-topped desk between him and the Notaro Perini, who was studying him through his gold-rimmed glasses.

'The Marchese's asking price is completely unrealistic, given the state of the villa. I didn't even have time to inspect the roof, but I'm sure it will need replacing. That alone will cost . . .' He took his calculator from his pocket, 'should we say another thirty million lire? No,' he said, shaking his head, 'my offer is final.' His mind reverted to the derelict villa that he had visited alone while Cotton was lunching with William.

Perini, a dour, middle-aged man with curly grey hair, thought it over for a moment. For the last half-hour they had been bargaining back and forth about the purchase price of the Villa Robbiano, and Prospero sensed he was beginning to weaken.

'Tell me,' Prospero interjected, 'just how long has it been since you visited the villa?'

'Oh, I don't know – a year, perhaps.' He shrugged.

'And yet the villa has been for sale for two years,' Prospero reminded him. 'It's not improving with age, you know, like vintage wine. My friend, every time it rains, every time the wind blows, it adds something to the cost of repairs.'

'All I can say is that I will contact the Marchese and inform him of your offer. As I've told you, he has refused other offers in the past, preferring to hold out for the asking price. Now that times are so good in Italy, I think he has every chance of getting it.'

'Come, come . . .' Prospero chided with a wave of his hand, unimpressed by his arguments. 'Good times, bad times, that has little to do with the fact that he wants too much money. Are people willing to pay more than something is worth just because times are good? I doubt it.' He gave a disparaging smile.

'The truth is that the Marchese is not always a reasonable man, signor. He's often difficult to persuade.' Perini gave a tired sigh, indicating he would be glad to rid himself of the tiresome Villa Robbiano and get his commission, knowing Prospero's offer was more than reasonable for a property that was decaying with every passing day. When Prospero had handed him his card, he had recognized the name Vallone and had registered that everything about him spelled money.

Prospero played his final card. 'By the way, you might mention to the Marchese that if it would suit him, I could deposit a portion of the asking price abroad, say in Switzerland.'

'I'll convey that to him, but of course that should have nothing to do with the price,' Perini added, though they both knew that Prospero's offer of foreign funds was an added attraction.

'Bear in mind, Dottore Perini, that I have acted on what you might call a whim. I saw the villa and it pleased me. But even at this moment I'm telling myself that I must be crazy to want the villa at all. In fact, I will probably live to regret it. However, right now the idea amuses me,' he remarked as if to himself. He pinned down the lawyer with a shrewd glance, conveying that he meant business. Even now Prospero was half-tempted to close the matter, get it over with by offering the asking price just so he could surprise Cotton with the news; but it was his nature to drive a proper bargain, particularly when he knew he had the advantage.

He rose to leave. 'There seems nothing more to say, so I will wait for your answer by, shall we say, tomorrow evening? I shall be at the Villa Cora.'

The notary regarded him with a shocked expression. 'But signor, that's hardly enough time to decide upon a matter of this importance.'

'Suit yourself. I'm going back to Rome the day after, and I'll have to know before then so I can instruct my lawyers. Here – let me jot down the name just in case,' he said casually. Shaking the notary's outstretched hand he remarked: 'I have every confidence in your powers of persuasion.'

When they had said goodbye, Prospero ran down the stairs into the street below, humming a little tune. He had a strong hunch that the villa would be his by the following evening, leaving them time to celebrate his newest acquisition.

Striding into the sunlight, Prospero was smiling to himself as he thought of Cotton's face when he broke the news, reflecting that it might be bad luck to mention it now, in case he was disappointed. But he rejected such a negative idea, determined to possess the villa at all costs. He would tell Cotton today, now, about the Villa Robbiano. In the unlikely event of his offer being rejected, he would simply make a counter offer after a suitable time had elapsed. He was determined to live there with the woman he loved.

He was startled to find himself colliding with a woman sailing down the street.

'Prospero!'

He blinked, realizing the woman was Chiara.

'What are you doing here?' he asked in disbelief.

She returned his look of utter astonishment as she caught her breath. About to blurt out that she was on her way to a notary in the Via Strozzi, she caught herself in time.

She gave a little laugh of pure delight, her heart pounding as she felt herself melt under the sweep of his blue eyes. She tried to interpret their expression.

'You don't look very pleased to see me.'

'I'm just surprised, that's all,' he said, suspicion creeping into his voice.

'Come now, do you think I'm following you? I've been here for a week with the crew, scouting for locations.' She turned the full force of her charm on him, displaying no sign of the hurt and anger that he hadn't called for weeks. If it was meekness he needed to salvage his pride, then she would give it.

As she chatted, Prospero regarded her kittenish smile and her beautiful cloudless eyes, now very different from the night of the Embassy reception. Her cheeks were flushed with genuine happiness at their chance meeting, and as she rested her hand on his arm, his coldness melted somewhat.

'You look very well, Prospero. No, I'm not flattering you. I mean it. You look so fit, so relaxed, and it makes me very happy.'

'And you look well, too, Chiara,' he answered, surprised that she didn't seem to hold a grudge against him; but then he reminded himself that he had never understood Chiara, nor she him. All of her venomous jealousy seemed to have vanished, and in its place was a gentleness he didn't entirely trust. It crossed his mind that she might be in love again, but he had no inclination to ask with whom. He had not seen her dressed with such simple but appealing elegance since that first day when they met in the Via Condotti in Rome and she was in jeans and sneakers. In a dark cotton dress, her hair drawn back smoothly, she wore very little jewellery and none of the showy accessories she was so fond of. He remarked to himself that whoever her new lover was, he had trimmed the excesses of her flamboyant taste.

'Can't we have a drink together, or even dinner?' asked Chiara, glancing at her watch. There was a pleading softness in her voice. She had already made up her mind she would put off seeing the Notaro Perini, until tomorrow, if necessary.

Prospero looked at his own watch, then down the Via Tornabuoni for any sign of Cotton. 'I'm sorry, but I can't. I've got a meeting,' he said, indicating the opposite direction.

Chiara concealed her disappointment, conscious of just how much was at stake. Though Prospero was polite and not over friendly, she was sure that now she only needed time to woo him back.

'In that case, do you mind if I walk with you?' she said, as if it didn't matter to her one way or the other. 'There's a shop on the way there I wanted to visit.'

'Sure, come on,' he said pleasantly, but inwardly irritated at being trapped in the little charade. Casting a restless glance over his shoulder to make sure Cotton hadn't arrived, he started to walk briskly away from their meeting-point with Chiara close to his side. Before they had gone very far she drew him back, looping her arm through his.

'Just one moment. There's a handbag in this window that I think I prefer to the one in the shop I was about to go to. But what a pity they're still closed,' she said, seeing the locked grille door.

He waited impatiently, keeping his back turned to the direction from which he expected Cotton at any minute. Trying to keep his temper he said: 'Chiara, you can come back later. Please, I'm already late and I must go . . .'

'It's all right, I'm coming,' she said, laughter bubbling from her.

At that moment Cotton turned the corner of the small side street that led on to the Via Tornabuoni, searching the opposite side of the road for some sign of Prospero. As she darted across the street she saw no sign of him on the corner of the Via Strozzi where they had arranged to meet. On the pavement, she stopped suddenly. There he was, no more than thirty feet away, and she was taken aback to see that he was with a woman. He hadn't seen her, and Cotton turned abruptly, pretending to look in a shop window as it dawned on her that the woman was Chiara Galla. There was no mistaking it, she saw, glancing again. Even at a distance she was instantly recognizable. She had the kind of face and figure that turned heads as she passed.

Cotton froze, wondering what to do. Should she stride up to them and pretend that nothing was out of the ordinary? Or should she melt into the crowd and return in a few moments? The news about her real mother and father was eclipsed by the unexpected encounter.

Telling herself not to be a fool, Cotton turned, intending to brazen it out, when she saw Chiara slip her arm under Prospero's jacket and around his waist. Her laughter echoed down the street as she reached up to kiss him on the cheek, an intimate gesture that threw Cotton into confusion. She was left speechless as they disappeared down the street. Prospero hadn't given so much as a backward glance to see if she was coming. Staggered, Cotton stepped into a shop entrance while she took hold of herself, but anger and hurt were coursing through her. Without looking, she dashed across the street the way she had come. She hardly heard the squeal of the brakes or the angry cries of a driver shouting after her. Hailing the first taxi she saw, she leapt in and ordered him to return to the Villa Cora.

All of Florence and its splendour passed by, its ancient streets flooded by the brilliant sun of a day in June, but Cotton saw none of it. She stared stoically beyond the Uffizi, the Ponte Vecchio, forcing herself to confront the unpalatable truth. How could she have been so blind, she wondered. Prospero's philandering nature had been as clearly marked as the skull and crossbones on a bottle of poison, as barbed wire in no man's land. She couldn't shake off the notion that the moment he left her on the street that morning he had hurried to a hotel somewhere to meet Chiara, to achieve a double seduction that must have given him some perverse satisfaction. He had probably collected a stable of willing women, too dazzled by his charm to see him for what he really was, too drugged by his passionate love-making to care.

But it wasn't only her body Cotton regretted surrendering to a man who had duped her. Thinking over the last twenty-four hours, she had given him much, much more of greater value, confiding things about herself that she had never told anyone. It was betraying her spiritual nakedness that she regretted, exposing all her fears and weaknesses. Shame coursed through her at the thought. She could only wonder how Cotton Castello, with years of experience behind her, could have made such a colossal mistake.

Her mind reverted to the time she breezed into Prospero's office, the day she had discovered how heartless and arrogant he really was, now that he had made his millions. It was a brilliant stroke, she had to admit, putting her off guard with a bunch of flowers, phone calls and an invitation to dinner, not to mention the profuse apology which had taken her in. He was far cleverer than she had realized, waiting until he was very sure of himself before he made the first move.

As the taxi sped through the Boboli Gardens, Cotton gave a bitter little laugh; she had to hand it to Prospero. It had taken him years, but he had extracted his revenge on her with all the smoothness of a born con-man. He'd killed two fledglings with one blow – first Herron, then her.

In retrospect, she wondered if she had disappointed such a great and skilful seducer as Vallone by capitulating so easily, so soon. He had probably relished the idea of a difficult conquest, but she had been a pushover. It was possible that Chiara had put him up to it. She could imagine the two of them laughing in triumph at her naïvety, as he recounted how she burst into sentimental tears in his arms at the Villa Robbiano.

Jumping out of the taxi at the Villa Cora, she asked the driver to wait. Moments later, she returned to the lobby having thrown all her clothes and make-up into her overnight bag. Long training had taught her how to pack and make a getaway with only a moment's notice. The doorman opened the door of the taxi and she jumped in. As they drove away, she said to the driver, '*I termini, per favore.*'

She thought of William as they sped along. She would call him before she boarded a train north, to Paris. That's where she would go, she decided. All she wanted to do at that moment was to excise the events of the last week from her mind. And yet, there was one visit she had to make before leaving Florence.

'Driver, before we go to the station, please drive to the village of Robbiano.' She had to say farewell to the Villa Robbiano, and to the dream that had been rekindled there.

After Prospero had entered an office building at random to get rid of Chiara, he raced back to the street corner, where he expected to find Cotton. He began to pace up and down, glancing continually at his watch. Hands in his pockets, he looked past the smart Florentines, who streamed down the pavement, his eyes trained on the distance for some sign of Cotton's inimitable walk, her honey-coloured hair catching the sun. He realized now that if he hadn't been so distracted he would have told Chiara frankly that he was waiting for a woman – the woman he had begun to fall in love with the night they quarrelled. After all, he had nothing to hide. Instead, he had doltishly allowed Chiara to manipulate him as she so often had in the past, even pretending to be amused when she surprised him with a kiss on the crowded street. As he searched the passers-by coming down the pavement, he longed for the first sight of Cotton to erase his irritation.

Where was she? he asked himself when he saw by his watch that it was nearly four-thirty. Finally, when he could bear it no longer, he crossed the street towards William Partridge's studio, telling himself she was bound to come by the shortest direct route. He looked for Cotton to come running towards him at any moment with an apologetic smile on her face. But, when he arrived at the entrance to William's studio, an inner foreboding told him Cotton wasn't there. The only plausible explanation for her failure to keep their appointment gnawed at his mind, but he suppressed it as he pounded the door of the studio. That fawning, poisonous kiss Chiara had given him stuck in his mind; Cotton might have seen it and jumped to the wrong conclusion.

When William opened the door of the studio in response to his knock, he looked surprised to see him standing there.

'Sir William Partridge?'

'Yes. May I help you.'

Prospero extended his hand and forced a smile. 'I'm Prospero Vallone.'

William's face broke into an answering smile. 'Ah yes, Prospero. Cotton has been telling me all about you this morning. We met years ago, and I know your cousin Cardinal Giannini. I understand we're dining together tonight.' He looked at him questioningly, sensing his agitation.

'Yes, I believe so. I'm looking for Cotton,' said Prospero worriedly.

'Cotton? She left here, half-an-hour or more ago, telling me she had arranged to meet you.'

Prospero pressed his hand to his temples. 'I see. Now I don't know what to do,' he muttered.

'What's wrong? Has anything happened?' asked William, puzzled.

'She didn't show up.'

'Well, I wouldn't worry if I were you. You probably missed each other somehow. Perhaps there was a misunderstanding about the time or place.'

'No, no, it was very clear. The corner of the Via Strozzi and Tornabuoni at four. There was no mistake.'

'Well, in that case I suggest you go back. She's probably standing there right now, wondering what's happened to you.'

Prospero tried to force a laugh. 'Yeah, that's probably it. Sorry to bother you. It was a pleasure to meet you, and I look forward to seeing you tonight,' he said, turning with a pre-occupied air. As it dawned on Prospero what had happened, he was filled with panic.

'Goodbye,' William called after him as he clattered down the stairs. He clucked his tongue at the absurdity of love. The two of them had been separated for only a morning, and already Prospero was in a state of panic that Cotton was late for their meeting, reassuring William that he was as besotted with her as she was with him.

By the time he leapt out of the cab at the station entrance Prospero was exasperated to realize he had lost a lot of valuable time. It was now after five o'clock, and he reckoned that if Cotton had come to the station she would have had ample time to catch a train headed somewhere – anywhere. He rushed into the crowded station. For a moment he stood helplessly in the mêlée, searching the hundreds of passing faces for Cotton. It dawned on him that she could be on her way to Rome, London, Paris, if she were running away and didn't want to be found. With a sinking heart, he realized he didn't even have her address in London. He knew he had to find her before too much time had elapsed. Timing, timing was everything. And so was luck; he needed luck at this crucial moment in his life.

He approached the ticket windows, where there were long queues. Barging to the front of one of them, he said impatiently to the person next in line:

'Excuse me – this is an emergency.'

Shoving his way to the window, he said to the clerk: 'I'm looking for an American woman in her late twenties – tall, blonde. Can you ask the other clerks behind the counters if she bought a ticket in the last half-hour, and where to? It's a matter of life and death that I find her.'

The man looked at him blankly and then shrugged at the absurdity of the request. 'Are you serious?'

Looking around, Prospero came to his senses, realizing how ridiculously inadequate his description was. It was true. In the hall milling with travellers he could see more than a dozen women who could fit his description. Leaving the ticket counter, he dashed to the arrival and departure board, scanning it for some clue, but not knowing what. There was a train to Paris in ten minutes, a train departing for Rome at nearly the same time. Logic told him that Cotton should be on the train to Rome, but nothing that had happened during the past hour was logical. Again and again his eyes kept reverting to the Palatine Express, scheduled to depart for Paris. He stood for a moment, trying to get inside Cotton's mind, reasoning that if she was running away and didn't want to be caught she would head north. Not wasting another moment, Prospero noted the platform numbers of the two trains.

Striding through the barrier, he came first to the train for Rome and began to walk rapidly past all the carriages lined along the quay. It soon became clear that it would be a hopeless task to locate Cotton before the train pulled out of the station. Seeing a conductor, he bounded up the steps of the car and questioned him, but the man regarded him with the same incredulity as had the ticket clerk.

He was forced to wait while embarking passengers jostled past him with suitcases and rucksacks. Looking out of the window, he found himself once more regarding the sleek Palatine Express on the opposite platform. He was startled by the sight of a head of blonde hair and the momentary image of a girl who looked just like Cotton. He lost more precious time while a man with a big suitcase jammed the exit. Then, darting out of the exit, he sprinted as fast as he could to the adjacent platform and leapt on to the Paris train. As he stood in the corridor to catch his breath, he heard the whistle blow, and was immediately greeted by the conductor.

'It looks like you just made it,' he said with a friendly smile.

'Yes, I was lucky,' Prospero said absently, peering through the glass doors of the next carriage for some sign of Cotton.

'And lucky you didn't have any luggage. May I see your ticket, please? I'll direct you to your seat.' The conductor noted Prospero's expensive clothes and shoes, his gold watch, as the train glided smoothly out of the station.

There was nothing to do but admit the truth.

'I don't have a ticket,' Prospero said with a disarming shrug.

The conductor frowned. 'All seats on the train are strictly reserved, signor.'

Prospero jammed his hand into his pocket and withdrew a wad of lire notes, wasting no time on explanations.

The conductor held up his hand, about to protest, his eyes shifting from the money to the determination on Prospero's face.

'I'm looking for an American woman . . .' He described Cotton as well as he could, described what she was wearing.

'I think there might be a woman answering that description on the train. She boarded late and asked me if a compartment became available, she would like to exchange her first-class seat for a compartment.'

Prospero was electrified by the information. 'Do you have a compartment?'

'They're all booked, signor. The Palatine Express – two months in advance, if you're lucky . . .'

When Prospero began to count out ten-thousand-lire notes the conductor said: 'I think there might be a compartment undergoing repairs.' He muttered, waiting to see how many more notes Prospero would be willing to part with.

'Here,' he barked, stuffing the wad of money into the conductor's hand.

Stashing the notes discreetly in his breast pocket, he said, 'Number one hundred and ten, two carriages down. I'll go and unlock it for you now. But I think you want to go that way in search of your friend.'

Prospero finally found Cotton in the crowded carriage, slouched down in her seat, her arms folded as she stared out at the Tuscan hills. At the sight of her, he was filled with relief that boiled into anger when he saw the placid distant expression on her face, as if she didn't have a care in the world.

Aware that someone was standing in the aisle, she turned her head abruptly. When she saw Prospero, her eyes widened in shock.

'Hello, Cotton,' he said in a tight, controlled voice. 'Would you come with me? I'd like to speak to you.'

Her face hardened at the thinly disguised anger in his voice, but the sight of him had thrown her into confusion.

'Whatever you have to say to me you can say here,' she replied. A large grey-haired woman next to her looked at them in astonishment over her magazine, and people in the carriage began to turn their heads in curiosity.

'I want to see you alone, if you don't mind,' he said determinedly. Reaching over, he grabbed her wrist roughly.

'Eh? *Che cosa?* What is this?' said the woman angrily as Prospero brushed against her.

Sensing that his seething anger was barely held in check, Cotton climbed reluctantly out of her seat. All the strong emotions she had experienced over the last few days had simmered down to determination not to let him get the better of her. Though she was amazed he had followed her, everything she had once felt for Prospero had now gone underground, and she vowed she wouldn't allow him to reach her again. She struggled to pull her hand away as he tugged her down the narrow aisle, all the passengers staring after them.

When they were in the passage between carriages, she cried over the clatter: 'Just where do you think you're taking me?'

He didn't reply, but tightened his fingers around her wrist and pulled her stumblingly down the aisle of the next carriage to the compartment. Opening the door, he dragged her inside and slammed it behind them.

'How the hell did you get this compartment?' was all she could think to say.

He didn't trust himself to reply. Glowering at her, he tore off his jacket, pulled off his tie and rolled up his shirtsleeves without taking his eyes off her.

She scowled and turned away, moved unwillingly by the sight of the strong brown arms and hands that had held her, touched her, that morning in bed.

'Sit down,' he ordered, nodding at the banquettes.

'I'll stand. I don't intend to stay.'

'What you intend is neither here nor there,' he said with icy control as he pulled down the blinds and locked the door.

'Just one minute . . .' she protested.

As they faced each other his expression was not what she had anticipated. His temples glistened with sweat and his blue eyes, though full of rage, glinted with a kind of desperation that made her knees go weak.

'Look, I don't know what you intend to prove by this melodramatic train chase,' she began, a tremor in her voice. 'Can't you get the message? I want to be on my own. It's over, whatever it was.'

'Oh yeah? What's the last twenty-four hours been all about, anyway?'

'Temporary insanity, a lapse of judgement. I don't give a damn what you call it,' she cried. She would have died rather than admit she was hurt, and why she had run away.

'That's not good enough. What kind of a bitch are you, anyway?'

'I'm not a bitch,' she flared. 'But you're a bastard. Get this straight, Prospero – I'm not like, and never was like, all your other women . . .'

He grabbed her by the shoulders and gave her a violent shake.

'Who the hell do you think you are, anyway? You can't do this to me, make me feel about you like I do for the first time in my life, then disappear on me.'

She pushed him away roughly. 'I had an assignment, okay? It's my life, and I can do what I want with it.' Her eyes blazed with rage that none of her perfectly reasonable explanations had phased him. She knew her voice lacked conviction. 'An urgent call came while I was at William's and I have to be in Paris by tomorrow morning.'

'Oh yeah? Don't make me laugh.'

'I don't owe you any explanations.'

'You couldn't leave me a note or anything, you were in such a hurry? You're lying,' he hissed. 'I went to William's, looking for you; then I called the hotel.'

'How dare you pry into my life, how dare you? Now get out of here and leave me alone. No – I'll get out. Let me by.' She lurched past him, but he barred the door.

'You disappoint me, Cotton,' he said quietly, his chest heaving, his voice spiked with contempt. 'You pretend to be so damn brave, so independent, but you don't have the guts to confront me with the truth. You think I'm stupid? I put two and two together. You saw me and Chiara on the street and you jumped to conclusions, right?'

She tossed her head, but didn't answer. She seemed to be burning all over with the strangest feeling, and the motion of the train made her light-headed.

'That's right, isn't it? Instead of giving me a chance to explain, you turned on your heels and ran out on me because you just can't face it. You're so goddamned courageous when it comes to being kidnapped or dodging bullets. Oh yeah, you're a brave little lady under fire, a real heroine. But Christ, when it comes to loving you're a coward. The first sign of trouble and you turn and run a mile, your tail between your legs.'

Now she was quaking. 'Oh, shut up! Shut up! You don't know a damn thing about me.' Her eyes studded with tears, she stumbled back and pressed against the window of the swaying train. 'Do you really expect me to believe that the two of you just ran into each other, just like that?'

'Yes, I do. Because I'm telling you so, that's why.'

She gave a snort of indignant laughter. 'You must think I'm as dumb as they come. I saw the way you looked at each other, the way you touched, kissed. And I'm not buying it. So what are you looking at me like that for, anyway?' she cried. 'You got what you wanted last night, so why are you here?'

'Is that what you think? Is that it?' The slow burn inside him reignited. 'Sure, that's why I chased you all the way here. That's why I drove like a bat out of hell to the station. I came back for more.' He lifted her suddenly and pushed her on to the banquette.

She looked up at him with naked shock. He plunged down and crushed his lips to hers, drawing the breath from her before she could speak.

When she tried to bite his lips he kissed her harder, enraged by the fight in her. He kissed her again, thrusting his tongue between her teeth, his hand searching eagerly between her legs which he began to prise open.

'I love you, damn you, do you hear?' he muttered.

She had been furiously digging her nails into his shoulders, but at the taste of his kiss, the feel of his hands touching her bare flesh, an unexpected response suffused her body, dissolving all her resistance. Unhinged, confused, she cried out, her desire fanned by a perverse, and insistent need. As their mouths met hungrily, their bodies clung, separated only by a few thin layers of clothes, the most violent spasm of lust Cotton had ever known ripped through her, churning up a tormented longing. She couldn't wait to have him inside her, to punish him, wound him with the violence of her strange, muddled emotions. In a frenzy she tore at his trousers. He roughly pushed her dress above her waist, still only half-aware their struggle had changed course. Wrenching her legs apart, he thrust himself into her, finding her hot and eager. She responded with a sob that brought tears to her eyes. As he buried his face in her hair she reared towards him to draw his power deep inside her. They were seared together in a pulsating movement of ecstasy, the rocking of the train heightening their frenzied movements. As his hips drove back and forth, Cotton tore at his shirt, hungering for his bare skin against her breasts.

All the while she was thrusting beneath him, riding the wave that overcame her with such force. His every movement gorged her with an exaltation expressed with a gasping little cry that gave him the strength to drag her to the summit, while delaying his own climax. He fought to hold himself until they had exhausted the wild need that drove them. He had never before felt such power, as he proved all the force of his love, his fears, his needs. When, and only when, he sensed she was with him, did he let himself go.

Cotton shuddered as they soared together, then sank, then

dropped against each other, drained and stunned like two war-riors who had fallen in combat.

Later, when they were lying quietly in each other's arms listening to the muted clatter of the train speeding over the rails he said softly, kissing her ear,

'Yes, I knew Chiara was in Florence, but I never expected to run into her. She cornered me, and everything you saw be-tween us was her doing, not mine. I haven't talked to her or seen her since the night we met. You've got to believe me, Cotton, because if you don't . . .'

She waited an eternity for him to finish the sentence.

'. . . because if you don't, my life will never be the same.'

His declaration seemed to hang in the air as they regarded each other in the compartment filled with golden light. As he stroked her cheek, she melted, pressing her lips into his palm. She drank in the smell and taste of him as he kissed her.

'I love you, and I want to get married.'

Cupping her chin, he looked deeply into her eyes, where he recognized at last the naked loneliness that had manifested itself as pride. Her need reached out to him and planted itself like a seed in an empty furrow. As they lay together, lulled by the motion of the train, Prospero felt the floodgates of understand-ing open between them, drowning all his fears.

'Marriage – I don't know. It's too soon, much too soon,' she replied uncertainly, adding in a small voice, 'isn't it?'

'This is our time, and we have to seize it and make the most of it. It may never come again.' He kissed her once more, finding her answer as she laid her head on his chest.

'And, Cotton . . .'

'Yes?' she murmured, stroking his hair.

'Promise me, please, you'll never do that again. Don't ever run away without asking for explanations.'

As he spoke, she wanted to believe his every word, to float freely on a tide of simple faith. Feeling his arms wrapped protectively around her, she clung to him with all her strength, trustful of all he had proved in the last twenty-four hours. She was too happy to wonder how he knew so much about her. All that counted was that he did know, and that he had come running after her when she had so foolishly fled. What greater proof could she have than this anger, which she knew was fuelled by pain.

'It's a wonder you can care for me after what I've done. I'll never let you down again, never,' she vowed.

Later, just before the train pulled into Genoa, where they planned to get off, Cotton set about repairing her smeared mascara and trying to tame her dishevelled hair. Looking over his shoulder from the window, where he stood to observe the passing landscape, Prospero gave her a smile. Cotton glanced up from the compact in her hand. Reaching into her bag, she handed him a comb, then tried to smooth her dress.

Slicking back his hair, Prospero laughed. 'Forget it – it won't do any good. Just look.' He gestured at his shirt, open to the waist, and plucked off one hanging button.

Cotton laughed as she stood to shake her hair.

'I must look like I've been savaged by a lion,' she said play-fully, putting her arms around his neck. 'I guess in a way you could say I have.'

Laughing, he kissed her forehead. 'We should be pulling into the station soon. We'll have to get off this train with as much dignity as we can.'

'I don't give a damn. I want the whole world to know,' she replied, hugging him.

'If you returned to your seat looking like that, you'd get a round of applause,' he remarked. 'They probably thought we were going to kill each other.'

'Maybe I should go back, just for kicks. We don't want to deprive them of knowing our lovers' quarrel had a happy ending, do we?' She looked at her watch. 'If we hurry we can make it back to Florence in time for dinner with William and he'll never know the difference.' At the mention of William, she gasped.

'What's the matter?'

She was laughing, clutching her throat in surprise. 'I haven't even had a chance to tell you what happened this morning. William finally told me after all these years who my real father and mother were.' Astonished anew, Cotton's voice dropped to a whisper.

'What? You mean he knew, and kept it from you all this time? Well, tell me, who were they?' he asked, sitting beside her on the banquette.

'I think that might explain why I reacted like I did when I saw you and Chiara. I must have been in a state of shock. Apparently my father was one of William's students, a young American named Matthew Swope. And listen to this – my mother was a maid at the villa. Prospero, she was only fourteen. Her name was Anna Gagliani.'

Prospero looked at her blankly, a little frown digging into his brow.

'You didn't know her by any chance, did you? I'm hoping you might remember her,' she added, biting her lip, 'because she's disappeared without a trace.'

'No, no,' he said, after a moment's hesitation. 'I don't remember her. But don't forget, I was only there for a short time.'

Disappointment crossed her face. 'I was really hoping you would. Apparently she was lovely . . .'

'No kidding? I don't know how I could have missed her, in that case. But then my luck ran out that summer, remember?' He gave a wry smile, patting her cheek.

He rose and shoved his hands in his pockets, staring out of the window as the train ran through the sprawling suburbs of Genoa. Smiling at Cotton over his shoulder, he felt himself break out in a cold sweat, thinking that if his family hadn't left Robbiano when they did that summer, he could easily have been Cotton's father rather than Matthew Swope.

Trying to interpret the peculiar expression on his face she said: 'What's the matter?'

'Nothing – nothing. What you've told me has taken me by surprise, that's all. I'm glad you found out who your real parents were. It's important for you to know,' he said, gathering her in his arms; but his mind was still spinning around the memory of Anna Gagliani. 'Speaking of surprises, I've got one of my own.'

When he told her about his offer for the Villa Robbiano, Cotton's momentary disbelief blossomed into passionate enthusiasm.

'I don't believe it; I just don't believe it. Prospero – just like that, you've bought it?' she gasped, hugging him tight.

'Hang on, the offer hasn't been accepted yet, but it will be. I'm confident of that. It is what you want, *cara*, isn't it?' he added, suddenly conscious that her amber eyes were deeply serious.

'Prospero, if you're doing this just for me . . .' She broke off with a smile and gazed up at him. 'Don't forget, I'm a hard-working girl, not used to this kind of thing.' She stopped abruptly and sucked in her breath, 'God, what a wonderful, exciting thing to do!' His grand gesture had staggered her.

'I'm doing it for us, so let's hear no more about it. And anyway, it's no bagatelle renovating a house that size. It may take years to complete. Unless you're busy doing something else,' he said in a whisper. Their lips met in a lingering kiss as the train swayed.

'Actually, I'm not doing a thing for the rest of my life,' she replied, kissing him again.

'That sounds promising. I'll take it,' he replied. 'Say, I was thinking. Maybe instead of going back to Florence now, straight away, we should rent a car and visit my mother in Livorno so I can introduce you. What do you say?' he teased, breaking into a mischievous grin.

Looking down at her crushed dress, Cotton laughed, 'Oh yeah? Not bloody likely.'

....
....
....
....

Chapter 24

The shutters of Chiara's bedroom were closed against the heat of a Roman afternoon, casting a premature twilight on the flowered carpet. From her bed, propped up against a pile of lacy pillows, Chiara stared accusingly at the telephone on the bedside table which had stubbornly refused to ring for four days. She shifted her legs restlessly between the cool sheets drawn up over her tanned body, and tried to concentrate on the script propped on her taut stomach, though the silence of the villa all around her made it difficult. Tossing the script aside, she sighed deeply and was seized by self-pity. During the long month of August, now in its third week, every day was just like every other.

Until that summer she had forgotten how empty Rome could be during the holidays, when the population migrated in droves to the seaside or the northern lakes. Sandy Vincent had already left the city for the Adriatic, as he did seasonally with his brood of children and relatives. He had invited her to come along, but she had replied breezily that she already had a number of invitations from friends — St Tropez, the Greek islands, Sardinia. She was reluctant to admit, even to Sandy, that she had nowhere to go, nothing to do, until filming of the mini-series began in September. There had been a momentary look of pity in Sandy's eyes when she had refused his offer, a look that even now made her angry when she thought of it. Of all human emotions, Chiara considered pity the most despicable. Yet, alone in her villa in the dead of afternoon, she found it hard to admit even to herself that she, Chiara Galla, had cloistered herself in her house because she was desperately hoping to hear from Prospero. Her hopes were fading as fast as the light dying beyond the closed shutters.

Since she had seen Prospero in Florence at the end of June, Chiara had come to realize that she had bought the Villa Robbiano for him, knowing what it meant to him. She had imagined at last revealing who she was, when she told him that she had bought the house that figured so evocatively in their past. Then they would start all over again, righting what had gone wrong between them. When she had bought the villa, it had seemed a sign that the past was dead and that she had risen from the ashes to take what she wanted from life.

By the time she had found out that Prospero was the other party trying to buy the villa, it was too late to do anything. She had been deeply puzzled and hurt that he hadn't called her after the deal was closed. She was sure he was aware that she was the new owner of the Villa Robbiano, and she knew him well enough to guess that when he discovered he had been competing against the woman who loved and adored him, he would contact her immediately. She could almost hear his rich laughter at the absurdity, as he made the incident a pretext for ending the agonizing silence she had endured since they ran into each other in Florence. How often she had berated herself for not pinning him down for a drink, for dinner, instead of letting him slip away to a meeting. But she had been too preoccupied with buying the villa and with the strong emotions her confrontation with the past had aroused.

With a gasp of dissatisfaction, she slipped out of bed and shook her hair. A shaft of stray sunlight crossed her full breasts, filling her with longing and carrying her thoughts to Portofino, where Prospero was undoubtedly spending his usual holiday with his family. They should have been there together, making up for all the years they had missed. The sight of the telephone in a pool of lamplight by her bedside made her resolve to wait until the following day for his call. If he hadn't contacted her by then, she would break down and call him. Too much was at stake to let more valuable time be lost. Though she believed in bringing a man to his knees with the waiting game, a ploy that had always succeeded before, Chiara knew Prospero had defeated her. Like it or not, she would have to give in.

Her heart skipped a beat when she thought she heard wheels in the courtyard below. Going to the window, she tugged at the brocade curtain and peered through the shutters to see the tall gates locked and the courtyard empty. She decided the only thing that would break the monotony would be a long, exhausting swim in the pool. Pulling open a drawer lined with satin, she chose a swim suit from the dozen carefully arranged by her maid.

When she descended the stairs to the darkened hallway, illuminated only by doors of thick glass and wrought iron, Chiara paused at the table where the mail was always laid out by the butler. She sorted through the pile. There was nothing interesting, but her mood brightened when she saw the latest issue of *Gente*. She slipped it into her bag to take to the pool, wondering if there was anything about herself. The previous week a paparazzo had surprised her as she drove through the gates of the villa in her chauffeured car, and she hoped that if they published the photograph the startled look on her face wouldn't be too unflattering.

An hour later she was lying on the sunbed in the dappled shade near the gazebo, her chest heaving with exhaustion, her golden skin beaded with water. Every muscle throbbed from her relentless workout in the pool. For a moment she felt release from anxiety as the blood pumped through her body. Through half-closed eyes she followed the reflections of the sun-veined water weaving across the trees overhead. After several moments' relaxation, when she successfully blanked any troubling thoughts from her mind, she put on her sunglasses. Reaching for the copy of *Gente*, she settled back to read, thumbing idly through the magazine, pausing now and then to read a caption or study a familiar face. She found herself distracted by the cordless telephone she had left within easy reach.

Turning a page, she was catapulted fully to her senses by a picture of the harbour at Portofino, and a blurred long-range photograph of Prospero Vallone and his family on his gleaming white cruiser, the *Elphiandro*. Her eyes raced across the two-page spread to try and make sense of the photographs accompanying the feature. There was a small picture of herself looking out of the car window in open-mouthed astonishment, an ugly, unflattering grimace, and a close-up of Prospero Vallone walking along the harbour with his arm around a willowy blonde, identified as a young journalist on the *Washington Herald* now posted to Rome. Chiara read her name with disbelief: Cotton Castello.

She fell back on the sunbed, warding off the vertigo brought on by the revelations labelled as a 'love triangle'. The article dubbed her the 'discarded mistress', and there was a small photo of her villa taken at a distance, as well as a stamp-sized portrait of her when she had starred in *Ciao, Senator*. She was portrayed in a few cruel phrases as a pathetic recluse who had schemed her way into a fortune and had now lost one of Rome's most glamorous men to an American mystery girl half her age. Chiara choked with disbelief when she read that Cotton Castello and Prospero Vallone would marry as soon as his divorce from Swiss heiress Ghisela Schmidt became final.

At six o'clock, after taking twenty milligrams of Valium, Chiara was just sliding into blessed unconsciousness when the telephone rang. For a moment she didn't know who she was or where she was, but the piercing ring at her bedside cut through her numbness. She fumbled for the phone in the darkness and as she picked it up she struggled to clear her mind.

'*Pronto?*' she breathed, knowing it was Prospero on the other end of the line, calling to tell her the story in *Gente* was all lies. The lamp blinded her as she found the switch, her heart beating with expectation.

'Chiara? Is that you? How are you?' came a hearty American voice. 'Can you hear me? This is a bad connection.'

'Hello?' she repeated desperately.

'Darling, it's Herron.'

'Oh, Herron, it's you,' she replied dully, drained with disappointment. She let out an involuntary sob.

'Are you all right, Chiara? You sound so far away. I didn't disturb you, did I?' he said, with a suggestive little laugh.

'No, you didn't disturb me.' Tears began to roll down her cheeks. 'I had to run to the telephone, that's all. I was getting ready to go out, and the maid isn't here . . .' She struggled to pull herself together.

'Listen, Chiara, I'm calling from Geneva.'

'Geneva?'

'Yes. I had to fly over for a meeting on short notice. I didn't even have time to let you know I was coming, and in fact I thought I might even have to get back to the States right away and join the kids in Maine, but I've decided to spend the weekend.' When she didn't reply, he went on: 'I had a terrific brainstorm. It's all very last minute, but it occurred to me that I'd like to see you if you were free, though I suppose there wouldn't be a chance in hell you could make it at such short notice?'

When she still didn't reply, he continued: 'I know it's a hell of a nerve to ask you like this, but I'm flying to Paris in a little while. I'm just leaving the hotel, and I've booked a suite at the Crillon. I'd love you to come too. By the way, did you get the flowers I sent?'

'Yes, yes, I got them. They are lovely,' she answered vaguely, glancing at the sunburst of long-stemmed freesias, ten dozen at least, whose scent filled her room.

As she heard Herron's enthusiastic voice, it took her a moment to remember she had slept with him twice when he was in Rome. He had been an ardent and virile lover, and in the past weeks had sent flowers repeatedly and had called her. But, she recalled with despair, she had only started the affair to drive Prospero mad with jealousy.

'Well, what about it?' he was saying. 'Any chance I can persuade you? If Paris doesn't appeal to you, we could go down to the Riviera. Or we could pop over to London and take in a couple of plays. The important thing is that I want to see you so much it hurts. I've been thinking about you all summer.'

'I don't know. When did you have in mind?' Her own voice seemed like a distant echo.

'It sounds crazy, but why not catch a plane tonight?'

'No, not tonight. There's a big opening I must attend.' As she paused, the prospect of an empty weekend stretching ahead closed in on her. Picking up a mirror, she focused on her swollen face peering back at her from the shadows. 'But what about tomorrow? I could come tomorrow,' she replied, grasping the lifeline he had offered her.

'Can you really? That's terrific, Chiara.'

For a moment the gratitude in his voice made up for the fact that Herron meant nothing to her. She felt compelled to add: 'I was supposed to go to Portofino, but I cancelled. It's so crowded there in August.'

He laughed heartily. 'I wouldn't worry about that. At the Crillon you won't be bothered by crowds. There'll just be you and me.'

PORTOFINO

A warm sea breeze penetrated the closed shutters, ruffling the gauze draped around the four fluted columns of the Egyptian bed. Cotton opened her eyes and looked at Prospero sleeping naked beside her – a sight that reawakened all her senses. Longing for his touch, she moved languorously against him, causing him to open his eyes. As he reached out to stroke her breasts, she let her hand wander lazily down his torso to play with him.

'It's been one hell of a long time,' he murmured as desire surged in him again.

'I'd almost forgotten what you look like, what it feels to touch you,' she whispered.

'If you keep that up you'll have to do something about it,' he said, his voice thick with arousal. As he stretched and pressed himself against her they shared a private little laugh of pleasure. Their limbs intertwined and the world fell away as they exchanged hot teasing kisses. Cotton pulled him to her, unable to wait another moment longer when there was an insistent knock at the door. They broke apart, their eyes flying to the doorknob that was moving back and forth. Violently hurled from the world of the senses, they stared in shock for a moment at the door.

'*Zio Prospero*,' came a small child's voice in Italian, 'Mama said to tell you that *Zia Ghisela* is here.'

Prospero froze. '*Porco miseria*,' he cursed.

'What's she doing here?' asked Cotton incredulously. Descending from the peak of arousal, she had the dazed recollection that Prospero's wife had arranged to pick up their daughters late that afternoon.

Cotton turned with a sigh and watched Prospero leap from the bed and pull on his trousers.

'She's early, damn her. It's typical of Ghisela. She assured me she wouldn't be here until five,' he muttered angrily.

Sitting up, Cotton brushed her hair from her face. 'What do you suppose she wants, anyway?'

'She knows you're here. Knowing her, she probably hoped to take us by surprise after lunch, just like this,' he replied, hastily buttoning his shirt and rolling up his sleeves. 'But don't worry. I'll get rid of her and be back in a moment.' Bending over the bed, he kissed her shoulder.

'I don't know if I can wait that long,' she whispered, seizing his head in her hands and kissing him urgently.

'Christ – ' he said with a laugh, glancing at the bulge in his trousers. 'Listen – stay right where you are. When I come back I want to find you exactly like that. Got it? Don't move.' Cupping her chin in his hand, he kissed her again.

Cotton watched him leave, then leaned back with a sigh. For a moment she lay in a daze, looking at the huge, airy room furnished in Ghisela's starkly elegant taste. It was too pure, too cold for Cotton, but, none the less, she admired the exquisite hand-carved bed made to exact specifications in Cairo. Old Syrian commodes inlaid with mother-of-pearl, mirrors of hammered silver, priceless rugs and lamps shaped like amphorae were among the other striking pieces painstakingly collected to furnish the room. But Cotton's glance kept returning to the phallic lotus columns of the bed, their suggestive lines filling her with a sense of amused irony that would be wasted until her lover returned. In the week she and Prospero had been staying at his villa in Portofino, surrounded by the entire Vallone clan, they had had very few chances to use the luxurious bed, and it seemed farcical that Ghisela, whom Cotton had never met, had chanced upon their love-making.

If anyone had ever suggested to Cotton that she would agree to being separated from Prospero every night by a corridor of bedrooms filled with brothers, sisters-in-law, children and his mother, she would have laughed out loud. She had pontificated on their first date about the joys of a big, happy family, and now she was only too familiar with the drawbacks.

She had arrived to meet the family in high spirits after Prospero had picked her up at Genoa Airport. They had been separated for nearly a month; she had gone to Sweden on an assignment, and then returned to Washington for a last briefing before being posted to Rome in September, a transfer she had proudly achieved in record time. She had been stunned to discover that they wouldn't be sharing a bed in Portofino. Prospero had tried to blame the bizarre arrangement on his mother's sense of propriety, but now Cotton knew better. She had discovered that, in spite of his dashing public image, Prospero was a strict and somewhat old-fashioned father to his two daughters and his son. At the thought of Sophia and Elysia, who were said to strongly resemble their mother, Cotton quickly got out of bed. She dabbed on some lip gloss, then gathered her hair into a pony-tail and tied it with a trailing scarf. As she did her hair, she pushed open one shutter and gazed out to the misty blue horizon where sea met sky beyond the harbour. In the distance, she could see a twin-masted ketch dancing on the waves, and for a moment she imagined drifting with Prospero far out to sea, away from the vigorous brawling Vallone clan whose feuds and rivalries and private jokes she had only begun to understand. Pulling on her jeans and a crumpled white shirt, she slipped into a pair of moccasins, then determinedly opened the door. It was one thing to be banished to a room down the hallway out of respect for the conventions but it wasn't her style to hide upstairs while Ghisela made a social call.

Descending the marble stairs, Cotton paused at an oval

window overlooking the gravelled forecourt of the house, where a sleek dark blue Mercedes was parked. A trim young chauffeur who doubled as a bodyguard, in grey uniform with gold piping, his handsome face shadowed by his cap, leaned against the silver grille of the car, telling Cotton more about Prospero's wife than any gossip column or paparazzi photograph. She heard Prospero's angry voice drifting up the stairwell from the drawing-room.

'Just tell me why you had to come here ahead of time? The arrangement was that you come at the end of your holiday to take an inventory – not now, not today.'

'There are certain measurements I need in order to plan what I want to remove in the autumn. That way, I'll have time to think about it while I'm in San Stefano,' was the unruffled reply.

Hearing the crisp, precise English, Cotton had a clear image of Ghisela. Taking in car and chauffeur, she had already observed that her taste for slim, clean lines extended to every stylish detail of her life.

'I know damn well why you're here,' Prospero said heatedly.

'I am here because this is still my house and because you are still my husband, and I am still your wife . . .'

Cotton felt herself go cold. The incident with Chiara in June that had nearly parted her from Prospero returned with jarring clarity. She ran silently down the stairs and along a corridor to escape the sound of their voices. She went into the terraced garden below the drawing-room balcony, glancing up to make sure she hadn't been seen. Beneath the tall pines, she paused, her knees suddenly weak with foreboding. Until now she had thought of Ghisela as a spoilt woman, as bored with the marriage as Prospero, but the determination behind the voice belonging to a woman she had never set eyes on filled Cotton with uncertainty.

Not wanting to eavesdrop on the argument raging inside the house, Cotton followed a path shielded from the house by a grove of oleanders, but though she could no longer make out their words, the sound of their voices followed her.

Hearing a movement ahead, she stopped. There was Alessandro, Prospero's small son, crouching in the dust on all fours, his shiny dark hair tumbling over his eyes. He was stealthily dragging a cork tied to a string to and fro in front of the bushes. After a moment, Cotton saw a black and white kitten dart through the leaves, its eyes wide with curiosity. Cotton forgot for a moment that Alessandro could hear nothing and tiptoed towards him.

As soon as she had met Alessandro, Cotton had sensed his pain and isolation. She had been moved by the sweetness of his face and the inner self-reliance which was, she guessed, won from his realization that he was different from other children. He had offered her his cool little hand with a dignity that went straight to her heart. Then, as now, she stifled the urge to take him in her arms.

During the last two weeks, Cotton had felt uneasy at the false heartiness with which Prospero treated his son. She had reassured herself that Prospero's awkwardness came from a deep pain that he could share with no one, not even her. Only now was she beginning to understand what a catastrophe it was for Prospero, a man who had everything, that his beautiful child had been born imperfect. She had planned to face the problem in time. But, watching Alessandro's patience, his deft movements as he coaxed the half-wild kitten, she knew that she could avoid the issue no longer. Alessandro was treated by the Vallone clan with affectionate indulgence, like a favourite pet instead of as an intelligent child confronting the world with enormous odds against him.

Prospero, in his bitterness, had left Alessandro's education to Ghisela. But surely, thought Cotton, there was infinitely more to be done for him. He would stay locked in his own world unless they all joined forces to free his spirit. And the most important key, Cotton suddenly understood, was his father's love, his time, his patience, which were essential to bring about this miracle. Already their life together was bursting with all the good things within their reach. But Cotton realized she wanted one truly important thing – to feel the arms of Prospero's son entwine around her neck in affection and trust. And without that miracle their love would be less meaningful.

She made a movement to attract Alessandro's attention. He turned his head sharply and when he saw it was Cotton his eyes softened in recognition. She could see he was undecided whether to scamper away or continue his pursuit of the kitten. But the kitten proved irresistible. He turned away and cast the cork towards the bushes again as Cotton crouched behind him. Alessandro's patience was inexhaustible as again and again he cast the cork to entice the kitten. When it finally pounced on the cork, he scooped it up and pressed it lovingly to his chest. He stroked its chin evoking a deep purr that Cotton realized must be reverberating against his heart, perhaps in some way breaking the perpetual silence in which he lived.

He sprawled happily in the dust, with a delighted grin brightening his serious expression. Cotton reached out and gently stroked the kitten's spine. She stopped as her fingers touched Alessandro's. She entwined her hand round his for a moment, surprised that he didn't draw away. Sensing the small sign was enough for the moment, Cotton rose to her feet. He seemed sorry to see her go. As she waved and smiled, she wondered if he knew just how happy he had made her.

Walking back towards the house, she looked up at the drawing-room balcony. Cotton judged from the silence that Ghisela must be gone. She went up the stairs and through the open doors thinking what a fool she had been to give a damn about Prospero's wife when he was probably waiting for her at that moment between the sheets upstairs.

But Ghisela hadn't gone. At the sound of Cotton's footsteps, she turned from the Chinese lacquered cabinet that she was measuring. They regarded each other for an instant. At a distance Ghisela projected a striking fragility, with her pale silky hair swept neatly away from her Dresden china face. Her elegant pleated ensemble of black spotted silk, her pearls and kid shoes seemed more appropriate to Park Avenue than Italy in August. Cotton couldn't avoid the uncomfortable contrast between Ghisela's moneyed elegance and her own jeans and rumpled white shirt, her hair carelessly tied back into a ponytail. But she gathered her confidence and said in her best East Coast contralto,

'Hello, my name is Cotton Castello. You must be Ghisela Vallone.'

Ghisela seemed to freeze at her presumption. Cotton returned her diamond-hard glance with the unshakable social confidence she had learned at Delilah's knee, conveying that she was every inch Ghisela's equal, not just an American tourist in blue jeans that Prospero had picked up for the holiday.

Ghisela ignored Cotton's outstretched hand and returned coolly to measuring the cabinet.

'I'm sure this must be awkward for you.' Glancing over her shoulder she cast Cotton a pitying look. 'Meeting you I can see you're mature enough, perhaps worldly enough, not to take your affair with my husband too seriously. His girlfriends aren't always old enough to understand the situation and Prospero can be rather inconsiderate sometimes.'

'I'm afraid I have no idea what you're talking about,' replied Cotton coolly, but inwardly she was taken aback by Ghisela's bluntness.

'What I'm trying to tell you is that this sort of thing has happened often during our marriage and will probably happen again. You've heard about Italian men, haven't you? Well it's true what people say. They are forever chasing an illusion like little boys.' Casting Cotton a thin smile she began calmly winding up her tape measure. 'We've been through this before and will probably go through it again. But we've survived. We're still married. This time next year, who knows? I might be standing here with somebody else.' She shook her head and gave a little laugh. 'This is just another little storm we will have to weather. But from the look on your face you don't believe me.'

Cotton shook her head slowly. 'Uh-uh. I don't believe you.'

'Of course you don't understand. How could you? In America things are very different, I know. In your country, everyone changes husbands and wives as casually as they change their clothes. But in Europe family solidarity survives everything. It is the basis of our lives. A woman like you couldn't possibly realize that in times of trouble, families stick together . . .'

Cotton could see by the angry flush on Ghisela's fair skin that she wasn't as detached as she would have her believe. For a moment Cotton had the devilish urge to rip the pearls from her neck. She imagined what it would be like to fight her then and there on the tiled floor. There was no doubt that she would emerge the winner. Then she schooled herself into icy contempt.

'You have one hell of a nerve. How could you know anything about me, or what I mean to Prospero? As for your platitudes about family solidarity, that's a crude little ploy that won't work with me. And, by the way, I'm not the least bit interested in the women in Prospero's life before we met. I'm with him here and now and that's what counts, so don't give me all this garbage about your home, and husband. I'm the woman who is in his house, in his bed, and that's where I intend to stay.'

The words reeled off her tongue crisply and with a confidence that left Ghisela staring with impotent hatred.

'Perhaps,' she said at last. 'You may be here at this moment, but not for long, I assure you.'

'Is that right?' replied Cotton scornfully. She wondered impatiently where Prospero was and why he didn't come to her aid. Only the thought of Alessandro restrained her. If she antagonized his mother irrevocably, she could threaten his precious chance for a better life. Common sense told her it probably wouldn't make any difference, but she held her tongue for a vital second.

At last Prospero came through the terrace doors from the garden. Cotton suppressed her amusement at his startled expression. He looked warily from one woman to the other, Ghisela as cold as crystal, Cotton blazing with anger.

As Prospero looked at Cotton across the room, her feet planted firmly on the floor, her arms folded defiantly across her chest, he sensed he had never understood her so profoundly as at that moment. The two of them lived by the same creed, fighting like tigers to protect their interests when the stakes were high. They were minted from the same rare alloy, risking all in one toss with a deceptive insouciance that disguised how much they really cared. As she waited for him to speak, a current of intimate recognition passed between them.

He turned to Ghisela. 'I guess this is as good a time as any. Ghisela, I think you should know that Cotton and I are going to get married as soon as the divorce is final.'

Two hot little circles of anger appeared on her cheeks but, even in defeat, there was a steely purity about Ghisela that Cotton found chilling, although she began to understand that Prospero had fallen for her self possession as well as her beauty. Now the enigmatic Ghisela represented one last chapter of Prospero's life which they both had to come to terms with.

Ignoring Cotton, Ghisela said impatiently: 'How much longer will you be here, Prospero, in case I need to contact you?'

His arm firmly around Cotton, Prospero replied, 'We're staying here for another week, until Cotton goes to Moscow on an assignment for the *Herald*. I might stay on a while after that, but I have to be in Rome by the first week in September.'

His voice filled Cotton with an unshakable sense of her place in his life. If she had ever doubted his love, he was reaffirming it now. She was aware that in a few short moments, something of lasting importance had been resolved.

Undefeated, Ghisela gave her a sharp critical glance. 'I have no more time to waste.'

As she sailed past, Ghisela emitted sparks of impotent anger. Her eyes slid over Cotton in a last attempt to put her in her place. She went out, leaving a trail of her perfume and the echo of her heels on the tiled floor.

They heard the front door slam and the chauffeur starting the engine of the car. Ghisela had left the house without even bothering to say goodbye to her children. Cotton stared in the direction of the hall, then turned her head to see Prospero smiling at her.

With a shake of his own head, he remarked: 'You are one hell of a beautiful ball breaker, do you know that, Miss Castello?'

'Me?' she replied, wide-eyed. 'What a vulgar thing to say.'

Smacking her bottom affectionately, he said proudly: 'You've just done in five minutes what it took me eighteen years to do.'

She felt his arm slip surely around her waist as he led her back upstairs.

Resting his hand on the balcony of the suite at the Crillon, Herron looked up at the pink blush cast by the city lights.

'You know,' he said thoughtfully to Chiara, 'this city has always had an amazing effect on me, ever since I was a kid. I used to come here with my parents in the summer, on the way to see an aunt of mine who lived in Monte Carlo. I remember hating to leave, looking out of the back window of the taxi as it left the hotel, feeling that nothing that lay ahead was as exciting as what we were leaving behind. And now, if I don't renew my acquaintance with this grand metropolis once every two years or so, I feel cheated of the good things in life.'

He took a sip of his brandy, his eyes fixed on Chiara, incandescent in white silk jersey that revealed her smooth brown shoulders and the swell of her breasts. He brushed her hair back with a caressing hand. 'It's pure enchantment, isn't it?'

'Yes, I know exactly what you mean. I feel that way, too,' she replied with a preoccupied expression. Even though she had never been to Paris in her life, she pretended she had.

Years before, as a young starlet in Rome, she had dreamed of the Cannes film festival, eagerly absorbing pictures of Bardot and Anita Ekberg frolicking on the beach. From there, her thoughts had automatically moved to Paris. When she had married Abner, he had promised faithfully to take her there, but they had never made it. The reality she was experiencing at that moment could not have come closer to her dream had she ordered it down to every exact detail. Here she was in evening dress and diamonds, standing on the terrace of a luxurious hotel suite in the fabled city, with a man as rich and powerful and handsome as she could ever have desired. Yet this fantasy, now sprung to life, was empty, robbing her of all the joy of fulfilment. The Étoile at night, the Place de la Concorde, the Seine criss-crossed with lights, had seemed as two-dimensional as a movie set, and the man at her side might as well be made of straw. She realized dully that the only reason she was standing there on that balcony, the only reason she had come to Paris, was to ask Herron about Cotton Castello.

'Are you sure I can't get you something, a liqueur, a glass of champagne?' asked Herron attentively.

'No, thank you,' she said, clutching her cool bare arms as she gazed at the coral dome of sky.

'I admire your self-control, but hey, listen, you don't want to go overboard,' he murmured. The smell of cognac reached her nose as he bent to kiss her shoulder. She turned to him, remembering to smile.

'I believe in moderation, that's all,' she said. She had taken another Valium before dinner, and now she felt numb enough to go through with the rest of the evening. She did have admirable self-control, it was true, only giving in to tranquillizers when the fluttering in her stomach became unbearable. When the effects began to wear off, she could no longer cope with the ever-present image of Prospero with Cotton Castello; the panic, jealousy and hurt formed a three-edged sword that was cutting her life in pieces.

By the time she and Herron had arrived at Lasserre for dinner that evening her mind was functioning on two levels. She had caused a stir in the restaurant when she had entered on Senator Easton's arm in a clinging white silk jersey Valentino with diamonds glittering at her throat and ears. If she hadn't stumbled across the article in *Gente* the day before, Chiara would have at least managed to blank Prospero out of her mind just for the occasion; but knowing he was at that moment in Portofino with another woman had catapulted her on to a desperate course. There were murmurs from a table where some Americans recognized the handsome, tanned Senator Easton, accompanied by Chiara Galla. Together they were a publicist's dream.

'Nice to see you in Paris, Senator Easton. Enjoy your stay,' one man had remarked as they passed his table, giving them a smile of recognition. 'Miss Galla,' he had added with a deferential nod.

Normally Chiara would have been thrilled to be recognized in Herron's company. She was Gina in real life for a moment, and Herron was the genuine article. But none of it seemed to matter. She had barely tasted the exquisite five-course dinner or the vintage wines. It had all passed in a glittering blur, woven with the recollection of her own laughter and Herron's face dancing seductively across the table. The way Herron was looking down at her now, on the terrace, in the sumptuous suite of the Crillon, told her she had proved she was irresistible, even though the warm giving woman in her had been elsewhere. Edging away from him, she murmured throatily:

'Isn't it a lovely night?'

'Magnificent,' he replied, following close behind her.

Lifting her hair, he kissed the back of her neck, conveying his impatience to possess her after their long separation: but she wanted to put him off a while longer. From the moment he had met her at Charles de Gaulle airport he had behaved with an intimacy that implied they were two lovers reunited after a long absence. He failed to sense behind her smiles, her laughter, the reserve that indicated he was taking too much for granted. None of these thoughts registered in Chiara's face as she looked up at him with the flirtatiousness that was second nature to her. Toying seductively with his lapel, she suppressed hysterical laughter at his ignorance of her true feelings. She had no desire for him whatsoever, but it was easier to capitulate than to resist. And then, when he was sated with her, she would ask him about Cotton Castello.

She shrank involuntarily as he brushed her lips with his. She drew back and opened her eyes. His kiss had made her feel nothing. Appraising Herron frankly, she had to admit that with his broad shoulders, his finely made head, he was handsome enough to be a leading man. More than that, Herron was rich, and he was famous. With an effort of will she could superimpose Herron's smoothly handsome features on Prospero's roughly virile face. As Herron kissed her again, this time more insistently, she had the feeling that something was wrong, as if rain was falling upwards, shadows cast on the wrong side of the sun. When she responded to his touch, he tightened his embrace, searching her mouth with his tongue, and pressing against her.

Gathering her in his arms, he began to dance her across the square of paving secluded by walls and trellises, in time to the music playing somewhere in the distance. As he kissed her temples, her hair, he pushed his erection more insistently against her and she could feel his heart pounding in excitement.

'It's getting late,' he murmured, stopping. 'Are you ready for bed?' His voice was thick with desire.

Her answer was to smile thinly and drop her eyes drowsily, as she ran her fingers through her hair.

When they slipped into bed, Chiara breathed, 'I want us to take our time.'

She slid deep into the cool sheets. As he gathered her in his arms she emitted a little cry at the contact with his strong body – not of passion, but of protest.

Entwining his feet playfully with hers, he murmured, 'I haven't thought of you all this time, Chiara, to rush anything, now that I'm here with you at last.' As he spoke, he planted biting little kisses on her neck.

She emitted the kittenish little moan he expected, and which sent a jolt of fresh desire through him. He slipped his fingers between her legs and she allowed him to stroke her. When he started to kiss her breasts, she said in a husky voice:

'Have you had very many women in your life, Herron?'

'I've never counted,' he replied with a little laugh. Raising his head, he studied the fine cameo of her bare shoulders and magnificent face caught in a shaft of amber light falling through the window. 'But you know damn well there's never been anyone in my life, Chiara, to compare with you. And I want to prove it to you now,' he said with whispered urgency.

She began to toy with his thick, hard penis in the cleft of her fingers. Sighing as if in ecstasy at this foretaste of his power, a look that resembled desire glazed her eyes and a shudder of pretended anticipation shook her body which couldn't dispel the gnawing emptiness she felt.

As his hands explored her body she edged away. Injecting her voice with sultry innuendo, she said,

'What about that beautiful young American girl you were with the night we met?'

'You mean Cotton?' he said distractedly, burrowing his tongue between her breasts and down towards her navel.

'Didn't you say you were engaged to her once?'

'Mmm,' he replied.

Between kisses Chiara said, 'I didn't tell you that she came to my villa that first day we had lunch, when you sent me flowers. I think she must have guessed about us. She pretended to ask for money for some charity, but I knew what she was after. She's not going to let you go so easily this time, Herron . . .'

He gave an amused laugh, cupping her magnificent breasts in his hands. 'You aren't jealous, are you? Cotton was another lifetime. She's just an old friend, nothing more, I swear. I like you when you're jealous. It makes me want you more.'

'No, I'm not jealous,' she said. She eased him between her legs but resisted the urgency of his athletic body on hers for just a little longer.

'Tell me about Cotton Castello. Does she have a pretty figure?'

He sighed, and drew away. 'Oh, so that's what you're getting at? Does a threesome turn you on?' He laughed. 'Christ, I doubt if Cotton would be interested, but I'm sure we could find someone to accommodate us. After all, we're in Paris. Anything goes, *chérie*.'

She gave a hollow little laugh, shocked at the thought.

'Should we adjourn the subject until later?' Scooping his hands beneath her buttocks, he entered her in a powerful thrust that ended all conversation.

Afterwards, when they were lying in each other's arms, she stroked Herron's damp forehead absently as he released a shuddering sigh of contentment.

'Chiara, that was the best ever yet.' His strong hands searched her body anew. 'You've never been so wild with me as you were a few moments ago. It shows how much you've missed me.'

'Oh, I have, I have. And the more I know you, the more I can respond to you. Now I've learned to trust you, Herron, I want you to possess all of me, all.' She had said the same thing to Abner once, and to her other husbands, and now to Herron; yet the time she had made that same vow to Prospero was the only time that counted. It was easy to enslave a man you didn't care for, she reflected. If Herron had risen from the bed and walked from the hotel that moment, she would hardly have noticed.

'Tell me about yourself, so I can know you better.'

Pivoting her exquisite body, she arranged herself seductively on the crumpled sheets. 'I need to know all about you, all about your past.' Stroking the hair on his chest, she said thoughtfully. 'You've never told me why you didn't marry Cotton Castello. And yet the night I met you, you seemed such good friends. What happened? Why did you break up?'

Chiara was gazing at him with eyes luminous in the dimness, portraying the tenderness and passion of a woman in love. Smiling, he traced the outline of her lips with his fingertips.

'We just had different goals, that's all. It turned out that we didn't want the same things from life.'

'But tell me from the beginning. I'm intrigued.' Her heart began to beat with anxiety.

'Do you really want to hear this now?'

'Mmm,' she crooned.

'Well, I think the day I first really noticed her was the day her mother died. We were all having lunch at a country club on Long Island when the news came. She was about twelve, I think. Very cute, and bright as a button. It seems like only yesterday that her cousin Biddle carried her kicking and screaming from the club after we heard that Delilah – that's her mother – had had a fatal stroke. Delilah was Biddle's aunt, an American married to a titled Italian, and she adopted Cotton so she grew up in Italy.'

'Italy? She grew up in Italy?' whispered Chiara. A chill travelled through her, triggered by the unusual name of 'Delilah'.

Propping his head on the pillow, Herron warmed to the story. In the darkness he couldn't see the haunted expression in Chiara's eyes. 'You may not realize it, but Cotton and Prospero Vallone were bitter enemies at one time. You'd probably find this very funny, if you haven't already heard it from Prospero.'

'No – Prospero told me nothing,' she said in a blank whisper. As he related the incident, Chiara was only half-listening. Her mind was coldly fixed on what he had said earlier. Deep inside her, a dark, tortuous spool had begun to unwind. She said:

'So they're enemies, Cotton and Prospero . . .'

'I'm sure he doesn't give a damn any more, it was all so long ago. It's a long story. I'll tell you about it some time. And anyway, I saw them talking at the party. Some grudges he doesn't forget, though,' he said with a wry smile, stroking his jaw. 'If it hadn't been a party at the Embassy that night, I would have given him a run for his money. I had to wear pancake for three weeks to cover the bruise he left on my jaw.'

His fingers lightly circling her nipples, he began to exhibit the stirrings of desire again. 'You do something to me, gorgeous,' he murmured, turning to Chiara as she lay flat on her back staring at the lights dancing on the ceiling.

'What did you say her mother's full name was?'

'Oh, I can't remember. She was a Contessa or a Marchesa, or maybe even a Principessa.'

'Please try. Try and remember.' Her voice was hollow.

'Does it really matter?'

'Yes, it matters.'

'Okay, Easton, comb that memory bank of yours,' he said, narrowing his eyes in concentration. As his mind worked, passion began stoking wildly through him as his fingers invaded the smooth downy furrow between Chiara's legs.

'Please, please, remember. I want to know,' she said in a small pleading whisper.

'I know – I've got it,' he said at last. 'Delilah, Marchesa di Castello di Montefiore. That's it. Now, beautiful, can we drop the subject?' Laughing, he thrust his tongue between lips parted in shock.

As Herron made love to her, tears streamed down her temples and on to the sheets. Sobs that might have been mistaken for passionate fulfilment racked Chiara's body as the harpies of the past caught up with her. Herron moved inside her with a violent rhythm, while part of her spun away in a black void, pierced by knowledge that she would have given her life not to possess.

★

In the evening, the entire Vallone family gathered for dinner at a long table set under a vine-covered pergola. It gave on to the terraced garden lush with palm trees, rosemary and oleander. Prospero sat at the head of the table and, next to him, Cotton watched the children run to the garden to catch fireflies as the maid cleared away the pasta plates. Shouts from the children echoed through the night, above the conversation between Prospero's mother and his two teenage daughters, and the wives of his two brothers.

Enrico Vallone, the middle brother of three, was expounding his ideas for extending the Vallone freight and container business after the August holiday. Cotton glanced from Enrico to Roberto, both of them quite different from their elder brother. Neither of them had his physical magnetism, nor his strength of personality. They deferred to his authority as the eldest, and as head of the business empire he had founded; yet underneath, Cotton suspected she would discover rivalries and jealousies between them when she knew them better.

Enrico was a lawyer by profession, and the livelier of the two. Slight and dark, with receding hair, his methodical mind was a complement to Prospero's quicksilver shrewdness. When Roberto, the youngest, entered the conversation, she listened to what he was saying. A quiet, paunchy man who looked older than forty, he had become an accountant and had the financial expertise to back their ambitious plans for expansion. Quieter and more cautious than Enrico, he had a sincerity of manner which Cotton liked. As talk shifted to the reinvestment of last year's profits in a bid for a travel and leisure company, rather than diverting capital to tax shelters, Cotton tentatively suggested that the brothers ought to take a second opinion from a reputable firm of international accountants where she had a contact.

'You know, I think she's right,' said Roberto approvingly. 'Before we make a move, we should look into it more carefully.'

'If we went into such a detail before making a deal, we'd lose every opportunity that came our way,' disagreed Enrico. 'We'll have to move fast on this one, or it will be too late.'

'Him, he's a dreamer,' said Prospero, with a nod towards Enrico.

'I think you're all doers, not dreamers,' said Cotton with a laugh, taking a sip of wine.

'No, I think Cotton is right,' said Prospero, slipping his arm around her shoulder. 'Let's do it first thing when we get back to the office after the holidays. You know, Rico, she's not just a pretty face.' Laughing good-humouredly he pinched her cheek. Enrico smiled at them and shrugged good-naturedly.

Cotton gave Prospero a look of amusement, taking his comment in the spirit in which it was intended. Just then she caught Maria Vallone's glance for a second. The striking blue eyes, which she had bequeathed to Prospero, seemed to say that a woman's area of influence should be the home, not business. She glanced away when Cotton caught her eye, directing a remark to Gina, Enrico's wife, who was breast-feeding her baby daughter. Cotton reminded herself that patience was needed to break down the barriers between herself and Prospero's mother, contenting herself with her small victory over Ghisela that afternoon. News about their meeting had travelled through the house immediately, and when the family gathered around the table for dinner, Cotton sensed she had won a new measure of respect from all of them. She gazed at Maria Vallone, who radiated matriarchal authority. Her dyed gold tresses were piled up on her head, her ample figure was swathed in a black linen dress. Around her lined neck she wore a heavy gold necklace and her hand was studded with a large diamond ring. Her will was law when the family gathered at Portofino. Cotton observed that everyone deferred to her, especially Flavia, Roberto's wife, and Gina.

From the day they had met, Cotton was aware that Signora Vallone harboured prejudices about her that might take years to eradicate. Looking at herself from the older woman's point of view, Cotton had to admit she wasn't exactly the most suitable mate for her first-born son. She had numerous points against her: she was nearly thirty and her life had been devoted to a career that had brought her plenty of notoriety. Early on in her visit, when her origins had been mentioned, Cotton detected that Maria Vallone covertly disapproved of her because she was adopted. Her eyes seemed to question who Cotton's parents were and where she had come from, even though Signora Vallone knew she had grown up as the adopted daughter of Robbiano's most illustrious aristocrat. Cotton and Prospero had decided to keep her real parentage secret, concluding that no purpose would be served by bringing it out in the open. As a sea breeze crossed the terrace, Cotton looked around the table with a growing conviction that in spite of everything this was what she wanted, to be in the heart of a large, boisterous family. She told herself that all she needed to establish herself among them was time, time to know their ways, their prejudices, their likes and dislikes, time to speak fluent Italian again so that she could take part in their unremitting stream of conversation, peppered with references she couldn't catch.

She watched Elysia, Prospero's youngest daughter, as she helped the maid hand round plates of roast veal. Her eyes rested for a moment on her father's hand entwined with Cotton's. Since their mother had come to the villa that afternoon, Cotton was surprised to sense a new curiosity in her attitude towards Prospero's daughters. She had expected them to be typical teenagers, but instead she had been confronted with two blonde sophisticates with knockout figures, on the brink of womanhood. She had come to Portofino fully armed against their challenging coolness, even the hostility they were bound to show any woman who was a rival to their mother. Cotton was reminded how sure of herself and her own opinions she had been at their age, realizing how much she would have hated it if Delilah had suddenly produced a new man who might come between them. She would have made life hell for everybody, Cotton thought, directing a smile towards Sophia. Taken by surprise, Prospero's elder daughter smiled back, revealing that beneath her precocious sophistication lurked the responsiveness of an ordinary teenager. Whatever pangs of adjustment lay ahead between herself and Prospero's daughters, Cotton was determined to meet them all the way.

As a tureen of summer vegetables made the round of the table, Prospero rose and called the remaining stray children back to the dinner-table.

'They should all sit here until we have finished, not go running off into the bushes,' he shot at Gina in rapid Italian.

Cotton saw Gina frown at his impatience, but the disgruntled look on Prospero's face changed to a smile when one of her sons ran by, and he smacked him on the bottom. Clucking like broody hens, she and Flavia gathered their children around them. Cotton imagined the day when her own children would be seated at that same table among the other Vallone children. Flavia, younger than Gina and married to Roberto, was the prettier of the two. Cotton foresaw that Flavia, with her commercial law degree, would make waves some day when the children were grown. Gina, brown-haired, vivacious Gina, had shown Cotton the most friendliness and she hoped that some day they would be close. Neither of the two conformed to the stereotype of rich, cosmopolitan women who frequented the chic little port, but they radiated a quiet confidence that protected them like a wall, and couldn't be quickly breached with womanly small talk. Their lives revolved around being the mothers of families and mistresses of homes. Cotton wondered what they thought of an American woman who had led such a rootless, independent existence until now, and who was so different from Prospero's first wife.

While Enrico filled her glass with wine, Cotton saw Alessandro run late to his place between his cousins. He blushed and glanced down as he caught his father's look of disapproval. He had retreated to his silent world, eyes cast down as he ate, his long dark lashes casting fringed shadows on cheeks browned by the sun. Then, sensing Cotton was observing him, he looked up quizzically.

Their eyes locked for a moment in complicity, then with a shy smile he cupped his hands beneath his chin and began to stroke an invisible kitten in perfect mime. She returned his secret gesture by holding up her hands and moving her lips as she said in Italian, 'May I hold him, please?'

Cotton felt a warm glow of recognition as Alessandro nodded eagerly, opening his hands towards her, the first indication since she had been there that he could read her lips. It was all she could do not to announce to the entire family that something extraordinary had happened. Before turning away she was inspired to wince, puckering her lips, pretending that the make-believe kitten had scratched her which elicited a smile of delight from Alessandro.

Glancing at Prospero she realized that he had been watching their little exchange with an unreadable expression on his face. Time, give him time, she told herself, moving closer to him and tucking her hand into his. Though they hadn't as a couple begun to come to terms with Alessandro's problem, Cotton was sure at that moment that they were on the verge of a breakthrough.

After dinner, laughter was echoing around the table at one of Enrico's silly jokes. Even Maria Vallone was shaking with amusement, which amazed Cotton who had never seen her laugh openly. Suddenly she noticed the maid coming on to the terrace balancing a tray with a magnum of champagne surrounded by crystal glasses.

'What's this, Prospero?' asked Maria, looking over her shoulder. Excited whispers went around the table.

Prospero, beaming with satisfaction at everybody's surprise, gave a rich laugh as he signalled the maid to bring the bottle to him.

'Roderer, '76,' he said as he began to uncork the bottle expertly. 'The children are going to have some, too,' he announced. 'Claudio, Bruno – all of you, bring me your glasses.' When Gina and Flavia protested that they were too young, Prospero said, 'It's never too soon to acquire good taste.' He was immediately surrounded by the children, holding up their glasses.

Observing his largesse, Cotton knew the scene would have been the same had it been animal crackers or chocolate. Glancing round the table, she felt a sense of pride at being in a family whose greatest virtue was its solid simplicity and its sense of belonging, unchanged by recent wealth.

When everyone, down to the smallest child, had been served with champagne, Prospero touched his glass to Cotton's in a private little salute. When he tugged her to her feet and roughly slipped his arm around her waist there was laughter at the blush of sudden shyness that came across her cheeks.

'It's no secret by now, but we wanted it to be official. Some day this year, when the time is right, Cotton and I plan to get married. From now on, she's a Vallone.'

There was applause as Enrico stood and raised his glass. Meeting their eyes, he said in English and Italian, 'I propose a toast to Cotton and Prospero. May they have a long and happy life together.'

There was more delighted applause, followed by murmurs of '*auguri*', as everyone drank their champagne.

The entire family was looking at Cotton who had to bite her lower lip to hold back the tears. When she had regained her composure, she slipped her arm around Prospero and smiled radiantly to express all the joy and happiness that fate had compressed into that one moment. Her entire life seemed to have been leading to this private ritual of welcome. Though the Vallones were still strangers, she was poignantly aware that she would know them for the rest of her life. In carefully chosen Italian words, she proceeded to express what she felt:

'I want to thank all of you for welcoming me here among you, and to say how much I look forward to being part of this wonderful warm family. You see – I've never had a family in exactly that sense of the word, but I'm very, very happy to know that I have one now. Thank you, all of you . . .' She broke off, perilously close to tears again. Prospero pulled her to him and planted an exuberant kiss on her lips, a spontaneous gesture that made the family applaud and laugh with delight.

After dinner Cotton and Prospero slipped away to the drawing-room balcony nestled high above terraces of shading olive trees sloping down the hillside. The shimmering black bay at the foot of the hill was inlaid with a column of white moonlight dissolving into the dark water strewn with the lights of numerous boats. A warm herb-scented breeze whispered its way up the hill, bringing a suggestion of the sea in its wake and ruffling Cotton's hair which she had loosened on to her shoulders. Toying with the ribbon in her hand, she took in the magnificent sweep of the harbour at night, knowing she would never grow tired of it.

'I was proud of you tonight, *cara*,' murmured Prospero pressing his hand on her shoulder. He spoke in a tone he had never used before. 'I know it isn't always easy with Mamma and the rest of the family, not to mention Ghisela. But I want you to know how much it means to me, all the effort you made.'

She nestled closer as his warm hand caressed the back of her neck. Prospero's gentle touch, his strength, had endowed her life with a certainty it had missed until then, fulfilling her dormant need to be held and loved. In that rare moment, in their private eyrie above the world, they were free from every distraction. She uttered a sigh of contentment, feeling as sublimely untouchable as if she had won a race, passed a hurdle, beaten a deadline. She looked forward to the future that lay ahead of them, an endless vista of years as pure and uncharted as the horizon melting into the sea. It would be tempting fate to express her new-found invincibility aloud, but she knew that now they had left the difficult beginnings of their relationship behind them, nothing could destroy their happiness.

Absently brushing the sunbleached hair at Cotton's temples, Prospero was at that moment suppressing an unwanted image of Anna Gagliani. Sometimes the realization hit him that she was Cotton's mother and it gave him a feeling of niggling disquiet. The day Cotton had asked him whether he knew Anna, an instinctive lie had sprung easily to his lips. Later, when he thought it over, he decided that he was right not to confess to Cotton that he had once slept with her mother, a revelation that could only make her unhappy.

He was secure in the knowledge that at least no one had ever known about him and Anna except themselves but he was ashamed to admit that he couldn't even remember what she looked like. The blank in his mind made him feel less uncomfortable about the lie he had told Cotton. In a sense, he told himself, it was true. All he had left of Anna after so many years was the lingering impression of his own turbulent emotions that summer, and Anna's rejection of him when he had needed her so desperately.

But in the light of what happened, he could no longer bear any sort of grudge. It was a sweet irony that she had bequeathed to him her daughter, she and the tall blonde stranger he remembered her walking with on the night he left Robbiano. As he gathered Cotton in his arms, he wondered if Anna, wherever she was, was as happy as he.

'As soon as you come back from Moscow, we've got to make some solid plans for the future,' he began, his mind fixed on the Villa Robbiano. He disliked the thought of spoiling their mood of contentment, but the time had come to tell Cotton what had happened.

Resting her cheek against his, she was saying: 'I hope there are no last-minute hitches in my posting to Rome. The *Herald* has ways of springing surprises on me. Two years ago, when I was sent to London, I was scheduled to move to Paris. Good thing I didn't, or we might not have met that night at the party. I wouldn't have been covering Ethiopia from there.'

'We would have met somewhere, some time, there's no doubt about it.' As he spoke, they looked at each other in the darkness, aware of the narrow margin that had determined their fate. Their lips met, and Cotton was filled with the courage to face whatever came.

'Do you know something? You and I are the luckiest people on earth. I never thought I'd say that about myself, ever,' she whispered.

'Cotton – *cara*, we do have everything, but there's one thing we won't have. One thing that means a lot to you.' He released a pent-up sigh, filled with regret that he had to mar her perfect world. 'It's the Villa Robbiano. We've lost it.'

She stared at him incredulously.

'What happened?'

Pained at her disappointment even though he had expected it, Prospero took her hands in his. 'Apparently another buyer came along almost immediately after I saw Perini, and offered the asking price in cash.' He shook his head. As they looked at each other, he was weighing up whether he should tell her the buyer was Chiara, but he held back, aware that she had already come between them once.

'But when did you find out?' asked Cotton, unable to disguise her devastation.

'I confess I've known about it for nearly two weeks, but I didn't have the heart to tell you with so many other things on your mind. Forgive me, maybe I was wrong. That day in Florence, when I told you about the villa, it never entered my head this might happen. It's obvious to me now that the notary was playing each of us off against the other.'

Cotton faced her crushing disappointment, steeling herself against the pain the news caused her. During the two months since they visited the villa, they had allowed themselves to dream, building their future around the grand illusion of restoring it and living there for part of the year when they were married. It had never occurred to Cotton that an interloper could sweep in and prise away the Villa Robbiano from her, now she had found it again.

'I can't bear the thought of somebody else living there,' she said bitterly. Outsiders, no matter who they were, could never understand the Villa Robbiano as she did. How could they appreciate its rich history? How could they possibly be the keepers of its private grief and happiness, its legend locked between the walls, which was her exclusive legacy? Cotton came to her senses abruptly when she saw the disappointment on Prospero's face. She ordered herself to stop harking back to the past, determining that henceforth the Villa Robbiano was a closed chapter in her existence.

'It doesn't really matter, Prospero,' she said resolutely. 'It's only a house.'

As she hugged him he clenched his jaw in anger, not wanting her to see the fury sparkling in his eyes as he thought of Chiara. 'I even tried to offer a premium to the buyer in the hope of persuading them to sell it back to me. I offered forty per cent over the asking price to get it back, but they refused. I'm kicking myself now for not tying the whole thing up then and there, that first day. It would be ours now, if I had.'

'Well, no matter. It's too late to change things,' she replied. 'Who bought it, do you know?'

'No, I don't know,' he said with a shrug. 'Does it matter?' Some day Cotton was bound to find out, but not now and not from him.

He swallowed a poisonous resentment against Chiara for what she had done, vowing he could never forgive her spiteful, heartless action. He remembered the day their paths had crossed in Florence. When his lawyer had revealed that Chiara was behind the battle over the villa, Prospero had been deeply shocked to realize how deadly the grudge she bore against him was. He could not imagine how she had discovered that he had made an offer to Perini, and the only explanation he could think of was that she had deliberately nosed around Robbiano, knowing he had spent the summer of his father's murder there. She must have wheedled information from Giuseppe the gardener about himself and Cotton, and realizing finally that there was no chance of a reconciliation, had taken a bitter revenge.

Prospero's mood lifted as he began to talk optimistically of another villa they would buy. Cotton listened with a sense of unreality, aware that it was going to take her a long time to adjust to the idea that she was marrying a man who could buy anything he wanted. But she was determined never to be in awe of the power of Prospero's wealth, knowing that if she was, it would come between them.

They were interrupted by the family gathering in the living-room again. Maria Vallone stationed herself in her usual armchair before the television, her eye on Cotton and Prospero, and Flavia and Gina came downstairs after putting the children to bed.

Cotton was just about to slip upstairs to say goodnight to Alessandro, when she saw Prospero cross his arms and frown, a brooding stance she knew well by now. Following his eyes, she saw Sophia and Elysia flitting across the room together, having undergone a dazzling transformation since dinner. They had tousled their blonde hair with gel and slipped into mini-skirts with black, silver-studded belts on their narrow hips. Their pretty oval faces were plastered with make-up and their high breasts were provocatively outlined by tight, clinging jersey halters. Smiling brightly, they joined Cotton and Prospero. Their faces fell when Prospero said:

'You're not going anywhere looking like that.'

'But, Papa, everybody dresses like this,' protested Sophia. 'You said we could go down to the port if Tommaso comes with us.'

Cotton waited for Prospero's reaction. Like all rich Italians, he lived with a gnawing fear of kidnappers, and his children were never allowed anywhere unless accompanied by the brawny chauffeur–bodyguard, Tommaso.

'I said you could go to the port for half an hour, but not dressed like that. Go upstairs and change back to what you were wearing at dinner,' he ordered, his face set determinedly.

'Why don't we all go?' suggested Cotton in a sudden inspiration. 'We could go for a drink at La Gritta, or to the *gelateria*.'

'Yes, we could all go,' chorused the girls. They began dancing around Prospero, to get him in a good humour. He looked at Cotton to see if she really meant what she said.

'Well,' he said, his voice softening. 'I guess we could all go, then.' He broke into a smile and his daughters squealed with delight. 'But go upstairs and tone down that make-up, or I won't take you,' he added.

Cotton was reminded that Prospero was an old-fashioned father who tempered his affection for his children with strict discipline very much, she imagined, as Franco Vallone had raised his sons. When the girls had gone she said:

'Do you know, if Delilah had stuck to her word and banished me to my room the night you came to the villa, the entire course of our lives might have been altered. Think of that.'

He kissed her on the forehead and said with a laugh, 'So, you think the entire course of their lives will be altered if they don't go to the *gelateria* tonight?'

They were interrupted by the insistent blaring of a car horn that echoed from the other side of the villa, cutting through the tranquil night. Everybody looked towards the vestibule in surprise that a caller would arrive so late and unannounced. Prospero strode towards the hall, where the sound of voices could be heard. As footsteps approached, all eyes went to the threshold of the room.

'*Benvenuto*, come in!' cried Prospero, who had seen the visitor first.

It was the last person Cotton expected to see. Cardinal Pietro Giannini came towards them in a black soutane warming the room immediately with his presence. Gina and Flavia rose with welcoming smiles on their faces and hastened to kiss his ring, and Roberto and Enrico greeted their cousin effusively. Maria Vallone rose from her chair, her dour expression transformed with enthusiasm. For several moments the big room was filled with a chattering welcome as the entire family clustered around the great man. Even at a distance, Cotton saw that Pietro Giannini projected a humanity and vitality that had only deepened with the years. The Vallones treated him more with affection than with awe, even Prospero's daughters, who rushed to greet him.

Cotton stood apart. The sight of the priest from Robbiano who had risen to become a cardinal took her straight back to the past and another window in her mind opened unexpectedly, admitting vivid memories that she had all but lost in the intervening years. As she regarded the handsome, greying Giannini whose waistline had thickened a little with a lifetime of good living as a prince of the Church, she could see why Delilah had dubbed him a notorious heartbreaker. The worldly charm he exuded was in intriguing contrast to his religious vocation. Cotton remembered William saying caustically to Delilah that any number of girls in the convents surrounding Robbiano had pledged themselves to Christ after gazing into Giannini's liquid brown eyes.

When all the commotion had died down, Giannini singled out Cotton with an affectionate regard. 'Well, well,' he said in English, 'if it isn't *la piccola Cotton*.'

She moved to embrace him, feeling the warmth of their reunion.

'Cotton Clotilda Castello di Montefiore,' he intoned, his hand on her shoulder. 'How good it is to see you, how very good.' He gave her a hug. 'When I heard the news about you and Prospero, I was absolutely delighted. Let me look at you.' He held her by the shoulders. 'You are still the girl I remember, but how you've grown.' Everyone laughed. 'Are you still as strong-willed and stubborn as ever?'

'I don't know. Ask him,' she replied laughingly, nodding towards Prospero. 'It's so good to see you,' she added, clutching his hand.

'This little one, do you know I held her in my arms when she was only a week old?' he informed them all with a chuckle. 'I tell you, Prospero, you've got your hands full with her. Yes, I can see that at last Prospero Vallone has met his match.'

Cotton wiped away her tears. 'I feel like such an idiot,' she murmured in embarrassment. Gina slipped her arm comfortingly around her, and to her surprise Maria came forward and patted her affectionately on the cheek.

As the Vallone clan encircled her protectively, Cotton knew she had ceased to be a stranger and she was filled with a sense of belonging that had eluded her all her life.

Chapter 25

When the telephone rang at the Villa Flavia, Diane trotted down the marble hall on tiptoe, worried that her footsteps might disturb Chiara upstairs.

'Hello? *Pronto?*' she said in a breathy voice, glancing up at the landing.

'Diane, it's Sandy. Can I speak to Chiara?'

'I'm sorry, but I'm afraid she's still indisposed.'

'Indisposed? What the hell does that mean? Tell her to pick up the phone. I've got to talk to her. Come on – I'm calling from a goddam callbox in San Treviano.'

'Please, Sandy – I don't want to disturb her,' said Diane in an anxious whisper.

'Listen, Diane, this is getting to be serious. I've shot around her as much as I can, and if she wants this thing under budget she'd better get up here quick. If she's sick, then call a doctor, if she's not, tell her to snap out of it. Do I have to come down there in person to drag her out of bed? What is this, a nervous collapse because she's suddenly camera shy?'

'Please, I'm in a very difficult position. You know what it's like.' Diane's eyes darted to the landing where she half-expected to see Chiara appear like an angry wraith. 'To be honest, she looks awful,' she whispered.

'Look, Diane,' said Sandy, his voice dropping. 'I don't mean to take it out on you, but we've got to do something. If it's a case of last-minute jitters, tell me. I'll come down and coax her out of it. If she needs medical attention, then call a doctor. Just do something – anything.'

Diane agonized for a moment. 'She hardly speaks to me, Sandy. She's fallen into a deep depression for some reason. I really don't know how much longer I can take it . . .' Her voice broke. 'I'm seriously thinking of going back to the States.'

Discretion kept her from mentioning that Chiara wouldn't even speak to Senator Easton who had called repeatedly from Washington. For two weeks she had imprisoned herself in her bedroom with the curtains drawn, stretched out on the bed in her dressing-gown. She was eating hardly anything, and the only time she left her room was for an occasional swim, something she hadn't done for the last three days. What alarmed Diane most was that the bottle of Valium on her bedside table was emptying fast. Whenever the secretary had summoned the courage to ask her what was wrong, if she wanted anything, Chiara had replied in a ghostly, defeated voice:

'No, nothing, thank you, Diane. I just want to be alone. Keep everybody away.'

Upstairs in the darkened room, Chiara slipped from the bed and glided quietly across the floor. Carefully opening the door a crack, she closed it when she heard Diane walk down the hall. Returning to her bedside, she picked up the telephone receiver and turned on the lamp. A little flutter rose in her stomach as she dialled Prospero's private number in Rome. It rang only twice before she heard his voice at the other end. Putting her hand over the receiver, she held her breath as he spoke.

'*Pronto?*' came his deep, familiar voice. When there was no reply he repeated the word sharply, '*Pronto?* Who is this? Is anyone there?'

She quickly hung up the receiver as if the telephone was burning, afraid Prospero might suspect it was her. Her stomach churning, her heart pounding, she sat on the bed, deeply shaken by the sound of his voice.

She had called his number repeatedly every day for the last week, and today was the first time he had answered, confirming what she was waiting to know, that he was back from Porto-fino. She felt nauseated at the thought that he and Cotton might even be in his apartment together. Knowing what she had to do, she flipped through her Filofax and located the number of the Rome bureau of the *Washington Herald* which she had noted down two weeks before, when she came back from Paris.

When the bureau chief came on the line, she said in a silky voice, 'I'd like to speak to Miss Cotton Castello, please. This is Chiara Galla calling.'

'Cotton? Let me see, she's not due here for another week or so to take up her post,' came a man's friendly voice. 'What's it about? Maybe I could help you, Miss Galla.'

Reassured that he seemed to know who she was, she said smoothly, 'Miss Castello came to interview me in June, and I promised to contact her in the autumn about a project of hers.'

'Sure, I see. Well, as far as I know she's still in Moscow on an assignment, but you could try the London bureau. They would certainly know her movements. Let me give you the number.'

The moment she had hung up, Chiara feverishly dialled the *Washington Herald* in London. Each long-distance ring of the telephone seemed to pierce her chest, wounding her afresh with the heartache of the last weeks.

After a short conversation that told her all she needed to know, Chiara hung up the telephone and sat thinking for a moment. Then she stood erect and walked purposefully to the hall to summon her secretary.

Diane came hurrying breathlessly into the room, astonished to see Chiara in her dressing-gown, energetically drawing back the curtains.

'Why, Miss Galla – I'm so glad to see you're feeling better,' she cried, relief flooding through her. When Chiara turned to give her a withering look, Diane knew for certain that she was her old self again.

In an imperious voice she said, 'Diane, I want you to book me a flight to London this afternoon. I also want you to book me a hotel. Something small and quiet close to this street.' She went to her desk, picked up a pen and jotted it down.

Diane regarded her in open-mouthed astonishment as she looked at the paper. 'Of course, Miss Galla. I'll do it right away. But when will you be coming back? Mr Vincent called again this morning and he seems very concerned that you're not on location. He said he'd come down today or tomorrow to talk to you in person. He'll be very upset if you're not here. What should I tell him?'

In the archway of the bathroom door Chiara was slipping off her dressing-gown. She regarded Diane with wilting incredulity across a shaft of sunlight flooding the room.

'If he insists on coming, I won't be here.' She relented. 'Just call him and say I'll be in San Treviano on Thursday morning. Now get my small Vuitton overnight case from the dressing-room, will you? Why are you looking at me like that? Please do as I say.'

'Yes, Miss Galla,' said Diane obediently. She was startled by the strange metallic emptiness of her employer's voice, but relieved that she had snapped out of her inexplicable mood.

From her seat in the first-class section of the plane, Chiara observed the fields of France stretching endlessly below on a clear September day. Her mind was as cloudless as the curving blue-green horizon and her hand was steady as she took a glass of champagne from the stewardess, enjoying its flowery fragrance as she sipped it. It was the first alcohol she had had since she'd been in Paris with Herron and it instantly revived her.

Reaching for her compact, she tilted the large sunglasses on her nose and checked her make-up which was immaculately applied. Her eyes were highlighted by golden taupe shadow, her mouth was perfectly glazed a deep russet, her flawless complexion highlighted with blusher. A hairdresser had rushed to the villa to style her hair before her departure, and Diane had packed in tissue paper the few things she would need for an overnight stay in London. In a reflective gesture, she brushed the skirt of her bronze gaberdine suit and toyed with the gold buttons on the cream silk shirt she had selected as being appropriate for London. She was glad she had had Diane check the weather in England, which was reported to be cool and showery, and she had brought her Burberry and umbrella. She was looking forward to the English climate, even if it was only for a day, after the punishing heat of Rome. Leaning back in the comfortable seat, she pondered the novelty of travelling alone, a thing she had rarely done during the last fifteen years, deciding she rather enjoyed it. There was no secretary, nurse or tiresome assistant to distract her from what lay ahead. It was only she, Chiara, travelling discreetly, without fanfare and with a purpose.

Stroking her nails, Chiara studied the topaz and diamond ring which, apart from her gold Piaget watch and earrings, was all she had chosen from the velvet jewel cases in the safe. She had been tempted to wear her big diamond solitaire, her engagement ring from Abner, but she had rejected it on the grounds that it would have been too overpowering for her meeting with Cotton Castello, a very important occasion for both of them. Chiara had blanked out the word 'daughter' from her mind entirely; it was a tie which seemed incidental. She stretched her legs forward, obliquely aware of an appreciative glance from the businessman sitting next to her. After her week of seclusion, she discovered she was ready to face the world again. Like cold hands slipping eagerly into warm gloves, she had stepped back into her old self and was in command of her emotions once more.

Two weeks ago, when she had fled Paris and a baffled Herron Easton, claiming to be ill, she had retreated instinctively to her bedroom at the Villa Flavia. Once she had closed the door, the shutters, the curtains, she had entered the chamber of her own mind. As the hours and days ticked by, she became aware that her life lay in chaos like a random pile of toys. Slowly, very slowly, she had begun to rebuild a structure to support her existence, putting each piece in place and making sure it was correctly aligned before adding the next one – a mental discipline that had saved her in the past. Two weeks ago her will to live had been annihilated, but gradually she began to understand what she must do to survive. It had been a long time since she had needed to call on her wits so crucially. She reckoned it hadn't happened since the final days of her marriage to Abner, at the time when she realized she would be alone in life once again. As was her habit, when Chiara determined a course of action, not a shred of doubt clouded her objectives.

Once it became clear that she could not let a marriage occur between Prospero Vallone and Cotton Castello, the only thing that remained to decide was how to go about stopping it. The solution turned out to be simple. Distasteful as Chiara found her errand to London, she would go through with it, resolving that once it was behind her she would get on with her own life again. If everything went according to plan, she would be back in Rome and on her way to location in Tuscany by the same time the next day. A great burst of energy overtook her whenever she thought of the work that lay ahead, which henceforth would be her dynamo, her reason for living.

Until the moment she had contacted the *Herald*, Chiara had hoped there might be a way to avoid a confrontation with Cotton Castello. When she had heard that she was returning from Moscow that same evening, the thought crossed her mind that Cotton's affair with Prospero might even be over, but then the bureau chief in London let slip that she was getting married and would be posted to Rome. Chiara's worst fears were confirmed.

A few hours later she had checked into a small, comfortable hotel around the corner from Cotton's flat in Onslow Square in South Kensington. The first thing Chiara did was to call Aeroflot to confirm that the flight was due at Heathrow on time. Ordering tea to be brought to her room she pulled aside the chintz curtain and looked down on the pavement glistening with rain. The hotel was in a typical London street lined with elegant white town houses in a neat row behind freshly painted black railings. They were decked with window-boxes crammed with geraniums and lobelia, and people were hurrying by, umbrellas unfurled against the elements, wrapped up in raincoats, walking dogs; a scene very different from the dusty grandeur of Rome in September, where a lazy holiday feeling still lingered.

When the hour approached seven, Chiara slipped into the bathroom to retouch her make-up. Tying a richly patterned Hermès scarf around her head, she slipped on her Burberry and picked up her matching umbrella. As she left the hotel she felt every inch a Londoner, even though she had never been in the city before. Walking down the pavement she sniffed the air with its distinctive aroma of wet leaves, taxis' exhaust and wood smoke.

When she came to the tall white house divided into flats where Cotton lived, Chiara climbed the steps and searched the brass plate for her name. Without hesitation she rang the bell and waited, ignoring the fluttering that rose in her stomach. When she had rung the bell a second time, then a third, Chiara peeked round the corner of the pillared porch and saw that the interior shutters of the ground-floor flat where Cotton evidently lived were closed. She stood in a quandary for a moment, wondering what to do.

Looking at the time, Chiara impatiently calculated that Cotton should have had plenty of time to get through Customs and take a taxi from the airport. For a moment she panicked, wondering if Cotton might have changed her plans and flown directly to Rome, or even missed the flight from Moscow. For an instant, Chiara was terrified by the prospect of confronting Cotton suddenly unawares, but she pulled herself together. She didn't dare return to the hotel in case she missed Cotton, nor did she dare stray too far. She decided the only thing to do was to walk casually up and down the quiet street until Cotton arrived, which could only be a matter of minutes.

For the next half-hour she walked methodically up and down the opposite pavement, like an actress pacing in the wings for her cue. She went over in her mind the speech she had prepared, once avoiding the glance of a London bobby who was patrolling the square, an excuse on her tongue if he should question her. She had just put up her umbrella against the drizzle when she heard the distinct rattle of a London taxi. She stopped abruptly when she saw the black Austin screech to a halt in front of Cotton's flat. She recognized Cotton at once by her fair hair and coltish figure draped in a stylish black raincoat, as she leapt out, dragging her bag after her. Tipping the driver, she flashed him a smile.

'Thanks a lot,' she heard her call as the taxi drove away.

Chiara stood transfixed, watching her as she searched in her bag for her keys, her face and golden head silhouetted by the lamps overhead. Chiara was fascinated by her every movement. For an instant she felt a tug of indecision, which was over-shadowed by a small voice inside her dictating that she had no choice but to go through with it. She, Chiara Galla, had given life to the beautiful, confident creature who was blissfully ignor-ant of her mother's suffering. She had withstood humiliation, pain and loneliness, a pattern that had repeated itself in her life again and again. Everything she had achieved in life she had accomplished the hard way, from learning English to starting on the bottom rung of the movie business, having no one to advise or help her. And all the time Chiara had been struggling, learning, trying to make something of herself, Cotton Castello had lived a charmed life which offered her every luxury and opportunity her heart could desire. Cotton Castello had always had everything she wanted, but there was one thing Chiara was determined she would never have. The ground seemed to move beneath her feet as she stood there, giddy with anger and self-righteousness, watching the interior lights of the flat come on. She folded her umbrella, prepared to wait a moment or two before she paid her call.

Cotton entered her flat and dropped her bags, almost tripping over the pile of bills, letters and magazines on the mat. Sighing with exhaustion, she slipped off her raincoat and hung it on the hall peg, then went into the sitting-room to turn on the lamps. Rolling up the sleeves of her shirt, she walked down the hall to the small kitchen and looked inside the refrigerator which was pathetically empty. Fetching a Coke, she returned to the com-fortable but soulless living-room. She had furnished it in a hurry when she moved in, with a pale upholstered sofa and chairs around a modern coffee table, and ceramic lamps with pleated shades, a big shelf full of books. But in all the months she had lived there, she had never bothered to completely unpack the paintings and bric-à-brac she had collected during her travels around the world. Running her hands through her hair with a smile, she reflected that it no longer mattered. This time, returning to her flat wasn't the anticlimax it had so often been in the past, now she knew she would be decorating a home for herself and Prospero. Kicking off her shoes, she grabbed a shrivelled apple from the fruit bowl on the pine table, to stave off her hunger. When she saw the repeated flash of the answering machine she turned it on. There were several messages from Prospero in a heavily disguised voice. She burst out laughing at his last message. It was so funny she played it back again: 'This is the KGB – we're on your tail. Bring back the Beluga you smuggled out, or else . . .' he breathed in a comic Russian accent. She hooted with laughter at the post-script as he sang a snatch of a Mario Lanza tune, 'Be My Love', to the sound of his shower running in the background. As soon as she had brushed her teeth, she would call him.

Pulling her cosmetic bag from her hand luggage, Cotton went to the bathroom. Unzipping the bag, she saw the preg-nancy indicator she had prudently bought before departing for Moscow, whose results she had saved for posterity. It had seemed heartless to throw it in the waste-paper basket of a Moscow hotel room, and now she propped it on the bathroom shelf and gazed at it as if it were a precious icon. Cotton guessed it was going to take all her self-control not to tell Prospero she was pregnant before she had had proper confirma-tion from the doctor.

She was just thinking to herself how she would fly to Rome and thrust the bottle of pink liquid into his hand in lieu of a formal announcement when the doorbell rang. Wondering who it could be, she wiped her mouth with a towel and started across the sitting-room. Passing the bouquet of wilted roses Prospero had sent before she left for Moscow, she wondered if the caller might be a florist. Pressing the entry button, she peeked around the door with an expectant look on her face. A woman entered, her face shadowed by her headscarf. When she took off the scarf, Cotton was startled to recognize Chiara Galla, uncharacteristically garbed in an English trench coat. It crossed her mind that the last time she had seen her she had been wearing a parrot-green bathing suit by her pool in Rome. But then she corrected herself. She had last seen Chiara kissing

Prospero on a street corner in Florence – an incident she preferred to forget.

'May I come in?' said Chiara, her face blank and unsmiling.

Mystified and apprehensive, Cotton nodded and she walked through the door.

'What a charming flat,' she commented, shaking her umbrella on the mat. Chiara glanced around at the predictable and uninteresting modern décor, finding nothing remarkable, noticing that an entire unattractive wall of books dominated the smallish sitting-room. There was a simplicity about Cotton's home that was totally alien to Chiara's own love of rich decoration.

Cotton watched her warily, taken aback by her purposeful manner. There seemed no sign of the simpering femininity she remembered on the night of the Embassy reception, or even the condescension she had shown when she received Cotton at her villa. As they regarded one another, Cotton sensed a directness that seemed out of character.

'How did you know where I lived?' she asked, closing the front door.

'I called your newspaper.'

'May I ask why you want to see me?'

Chiara's reaction was to suck in her cheeks thoughtfully, and for one crazy moment Cotton wondered if she had come belatedly to offer money for Seamus's film. She was relieved she would be able to reply she didn't need her backing. Then something warned her that this visit had something to do with Prospero.

'May I sit down?'

'Yes, please do. Excuse me, Miss Galla, but I've just got in from Moscow and I wasn't expecting anybody,' Cotton said, determined to be polite, though her heart was racing furiously.

'Please call me Chiara.' She settled in the chair and put down her handbag. 'Yes, I heard you were in Moscow. Did you have a pleasant trip?'

'Yes, thank you. Don't you think you'd better tell me why you're here?'

'In a moment. Why don't you sit down so we can talk,' said Chiara, appraising her coolly.

Cotton did as she suggested, and as she sank into the chair opposite she was unnerved by the sense of a storm gathering between them.

'This is very difficult for me,' Chiara began, her accent more pronounced than usual. 'It was a hard decision to make, to come here. I must start at the beginning so you will understand.' Folding her arms, she settled back in the chair and began to reminisce in an even, quiet voice.

'Many years ago, when I was a young girl, I lived in the village of Robbiano where I had a job working as a maid at the villa belonging to the Marchesa di Castello di Montefiore . . .'

As she spoke, her words seemed to drop from a great height, like stones, hitting Cotton one after the other.

'One summer a boy of fifteen came to that village from America to visit relatives. He and I fell in love. We were both very young, but our happiness ended without warning one day when word came that his father had been murdered in New York. He and his family left the village suddenly, before either of us knew that I was carrying his child. My name was Anna Gagliani then. The man was Prospero Vallone – and you are that child.'

Chiara looked at Cotton with eyes full of compassion. Cotton felt a shudder of repulsion course through her. She cringed inwardly as the breath, the life, was momentarily knocked out of her. There were tears forming in Chiara's eyes, and as she leaned forward to touch her, Cotton shrank away instinctively. Her offering of pity twisted in an ugly tangle, sending out conflicting signals of falsehood, subterfuge and revenge that embedded themselves at the back of Cotton's mind. For a moment Cotton was in a state of complete immobility. A feeble cry rose in her throat, the only response she had to offer against the revelation which, her instincts told her, Chiara couldn't have invented. In the searing moment during which they regarded one another, the only thing that kept Cotton from hysteria was the knowledge that she didn't want to share this terrible grief with anyone, least of all with Chiara Galla. The fact that she had come there claiming to be Anna Gagliani, her mother, only dimly intruded on her consciousness.

'This doesn't make any sense,' she countered bravely. 'Why did you wait until now, when it's too late, when we love each other?' Unable to bear the sight of Chiara, she turned her head as she started to shake.

Chiara continued in a soft, unassuming voice. 'I only recently learned about you and Prospero, and even more recently discovered you were my daughter. This all happened some time after you came to see me. At the time I had no idea, none.'

Her voice conveyed a caressing regret as she delivered the truth overgrown with lies, though as she spoke, Chiara no longer recognized the difference. What she told Cotton and what had happened in reality had become intertwined in her mind. Watching Cotton's face twisted with shock, she searched for something of herself or Prospero. She wished at that moment she had been more careful in counting the months, but it had all happened so long ago, and she had been so young.

Cotton was standing with her back to Chiara, her shoulders hunched, her arms clasped tight. 'Why did you say that Matthew Swope was my father, why?' Tears were falling down her cheeks that she didn't want Chiara to see.

Chiara shrugged helplessly. 'Imagine for yourself. I was fourteen years old, poor, and in disgrace. Remember – it was 1955, not 1985. What was I to do? Matthew Swope fell in love with me days after Prospero left the village; and anyway, what could Prospero have done? It was my chance, our chance, to be saved. But before he could marry me, Matthew was killed. Obviously, you know the rest . . .'

Feeling herself starting to tremble uncontrollably, Cotton had the presence of mind to say in a steady voice, 'If you don't mind, I would like you to leave now. I really have to be alone.' Turning to Chiara, she looked at her with a tear-stained face, unable to summon up a single drop of curiosity or affection. The daydream she had woven round Anna Gagliani withered and died.

'Wouldn't it be better if we talked more? You're upset, and maybe I can help you,' said Chiara, at a momentary loss.

'You can't help me. Now, please go, will you?'

Chiara sighed and rose to her feet. 'I regret that you're taking it like this. I hope you will believe me when I say that one day I want us to be friends. This has been the most painful duty of my life and, believe me, if there was any way to change things, I would.'

There was a tragic emptiness in her perfect face that conveyed a deep private suffering. Cotton was chilled by the conviction that Chiara's motives were sincere. She felt guilt at her own callousness but was unable to deal with it there and then.

'Friends?' she replied, swallowing a mad desire to laugh. 'Are you serious? Friends?' The moment she spoke, she wanted to take it back, seeing the veiled hurt in Chiara's eyes. Through the web of her confusion she struggled to grasp that this woman was her mother.

'I was hoping you wouldn't feel that way, but I guess I must not blame you. In that case, there is nothing further for me to say to you now. Goodbye.' Drawing herself up, she walked towards the door where Cotton was standing, stricken.

'But one more thing,' she murmured, touching Cotton's hand. 'It isn't necessary to tell Prospero about this. As far as I am concerned, it will be a secret between us and no one else need ever know. If you love him as you say, you won't want to hurt him unless it's necessary. Isn't that true? There are easier ways to break off your relationship, much easier. Why cause more pain?'

'I can't even think that far ahead now, don't you understand?' Cotton replied desperately.

Chiara nodded, then slipped out of the door. When she was on the pavement she walked down the dimly lit street towards the hotel, her tears mingling with the falling rain. Glancing at her watch by the street light, she decided with a shudder she couldn't endure a night in the cosy English hotel, that she would collect her bags and return to Rome that evening.

When Cotton closed the door behind Chiara she stood for a moment, her back flattened against the cold wood, wishing with all her heart that she was dead. She went to the sofa and lay down, feeling empty, finished. The idea of going to bed, of waking up in the morning and going through the motions of life seemed unthinkable. An hour ago she had possessed everything, and now she had less than nothing. In an absent gesture, she touched her hand to her stomach, trying to stroke away the gnawing sadness that seemed to have sprung to life inside her, quickening with more vitality and reality than the baby she had hoped she was carrying. Closing her eyes, she let the tears fall as she whispered a prayer that she wasn't really pregnant after all; but she knew in her heart that she was. She had lived with a feeling of fullness, of completeness for the last few weeks, and all the little signs were there. She groped through memory, searching back to the moment she had asked Prospero whether he had known Anna Gagliani, the most beautiful girl in the village. The recollection came back, bringing more pain with it. She could see Prospero's face, sense his hesitation that lasted one skipped heartbeat, the give-away that he wasn't telling the truth, though she hadn't even thought about it at the time. All summer he had known she was Anna's daughter. She could only wonder now why it hadn't crossed his mind that he might have fathered her child. For a minute Cotton wished desperately that Anna Gagliani had disappeared without a trace, instead of being resurrected as Chiara Galla. Then she would never have been aware of that most ancient and rigid taboo that now divided herself and the man she loved.

She lay on the couch for a long time, dry-eyed and empty as she stared sightlessly at the mouldings on the ceiling. The future was enclosed in gathering darkness and, try as she would, she couldn't see ahead, even to the next moment. She could feel herself breathing, she could see, she could hear, but there seemed no proof she really existed. The weight of her own body seemed to sink into nothingness where she wished her mind would follow; but it kept turning, turning, on the fulcrum of Chiara's words which were embedded in her heart.

Moving her head, she saw the room as if through a fish-eye lens, picking out the objects that symbolized her wandering existence: a Balinese temple carving, a naïve painting from Ethiopia depicting the marriage of Solomon and Sheba, a bowl of bangles from the Middle East, a pile of tapestry cushions she had bought when she came to London, in a fit of domesticity. She had wondered how her possessions, some of which were eccentric and shabby, would fit into her new life with Prospero. She needn't worry about that any more. She scanned the hundreds of books she wouldn't have to crate and send to Rome. Rome reminded her of the re-posting she had battled for that summer in Washington, and she wondered where she would find the strength and energy to reverse the forces she had set in motion. A moment later, when the phone started to ring she died inwardly. A shiver coursed through her as the answering machine clicked on after several rings, and she heard Prospero's beloved voice.

'Hi, Cottontail. I just checked the flight to see if it came in on time, and it did.' He gave a little laugh that cut her in two. 'So where are you, anyway? When your feet touch ground, do you think you could give the guy who loves you a call? You know, the one who left the other messages. *Ciao, bellissima.*'

When he rang off, tears were rolling from her eyes.

The next morning Cotton woke up as the pale dawn filtered through a crack in the shutters. Some time during the night she had slipped into a shallow doze that resembled sleep. She got up heavily and steadied herself to get her bearings, her head throbbing, her bones aching. Trying to shrug off an unkempt, dishevelled feeling, she wandered to the kitchen to make a cup of tea, knowing that somehow she had to find the courage to face the day. She was sitting at the kitchen table when the phone began to ring, sending the adrenalin through her. She rushed to the sitting room instinctively, knowing it was Prospero. When she picked up the phone, his voice vibrated down the line.

'Cotton? Why the hell didn't you call me last night?' His voice was full of relief. 'I was worried about you. Did you get my messages?'

'Prospero, hello. Yes, of course I got your messages. I'm sorry, but I got in so late. I went out with some colleagues from the office and we had dinner. We were all starving after a week of Russian food.' She gave a hollow laugh. She astonished herself how normal she sounded.

'Oh, I see, that's why.' He was unable to disguise a note of irritation in his voice. 'How was Moscow, anyway?'

'Fine. Just great. I gathered a lot of good material. In fact I was up early this morning to start working. I want to file at least two more articles on the trip. I have to get moving right away.'

'And how was Kiev?'

A note of suspicion crept into his voice and she felt suddenly frantic. The tension built up inside her unbearably, twisting her in knots as she struggled to formulate what she was going to say.

'Oh, Kiev was fascinating, and frightening. We went to two hospitals and I talked to the American medical team operating on the Chernobyl radiation victims . . .'

He broke across her monologue. 'Listen, Cotton, are you sure you're okay? You sound . . .'

She interrupted him shrilly. 'Prospero, I can't carry this charade any further. While I was there I did some soul-searching, some serious thinking . . .'

'Yeah? And?'

'I don't know how to tell you this, but I've come to the conclusion that it's just not going to work between us . . .' Her voice was quivering badly.

'What are you talking about?' he replied, dumbfounded.

The whispering echo of his voice crossed the distance, making her feel as if she had been punched in the stomach.

'You've got to hear me out. It was a wonderful summer, wonderful.' Taking a deep breath, she knew she couldn't let him stop her now. 'But in spite of everything, in spite of the affection I hold for you . . .'

'Affection? Affection?' He gave a snort of disbelief.

'Let me finish, please,' she begged. 'I realized on my trip that my career means more than anything to me. I'm not cut out for marriage, that's all. It's nothing to do with you, really, but I can't see myself settling down to make that kind of commitment. There are places I want to go, things I want to see.' A sigh escaped her that held the tears in check. 'In short, I guess I need my space. And that means that marriage and children are . . .' At this, her voice gave out.

There was complete silence for a moment, then Prospero exploded. 'Don't give me that crap. Who is he? You met somebody while you were away and that's where you were last night. Just how dumb do you think I am, anyway?'

A howl escaped her. 'No, no,' she protested. 'You mustn't think that. It's nothing to do with it. Please – don't ever call me again. Just leave me alone, I beg you . . .' Her voice breaking, she hung up on him and sobbed, her head in her hands. When the phone rang again in a minute, then again, she didn't pick it up, but turned the answering machine down low so she wouldn't have to hear his voice.

At three o'clock a black taxi pulled up in front of Cotton's flat and deposited Prospero. He climbed out carrying an overnight bag and paid the driver with a hurried gesture as he glanced towards the flat.

When the taxi had driven away he climbed the steps, noticing the shutters of the drawing-room were firmly closed, yet he knew she was there. Ringing the doorbell, he told himself that if she didn't answer he would station himself on her doorstep until she decided to appear. The lines at the corners of his mouth and on his forehead had deepened, giving him a dark, brooding intensity, and his blue eyes were murky, like water on a cloudy day.

Jamming the doorbell down repeatedly, he listened for some sign of life within the flat. There was no response for several moments, then finally he felt a surge of relief when the automatic lock clicked and the black door set with a polished brass knob and knocker swung open.

Entering the darkened hall, he saw Cotton waiting at the threshold of her apartment in a shaft of light flooding through the front door. Even at a distance he could read the broken expression on her face. She looked as bewildered and as uncomprehending as an abandoned child. He had been ready to rage, to shout, to shake her to her senses, even to insult her, but all his anger dissolved at the sight of her. Without a word, he strode down the hall and gathered her in his arms. They stood locked tightly together until the relief they both felt was broken by a dry sob that escaped her throat.

'Whatever it is, we can solve it together. For God's sake, you have to tell me what it is,' he whispered, stroking her hair.

She nodded, swallowing hard, not trusting herself to speak. Something urgent and unexplained in her voice had communicated itself to Prospero that morning, leaping across space, and he had come to her side as quickly as he could. Cotton allowed herself only a moment's respite in Prospero's arms before she felt herself overpowered by the force that was about to drive them apart. The moment he released her, she felt tainted with guilt. She had to put a distance between them, without delay.

'Come on,' she murmured. 'We've got to get out of here, Prospero. I'll explain why in a minute. Just let me get my coat.'

They took a taxi that dropped them in the middle of Hyde Park. They didn't exchange a word until they had arrived at a wide alley shaded by chestnut trees whose leaves were just beginning to turn. Picking out a bench, Cotton motioned him to sit beside her. She avoided his eyes for a moment, searching the green grass that met the grey horizon where children played ball and dogs chased each other. She shivered involuntarily at the penetrating damp of the gloomy afternoon. Prospero reached out to put his arm around her, but she pulled away.

'Now tell me, what's all this about?'

Cotton looked at him with tortured eyes. She felt utterly inadequate to shield him against the pain her relevation was about to cause. When morning came, she had decided she had been right to keep Chiara's visit a secret, but now he had come she was overjoyed. They would share the truth, no matter how damning. In a hushed voice, her eyes lowered, she said: 'Why did you lie to me when I asked if you knew my mother, Anna Gagliani?'

He thought a moment. 'I don't know. I can't really tell you until you tell me why you're asking me this.'

'It shouldn't really make any difference. The truth is all I ask. You had an affair with her, didn't you?'

'Christ,' he muttered under his breath. 'Is that what it is? How did you find out about it? Nobody knew but me and her . . .' His mind was racing, how it had all happened during the week Cotton was in Moscow. 'You tracked Anna down, is that it?' he asked incredulously.

'No.' Cotton shook her head. 'No – in fact, she found me. She came to my flat last night, just as I got in.'

'She came to your flat? What are you talking about?' he demanded.

'Prospero – there's no way to prepare you for this shock, but Anna is Chiara Galla.'

He looked at her uncomprehendingly. 'That's impossible,' he replied with an astonished laugh.

'I'm afraid it's true.' When he looked at her, thunderstruck, she said, 'Why would she lie? She has no reason to lie. She knows all about Delilah, you, your father's murder, William, Matthew Swope. And yet you didn't recognize her.' Her hands suddenly twisted in despair. 'For God's sake, you made love to her,' she cried.

'Wait a minute. I'm not denying that. But it was thirty years ago. We were kids. Anna . . . Chiara,' he repeated in astonishment. 'She's nothing like she was then, believe me. Tell me the truth, would you have known I was the same guy you knew years ago, if you hadn't known my name?'

'You still haven't explained why you lied to me.' She found a release in the anger she felt, postponing the moment when she would have to wound him with the full story.

'Well, look how upset you are. Doesn't that explain it? You're upset, really upset that I slept with your mother, and I can't blame you. That's why I didn't tell you, knowing the effect it would have on you – so I kept it a secret. But, sweetheart, we can overcome that. It's absolutely nothing to do with us. Christ – for a minute you had me worried.' Relief swept over him, and he burst out laughing.

'Anna Gagliani – Chiara Galla. She must be feeling so fucking smug. What a bitch,' he remarked, thinking of her underhand purchase of the Villa Robbiano. Now everything was clear. 'Tell me, why didn't she mention that she was your mother until now? Why didn't she tell me who she was? Don't answer that. It's because that's the kind of woman she is. The night I heard my father had been killed I turned to her. I was desperate. And do you know what? I didn't get an ounce of sympathy. She said I had ruined her good name – her good name, for God's sake! Now she's changed it. What a laugh. Yeah, she was as cold as ice. So it's easy to see why when we met last spring she didn't let on who she was. By that time, thirty years later, she had changed her mind about me. I was good enough for her after all. God, she must really be pissed off that I'm in love with her daughter. No wonder she's so furious, Cotton – she's jealous. That's why she told you now. Anyway, so what? What do we care?'

All the time he spoke Cotton was staring numbly at the path. When he reached for her, she moved away.

'No, Prospero. She didn't know who I was until a week ago.'

'Are you sure? Well, what the hell . . .'

'It's not that simple, Prospero.' She paused, aware she would have given anything at that moment not to shatter his buoyant expression. 'The reason she came to see me was to inform me that you, not Matthew Swope, are my father.'

When she had spoken the terrible words that until now she hadn't allowed to form in her head, Cotton forced herself to look into Prospero's eyes and to endure the moment to its very end. Her eyes filled with tears and her heart pounded in agony as she witnessed his spirit fall like a tree to the axe.

Her words made no sense to Prospero whatsoever. The idea was so far-fetched, so ugly, that he couldn't form a coherent reply. From the gravity on Cotton's face he comprehended she had no doubt about what she had told him.

'Cotton, that's impossible, ridiculous.' As he groped for a rebuttal he had the suffocating feeling he was helplessly caught in an avalanche. He racked his brain for some connection between the young innocent Anna he could only half remember and Chiara but the harder he tried to conjure up the past the more elusive it seemed.

'She's lying. The bitch is lying,' he muttered, then cried aloud. 'She's goddam lying, I tell you.' His words echoed down the leaf-strewn path and over the gently rolling parkland. A uniformed nanny wheeling a baby in a perambulator festooned with chrome turned to glance disapprovingly over her shoulder.

Prospero leapt to his feet, his fists clenched defiantly in a primitive gesture of helpless rage.

'It's not true, Cotton. There's not one shred of truth in this.' He looked at Cotton in desperation.

'And – Prospero – I think I'm pregnant.'

Something twisted and died in him as he comprehended what she said. Dropping beside her on the bench, he clung to her, tears streaming down his face. He hadn't cried since his father had been killed. Dry, harsh sobs racked his body as Cotton held him tremblingly. The earth seemed to be swaying around them, while trees, birds and statues remained oblivious.

Still holding him tight, Cotton said in a small voice:

'What are we going to do?'

'I don't know, I don't know. But for the moment we're going to hold tight.'

Chapter 26

When Prospero stopped his car at the shady edge of the tree-lined space outside the village, he released his grip on the steering-wheel which he had clenched since leaving Rome early that morning, stopping only once for petrol. Getting out of his car stiffly, he could already see evidence of the film crew who had taken over the village. Electronic vans and mobile wardrobe and dressing-room units littered the parking space allotted to tourists, and a catering van, its hatch open, was dispensing snacks and drinks to the technicians and extras. Prospero didn't need to ask where to go, but followed his instincts to track down Chiara. He walked resolutely down a narrow, cool street lined with ancient stone houses towards the medieval central piazza that she had told him about. As he passed members of the cast and crew of *Village in the Sun* he looked beyond them unseeingly, his face set hard and unsmiling. Prospero was a man whose life was no longer his own and beneath his unruffled surface was a determination to get it back.

During the past forty-eight hours he had raked over every detail of the past months since he had met Chiara, searching for some clue that would release him miraculously from his anguish. He remembered his casual remark that she reminded him of someone and how she had countered with a similar admission of her own. At the time their exchange had passed for flirtation. But now he asked himself why he had ever said such a thing in the first place. Had Chiara, in fact, reminded him of Anna Gagliani and had he submerged the truth at the back of his mind as their affair blossomed? Searching his soul Prospero asked himself if he was capable of such self-deception. No. He would never have guessed the truth about Chiara unless she had chosen to tell him. He had had no reason to question the past she had invented for herself, and Sandy Vincent had known her for years. Prospero began to wonder why Chiara had concealed her identity. He was certain, looking back, that she must have known all along who he was. He hadn't changed his name, his past, altered his appearance. He had only aged, unlike Chiara, whose looks had been utterly changed by art and artifice. Finally, he asked himself whether Chiara had really fallen in love with him, or whether she had faked that too and, if so, why? He had no answer. The only part of the mystery that had been solved was Chiara Galla's motive for acquiring the Villa Robbiano from under his nose. The little servant girl from the big house returning as a rich and famous woman to take possession might have summoned up a measure of pity were it not for Prospero's anger and disgust. Last, first and always – was she lying? He could hardly bear to think that Chiara was telling the truth about the three of them. If she was, how could he accept it, and if she wasn't how could he prove it?

His ordeal had been prolonged when he had returned to Rome only to discover that Chiara had departed for location the morning he arrived. Another long day had passed, while he and Cotton were forced to live with the horror that stalked them.

He spotted Sandy Vincent right away, in a blue bush suit and baseball hat, standing in a swirl of cables near a camera as he consulted with a technician. Raking the sunlit piazza with its fine old buildings clustered around a gushing fountain set in a wide cobbled arena, he could see no sign of Chiara. For an instant he was distracted by the startling sight of a group of actors in German SS officers' uniform, swastikas on their sleeves and wearing peaked caps. The red flag of the Third Reich, with the black swastika on a field of white, was hanging from the town hall, and all the extras waiting for the next take to begin had been sent back in time to the forties. The men sported baggy trousers and braces and the women wore short, puffed sleeved dresses, dark red lips and plucked eyebrows, their hair coiled in the severe styles of the day. A further tribute to the past were the ancient, immaculately kept motor-bikes with sidecars, and open-topped pre-war Mercedes in mint condition parked around the square.

Sandy spotted Prospero standing ominously at the edge of the crowd, his hands in his pockets.

'That's all we need,' he muttered to the assistant. 'She's giving the performance of her life, and he has to come and fuck it up.' Smiling, Sandy waved and walked in his direction.

'Prospero, good to see you. What brings you here?' he said heartily when they were face to face. 'Chiara didn't tell me you were coming.'

'No, I wanted to surprise her,' he replied with a cold smile, patting Sandy on the shoulder. 'Where is she?'

Narrowing his eyes, Sandy tried to penetrate the surface of Prospero's shallow amiability. He could immediately sense a dangerous undertone to his manner, and there was a killing sharpness in his eyes.

'The thing is, she's in her dressing-room, but she's due on the set for the next take the minute she's ready,' he said, glancing at his watch.

Prospero was not to be deterred.

'In that case, I'll wait on the sidelines until she's free.'

'Sure, go ahead. It might be a while. Look, Prospero . . .' began Sandy. They were interrupted by the assistant director, who called,

'Hey, this set-up is going to take a little longer than I thought. Why don't we break for lunch now and pick up where we left off? Make it forty-five minutes.'

'But the light,' protested Sandy, squinting at the blazing sun.

'It's the best we can do,' yelled Sandy's assistant.

'Where's her dressing-room?' asked Prospero.

Sandy sighed. 'It's over there, through that archway on the corner. You can't miss it. But listen, Prospero,' he said, catching his sleeve. 'Give me a break, will you? Please don't rock the boat. This is her first day on the set. We've had to delay shooting because of her mental state, and now I'm pleased to say she seems to have ironed out her personal problems,' he added pointedly. 'I'd like things to stay that way, okay?'

Prospero gave him a little smirk. 'Don't worry, Sandy. This won't take long. I just came to ask her one question, that's all.'

Going through the stone arch, Prospero approached the empty shop that had been turned into a dressing-room. He didn't recognize Chiara at first. In a dark wig coiled at the nape of her neck, she was portraying an Italian war widow, mother of a sixteen-year-old girl. A shapeless dark print dress disguised her ripe figure and clumsy black lace-up shoes gave her a provincial awkwardness appropriate to the character she was playing.

'Hand me that black sweater — maybe it will look better with the sweater over my shoulders,' she said to her dresser, impatiently.

Prospero watched unseen while the woman did as she was told, then tied on a soiled apron. When she swivelled the long glass for Chiara to see her reflection, Chiara froze, seeing Prospero's image over her shoulder. Whirling around, she said,

'Why, Prospero, how lovely to see you,' A tentative smile crossed her face which paled beneath the thick make-up.

He made no reply, but watched her closely for some clue to what was going on in her mind. A faint tic under her eye revealed a fear she couldn't quite disguise. He superimposed the image of a girl he had known briefly thirty years ago on the woman who had excited him in the spring, still unable to register that they were one and the same person. It wasn't the cosmetic surgery that had subtly altered her face, or her hair-colouring, make-up or clothes — even her age. Looking at Chiara he realized that every trace of the fresh, exuberant Anna, so hungry for life and love, had gone. Ambition had consumed her, leaving this accomplished but empty woman in her place. The last thing he expected to feel for Chiara was pity, but he felt it now for a second, momentarily displacing the anger and grief at what she had done.

'I have to talk to you alone,' he said, nodding towards the wardrobe woman. His eyes flashed a warning and there was danger in his voice.

'I'm sorry, but I can't. I have a scene in a few moments,' came her clipped reply as she pretended to fuss with her wig.

'I've just talked to Sandy. They've decided to break for lunch,' he said flatly.

She hesitated. 'Very well. But I can't imagine what is so important that you have to come here without announcing yourself.' She pretended to be annoyed, but he sensed she was unsure of herself, on the defensive. She visibly shrank from his black mood and a murderous stillness fell between them.

Outside she said brusquely, 'We could walk up those stone steps through that alley, if you insist on being alone. That leads to a little park overlooking the ramparts.'

When they reached the raised battlements of the ramparts skirted by a low stone wall, Chiara sat on the wall and gazed out unseeingly at the rolling hills of Tuscany which melted away in the distance in layer after layer of delicate greens. The unchanging and ancient landscape was criss-crossed with olive groves and vineyards, broken by cypresses and umbrella pines protecting farmhouses that had been there for centuries. The ripe golden haze of approaching autumn hung in the air and a suggestion of coolness signalled that summer would soon be at an end.

'I've just come from London where I saw Cotton,' said Prospero. 'I had a hard time tracking you down. Nobody would tell me where you went.'

'Ah, yes, Cotton,' Chiara said thoughtfully.

Something in her composure chilled him.

'She told me that you came to see her,' he said, barely keeping his anger in check. 'And she told me what you said.'

'So, she told you, did she? I was hoping she would have the courage to keep the secret. It was terribly painful for her, for me.' She shrugged. 'It's too late now, anyway.'

Towering over her, Prospero gathered every ounce of strength and will he possessed. 'Cotton and I tell each other everything, bad and good – something you wouldn't under-stand. And now I'm here I want you to repeat that evil lie you told her. I want to hear you say it, Chiara – or should I call you Anna?'

Holding his gaze unswervingly, she said,

'All right, I'll say it if you want me to. Yes, you are Cotton's father. There. Now you can go.'

He gave an ominous laugh, trying to dispel the hatred that flooded him. 'Oh no, Chiara. It's not going to be as simple as that.'

She narrowed her eyes angrily.

'I suppose you think I'm lying. Why would I lie, why?' Her temper flared. 'When your father was killed I was already a few days late. That night when you came to my house, the last time we met, I was frightened. That's why I was unkind to you. And I'm sorry for it now, thirty years later. When we met this spring I thought life had given me a second chance, a chance to make it up; and that's why I didn't tell you who I was. I was afraid, afraid you would turn from me, against me, and not forgive me. Because after all those years, Prospero, I still loved you.' She sighed resignedly, looking away as if she had exhausted all her energy.

Prospero was thrown off-balance for a moment at the strength of a conviction which he had never expected to encounter. He said gruffly,

'How did you find out who Cotton was, and when?'

'Since you insist, it was Herron Easton who told me. I saw him in Paris two weeks ago. He happened to mention the Marchesa's name, saying she was Cotton's mother, and of course, then, I knew right away. It came as a terrible, terrible shock to me. I didn't tell him who I was, of course. Nobody knows who I really am, Prospero. Nobody except Cotton, and now you.'

'Why did you say that Matthew Swope was Cotton's father, why?' he cried. It was a plea uttered as he stared down a black chute of hopelessness.

Turning to him, she folded her arms protectively across her breasts. There was recrimination in her eyes. 'Because I had to find a father for your child. I was alone, unprotected, friendless. And what could you have done to help, a penniless fifteen-year-old boy? Nothing! You know what it was like for me in Robbiano. Matthew was a way out. Perhaps I was wrong, but he was in love with me. Not long after that last time I saw you in the piazza with your brother, I allowed him to seduce me. When he went back to America I wrote to him that I was pregnant and he offered to marry me. But his death in a car accident changed everything. I did then what I had to do, what any girl would have done without a family to protect her. I went to the Marchesa for help; and now I'm not sorry for what I did. I gave my daughter everything when I had nothing.'

'That's why you hate her, isn't it, Chiara? It's not just her, it's me too. You hate us because we're happy, because we found each other. You're lying, Chiara. And I'm going to prove it.' His eyes, darting with violence, penetrated her, stripping her bare. He didn't have a shred of proof to back up his conviction, but an inexplicable faith seemed to come from outside himself, bridging the chasm that threatened his life, his sanity.

She shook her head and looked at him pityingly, knowing it was probably for the last time.

'I'm very sorry for you, Prospero, but you can't always have everything you want in life. I myself learned that a long time ago.'

He turned, pausing to take one last glimpse of Chiara perched on the ramparts like a woman resurrected from another age. If it would have solved anything, he might have pushed her over the edge of the wall.

'You haven't won yet, Chiara,' were his last words as he disappeared down the steps.

The following day, Prospero entered Pietro Giannini's residence in the Vatican, where he was attached to the Curia. The Cardinal's secretary, a Monsignor in a long black soutane, greeted him cheerfully and led him down a marble hallway with a gilded ceiling to the double doors of a huge vaulted chamber overlooking the Vatican gardens behind the Sistine Basilica. Even though Giannini was a tall, broadly built man, his black-robed form was dwarfed by the massive cinquecento chair with curling arms in front of a massive desk. His reception room was like the inner sanctum of a Renaissance prince, rich with wall hangings, gilt sconces and vast dark paintings of saints in scrolled gilt frames. Prospero always found the mellow grandeur of past centuries an inappropriate background to his cousin's simplicity of manner, but the imbalance was redressed in his mind by the knowledge that Pietro preferred to sleep in a hard bed in a small whitewashed room, a crucifix above his head.

When he saw Prospero, Pietro stood up and removed his wire-rimmed glasses, a surprised but welcoming expression on his face. There was a shock of white hair at his temples and the lines engraved on his face gave it a leonine cast.

Hearing the door close quietly behind him, Prospero said: 'I'm sorry I didn't telephone, Pietro, but I had something very urgent to discuss with you, so I took the chance you might be in.'

'You know you don't have to call me. I'm always delighted to see you. What a wonderful surprise, Prospero. I take it the remainder of your holiday in Portofino ended as pleasantly as it promised when I last saw you.'

Patting him on the back with a smile, Giannini knew instantly that his cousin was deeply troubled.

'I drove directly here from Tuscany,' Prospero said, breaking into Italian. 'I hope I'm not disturbing you.' He nodded at the pile of papers on the embossed blotter beside a gilded inkstand that held the big bronze and cornelian cardinal's seal.

'Nothing that won't keep. I'm always happy to find an excuse to get away from paperwork. Especially anything to do with the Banco Ambrosiano,' he remarked with a weary smile.

Prospero nodded sympathetically and shook his hand. He and Pietro had spent many hours discussing the current Vatican conundrum, the banking scandal that had caused international repercussions. Now, as he looked at his cousin the cardinal, it seemed that this complex matter was child's play compared to his own impossible dilemma.

'I need your advice badly, Pietro.'

'Come, come and sit down and tell me what's on your mind,' said Pietro, gesturing towards two gilded armchairs set near a long, open window overlooking the lush gardens streaked with lengthening shadows. The huge park adjacent to the Vatican was sequestered by a high, ancient wall that muted the sound of the rush-hour traffic.

As he collected his thoughts, Prospero said: 'Pietro, bear with me if you can. In order to explain everything I have to go back nearly thirty years to the time Papa was killed – that summer when we all came over for the Fontini wedding. You're the one person in the world who might be able to advise me.'

'By all means, go ahead. I have all the time you need,' he replied, settling back into the high chair. Steepling his finger-tips, he listened intently as Prospero began to speak in a flat empty voice that could not veil his distress.

Some time later, when Prospero had unburdened himself, a silence fell between them. He sat, his elbows resting on his knees, his head hanging forward, as Pietro stroked his chin thoughtfully for a moment. Prospero, who had relived the agony of the crisis in relating it to his cousin, was overtaken by a fresh spurt of anger.

'Something tells me Chiara is not telling the truth,' he blurted out. 'I don't know what it is, but there's that niggling doubt at the back of my mind I can't ignore. It won't let me rest. And yet, and yet, tell me, Pietro,' he implored, searching his face, 'am I just making myself believe it because I need to hope? Am I grasping at straws because I can't face the ugly truth? I looked at Cotton in London, then at Chiara today, trying to remember Anna, trying to resurrect her from memory, but it was so long ago. And I know, I know I wasn't the father of her baby. The thing is, how can I get evidence, proof? Should I hire a detective to try and piece this all to-gether? I've thought of blood tests, but they're not conclusive in every case. It boils down to the fact that we're all at Chiara's mercy. If she wants to conceal what really happened, then there is absolutely nothing I can do. Pietro – there are three lives at stake: a man, a woman and their child, and time will run out so quickly.' He broke off in exasperation. Tact kept him from mentioning that Cotton would surely have an abortion if something couldn't prove their case in time.

'I'm thinking. I'm thinking back to that time,' murmured Pietro, his dark intelligent eyes glazed with recollection. In a moment he rose from his chair and put his hand on Prospero's shoulder while he gazed out of the window at the haven of greenery which kept the modern world at bay. Yet a human dilemma could still find its way inside the heavy gilded doors of the cardinal's chamber, and now he wrestled with it.

He studied Prospero, whom he had known since he was a child. In the intervening years he had watched him through countless stages, discarding each new-found identity for an even stronger persona. Pietro surmised that at forty-five Prospero had found himself, and would remain the same, give or take a grey hair or two and deeper lines on his face. His character was formed. Here was the successful international magnate, the cosmopolitan man of means with vast power, wealth and influence though born the son of a mafioso who had been gunned down in the streets. And yet, all his struggles and achievements seemed to have led to that singular moment, that precipice where his happiness hung in suspension. If he lost the woman he loved, who was carrying his child, his life would shrink to nothing. His sudden vulnerability revealed to Pietro that though Prospero had mastered the forces stacked against him all his life, he was now at the mercy of a woman he hadn't seen for thirty years. The tragic irony of his circumstances and Prospero's own humility, learned from love, made Pietro feel a powerful surge of compassion for the man.

'I think I might be able to help you,' he said cautiously.

'How?' cried Prospero. 'You were there at the time. Do you remember anything? In the meantime, maybe I should get in touch with William Partridge. Maybe he knows something . . .'

'For the time being I counsel patience,' said Pietro, rising from his chair and laying his hand on Prospero's shoulder. 'I'm afraid I can say no more at the moment. Just put your trust in me, I'll do what I can.'

Prospero hesitated, then nodded, sensing in Pietro some secret machination that excluded him for the moment.

'I'll try and have some news for you, perhaps tomorrow. If not, the day after. Will you be at home?' Prospero nodded. 'Good – I'll contact you there.'

In the Hotel Le Barone, Chiara was sitting in her room with her feet propped up, trying to concentrate on her lines for the next day's shooting at San Treviano. She had returned to the luxurious hotel, an ancient restored manor house a few miles from San Treviano where most of the crew and cast were staying. She sighed, and looked out of the open window at the lemon-coloured sky, thinking of that day's satisfying shooting during which she had played one of her most important scenes. It had gone brilliantly but now, as she sat alone in her room, she fought an inner restlessness. In her comfortable room furnished in the Tuscan style, she had taken off her make-up, pushed her hair back with a band and had slipped into a caftan while she sipped a cup of herbal tea and studied the script. At the sound of laughter beneath her window, she suppressed a wish that she had the knack of cultivating familiarity with the cast and crew as Sandy and some of the others had. As the star and chief investor of the production she suffered a sense of isolation after working hours, unable to unwind with all the technicians and extras who frequented restaurants, trattorias or bars in the evenings.

Rising to look at the changing light over the hills, she was seized by acute depression. This was the time of day she hated most and the time dragged by until she had her solitary dinner, usually sent to her room, then went to bed early in order to be fresh for her make-up call at dawn. The silence of the isolated hotel was like a reproach, and instead of being lulled to sleep by the crickets and the cool country air, she was often awakened by whispering nightmares that left her sweating in terror, her heart pounding. The last two nights, since she had seen Prospero, had been the worst. She kept pushing the thought of him from her mind, but she harboured an insistent uneasiness. She fought against loving him, nor did she want to feel anything for Cotton Castello. If she weakened, she reasoned, she would be letting herself down. Her triumph on the set in the first few days, when she had stepped firmly into the shoes of the character she was playing, had bolstered her ego. The return of her professional confidence was proof that the hideous wound she had suffered was healing, and she assured herself that from now on every day would be better than the last. Gathering all her powers of concentration, Chiara returned to her script.

A short while later, when the phone rang, she stared at it in surprise. Not expecting, or even wanting anyone to call, she decided not to answer it. A few moments later, when it rang again, she rose irritably and picked up the receiver.

'*Signora Galla, buona sera,*' came the voice of the receptionist. 'A visitor has arrived, asking to see you at once.'

Thrown into confusion, Chiara interrupted him. 'If it is a Signor Vallone, tell him I cannot see him . . .'

'No, signora – the person asking to see you is Cardinal Pietro Giannini from Rome,' the man said in a respectful whisper.

She gave a gasp of astonishment.

'Signora? Will you see the Cardinal? He is in the small secluded loggia, the one on the far side of the pool, where you can meet undisturbed,' he added delicately.

Chiara gave a little cry of panic as she hung up, feeling as if lightning had struck without warning. All the time she was seeing Prospero during the spring, she had avoided ever meeting Cardinal Giannini, afraid to submit herself to his scrutiny, though more than once Prospero had suggested introducing them. She bit her lip in indecision, not knowing where to turn. It would be impossible to refuse to see Giannini now he had been announced. Fury coursed through her that Prospero and he had set the trap together, knowing she would be cornered. Of all the people from her past, he was the one she feared most. She went to the bathroom to take a Valium, then combed her hair and dabbed on some lip gloss as she stalled for time, her hand shaking visibly. Slipping on her shoes, she left her room, her mind turning over rapidly.

In the tranquil garden full of evening birdsong, she saw the Cardinal sitting on a bench in a corner completely secluded by greenery. The moment he recognized her he rose with a kind smile on his face that cracked the thin veneer of her composure. The woman who offered her hand to the tall, distinguished Cardinal, who could barely restrain herself from lowering her eyes to kiss his ring and genuflecting, had become a shy young girl with a heavy heart again.

'*Buona sera*, Cardinal. This is a very great honour, but you must excuse me,' she said graciously, seating herself on a bench opposite him. 'I can only assume there must be some mistake, as you and I have never met.'

Giannini said nothing, but gave her a pleasant nod, pinning her down with his unfathomable eyes. She tried to escape his perceptive, steady gaze, but it was unavoidable. She felt paralysed for a moment by the authority he communicated, as if he would pursue her wherever she tried to flee. When she could stand it no longer, she burst out,

'I can't imagine why you have come to see me. Forgive my surprise, but you see, I'm not even a Catholic any more, so . . .'

When he spoke his voice was gentle but his words contained a terrifying message.

'Anna, little Anna Gagliani. It's been a long, a very long time,' he said with a thoughtful nod, his hands knitted together.

A gasp escaped her throat and she recoiled in disbelief.

'There's some mistake,' she murmured feebly, but the Cardinal's eyes bored into her, compelling her to own up to the past. Defeated, she slouched back on the bench and waited.

'Anna – may I call you Anna? It pleases me somehow.'

She didn't reply, but regarded him numbly. Leaning forward, he said in a quiet voice, 'For the last twenty-four hours I have been thinking of you, praying for you. I have searched my heart, trying to understand you. And I have come here, not to judge but to ask you to open your heart to me. I come here in humility, as your priest and former confessor, even though it was a long time ago. What I have to say to you won't take long, but it must be said – Anna.'

As he began to speak, the cadence of his calm, rich voice hushed her fears.

'I remember that little girl whom unkind boys and girls

teased and called *la bastona*,' he said with a smile. 'And who would have guessed that she would grow up into such a beautiful and famous woman, a rich and successful woman? It seems to me an undeniable justice. One hopes that all these things showered on you have made some kind of reparation for your very difficult childhood. Yes, I know how unhappy you were. So often they say that hardship acts as a spur, and in your case you have profited . . .'

She listened intently as he recounted her own life, evoking incidents she had all but forgotten, and which she was astonished that he, now a cardinal, remembered so well. As he spoke, it gave her a strange sense of importance to know she still existed in the great man's mind as a little urchin, Anna Gagliani, filling her unexpectedly with a strange tenderness for something she once was. The small frightened girl inside her stopped crying as the taunts of cruel children died away. Her racing pulse calmed as she listened to his every word, evoking that spring when *la bastona* shed her rags and turned into a princess.

'Every boy, every man in Robbiano fell in love with this girl who had come into womanhood like a barren tree clothed with blossoms. How well I recall that summer. The Fontini wedding, remember? When the jolly pharmacist, Mario, my cousin, married his daughter to a builder's son. Do you know, they have four children now? One son is a doctor, the other an engineer. Even though it was over thirty years ago this summer, I can still see you and Prospero dancing together in the piazza, looking even more radiant than the bride and groom. How worried I was, I recall, about your innocence, seeing the passion that had sprung up between you. And I remember, too, the day the Vallones departed from Robbiano, how relieved I was that they would be spared any more problems, having heard your confession and absolved you.'

His voice dropped, and he regarded her across a chasm that he breached with the humanity in his eyes.

'I remember so well your response when I asked whether you were carrying Prospero's child, your gasp of embarrassment, and then the way you fervently assured me that you weren't. I could tell by the profound relief in your voice that you were telling me the truth when I asked this question not only as a priest but also as a member of Prospero's family.'

He had hauled her up like a woman hanging from a precipice inch by inch with strong sure hands, closer to reality and away from self-delusion. But when the final moment came he could do no more, and it was up to Chiara to climb the last step and plant her feet on safe ground. He waited for her answer.

She hesitated, terrified at the courage it entailed, courage she doubted she had. It would be so much easier to fall. She had been falling all her life. But slowly and miraculously she felt the life flowing back into her, bringing with it a strength she hadn't known she possessed. The lie she had lived and believed in, the lie within the lie, slipped from her like a second skin, bringing with it an exhilarating sense of renewal. It was a revelation. In one vital moment she was sickened by her own cruelty, then filled with immense relief that the charade was over. She suddenly knew she was too weak to shoulder such a burden, too lonely to live with the guilt for the rest of her life. She blinked as if seeing for the first time after living as a blind woman. Then she began to cry softly, releasing the pent-up conflicts that would take the rest of her life to understand.

Cardinal Giannini held out his square, thick hand and she reached for it, her fingers brushing his ring that had at one time symbolized for her all the force of what was good in life. The memory of her faith beat like a pulse at the back of her mind; it had never left her. A power flowed between them, not the power of the Church, but of compassion, bridging the gap between Chiara Galla and Anna Gagliani, reconciled at last.

'Prospero is waiting at this moment for you to call his apartment in Rome,' said Giannini.

'Will you wait here for me? I'll come right back.'

She walked quickly towards the hotel, her arms folded against her chest. When she was back in her room she dialled Prospero's number, anxiously awaiting the sound of his voice on the other end of the line. She wouldn't be able to start all over again until she had made that phone call.

When she heard him speak, she said in a rush: 'Prospero? It's Chiara, calling from Tuscany. Prospero, I am here with Car-

dinal Giannini. He came to see me a little while ago, and we
have had a long talk. I'm calling to tell you that what I said was
a lie – none of it was true. Please forgive me, please try – you,
and Cotton too.'

'Chiara . . .' was all he had time to exclaim before she hung
up, a sob caught in her throat.

Her chest heaving with emotion, Chiara began to laugh at
herself, wiping away the tears as she hurried back downstairs
to the Cardinal. He was waiting for her, hands behind his back,
his face a study. The moment he saw her hurrying towards
him his face brightened, knowing from her expression that she
had done what she promised.

'Chiara . . . God bless you,' he said, holding out his hands.
'You're a strong, courageous woman. You've done the right
thing and you will never regret it, I assure you.'

Embarrassed at the approval in his eyes which she didn't
deserve, she remembered her duties as a hostess.

'But Cardinal, please, what can I offer you? You have come
a long way, and I've offered you nothing. A drink? Tea, perhaps? Or maybe you would like to stay to dinner in a private
room in the hotel. It would make me so very happy if you
would stay a while. I feel that for the first time in a long while
I have something to celebrate.'

Cotton and Prospero, their arms around each other, watched
impatiently as Giuseppe sawed through the chain that locked
the gates of the Villa Robbiano.

'Are you sure I can't give you a hand?' asked Prospero.

'No, signor, it's all right. I'm almost finished,' said the gardener breathlessly. His sinewy forearm moved vigorously back
and forth.

Prospero hugged Cotton and smiled at her. Seeing her look
of rapt anticipation, mingled with apprehension, he said,

'You're not still thinking that you won't accept it?'

She shook her head and bit her lip. 'It's a bit late for that, I
guess, isn't it? It would be like taking the ribbon off a present,
then changing your mind.'

When they had driven there on a hazy late September day,

the last vestiges of doubt left Cotton's mind about accepting Chiara's gift to her, the Villa Robbiano. Her mother had relayed the offer in a simply worded, affectionate letter that had moved Cotton deeply, and she still hadn't found the words to answer it. After the day, that incredible day when Prospero had phoned her with the news of Chiara's repentance, it had taken her a long time to fully comprehend what had happened. She put the ownership of the villa at the back of her mind as something to think about when the time was right. There were other things so much more important, she had discovered. Plunging back into life again with astonishing energy and vigour, Cotton had wound up her post in London and sold her flat in record time to join Prospero in Rome. She had been so anxious to see the villa, whose big, medieval-looking keys she collected from the Notaro Perini's office, that they made their way to Florence the day after her arrival in Rome, a sure sign to Prospero that Cotton's heart had made up its mind about the villa even if she hadn't. When they arrived that afternoon she had insisted that they arouse Giuseppe to prise open the lock on the front gate so they could drive through, regardless of the brambles growing over the pebbled drive, the stray branches, the fallen statue. It was something she had to do. She squeezed Prospero's hand impatiently as she heard the lock give way.

'It's okay, signor,' announced Giuseppe proudly. The chain made a rattling noise as he pulled it through the bars of the gate, then the two men pushed the gates open, kicking the gravel to ease it back. Giuseppe stood ceremoniously to one side as Cotton and Prospero got into the car.

There were very few dreams in life that ever came true, Cotton thought, as the car passed slowly between the crumbling pillars, but for her the dream of homecoming lived up to all she had expected. The abandonment and decay of the garden and house could do nothing to shake her sense of fulfilment as she looked at Prospero.

Her heart leapt as they passed the dark twin cypresses, their straggly branches beckoning them on like outstretched hands.

'The first thing I'm going to do is have Giuseppe get busy

with those trees,' she said in a gruff whisper, incapable of expressing what she felt. 'And the next thing will be to get those statues upright, and then the fountain in working order.'

The tyres crackled on the pebbles and dry sticks as they crawled along. The golden crumbling façade of the villa came into view.

'It sounds to me as if you've made up your mind,' said Prospero.

Until the very last minute there had been a slim possibility that she might refuse the present offered by the woman who had entered her life as a rival and an enemy.

'How could I refuse?' she said simply, catching sight of the house overlaid with afternoon shadows.

'Then in that case I think you and I should consider this moment the beginning of our new life together,' he remarked as the car passed from the cool blue shade into the sun.

Cotton's reply was to reach out and gather a handful of wild angelica that cast up the fragrance of summer.